THE RISE OF
AEON NOUS

THE UTOPIAN CONSPIRACY

TONY TEORA

DEDICATION

This book is dedicated to those who fight for truth at the expense of their own lives. Those warriors are the true heroes on this shiny blue planet, safely situated at the distant edge of the Milky Way Galaxy, a planet called Earth by its allegedly intelligent inhabitants. A planet of intelligent people who are under two quarantines, both derived from the same source: its reputed intelligence. That intelligence not only does not prepare for viral pandemics, it inadvertently creates them. That intelligence is the reason for the second quarantine—a planetary quarantine from other, more ethereal intelligences who prefer a mostly wait-and-see strategy with regard to the intelligent inhabitants of planet Earth. Even though that strategy has been in place for millennia, do not give up hope; for as long as a few truth tellers survive, so will the chances of Earth and its people exiting both quarantines. The prison we create on Earth is nothing more than a prison of the mind. To break free, remember this:

"Prison is not a place; it is a state of mind."

–Tony Teora

SPECIAL DEDICATION

Special Dedication to Truth Teller Dr. Li Wenliang, who sent a warning regarding a dangerous virus to fellow medics on 30 December 2019; the police advised him to stop "making false comments." Planet Earth's largest medical and financial disaster might have been avoided had truth been valued more than corrupt earthly systems of power which, unfortunately, are ubiquitous throughout planet Earth.

ACKNOWLEDGEMENTS

I'd like to thank the universe for being such a mystical and curious place. I especially want to thank it for creating family and friends who supported and inspired me. Without knowing it, a few friends even gave me material for eccentric fictional characters...

Special thanks to Proofed to Perfection and Pamela Cangioli for the editorial brilliance and marketing ideas. Your team helped bring out the color in the story. The book wouldn't be the same without you and your team's expert support. Sincere thanks!

ETYMOLOGY OF "AEON NOUS"

Aeon: This noun is derived from Ancient Greek and has various meanings, including: "Life, age, ageless life (eternity) of the cosmos"; also, "a personified deity who later became understood as an emanation."

Nous: In the Aristotelian scheme, *nous* is the basic understanding or awareness that allows human beings to think rationally.

CONTENTS

PROLOGUE...

"The genie is out of the bottle. We need to move forward on artificial intelligence (AI) development, but we also need to be mindful of its very real dangers. I fear that AI may replace humans altogether. If people design computer viruses, someone will design AI that replicates itself. This will be a form of life that will outperform humans."

— Stephen Hawking, Wired Interview, 2017

"When in the valley of fools and you're the only one carrying a light, you see things others don't."

— Aeon Nous, Surviving the Apocalypse, 2045

Year: 2018

Location: Secret Underground Artificial Intelligence Super Computer Facility

"**M**y God!" exclaimed Professor Bradley Hull, examining the artificial intelligence computer program results. *You're either the forbidden fruit of light and understanding,* he thought, *or the poison berries of the dark, alien devil waiting in the shadows to destroy humanity—maybe both. Who are you? What are you? Where are you taking us?*

Hull looked at the AI data and knew he had either single-handedly saved the planet—or maybe destroyed it!

Working deep underground at a top-secret AI facility in the rugged hills of Mount Laguna, California, Hull pulled his long, sun-bleached hair to the side, allowing his hazel eyes, owlish behind his Buddy Holly-style specs, to clearly scrutinize the numbers on his LCD monitor. His childlike grimace turned into a frozen smile, like a face splashed with liquid nitrogen and immortalized in time. He broke his icy stare to look up at an old-fashioned wall clock. The clock's face displayed a black and white picture of Rod Serling, natty in a dark suit, superimposed over a graphic of a spiral vortex, with *The Twilight Zone*—the late writer's most celebrated creation—printed underneath in the familiar, stylized font. It was three a.m.

At the tender age of twenty-seven, Hull was already one of the world's most preeminent physicists. Now he had collaborated on the breakthrough that would align his name with the likes of Schrödinger, Dirac, and Feynman. But it was Serling who was Hull's muse—he called him the "impresario of imagination"—and he had to thank him.

"We've done it, Rod, old boy!" he said, giving the wordsmith a thumbs up. From the clock face, Serling—compact but sturdy, his face fiercely intelligent—gave his tacit approval.

Hull, tall and angular like a humanoid mantis, hopped over to Edward Jones' computer station on his long legs, bumping a half-empty mug of coffee emblazoned with a triangular logo and the acronym HART.

"Wake up, Jones!" Hull shouted, shaking the napping scientist's shoulders. "Q-Bit hit the jackpot! We have zero errors for the permutation! The rest of the years should fold into place. We can predict at least fifty years into the future!"

"Are you sure?" asked Jones, yawning prodigiously. As the senior member of the Historical Analytical Regression Technology team, otherwise known as HART, Jones had worked a good four years looking for historical convergence. Many had thought it happened on several occasions, but once he'd double-checked, something always missed the mark. The quirky, secret Q-Bit quantum computer worked a thousand times better than the best computers in their class, but the AI module acted like an idiot savant who could remember the weather at every Major League baseball game over the last hundred years, but then would tie his shoelaces together and fall flat on his face.

"I'm sure, I'm sure! The new AI 'extension' unit I had built at Tokyo Technologies did the trick."

"You mean AI *virus* application," said Jones with a frown.

"Well … yeah, it's kinda like a virus, but you know, Q-Bit wasn't really being helpful and needed some coaxing. In any event, we can now cross-reference down to the stock market with more than 99.99 percent accuracy. The big events close nicely for more than 150 years."

The "big events" interested Jones. His colleagues at HART thought he worked for the government. Although true, Jones also worked for a secret organization more important than any government on planet Earth—an organization of the rich and powerful only known as OPUS.

Jones gulped the last mouthful of his cold, stale coffee, then rose and hurried over to the HART station. "Come on, Brad—99.99 percent? Are you *really* sure?"

"Take a look," said Hull, grabbing a No Fear energy drink and popping open the can.

Jones, on the sunny side of fifty and a mite overweight, leaned over the console. He scratched his graying, longer-than-socially-acceptable beard and pushed up his Gooble ZoomX glasses to bring the screen's scrolling data into crystal clear focus. Using instinctive movements developed over many years, he swiped his hand over several motion sensor screens. The computer read the gestures and listed key historical economic and technological data. Another large, glass screen in front lit up with charts and numbers scrolling down. Finally, the screen stopped scrolling and results popped into view:

>> Economics — 99.9%
>> Technology Development — 99.9%
>> Pandemics — 99.9%

Jones straightened up and shook his raised fist triumphantly. "This looks great! We've never been able to forecast with this accuracy."

Hull sipped his energy drink, then twirled the can thoughtfully between his fingertips, regarding the baleful, winged-skull logo. "We could get rich using this data for investments. Hell, this thing just accurately predicted all stock movements at 99.9 percent from 1920 until 1970. It can surely predict the next hundred years with enough accuracy to get us richer than God."

Jones, immersed in his mental calculations, continued to make hand gestures while examining various charts. "The stock market's been rigged for years," he opined offhandedly. "A ten-year-old can make what he or she thinks is money."

"Well," said Hull, smiling, "if making money is so easy, why are you working here?"

Jones shot him an inscrutable glance. "Money will be worthless real soon. *That's* why I'm working here."

"What do you mean by that?" asked Hull, thinking that the strange Professor Jones was getting even stranger.

"Listen, Bradley, you're a good kid, but there're things common folks shouldn't know. Like some of the results I'm seeing in this AI data analysis."

Hull picked up his Rubik's Cube. With deft twitches of his fingers, faster than the eye, he solved the puzzle in eight seconds flat. Turning to examine the data Jones' board displayed, he noticed a big anomaly. "Wow, those are some strange predictions. We could definitely make money by putting out some stock shorts on dying companies—although we'll need to wait a few years."

Jones nodded. "Nothing's guaranteed in this kind of predictive analysis. But even if it's correct, we did sign those security agreements that forbid stock trading. Now, let me check one more regression test." Jones pulled out of his desk drawer a small black cube the size of a golf ball. When he pressed the center, it lit up with red and blue lights.

Hull eyed the device curiously. "What's that thingamabob, Jones?"

"Oh, it has a template for a few more big items—all classified. If this passes the test, we've hit gold."

Jones typed a code into his wrist band and a connector popped out of the cube. He inserted it into a high-speed port of the Q-Bit computer and typed in a password. Data raced down the screen. A table of historical events appeared, including: Beginning of Aviation, Great World War, Great World Depression, Rise of World Dictator, Second Great World War, Holocaust, Independence, Satellites, Manned Moon Landing, American Presidential Assassination, Loss of Independence, Nuclear Disasters, Imperialistic Wars, Tech Boom, Coronavirus Plagues, Greatest Depression, and finally Event X. The data filled the multiple computer screens. As the historical events were listed, the AI put in more specific terms and names such: "Adolf Hitler" for "Rise of World Dictator" and "John F. Kennedy" for "American Presidential Assassination." The screens filled with specific dates of world events and stopped scrolling in the year 2047, whereupon a blinking message popped up, filling the screen:

"Validated: Wars, Political Leaders, Population, Spiritual Leaders, Technology Development and Economics: 99.9%. All validated from 1920 until 2047 with 99.9% accuracy. High level probability of total system collapse validated for 2047."

Hull's eyes widened in surprise. "Are you serious, Jones? You have algorithms for wars, political leaders, and all that other stuff occurring in the future too?"

"It's classified, but I do. Been working on it for years. Needed to get the economic data right, as that's a precursor for the historical analytics."

Hull took an extra big gulp of this energy drink. He shook his head slowly, absorbing the immense ramifications of the algorithms. "Q-Bit just predicted politics and wars, too? From data only starting from 1920 and a little before?"

Jones nodded. "Yep, with a little help from another AI we integrated last week from Gal-X Systems at Gooble Labs. Can only imagine how well the accuracy is for the next twenty-seven years with that AI extension you had the folks at Tokyo Technologies write up."

Hull knew the ramifications of knowing the stock market at a 99.9 percent accuracy, but politics and wars were outright scary. "Gooble Labs? I wouldn't tell them it worked. This solution is *too* dangerous to share with those government- butt-kissing jerks. Anyone with this solution could control the future destiny of the world. Speaking of which, what was that system collapse at 2047? My data goes for seventy-five years at 99 percent. It doesn't break down at 2047."

"Here," said Jones, pulling up a chart. "You have data, but not all of it. You didn't consider planetary science. See what happens when you add in geologic seismic, geomagnetic field, solar activity, and meteorological historical data, including atmospheric chemistry? Did you extrapolate to see what that economic data was like after 2047 with that information included? Look here, it starts to drop in 2040 and hits bottom like a dead cat in 2046— and do you know why?"

Hull ignored the question. He'd been so excited to get the previous history working, he hadn't taken the time to view details of the future with all the parameters Jones added. He shook his head in dismay at the chart. "What's going on? This is horrible!"

"We'd hoped it was a later date," Jones said somberly, "but it's not the algorithmic system that breaks down. It's humanity. Nothing goes past 2047, because there are no human beings alive then to register any system activity. That's the 'big' prediction we're looking for from Q-Bit."

"What the hell are you talking about? What happens in 2047?" Hull's voice climbed an octave in anger and confusion.

"We added in some confidential data about unexpected radiation and weather patterns we're seeing related to a situation our scientists are calling Event X."

Event X, thought Hull. *That doesn't sound good.* "What," he said, gulping, "is Event X?"

"It's beyond my pay grade," Jones replied, "but since it's a complete human extinction event, predicted to wipe out all life on Earth, my team sardonically calls it Event X—gallows humor, you understand. Plus, there's a lot of Xbox enthusiasts on the team. In any case, we needed these other algorithms, and a whole bunch of other critical data points, to converge over 99.5 percent in order to calculate when the destruction of humanity would happen—and what, if anything, we might do to stop it. The year 2047 is much earlier than we'd expected. It will take something— or someone—very special to save the world."

Jones unlocked a cabinet with a pass code and pulled out a tranquilizer gun. "I'm sorry, Brad," he said coolly, pointing it at his colleague, "but I think I'm that special person who will save the world, and I can't let anyone stop me." He pulled the trigger, firing a hypo-dart into Hull's chest. Hull quickly pulled it out, but not before the sedative and amnesic agent had infiltrated his bloodstream.

"*Why, Jones?* What have you done?" Hull demanded as his vision blurred.

"This cannot stay with the government; it's too important. When you wake up in a few hours, you will have no memory of the events of the last hour, and after a virus I installed deletes all the programming, this project will get shut down and die, just like me. I'll be gone—'dead' in flaming car accident in the woods. My body, supposedly incinerated in the blaze, shall not be found. I'm gonna use this data to save the world. You should thank me now, as you'll never see me again."

Jones walked over to Hull's desk and pulled a book covered in strange symbols from a drawer. "You shouldn't have taken this book; no can read those alien codes anyhow." Jones threw it back on the desk. "Keep it, I already made a copy."

His mouth working like an oxygen-starved fish, Hull staggered toward Jones' hazy outline before collapsing atop his computer console. Upended, the can of No Fear disgorged a sticky puddle of overcaffeinated brew near Hull's cheek. The last thing he saw before all went black was the winged skull's mocking, hollow eyes.

Jones swung Hull's limp body into the swivel chair and put the energy drink upright. "Poor Brad," he commented. "You never could hold your energy drink."

ONE:

THE DARKNESS OF HUMANITY

"The only good is knowledge and the only evil is ignorance."

— Socrates

S hu Franklin, a smart and well-mannered (well, most of the time) twelve-year-old, touched the current date—December 11, 2096—on the holographic calendar in his study room. A history buff and science/technology wunderkind with a genius IQ, Shu had cobbled the device together from electronic odds and ends, mostly for his own amusement.

Instantly, an audiovisual slideshow of significant historical milestones began to play, just as he'd programmed the device to do. Having just showered after a vigorous mountain bike ride, and now getting dressed ahead of his Sophistry class, the preteen only half paid attention until the female narrator's sexy voice (also Shu's handiwork; his hormones were starting to kick in big time) informed him:

"Many believed humanity lived in darkness. A darkness of the mind, of the soul, and eventually, a complete darkness that would fill planet Earth with pestilence and destruction.

"But the Utopians were, at heart optimists, and prophesized that only in the darkest of times could people see the light.

"And so, it came to pass that in one of its darkest and most desperate years, humanity reached out to the stars and captured the light and knowledge they called the Illumination, officially creating Utopian society on planet Earth on December 11, 2084."

Wow! he mused. Today is exactly twelve years since the Illumination of mankind. What with his studies and recreational activities, the anniversary had somehow slipped his mind. Utopians didn't mark such events with garish hoopla, but rather observed them privately, in serene contemplation.

Shu had arrived into the world a few short months after that worldwide event, given birth by his mother, Maki. She named him "Shu" after her Japanese grandfather, Shu Yamada, who'd passed away when she was seven years old. At his deathbed, Shu Yamada told the young girl: "Maki, everyone dies, but not everyone lives, so enjoy a great life. Someday, create a family and fill the world with beauty. I'll be watching from above."

At school, Maki learned kanji and discovered that her grandfather's *kanji* name meant "beauty and excellence." After marriage, she decided she wanted something beautiful in her life. Maki told Shu that, before the Illumination, she and Shu's father, James, weren't sure conceiving a child made sense in a crazy and destructive world, but they believed in the Utopian movement and the eventual Illumination. Thus, Maki and James moved from a Utopian-based camp in the ex-Cleveland National Forest to the small mountain city of Julian to have a child. Months later, a fire engulfed the forest camp, killing the few adherents that remained. If they'd stayed at the camp, his father and mother would have perished. Shu's mom explained to Shu: "Timing is critical with all things in life. And if you value your life, then you'd better value your time, too—because that's what life is made up of."

Shu valued his time, certainly, but wished he had more of it for playing with his friends instead of studying six hours a day—much of it in preparation for his own Illumination.

Shu continued to listen to the calendar's litany of milestones, reminiscing back four years ago, when his father, then sixty, had observed wryly: "History laughs at humanity. Why else would the salvation of mankind, the Illumination, arrive one hundred years after 1984, the date used as a title in George Orwell's dystopian novel?"

It's all timing...and propaganda, thought Shu. He had heard that the founding of the Utopian Society had been delayed to 2084 and then almost went into 2085, but the Founders pushed ahead the legal ratification timeline. The Founders even cut back the original eleven Utopian commandments to ten; Shu supposed, they decided a good, round number was more impactful than an odd one. Shu learned through his studies that if you could rely on one principle in this world, it's trust nothing, verify everything. Almost everyone has a hidden agenda.

Four years ago, Shu couldn't answer why humanity needed the Illumination, George Orwell, or even *1984*. But things change.

Now, as a Utopian, Shu Franklin knew all about those things, and even more important ones, like how to fish, swim, fight, and ride a mountain bike. From his political expression class, he had learned to fluently discuss alternative viewpoints, which his parents drolly called "arguing." Shu liked using persuasive reasoning to argue his points, but his parents didn't seem to be as smart nor as logical as they used to be. Educated to the equivalent level of a freshman at an Old Earth Ivy League college, Shu felt he was an intellectual equal to his parents. Although they both had PhDs, they seemed to lack an appreciation of a young man's desire for freedom and equality—especially for some desperately needed reforms in the home.

For instance, when Shu asked his father for a meeting on democratic reforms related to chores and personal liberties, the meeting ended abruptly with the elder Franklin stating dictatorially: "When you can afford your own home, you can do what you want. Until then, you will follow the house rules and take out the garbage. No more discussion on the topic."

Shu later spoke privately to his mom about his frustrations (using skills acquired in his persuasive reasoning class), but to no avail. Even appealing to her maternal instincts proved fruitless. It didn't take a genius to see his parents were in cahoots in these matters. *Politics would not be an easy course to pass,* Shu realized, sighing. *People seem to have vested personal interests that conflict with reason and true reform.*

* * * * *

Shu enjoyed living in Julian, a quaint, California town teeming with trees and surrounded by mountains and apple orchards. He sat in his red, cushioned ball chair reading a digital book for a class called *The History of the World*. The unusual ball chair enclosed Shu inside a semi-globe. Inside were speakers and a microphone, which allowed Shu to interact with friends and his online Sophist professor. To become a full Utopian citizen, Shu would need to prove his worthiness through completion of his Illumination studies. He only had a few classes left to complete and couldn't wait to move on to the adventure he believed awaited him, beyond Julian's provincial confines. *Illumination* and adulthood occurred concurrently at the age of thirteen for all Utopian children, and required completion of a rigorous curriculum of reading, writing, scientific studies, special projects (ESP, remote viewing, telepathy, and mindflashing), rhetoric, philosophy, athletics, and music programs. Called the Ingenium, this curriculum commenced at the age of two and a half years and ended on the child's thirteenth birthday. It was a tremendous amount for these young minds to learn; the pressure exerted by parents, teachers, and counselors to succeed was often unbearable, but Shu excelled as an honor student. As much as he enjoyed Julian's bucolic charms, he also chafed at its cultural and social limitations. The personal restrictions imposed by his parents weighed even heavier on him. He already felt like a man. He wanted to get free from his parents and do what he wanted to do, when he wanted to do it.

Shu studied Earth history with interest and focus, comforted in reading that humanity had survived its darkest hours. Over the last three years, he'd read about the Black Death, the rise and fall of the Roman Empire, World War I and II (a combined class, as WWI set the foundation for WWII), the rise and fall of the American Empire, World War III, and the rise and fall of the Chinese Empire (the shortest empire in recorded history at only twenty years), and, finally, the new Golden Age of the Utopians.

At the age of thirteen, the year of his personal Illumination, he would move out for seven years of Outer World Education at a special training facility modeled after an old education system called "college." All Utopians who completed their Ingenium home studies were required to take this next step in their education. Shu planned to go to Maruyama Park in Hokkaido, Japan to lead a software development collective. Under Utopian policies, he required seven years of computer engineering studies to get a PhD. He would also study for a collaborative operations degree at what, in olden times, was known as "business school."

Shu had recently read two of British author George Orwell's most venerated works, the allegorical novella *Animal Farm*, and *1984*, his masterpiece of dystopian literature. He thought it amazing that a book written about the future could so closely mirror the historical records. It fascinated the young boy, now quickly approaching adulthood, that most of the pre-Utopian populace had failed to comprehend and heed the dire warnings of a man desperately trying to save humanity through his bleak prophesies, while himself dying of tuberculosis. Shu thought it a sad state of affairs that humanity slept for years in the dark. Orwell's books became required reading for all Utopians; a statue of Orwell towered over Lake Cuyamaca, with this quotation from the author inscribed upon the pedestal:

The further a society drifts from the truth, the more it will hate those that speak it.

The Utopians loved truth, especially disturbing and disruptive truth—the only path to enlightenment.

The class Analytical Orwell forced Shu to analyze the author's writings. This intrigued him, because he'd discovered secret hidden truths in the texts. Back during the dark ages of Old Earth, people banned books, movies, TV shows, blogs, social media, reporters, and especially words that forced people to think. Old Earth had retreated back to the times where people had to meet in secret to talk freely. But in Utopian society, you no longer had to live in such fear.

Shu glanced over at the home study telescreen waiting for his tutor, a Sophist named Donald Austin. His solar-powered digital desk clock read 10:55 a.m.; in less than five minutes, his instructor would be on U-NET. While waiting, Shu lackadaisically glanced out the 1 x 2 meter window in his study room, enjoying the view of the cedar and oaks trees swaying in the breeze and the bluish-gray mountains looming like ghostly sentinels in the distance. In between the trees and the Franklin home stood a standard, Old Earth-style greenhouse, with two geodesic dome greenhouses nearby. The geodesics housed various vegetables and fruits, including tasty heirloom tomatoes, zucchini, and lettuce. His father used the standard greenhouse for year-round strawberries and seasonal grapes to make wine. Shu thought the wine tasted like rotten, fermented fruit juice and stayed away from the concoction.

Near the window in his room stood a large aquarium with five gray piranha that swam together in a small school. Shu had begged his parents for years to buy him some piranha, ever since he'd been immersed in an augmented reality documentary in which he'd virtually been attacked by the fearsome fish—and loved every terrifying minute of it. Alas, his pleas fell on deaf ears. Luckily, Shu's paternal grandfather, James Sr.—Shu called him Grandpa J—had come through.

At eighty-seven, Grandpa J was a fun-loving and indulgent sort who understood the whims and fancies of boys, being an overgrown one himself. (Shu's father claimed Grandpa J was in his second childhood—or maybe even his third.) On Shu's twelfth birthday, Grandpa J brought the fish over to his house, and presented them to his parents, who accepted them like one accepts a bag of dog poop. "I know ya don't want the boy to have him," he'd said, "but hell, he's got his heart set on 'em. You only go 'round once, ya know." Shu's mom and dad knew there was no sense arguing with Grandpa J—especially since he'd provided not only the piranha but also a top-of-the-line aquarium—and they listened with sickly white faces to the old man's graphic instructions on feeding the carnivorous fish.

"These fish bite," he said, "so ya better keep your fingers outta the tank if ya wanna keep 'em. These buggers here are meat eaters—just like me. Ya gotta feed 'em live fish or meat." Grandpa J had looked at Shu and grinned impishly. "Course, if ya run outta meat, you can toss this here punk into the tank." Shu and Grandpa J laughed their butts off. Ma and Pa Franklin were not amused. Next to the aquarium stood another glass enclosure containing a miniature ant farm. The inhabitants were busy creating tunnels and fetching food for the queen.

Shu also had an enviable collection of antique toys, courtesy of Grandpa J, who was always "spoiling the boy," as his parents put it. They were against "corrupting" Shu with material things, but Grandpa J's generosity would not be denied. Curiously, the toys were from the 1960s, by and large, and in remarkably good condition for being nearly a century and a half old, although some no longer functioned and were merely display pieces. Many still had the original boxes, whose bright, action-filled graphics thrilled Shu almost as much as the toys themselves. Old Earth antiques of this vintage, particularly toys, were a rarity in 2096. Antique stores were uncommon and far-flung; Julian had none. When Shu pressed Grandpa J on how he came to acquire these rare artifacts, he would just smile mysteriously and say, "I have my ways."

The vintage toy collection was displayed in a glass case occupying most of one wall. Among Shu's favorites was a game called Rock 'Em Sock 'Em Robots, consisting of a miniature, bright yellow, plastic boxing ring in which two robot pugilists—the Blue Bomber and the Red Rocker—squared off, each trying to knock the other's rectangular head off. The robots were controlled by a primitive mechanism operated by the youthful players—in this case Shu and his best friend, Andy Blackwell, a boy prone to mischief and affectionately known as Braindead. While Utopians strongly disapproved of physical violence, the two boys loved nothing better than going toe-to-toe—over Shu's parents' protests, of course.

Hot Wheels were another favorite. These were 1:64-scale die-cast replicas of the petroleum-fueled cars once common on Old Earth, but now long obsolete. The little cars—some, perfect replicas of actual cars, and others, fantastically souped-up hot rods—fascinated Shu, who had never seen an actual "gas guzzler," as his dad called them, in operation.

Space-age toys had been extremely popular in the 1960s, when, as Shu had studied, the United States had engaged in a desperate space race with the Soviet Union to put a man on the moon. Now that NASA and the Space Force had been disbanded, the vintage Major Matt Mason (Mason was a moon-based astronaut) "action figures" and accessories in Shu's collection allowed him to go into space vicariously. The toys went hand-in-hand with his passion for Old Earth science fiction cinema and literature, which were largely *verboten* in Utopian society. Shu's father, something of a sci-fi buff himself, was known to bend this rule, as well as other Utopian edicts he found too cumbersome. Grandpa J enjoyed science fiction, too, and had a fragile collection of sci-fi magazines from the 1940s and '50s. Shu's fanaticism for all things science fiction came naturally.

Asleep on the floor were two canines, one real, the other a fantastically lifelike android. The real pooch was Buddy, the result of thousands of years of unregulated, noncertified dog reproduction. Buddy was a delightful mix of German shepherd, Labrador, pit bull, and husky—in other words, a big, lovable, hairy black mutt. The dog-bot was Spike, a black Labrador with programmable memory, skills, and a personality chip, which Shu had assembled from a kit. Spike was a mere plaything, a project that had turned out well. Shu's greatest and abiding affection was for Buddy, of course, being the real McCoy. Buddy accompanied his master wherever he was allowed to go, including this morning's bike ride. Now Buddy was pooped, and his sleep was genuine, whereas Spike's was an artificial state. Shu decided to let the real sleeping dog lie, and beckoned to the simulacrum.

"Wake up, Spike!" Shu said in a loud whisper. "Do a somersault!"

Spike instantly sprang to life, capering happily around his master/creator and wagging his tail. The dog-bot's breath was every bit as stinky as a real dog's; it even had doggie body odor and produced copious saliva—or something like it—which was dripping all over Shu's feet.

"Yechh!" Shu said, grimacing. "Now, do a somersault!"

Spike gave a couple of woofs and jumped in the air, doing a double flip and landing squarely on its legs with programmed balance and grace. Meanwhile, Buddy had awakened and was watching the scene with open and undisguised jealousy. His tan eyebrows were twitching like twin caterpillars on a griddle, which was a sure sign he was itching for a fight.

Shu cried, "Good job!" The dog-bot squatted on its haunches, tongue lolling out. "Oh, so you want a treat, eh? Here ..." Shu tossed him a "dog biscuit"—actually a biscuit-shaped, dissolving lubricant good for keeping the electronic innards oiled. Spike caught the treat expertly in his mouth.

Buddy couldn't stand it any longer. Growling, he leapt to his feet and lunged at Spike, bowling the dog-bot over. Shu hadn't programmed Spike for dog brawls. The bot just lay there stoically as Buddy went savagely for his throat.

"Buddy! Bad dog! Get off of Spike! *Now!*"

With downcast eyes, Buddy slunk away from Spike. The dog-bot picked up the biscuit in his synthetic teeth and lay down to chew on it between his front paws, just as if nothing had happened.

"Jealous again?" Shu asked Buddy. "You need to get over that."

Buddy inclined his head, listening, as dogs are wont to do. "Tell you what: I'll deactivate Spike and put him in the closet for a couple of months. How's that sound?" Buddy jumped up on his hind legs and put his front paws on Shu's shoulders, and kissed his master lavishly, his absurdly long tongue slinging saliva like a wet mop. "Okay, Okay, that's enough! You'll drown me!"

Shu eased Buddy to the ground and walked over to Spike, who was through with his biscuit. "Sorry, pal, but I guess this study room's not big enough for two dogs." He felt for the deactivation button on Spike's chest, pushed it, and the bot turned as rigid as stone. Shu carried Spike to his closet (the bot weighed only a fraction as much as a real Lab), unceremoniously shoved him inside, and shut the door. "Happy now?" he asked Buddy. The dog smiled in triumph and lay down to resume his snooze.

Only two and a half more months until Illumination, thought Shu in jubilant anticipation. It would finally be time to leave home for his Outer World Education.

Shu looked over at the telescreen and reviewed his next historical assignment: Economic History 1900-2084. In 2096, the economy didn't really mean anything to Shu except as a mathematical game. Sophist instructor Austin smiled at Shu on a 3-D telescreen. A glance at the desk clock showed it was eleven a.m. The prof was right on time. His outfit—a smart, black jacket with a mandarin collar and a crisp, white linen shirt underneath—was at odds with his hair, a battleship gray jungle that looked as if it'd been styled in a wind tunnel. He peered at Shu, his blue eyes dancing with warmth, intelligence, and humor.

"So, how is my best student doing today?" asked Austin.

"Am I really your best student, or am I just your *only* smart student?" asked Shu, laughing smugly.

"I don't want to give you a big head, Shu. That would look most unbecoming, especially with that long hair of yours," Austin deadpanned. "But out of fifteen students preparing for Illumination this year, I'm proud to say you are currently testing as my number one. However, I do take points off for rude manners, so it is possible that after this class, you might end up at number two." Austin's stern look melted into a fatherly smile.

Shu flushed scarlet. "I was just kidding, Mr. Austin. But as a Sophist, I know you can't change my Illumination score for joking with you."

"Hmm. You have me there, young man. But trust me when I say that good manners are every bit as important as a highly developed intellect. Being bright does not make you right. To truly succeed, one needs brains, of course, but one must also endure the agony of hard work. It is the arrogance of the wise that makes a man a fool. Do you understand my meaning?"

"I think I do, Mr. Austin," said Shu sincerely.

"Good. Now let's review our final studies."

Shu looked at the telescreen 3-D projection and reviewed the agenda for his final three months of study. It included the years 2000-2014, known as the Millennial Years, and then 2020-2030, known as the Ten Years of Economic Restructure (also known as the "Great Reset") which had been triggered by two global pandemics. Some called those years "the True Depression." The final era was 2030-2046, known as the Planetary Imbalance, a time during which the world lost 90 percent of its population. A world war in 2047, combined with global climate change and more widespread death at the hands of a United Nations Police-controlled, digitally-monitored planet, nearly rendered Earth uninhabitable.

The advent of the great Utopian leader, Aeon Nous—who came to power that year, presenting the current framework of Utopian society—saved humankind from extinction.

From 2047 to 2080, an uprising called the Utopian Movement took hold and changed the world. In 2084, the philosophy of the Utopian Movement became the official rule of law, albeit one without any real military force. Shu learned that when people became truly good, in the strictest sense of possessing and practicing moral virtue, they really didn't need the police or the military. It took until 2084 for that Utopian concept to be fulfilled. Shu's tutor, Austin, explained that learning from history isn't easy.

Austin stroked his Van Dyke beard meditatively. "If you do not understand history, it may repeat. And each time it repeats, what happens?"

Shu smirked at the simplicity of the question. "Every time history repeats, the cost goes up. The past should teach lessons for the correct future action."

"Good answer, because those who cannot remember the past are condemned to repeat it—and that, my boy, is costly and wasteful. For example, can you tell me what happened with France and Germany during World War I and World War II?"

Shu closed his eyes and recalled visual pictures and movies of World War I and negotiations he'd read about and seen on the telescreen. They were structured in an organized way, using a mind map with a mnemonic peg memory system. Mind-mapping classes with mnemonic peg integration were required studies for all Utopians. Shu had passed those classes when he was only nine years old. Utopian children and adults commonly used memory tools and methods to remember more effectively.

Some people on Old Earth had used those systems to secretly (and not so secretly) outsmart others for unfair advancement in education and business.

Shu opened his eyes and confidently answered: "After repeated wars with Germany, France never learned. She still demanded that Germany, as the vanquished nation, pay billions of dollars to the victors after the First World War. This set the foundation for the Second World War."

Austin arched one eyebrow. "A costly event, wouldn't you say?"

"Indeed, Mr. Austin. But as much as man talks about learning from history, my studies indicate humanity never really learned from the mistakes they made—did they?"

"No, in most circumstances, they did not. But we, as Utopians, must do so—not only to survive, but also to thrive. Remember, a Utopian must peel back the onion skin, layer by layer, to gain real truth. We must dig deeper than what's accepted as truth, as written by the victors, in history books.

"Think about this, Shu. I want you to peel back the layers on the World Wars and discover their root causes, then look at the top fifty world conflicts since 1945 and write a report on how you would have avoided such wars."

Shu looked out the window at the trees dancing in the wind. In a frenzied courtship ritual, a pair of squirrels raced up and down the bole of a black oak at breakneck speed. Shu watched, fascinated, until the smart clap of his tutor's hands fetched him back to reality.

"You will not find the answer outside your window, my boy," Austin admonished him. "Stay focused!"

"Sorry, Mr. Austin." He reflected a moment and said: "I'm curious as to why my last year is so focused on history. We've put checks and balances into our Utopian society. The Illumination and Utopian society are in balance. Do I really need to know so much history for a world at peace?"

Austin shook his head. "Peace on planet Earth is a rare historical event. You do not have a full understanding of the final test of your day of Illumination, which is really a day of enlightenment.

You do not know what challenges lay in front of you. I can assure you that you will need history, math, science, remote viewing, telepathy, and, above all, deep conviction and perseverance to complete the challenge and pass this examination. I remind you once again that, although you've mastered your sciences, rhetoric, music, and special projects, as a Utopian, your studies are a lifelong engagement. As of now, you have not fully mastered history in order to pass. This is an imperative study. As a free Utopian, you may choose to cancel your exam and stay a non-illuminated citizen, if you so wish."

Shu's jaw dropped in his lap. "Me, your best student? Stay here in Julian as a laborer? Not a chance! Why would I do that?"

"Well, I want to tell you something today in a secret oath. We discussed the Utopian Secret Oath weeks ago, as you'll recall."

Oh, jeez, thought Shu, remembering the discussion. "Secret Oath" meant he would be told something he could not tell others, except for his mother and father. He hated this because, if he slipped up, it would mean points off his final test. Whenever Shu asked about specific details on the test, he'd never gotten a straight answer—only that it was a test on everything studied and then maybe not everything. *What was this test?*

Shu frowned pensively. "After I learned about the secret oath, I did some further reading on the subject, because I value honesty and I value you as my tutor. Forgive me for being so impertinent, Mr. Austin, but I read that 'secret oaths' are dangerous."

"And where did you read that?" asked Austin suspiciously.

"From a speech by President John Kennedy in 1961, addressing the American Newspaper Association," said Shu. He shrugged, adding, "A newspaper, I learned, is an antiquated printed form of information dissemination, quite obsolete now. I had fun doing some extra studies."

"Well, if studies aren't fun, students aren't successful," said Austin, quoting the Utopian policy on education.

Shu thought the Kennedy speech to be a fitting warning. "I read a contradiction to Utopian secret oaths. I'd like to share it with you, if you don't mind."

"Not at all. Proceed."

"Very well," said Shu. "I thought it was important enough to put into memory, so I added it to my daily Sati mindfulness meditations. I have the key parts memorized. Kennedy said: *'The very word "secrecy" is repugnant in a free and open society; and we are, as a people, inherently and historically opposed to secret societies, to secret oaths and secret proceedings. We decided long ago that the dangers of excessive and unwarranted concealment of pertinent facts far outweighed the dangers which are cited to justify it. Even today, there is little value in opposing the threat of a closed society by imitating its arbitrary restrictions. Even today, there is little value in insuring the survival of our nation if our traditions do not survive with it. And there is very grave danger that an announced need for increased security will be seized upon by those anxious to expand its meaning to the very limits of official censorship and concealment. That I do not intend to permit, to the extent that it is in my control. And no official of my Administration, whether his rank is high or low, civilian or military, should interpret my words here tonight as an excuse to censor the news, to stifle dissent, to cover up our mistakes, or to withhold from the press and the public the facts they deserve to know.'*"

Austin nodded and raised an eyebrow. "I'll admit, I'm impressed with your recall, Shu. And I agree with President Kennedy—in principle. As you know, Kennedy was an idealist and a fearless champion of human rights. Unfortunately, after just over a thousand days in office, dark forces behind the scenes murdered him. Semi-secret government forces took over the old United States and used the country's economic and military might to control many other countries. Future US presidents ended up being mostly controlled by these secret forces." Austin couldn't exactly explain to Shu why, in an "open society" like Utopia, there needed to be secrets—but he tried.

"It sounds likes these secrets weren't in the people's interest," said Shu, frowning. "It makes me question why one is needed with my studies."

"Listen, my boy. Secrets are required to win wars," said Austin. "You are in a war to pass the Illumination, and part of the

Illumination is waiting to pass along facts when a candidate is ready. Passing on this information to those who are not ready is as foolhardy as giving a twentieth-century pistol to a three-year-old. The information I pass you is under the promise of Utopian Secret Oath. Upon passing Illumination, you will understand its importance."

Shu didn't like the logical runaround, but he knew some truths took time to understand. "Okay, Mr. Austin. I'll keep this information as a 'secret oath.' As a Utopian who values honesty, I must say, I don't like secrets. But I'll adhere to our customs and rules, unless we change them. Please tell me more about the test. I promise to keep it under secret oath."

Austin's voice had an ominous edge. "Failing your test will mean certain death."

TWO:
FATES WORSE
THAN DEATH

*"WE PROBABLY COULD HAVE SAVED OURSELVES,
BUT WERE TOO DAMNED LAZY TO TRY VERY
HARD ..."*

— Kurt Vonnegut, Fates Worse than Death

Shu swallowed the lump in his throat. "Uh, did you say ... death?"

"Yes," answered Austin. "I would strongly advise you to maintain your final months of studies in order to pass."

Shu's heart was racing. "Do you mean death as in drowning, or being eaten by a bear ... or do you mean it euphemistically, as in death of the soul?"

"I mean unequivocal death, as in a pesky bug squashed underfoot. Dead as a Dickensian doornail. Dead as—"

"I get the picture, Mr. Austin." Shu smiled, looking both nervous and excited. He'd been taught at a young age not to fear death but to plan to win at life. The precocious youth's eyes shone with self-confidence. "Death to the loser, you say?" he asked.

"Yes."

"Wow, that's pretty serious."

"It is."

Outside, the trees were still swaying balletically in the howling wind. Shu pondered the situation, his peach-fuzzed face belying an intellect superior to most adults. "I'm your best student," he said at length, smirking. "I can beat the test. Can you tell me how you passed it? I mean, if it wouldn't be giving me an unfair advantage. I wouldn't want to cheat."

"I didn't take the test," said Austin flatly.

"Didn't take it? Why not?"

"I choose to stay in Utopia and became a Sophist," Austin replied, somewhat glumly, "to help others pass a test I never took."

Shu laughed, stopping abruptly. "Excuse my poor manners, Mr. Austin. It's just that I find it ironic that you're my mentor for this monumental test for which the penalty of failure is death, yet you, yourself, are ... well, untested."

Austin bristled. "Your unspoken point being, how can I teach what I have not experienced? Your overweening self-confidence is not an attractive trait, young man."

"I didn't mean to question your qualifications, Mr. Austin," Shu said contritely. "You know how much I admire you. I'm always shooting my mouth off when I should be listening."

Austin's voice softened. "Please understand that there is no fixed test. It's adaptive and dynamic, and the perils are quite real. If I might make an analogy, I know how to build the car; I'm an engineer—but I need a driver. And my students are drivers. It is my job to turn them into *good* drivers."

Shu's mind was stuck on the nagging question. "I hate to beat a dead horse, Mr. Austin, but why didn't you take the test? I imagine not taking it would be an easier route, but Utopians are taught to take the smarter route, regardless of the difficulty."

Austin blushed slightly. "Shu, it was actually the hard route. I've never left Julian in order to fully focus my time on finding the right students, ones who could pass this special test. Many days, I wonder if I've chosen the right path. But I enjoy my life. Most of my classmates and friends left Julian. They run companies, build things, and live in more advanced towns outside of Julian. And when they come back to visit, they regale me with stories of their fulfilling lives and exciting adventures. I'm sometimes jealous, and sometimes I don't fully understand them. I'm truly an outsider."

Austin fell into a contemplative silence, stroking his beard. Shu sat respectfully for a time before blurting out, "How many died taking the test last year?"

"What? Oh yes, the test." Austin blinked himself back to the present. "In our Utopian collectives around the world, about one in ten million die each year. None in my class died, and only one, me, opted out of the test during my Illumination."

"Why is my test a life or death proposition?" Shu pressed. "My mom and dad are going to freak out."

Austin answered truthfully, the only way to answer for a Utopian. "I knew everyone in my class that passed, and their grades and abilities. As a Sophist instructor I analyzed all the students in Julian and worldwide who had failed—to learn from their mistakes. I work with tutors from other towns to evaluate the data. We look at characteristics of the ones who failed and try to ensure that students do not have those failings. You, Shu Franklin, have none of those weaknesses, except your arrogance. Academically, you're ranked at the top of your class in most subjects, not only in Julian, but worldwide. If you can work on developing humility, I'm confident you'll pass. But to answer your question, this is a special year; that's why it's a life-or-death test. LISA discovered six Alpha Primes scattered across the planet, one of which will someday become our Supreme Sovereign Ruler. And you, Shu Franklin, are listed as one of the Alpha Prime candidates."

Shu puffed out his chest. "Wow! Really? But we don't have a Supreme Sovereign Ruler! The concept was banned after we achieved Illumination. What's happened? The Supreme Sovereign Ruler law is only for times of dire need."

"My knowledge in this area is limited, but the Council, based on LISA's AI analysis, has chosen this path. I would be proud if you could become an Alpha Prime, but I'll understand if you decline. The likelihood of death for candidates taking this test is a coin flip—a fifty/fifty shot."

Shu's heart threatened to jackhammer out of his chest. The responsibility of the Supreme Sovereign was well-known: to save the Utopians from a major threat, whether it be physical, spiritual, or otherwise. *But what was the threat?*

Shu sat quietly for a while until Austin asked gently, "Do you understand the risk?"

"I do. I'd be honored, but I'm concerned. There must be some dire circumstances..." His voice trailed off.

"Courage is a virtue. Do you not have courage, young Franklin?"

"I'd like to think I do, but this is pretty heavy stuff, Mr. Austin. I think I'll need some time to truly prepare myself."

Austin nodded. "A wise decision. By giving you this secret oath, and telling you of your final weakness, I have completed your training for the day. I assume you will continue your historical studies according to your schedule, and we can talk tomorrow at the same time. I strongly advise you to add the importance of this test to your mindfulness meditations."

"I will, indeed. Thank you, Mr. Austin, for your assistance and patience."

The tutor smiled. "You're already sounding less arrogant. The knowledge of a potentially fatal test tends to have that humbling effect. Please study the materials I sent. I'll be back in one week's time to evaluate your progress." The telescreen went black.

Shu sat alone, wondering why failing the test meant certain death. His life now depended on becoming a Supreme Sovereign Ruler. The Utopian town of Julian just got a bit stranger.

Wanting to consult with his father, Shu rose from his bubble chair and walked outside. A cobblestone path wended its way through a lush Japanese garden—wisteria, peonies, styrax, ornamental cherry trees, maples and black pines, rhododendrons—thoughtfully designed and lovingly tended by his mother. Although it was December, Julian seemed warmer than usual. The planetary climate change made winter come later and later in Southern California. But at 4,500 feet, you never really knew when the first winter storm would hit. Sometimes it snowed in June, and sometimes you wore summer shorts in December. That's why his father had purchased two spacious geodesic greenhouses, each forty-two feet in diameter; they kept all the veggies at the right temperature, even with radical temperature swings. Providing even light distribution, the special polycarbonate glazing kept the greenhouse interior warm in the winter and cool in the summer. The healing planet still needed systems like these for proper temperature regulation and mitigation of harsh ultraviolet rays.

Shu followed a well-trodden path through the fescue lawn to the greenhouses, devoting some mindfulness time to admiring the purple flowers, the apple and apricot trees, and a flock of wild turkeys foraging for acorns in a grove of oaks. He plopped himself down on a mossy log and breathed in the sweet, fresh air, feeling the preciousness of life, savoring the moment. A Utopian maxim intruded on the youth's reverie: "Live and savor the present, but prepare now, or fail in the future."

Preparing for the future. That's all the Utopians ever really do! It seems to contradict living and savoring the present. Shu got up, turned, and walked into his father's private Garden of Illumination. There stood a nineteen-foot replica of a Utopian statue called the *Monument of Wisdom*. The original granite monument had been erected in 1980 under mysterious circumstances in the unlikely location of Elbert County, in the state of Georgia. Commissioned by a pseudonymous man representing an anonymous group of likeminded individuals, the Georgia Guidestones, as the installation came to be called, contained ten "guidelines" or "principles," inscribed in eight modern languages. (Owing to its astronomical features, it was sometimes also called the American Stonehenge.)

Over the decades, the Guidestones had become a magnet for controversy and speculation, inspiring diverse interpretations of the principles—everything from advocacy of a New World Order, to their somehow being linked to the Rosicrucians, the secretive seventeenth century society devoted to metaphysical studies. A popular theory held that the Guidestones represented the basic principles a failed society would require in order to rebuild itself.

In 2096, the identity of the benefactors who paid for the creation of the Guidestones remained a mystery to the world at large. In point of fact, the Guidestones were erected by proponents of utopianism, and the principles thereon were their creed. The Utopians of Shu's era didn't mind that the Guidestones—which they called the *Monument of Wisdom*—remained the subject of debate, as it allowed them to live as they preferred, unhindered by outsiders.

Upon the replica's granite surface, as on the original monument, were inscribed the following commandments:

Maintain humanity under 500,000,000 in perpetual balance with nature.

Guide reproduction wisely — improving fitness and diversity.

Unite humanity with a living new language.

Rule passion — faith — tradition — and all things with tempered reason.

Protect people and nations with fair laws and just courts.

Let all nations rule internally resolving external disputes in a world court.

Avoid petty laws and useless officials.

Balance personal rights with social duties.

Prize truth — beauty — love — seeking harmony with the infinite.

Be not a cancer on the earth — Leave room for nature — Leave room for nature.

Shu had studied the context of each and every commandment in detail; he'd need to explain them all during his final test. He reread them now, concentrating on the first and most controversial one.

Many Old Earthers despised and feared the first commandment because, at one time, the planet had ten billion plus people—or twenty times the 500 million suggested for balance with nature. In a more benighted era, many thought the first commandment cryptically referred to a conspiracy to murder "excess" people. While Utopians lent no credence to that extreme theory, early adherents prophesized that overpopulation threatened to ruin the fragile balance between mankind and his natural world. Those early prophesies—in reality, mathematical probabilistic models—proved mostly correct. The world's inefficient use of resources created waste.

Shu had read that when there were seven billion people, it would have taken five Earths to sustain the lifestyle of the average American in the twentieth century; thus, only about 1.5 billion people could live on Earth in such a manner. Further studies showed that even before the Illumination, only one or two billion people could be sustained at the old European standards without stripping resources out of balance. Threatened by workforce reduction, many governments and conglomerates argued vehemently against the limited population.

Most world citizens before the Illumination were labeled workers, employees, or subjects of the ruling systems in place—but in reality, they were slaves to the owner classes. But that changed and the population, although not at five hundred million, now stood at only one billion. In post-Illumination society, Utopian families were limited to a single child to maintain a balance with nature.

Shu walked past the monument and went into the first geodesic hydroponic greenhouse. Inside were various vegetables in a riot of colors: red heirloom tomatoes, green spinach, purple and green lettuce, and yellow squash. At the far end of the greenhouse stood a fish tank, twenty feet or so in diameter, bubbling up white foam. Shu watched avidly as an unwary fly skimmed the surface, inciting half a dozen salmon to an aquatic drag race. A silvery flash, a splash ... and to the fleetest went the spoils! Shu's father, James, stood next to tank's water filtering system, checking out some water lines. The lanky and fit six-footer had to rise onto his tiptoes to grab a flexible pipe from a nearby shelf. Shu stood five foot two and dreamed he'd someday grow taller than his father.

James saw Shu approaching and waved him over before bending down to continue his chore. His dad's attire always reminded Shu of a strange subculture he'd read about in one of his history textbooks: "hippies," rebellious youths of the 1960s who wore psychedelic clothing, rejected societal norms, took hallucinogenic drugs recreationally, and advocated free love. Today, his father wore brown leather moccasins, faded Levi's, and a long-sleeved cotton shirt embroidered with colorful, exotic birds flying upon a jungle mosaic, with the motto "I Got A Peaceful Easy Feeling" stitched across the chest. Shu kept to himself the opinion that the elder Franklin, at sixty-four, was too old to be aping the fashions of a bygone counterculture.

Shu observed his old man was struggling with a hose that connected to a filtration line. "Hi, Dad! Need any help?"

James turned his balding head and smiled affectionately. "Hi, son. Actually, your timing is perfect. Can you go and get me that adjustable wrench over there on the counter, please?"

"Will do."

Shu picked up the wrench and handed it to his father, who used it tighten up a valve. Next, James bent over and connected a tube under a panel. Once finished, he stood up and wiped his hands with a rag. "Tough day with Austin?"

"Yeah," said Shu, thinking that "tough" didn't begin to describe the day's bombshell news. "Hey, Dad, you went through the day of Illumination. What's the deal with failing?"

James laughed. "Let's go outside and take a seat in the garden." Draping his arm over Shu's shoulders, father and son exited the greenhouse and sat on a wooden bench overlooking the Utopian monument. "Well, I guess you found out that failure's not an option."

"Yeah. If I fail, I'll die."

"But you won't, son. You have the skills to pass."

"So there's no chance of me dying?"

"Son, we live each day with the specter of death hanging over us, whether it be something as commonplace as a car accident, as tragic as an unintentional poisoning, or as cataclysmic as a natural disaster. An asteroid wiped out the dinosaurs; another will hit someday. But do we let that unreasoning fear stop us from living? No! So yes, there's a *small* chance you might not survive— but if you finish your preparations, I'm 100 percent confident you'll pass."

"You passed the test, right, Dad?"

"I wouldn't be sitting here if I'd failed, now would I? Keep in mind, the test changes to accommodate new statistical models. Your test will be very different than the test I took. New skills are required for each Utopian generation. And you're in a very special test—one that decides the next Supreme Sovereign."

"Austin told you?"

"Yep. He also said you're at the top in your class." James brought the curled fingers of his fist to his open mouth and breathed extravagantly on his fingernails. "Chip off the old block," he said, polishing the nails against his flowery shirt.

Shu rolled his eyes at his dad's drollery. "So, because the test's adaptive and picks the Supreme Sovereign—neither you nor Mr. Austin can help me much?"

James chuckled. "Son, your mother and I have put our lives into you. In addition to your studies, the mundane chores you've performed here at home have been part and parcel of your preparation, as have our philosophical talks. Maybe now you can appreciate why we've been such strict taskmasters. It was for your own good. The last thing we want is for you to fail. Believe me, I understand your trepidation—but there're some things worse than death."

Shu looked at his father as if the old man had grown a second head. "What could be worse than death?"

"Well, for one thing, an evening at your Uncle Jack's, listening to him prattle on about his earthworm studies. For another ... Vogon poetry."

Shu grinned. His father quoted liberally and often from his favorite non-Utopian tome, *The Hitchhiker's Guide to the Galaxy*. The youth had sampled his dad's dog-eared paperback, a UK first edition from 1979, and liked to surprise him by rattling off trivia from the fictional encyclopedia.

"Ah," said the boy, affecting a pompous accent, "but it's only the *third worst* poetry in the universe."

"Quite," sniffed James, playing along. "Second only to the Azgoths of Kria—"

"And the absolute worst, Paula Nancy Millstone Jennings. But seriously, Dad, what *is* worse than death?"

"I'll tell you in a second. First, take a look at the natural splendor all around us." James made one sweeping gesture toward their backyard, from whence beckoned the autumn-muted hues of Maki's Japanese garden, and another toward the valley below, bathed in dappled sunlight, and Lake Cuyamaca mirroring the mountain peaks. "Isn't it beautiful?"

Shu was supremely annoyed by his evasiveness. "Yes, it is. But Dad, that doesn't answer my question. I'm an Alpha Prime candidate. And whether or not it's honorable for a Utopian to be fearful, well ..." It wasn't easy for the boy to admit it, much less say it aloud: "Dammit, Dad, I'm scared!"

The elder Franklin had drifted into a dreamy silence, a beatific smile gracing his gray-stubbled face. His son's uncharacteristic swearing fetched him rudely back to the present. He loved his son more than anything else in the world. He knew the consequences, but as a Utopian, he was also proud of his son. "This is a serious matter, Shu," he said, sucking back tears. "Only you can choose whether to go through with it."

Shu stood up from the bench and paced upon the hillock. A raucous chorus of honking arrested his attention. He looked skyward to see a flock of Canada geese, flying in a ragged V-formation, coming in for a landing on the lake. "The Supreme Sovereign is the most respected and important role in Utopian society," he said, as much to himself as to his father. "But death is quite final." The boy kicked idly at the ground, thinking he might end up taking a dirt nap all too soon.

James pointed toward the town center of Julian. "Julian was almost destroyed years back, before the Illumination. People sacrificed their lives to make this a better world for their children. They died so that we could live. You want to know what's worse than death? Not being remembered. Not living as a free man or a free woman. Each Utopian has a unique perspective on the world. Each and every day, we chose to make a difference. If you live life without a mindful purpose, you're already dead." He paused. Managing a wan smile, he added, "The world needs a Supreme Sovereign. And you, my son, would make a splendid one."

While Shu was reassured by his father's vote of confidence, he knew his mom would freak out once he told her of his Alpha Prime candidacy, and the deadly conditions of the Supreme Sovereign test. Shu glanced at a young acorn woodpecker, a handsome fellow with glossy black plumage and a red-capped head, banging his long beak into an oak snag riddled with hundreds of holes. The bird chiseled into the wood instinctively, undisturbed by the presence of Shu and his father. The bird had no misgivings; it only did what it had to in order to survive. Shu, for all his self-confidence, wished he possessed this peace of mind.

"Why is the Supreme Sovereign needed?" he said, turning back to his father. "What happened in 2047? And 2084? How was the Earth saved?"

James Franklin looked pitiably at his son, wanting to tell him the full story, but he couldn't. The Utopian laws forbade divulging this information before one had passed the Illumination. Explaining Event X at this stage in development would be illegal and potentially dangerous.

"Son," he answered carefully, "two things happened that changed humanity. One was the Illumination, which you will experience personally in a few months. The other is something that's only slightly understood by a select few of our elders, that could destroy humanity."

"*You're* an elder, Father. Do you know that secret?"

James sat for a long moment, gazing out upon the valley. *I do know the secret, son,* he reflected, *and it forever haunts me. You were specially chosen, and if you pass the test, I will pass this secret and its burden along to you. Oh, if you only knew how much I and the other elders are counting on you. If you knew the truth, you might be too scared to even take the test. If you understand the ramifications, you might understandably run for the hills.*

"All in good time," said James, standing upon creaking knees. "Now, let's go inside and see what your mother's made us for lunch."

THREE:
PRIZE TRUTH

"I cannot teach anybody anything;
I can only make them think."

— Socrates

Safely snuggled in the Julian Mountains, the sturdy Franklin home withstood the assault of 50-mph winds ripping at the roof shingles like gremlins even as it howled, banshee-like, under, around, and over the eaves and windowsills. Icy hailstones ricocheted off the exterior walls, pinging at first like a volley of BBs. As the hail grew larger, the cacophony became almost deafening.

Sounds like popcorn popping, thought Shu. He had spent the last three hours reading a textbook titled *The History of Poverty and its Scientific Solution,* and he was dog-tired. Yawning, he flipped the book closed as the hailstorm faded to the odd pop before stopping altogether; meanwhile, the gremlins and banshees weren't giving up so easily, and continued to make halfhearted sallies.

Shu meditated on his studies, thinking that the vicious cycle of poverty needlessly continued for years until the Utopians creatively solved the problem by attacking the root cause: stress. Before the Utopians, most people on Old Earth coped with financial stress or stress stemming to societal violence. The stressed worker class mothers produced stress chemicals that affected newborn children. Those stresses, mostly from poverty, essentially handicapped a baby for life—literally before birth. Those early fetal changes caused the brain to react in ways that led to riskier behavior, and to a higher likelihood of bad health, poor grades, lower earnings, and prison time.

Because most people on Old Earth did not properly understand neurobiology (nor care, if they did), the world lived in a vicious cycle of violence. Ultimately, the chickens came home to roost, creating violent worldwide uprisings that some opportunists secretly tried to exploit for financial gain. True reform did not occur until Aeon Nous and the Utopians found a better way.

Shu gazed out his bedroom window toward the clearing night sky. The moon, magnificent in its ochre-colored fullness, shimmered upon Lake Cuyamaca and cast a spooky veil upon the sleepy town of Julian. *This will be a great night to practice meditation and remote viewings,* he thought excitedly.

After throwing on his pajamas, he went to the bathroom to brush his teeth in advance of the night viewing session (in case he fell asleep, which he did often). He used a natural mint toothpaste, flossed, and rinsed his mouth twice. He lingered a moment, staring at himself in the mirror. He'd recently learned that there were many multiple universes, or copies of this reality, some exact and some not so exact. Shu made quick, erratic gestures with his hands, alert for any indication that the mirror missed a movement. Everything was copied exactly; it was just a mirror. Nothing to be discovered here.

Vaguely disappointed, he walked into the living room to say goodnight to his parents. They sat in matching recliners before a glass-fronted Franklin stove. Buddy was snoozing on a rug in front of it. His mother was absorbed in *The City of the Sun,* a seminal utopian work written by Tommaso Campanella in the seventeenth century. Maki Franklin, fluent in several languages, was reading the original Italian text; Shu had had a go at the English translation but found it unbearably turgid. Meanwhile, James Franklin was curled up with much lighter fare: his beloved copy of *The Hitchhiker's Guide to the Galaxy,* which amused Shu no end.

"Good night, Mom. Good night, Dad," he said from the doorway. Eager to get to his room, he took off down the chilly hallway without waiting for a reply.

"Not so fast!" Maki called after him.

The boy returned, scowling. "What?"

"Don't you 'what' me." Maki laid her book in her lap. Wearing a flannel nightgown, the petite woman looked doll-like in the firelight, her porcelain skin ageless and too perfect for words. "Did you brush your teeth?"

Shu exhaled an impatient breath. "Yes, Mother. Can I go now?"

"He's itching to get to his remote viewing," James cut in. "Right, son?"

"Right. Can I go? *Please?*"

Maki smiled. "Well ... I suppose you don't have time to give your poor old mother a kiss."

Shu trotted over and pecked her on the cheek. Maki seized him in a hug. The strength of those thin arms never failed to amaze him. His mother always smelled wonderfully of jasmine; he forgot all about his troubles and lingered in her warm embrace.

"Mom," he said, when at last they parted, "there's something important I need to tell you."

Maki and James exchanged a knowing glance. "I know, my darling," she said, stroking his face. "Your father told me."

Shu looked at his dad. "I thought she might take it better," said James, winking, "coming from me."

"Whew! That's a relief." Shu looked at his mom curiously. "And you didn't freak out?"

Maki's mahogany eyes glistened with tears. "No, darling, I didn't freak out. I have every faith in you."

"I love you, Mom."

"I love you, darling."

Before he started crying, Shu darted down the hallway and jumped into his bed. The cotton sheets and flannel comforter kept him warm, and the soft, duck down pillows allowed him to quickly drop into a meditative trance. Lying on his back, he relaxed and started his remote viewing session, letting his mind drift out of his body. He looked back at it, thinking: *Wow, my body looks asleep, but I'm awake. Now for the fun—time to fly!*

Like an ethereal superman, Shu flew out of his home and up into the clouds. His mind, a reflection of his body down below, floated above the dark skies of Julian with the power no Old Earthling could understand, except for a rare few working on secret government programs. High above the town, Shu saw scattered lights in the homes below, where people were up late, perhaps in bed reading books; most homes, though, looked peacefully dark and cozy, the occupants fast asleep. He zipped across Lake Cuyamaca, gorgeously moonlit, flying in tandem with a great horned owl, feeling upon his face the breeze from its massive, flapping wings.

Shu fancied he saw some lights down below on Paradise Island, at the center of the lake. No one lived on that wildlife preserve, so that didn't make sense. Illegal camping, maybe? Shu flew down and looked closer, and sure enough, there seemed to be a well-lit building. *That's strange,* he thought. Shu had promised to never invade a person's privacy with his remote viewing, so he went no further. A lighted building on an uninhabited island made no sense, but Shu honored his remote-viewing pledge and soared higher into the sky.

Gliding amidst the clouds, he followed the mountain range into Julian. On the town's outskirts grew a spruce tree forest. Honoring the tenth Utopian commandment—which urged devotees to "leave room for nature"—Shu paused in his journey to drink in the sweet, refreshing fragrance of the trees and the loamy aroma of the leaf mold blanketing the forest floor, and to hark to the night calls of the birds and animals and insects. He prayed that humanity would never repeat its mistake of almost destroying the world. He reviewed the Utopian commandments, one by one, reflecting on the meaning of each. Afterwards, he quickly flew back home and entered his body, whereupon he fell into a deep, restful sleep.

But his bliss was not to last. Around three a.m., Shu started to dream about the enigmatic role of the Supreme Sovereign in Utopian society. In a scene redolent of an Old Earth movie, he saw five elderly but robust men, perhaps in their early seventies. They wore white robes cinched at the waist with black, knotted belts. This strange troupe walked solemnly, single file, under a cloudless, cobalt blue sky across an arid desert, their figures hazy in the heat shimmer. Upon their robes were embroidered the same geometric symbol: a red circle encasing a triangle, and inside the triangle were three dots, one at each point.

The robe of only one man was unadorned in this fashion. The men hailed from diverse countries and spoke different languages, but they all spoke Latin as a common tongue. The troupe had trudged several miles when the desert abruptly ended, becoming a lush, green meadow. The men followed a path of golden stones to a rocky eminence overlooking a breathtaking teal ocean and halted upon a stone platform, broad and flat.

Upon this natural dais stood a gleaming obsidian plinth carved into the shape of a pentagon. At each point of the pentagon was a tome bound in brown leather, cracked and tattered with age. The five books bore the same title and the same text, written in the respective native languages of the weary travelers. Each of the men picked up the appropriate book. Sprinkled by the ocean spray, they read in silence for some minutes and then shared their reactions to the knowledge therein.

The first man, a man of strong religious faith, said, "We should burn these books. They should never see the light of day; this knowledge is too dangerous for humanity to have and to wield."

The second man, who was involved in political affairs, said, "First, I will read my book and learn how to better manage humanity, and then I shall burn it."

The third man, a man of science said, "I will read my book as well, and teach its knowledge only to those who are worthy. Should this knowledge fall into evil hands, it will destroy the world."

The fourth man, a man of wisdom, looked at his book and said, "I now know my level of ignorance. This knowledge can only be understood by the wise. You cannot be enlightened without this knowledge."

The last man, a common man of the people, was the sole pilgrim whose robe lacked the geometric symbol. Even though the book was in his native language, he couldn't even read the title, which appeared to him as gibberish. The interior text was likewise indecipherable. He snapped shut the ancient volume; a cloud of dust escaped, encircling his angry countenance. Cursing, the common man flung the book upon the plinth. The others looked upon him in bewilderment.

"What is this claptrap?" he demanded. "How can you read this infernal, coded book?"

The wise man spoke: "Why, the code is in your head. Was it not put there when you were a child? Are you not one of us?"

"I thought I was," said common man, "but I'm no longer sure I know any of you. Who are you, really?"

"We are the enlightened," said all four men in unison.

"How did you become enlightened and able to read these words?" asked the man of the people.

"You cannot understand the words of this book," answered the man of science, "unless you unlock your mind."

The common man pondered this. "I know my mind is locked," he said at length. "I have only one question: why is this book so dangerous? Can one of you please just answer that question?"

"The masses are unfit for abstract thinking," said the wise man. "They will need fables and allegories to catch a glimpse of the truth. They will not understand unless enlightened, so the answer will be meaningless."

"Even worse," said the politician, "it will create chaos."

"Tell me anyway," pleaded the common man.

"Very well," said the wise man. "Perhaps you will become enlightened one day and truly understand. Now, open the book."

The common man retrieved the book from the plinth and opened it. He leafed through the yellowed pages, his eyes blank and uncomprehending, just as before. "I cannot read this text, I tell you!" he cried in despair. "I beg you, tell me the intrinsic truth told here!"

"The intrinsic meaning," said the wise man, "is that *only* knowledge of the nature of the universe has any meaning. But this knowledge requires a love of wisdom, truth, and logic to properly harvest the fruits which are only shown to humanity through his limited consciousness. Without a strong and prepared mind, one will be unable to lift the veil of knowledge without incurring punishment."

"This still means nothing to me," said the common man. "Where is my God? Where is She in this equation? What does She want?"

"You are all that is," said the wise man.

"No! There is a Universe, and it was created by an almighty God!" screamed the common man.

"God is everywhere," said the man of religion. "But you are not prepared."

A jagged bolt of lightning knifed across the suddenly black sky. Rolling thunder boomed; the stone platform quaked under the pilgrims' feet. The rain came in drenching sheets. Below, the windswept sea churned. A colossal wave washed over the rocky eminence, striking only the common man, as if aimed at him. He staggered, struggling to remain standing. Another wave hit, knocking him to the hard ground. The receding water was pulling him away.

The man tried to rise but could not; his fellow pilgrims offered no aid. "God, why have you cursed me?" he entreated; only the thunder answered. A final wave engulfed the common man, washing him, and the book he still clutched, into the turbulent ocean. The remaining quartet solemnly walked down the golden path, their books tucked into the folds of their robes.

Shu awoke with a gasp, stroking his arms frantically against the freezing ocean water sweeping over the bed. When he finally recognized his room, he felt sublimely silly. His bedclothes were on the floor in a big wad; Buddy, deep in a doggie dream, lay underneath the pile, his ears and eyelids twitching. *A nightmare, that's all it was.*

The mouthwatering aroma of a savory breakfast wafted down the hall, bringing Shu to full wakefulness. Flinging on his robe and leaping into his bedroom slippers, he raced to the kitchen to warm up and fill his hungry belly.

The kitchen was toasty from his mom's cooking as Shu sat down at his accustomed place. Maki was busy at the stove, humming a Utopian hymn, for it was Sunday. "Good morning, sleepyhead," she said over her shoulder. "Thought you'd never get up."

"Morning, Mom. Guess I overslept. Sorry." The boy noticed his father's place was empty. "Where's Dad?"

"Up hours ago. Said he had tons of work to do, and he was burning daylight." That was one of James Franklin's pet phrases.

"He'll be in directly. Said there was a problem with a thingamajig in the filtration system again."

Shu looked at the weather forecast posted on the DigiWall. During the night, a wild temperature swing had hit Julian and the temperature had dropped below freezing. Clouds had rolled in like slow-moving ocean waves, dusting the Franklin farm with a powdery blanket of snow. Shu looked out the kitchen window at the mountains, upon whose peaks millions of ice crystals reflected light like miniature prisms. *Leave room for nature, leave room for nature* ... intoned a voice deep inside his head.

Maki placed in front of him a plate of greenhouse vegetables, scrambled eggs, chicken sausage, potatoes, strawberries, a small salad, and miso soup. A stick-to-your-ribs breakfast was customary on the Franklin farm, but on Sundays, Maki always outdid herself.

"Don't wolf it down," she admonished.

"I won't," said Shu with his mouth already full.

Buddy had followed his nose and sat under the spacious farmhouse table, secretly accepting handouts from his master—against house rules. Shu was feeding the dog a chicken sausage when his father and grandfather came through the kitchen door. Shu couldn't help noticing that Grandpa J carried a large paper bag and was "grinning like a 'possum," as the old man would say. Maki and James traded a private look of disapproval.

"What's that you've got?" Maki asked. "Not another gift for Shu, I hope."

"Bingo!" said Grandpa J.

He down beside Shu and tousled the boy's hair. Grandpa J looked every second of his eighty-seven years. As he was fond of saying himself, his face looked like forty miles of bad road, and the little hair he had left was as gossamer as the fluff on a dandelion; but his blue eyes twinkled as merrily as any young buck's. Aside from some understandable forgetfulness, Grandpa J was robust for his age—being a frequent guest for Maki's healthy meals helped in that respect. He had declined his son and daughter-in-law's many offers to move in with them (which Shu would have loved), reckoning the invitations were made only out of politeness.

The widower lived alone in a modest bungalow on the outskirts of Julian. He was infamous in the community as a bit of an iconoclast (James preferred the more tolerant word "crank") who didn't "cotton" to the strict tenets of Utopian society. He had pulled up stakes to be near his family, and he tolerated these "cockamamie notions" as much as his freethinking nature would allow.

James was saying, "Father, Maki and I wish you wouldn't spoil the boy."

Grandpa J winked at Shu. "You're not spoiled, are ya, boy?" the old man asked. "If ya was, you'd stink and I'd smell ya!" Grandfather and grandson shared a hearty laugh that James and Maki did not join in.

Maki sighed. "What's the occasion this time?"

Grandpa J shrugged. "Don't have to be no occasion to give my only grandson somethin' fun." He reached down, picked up the bag and put it on the table. "Here, boy. Dig in!"

Trembling in anticipation, Shu reached inside and pulled out a tall, yellow box, battered and torn but intact. At the top was a friendly robot face flanked by twin rockets. Big Loo was spelled out in gigantic red letters, and below that, smaller, giant moon robot. He hesitated to look inside; the toy *couldn't* be as cool as the box. But it was! Big Loo, with his missile-shaped head and goofy, piano-keyboard grin, stood an incredible three feet tall. Rubber darts protruded from his golden chest plate. Big Loo's left arm, truncated at the elbow, contained some kind of round projectile; his right hand was a grasping plastic claw. Shu goggled at the amazing relic, imagining all the fun its plethora of built-in gadgets promised.

"That robot can do it all," said Grandpa J proudly, as if reading Shu's mind. "Eyes flash. Says ten phrases. Fires balls and rockets. Hell, he even shoots water from his belly button! Course, this robot is from 1963. I'm not sure if all of them gizmos still work."

Shu hugged him. "I don't care, Grandpa. I love it. And I love you, too."

James had a strangely nostalgic look in his eyes. "It *is* pretty cool," he said, reaching out to fondle the toy.

"Well," said Maki, "I think it's the most ridiculous thing I've ever seen."

Her remark shattered the mood. James looked at Grandpa J and said, "Father, Shu doesn't need distractions like this—not now. His Illumination is coming up. He needs to focus on his studies."

Grandpa J snorted. "Yeah, yeah, I know all about that Illumination crap. That's exactly why I brought this over. Maybe you've heard the old expression, 'All work and no play makes Jack a dull boy.' Truer words were never spoken. And I don't hold with planning a whole boy's life out for him. For Pete's sake, he's only twelve! Let the boy have some fun for a change. You sure had your share of fun, Jimmy boy, when you were a kid."

The old man reared back in his chair and chuckled. "Jimmy boy, remember when me and you went to the picture show every Saturday, watching those monster movie matinees? Those were the days! Only cost fifty cents to get into the movies back in the 1960s. Fifty cents! Imagine that."

James noticed Shu looking curiously at his grandfather. Maki was chewing her lip. James laughed nervously and said, "Father, I believe you're confused again. Neither of us was even *alive* in the previous century, of course."

Grandpa J straightened up. "I know that!" he said, a little too defensively. "I guess I was thinking of something my grandpa told me. Yeah, that's it."

"Maybe you need to visit the Infirmary," said Maki. "Get some memory-enhancing herbs." She shot the old man a critical look, which he obviously didn't appreciate.

"Don't you have chores to do, son?" said James.

"Yes, sir."

"Well, finish your breakfast and get at 'em."

"You heard the warden," Grandpa J said, smirking.

Shu dived into the meal. Grandpa caught him sneaking morsels to Buddy and winked at him. Shu could feel the tension in the room and was grateful when he could excuse himself to do his chores. James and Maki said nothing when Buddy scurried out from underneath the table and followed him out the kitchen door.

"Well, Father," said James, "you almost let the cat out of the bag that time."

"So what if I did? How long are you goin' to keep up this deception? It ain't right, I tell you. It just ain't right."

"That's not for you to decide," said Maki firmly.

"Guess not." The old man's tone was frosty.

James said, "Just try to be more careful about what you say around Shu, okay?"

Grandpa J gave him a petulant look. "I'll try."

James had a dreamy look in his eyes. "Big Loo. Got to be one of the coolest toys ever." He reached out to fondle the toy. Maki slapped his hand away.

"Don't you go getting soft!" she snapped. She snatched up the robot and none too gently put him back in his box. "What a ridiculous monstrosity," she muttered. "I'll put it in Shu's study room where I don't have to look at it." She bustled off, still muttering to herself.

James poured himself a cup of coffee. "Want some, Father?" he asked, rather hoping he would decline.

Grandpa J rose from the table. "No, thanks," he said. "I'd better be moseying along. Believe I've had all the family warmth I can handle for one mornin'." The slamming of the door made James flinch.

Maki returned, looking relieved that Grandpa J had departed. "You didn't tell him about Shu's Alpha Prime candidacy, I hope," she said to James.

"Are you crazy? The less he knows about that, the better."

* * * * *

Shu got dressed, ran outside, and went through his list of chores: pick vegetables, feed the fish, take out and bury the compost garbage in the fertilizer patch, feed the chickens, and check the solar battery levels to report to his father. This usually took a good hour or so a day. When he was finished, he went to his designated section of the workshop, where he stored his rugged, custom-built mountain bike. After checking the tire pressure and chain tension (both A-OK), Shu flung back his curly, shoulder-length brown hair and donned a well-worn ski mask with small openings for his eyes, nose, and mouth. Although it was early December in the semi-desert lands of Julian, at 4,500 feet above sea level, there was always a chance for significant snow. Ominous clouds scudded over the mountains.

With Buddy hot on his heels, sensing adventure, Shu wheeled the bike around to the front of his home. His mom was on the front porch, sweeping away the dusting of snow from the night before.

"Heading out now?" she asked Shu.

"Yeah, I wanna go to Braindead's house and get some bike riding in today."

Maki frowned. "You mean Andy Blackwell, don't you? You shouldn't call him Braindead. It's not nice."

"I don't mean anything by it, Mom. Andy's not *really* brain-dead. He's not the smartest kid in the world—not the best student—but he's got a lot of what Grandpa J would call 'horse sense'. Anyway, we're best buds, and he doesn't mind. It's just a joke between us."

"All the same," said Maki, "since today's Sunday, the day of contemplation and mindfulness, I'd like you to think about the importance of friendship and manners."

"I will, Mom. Know what Andy calls me when grownups aren't around? Egghead. All the kids think I'm a brainiac." Shu couldn't keep from sounding pleased.

"Don't get too prideful, young man. Your nickname wouldn't have anything to do with the infamous egg farm fire, would it?"

"No, but now that you mention it, the nickname kinda fits."

I'll never understand kids, thought Maki. "I'm not sure nicknames are nice. Hold on just a minute while I go inside and get something for you." She sat her broom against a column and hurried into the house.

I hope Braindead didn't get grounded again, Shu thought. Half the time, his best friend's good intentions brought them bad luck—like two months ago, when Andy and Shu accidentally burned down

Mrs. Englewood's egg barn. She had hired the boys to dispose of what seemed like thousands of pounds of neglected leaves. But instead of raking the leaves into a ravine, as Mrs. Englewood had directed, Braindead had had the bright idea of burning them. As fate would have it, the shifting wind blew the impromptu bonfire into the barn and poof! Barn up in flames, resulting in two weeks of grounding and a month of cleaning Ms. Englewood's property.

With the memory of that calamity still smarting, Shu wanted to make sure he was prepared for his outing. He unzipped his bike's emergency kit and examined its contents: one extra tire tube and miniature pump in case of a flat, multi-use tool/knife, extra chain, compass, laminated map, lighter, thermal blanket, bottle of water—and, most importantly, two energy bars, which would definitely not last the day. Shu locked the bag into place with a snap on the back of his seat and hopped onto his mountain bike. His mother stepped out of the house and handed him an insulated bag.

"I made some apple peanut butter mini sandwiches for you and Andy."

Shu raised an inquisitive eyebrow. "Did you add raisins?"

Maki smiled. "Of course! I know how you like 'em."

Shu took the sack. "Awesome, Mom! Well, gotta run." Shu looked down at Buddy; drool poured from his jowls in anticipation of accompanying his beloved master. "Sorry, fella," said Shu. "You'll have to sit this one out. Go on, now!" Buddy understood, and moped up the stairs to the porch.

"Be careful!" Maki called as Shu went flying down the hill. "I hear there's a mountain lion in the area, and it might snow more in the afternoon."

Shu looked back and yelled, "I'll be fine! I'll stay at Andy's if it snows! Don't worry, I'll call later!"

He went bumping along an abandoned paved road, once used by petroleum vehicles, but now a crumbling, grass-grown path for cyclists and hikers. Apple Orchard Way took him past the namesake orchards, lovely with the sunshine on their snow-draped branches. The apples in the fall were smaller than the hot house apples, but they tasted better to Shu. *Food grown in Mother Nature's bosom has a way of tasting better*, he thought.

On the side of the road was a rusted-out Ford sports utility vehicle of indeterminate vintage. The hideous eyesore had littered the landscape for as long as Shu could remember. He had asked his dad why the city fathers didn't remove it; James Franklin had speculated that the old vehicle served as an object lesson, pointing up the folly of man. No petroleum cars were on the road these days, of course; the only mode of transportation still using petroleum were some older, non-solar airplanes. Those planes sprayed nanoparticles in the severely depleted ozone layer of the upper stratosphere to reflect out harmful rays from sun. Years of industrialization had forced the world to use solar radiation management tools to prevent crop damage, skin cancers, and deadly heatwaves.

Shu picked up more speed going down Apple Orchard Way and then made a sharp turn up onto Iron Hills Road. This was the spookiest leg of the journey, taking Shu past a sprawling cemetery of concrete foundations, all that was left of homes destroyed in massive California fires decades earlier. Here and there, stunted trees reared their twisted trunks amidst the ruins, resembling grotesque stick men haunting the ancient homes.

The 2.5-mile trek up a winding, hilly road to Andy's ranch required every ounce of Shu's stamina. Gravity, and a lactic acid buildup in his muscles, took their toll about halfway, so he stopped to rest and watch a worker drone flying around a data hub.

Shu put the bike's kickstand down and settled against an apple tree trunk. He reached into the insulated sack and pulled out an apple peanut butter sandwich: fresh apple slices layered with peanut butter and raisins, in between two slices of homemade, whole wheat bread. Savoring the healthy snack, he watched the drone hover over the local solar energy tower like an intelligent bee, stopping at a datacon point to connect into the data hub's computer. This hub connected to the adjacent well that supplied clean water to homes down the hill. The drone downloaded usage and system statistics, checking for any malfunctions that would require on-site human maintenance. The drones saved on underground cabling and had the ability to perform minor repairs via remote control. Shu knew all about drones, computers, and the need to balance nature and technology.

Well, at least I'm getting in some contemplation today, the boy mused. The sky was gunmetal gray. His breath made shapeless ghosts in the frosty air. It felt good, even refreshing. It'd probably snow later in the day or night, he hoped. *Might even have to stay overnight at Andy's house. That'd be fun; play some chess, watch the snow falling, get in some good snowboarding the next day—after classes, of course.* You couldn't get away from school like they did years ago because of snow. With the online educational vid-con through U-NET, there were no such thing as "snow days." Shu could borrow a TED terminal from Andy; he had three in his home.

The worker drone finished its job, kicked its four propellers into high gear, and flew away like a bee going to its next flower. Shu appreciated the way the Utopians had integrated technology with nature: *Be not a cancer on the earth — Leave room for nature — Leave room for nature.* That Utopian principle stuck in Shu's mind as the one most important for the survival of humanity. Shu knew previous generations had all but succeeded in completely the environment, fomenting almost unstoppable global warming with the Last Wars and killing billions in the process.

Shu looked at his watch; it was noon and high time he got to Andy's ranch. There were only four hours or so of daylight left, and Andy had promised they'd take a two-hour hike. Braindead had told him he'd found something in the mountains that required Shu's special help. Both boys loved nature and forever tried to outdo each other on their discoveries. Andy said this was a big one, and Shu couldn't wait to see what he'd found.

After the short rest, Shu pressed ahead with renewed energy and made it up to Blackwell Ranch in record time, entering the metal gates with the family name chiseled on the stone archway. About twenty yards further, Shu parked his bike and sprinted up the steps to the farmhouse's wraparound porch. He stabbed the doorbell, heard the chime. No answer. He rang again. Still no answer. *Don't tell me that dingleberry took off without me …*

"Grrr-owwwl!"

Only the ski mask kept Shu's hair from standing on end. He whirled around, expecting to see the mountain lion his mom had warned him about. Instead, there was Braindead Andy's freckled face, plastered with a jackass-eating-briars grin.

"Gotcha!" the redhead crowed, looking insufferably pleased with himself. "I snuck out the back door."

"Pretty lame, Braindead," said Shu, trying to salvage his dignity.

"Lame, huh? You just about shit your pants, Egghead!" He punched Shu playfully in the chest.

"Did not."

"Did too. And Himiko wet *her* pants when I pulled the same trick on her last week."

"Humph! I doubt that very much. Himiko's the bravest girl I know—plus, she's three inches taller than you and could kick your butt without batting an eyelash. She's a black belt in karate, too."

"Really?" said Andy, looking a bit amazed. "I thought she was only a brown belt."

"She just got her black belt, so you better watch out, or it'll be *you* that's shitting your pants." Shu glanced around the property, noticing two of their three horses were gone from the corral. Andy's horse, Boots was nibbling grain from the trough. "Hey, Braindead, where're your parents?"

"They went to see my Aunt Carolyn. Said they'd stay over if it snows tonight. I checked TODS; it said there's a 40 percent chance of precipitation. Personally, I don't think it's gonna snow."

Shu said, "I don't need that dumb Total Online Data System to tell me it's gonna snow. I saw a couple of dark, monster-sized nimbostratus clouds coming up from the west. They'll hit here in probably two or three hours."

Andy snorted. "Nimbostratus clouds? What happened, Egghead, did you swallow a dictionary or something? All I know is, the wind is going the other way from those nimbo-whatsis clouds you're talking about." Andy opened the main door and Shu followed him into the house. "Let me get my backpack. I can't wait to show you the treasure I found."

Shu's eyes gleamed with excitement. "What'd you find? Tell me!"

"Oh, this is some zappy snappy stuff, Shu," said Andy with a mischievous smile. "I found something from Old Earth that must be hundreds of years old. I think it's from an old Air Force Base."

"Wow! What is it?"

"I want to keep it a secret. I'll show you it up Mount Laguna road, near the top."

Shu shook his head. "Whoa, Braindead! You know Mount Laguna is off limits. It's only for illuminated adults. It's abandoned, except for an old firehouse museum."

"Tell me something I don't know," said Andy. "My discovery's in the woods, so we only need to go up the border of Mount Laguna. I heard there was an old secret military base there. Gotta be lots of cool ruins of Old Earth. We'll be all right, Shu. Trust me."

The egg barn blaze popped into Shu's head. "Famous last words! It'll take us at least two hours to bike up to Town Mount Laguna— not enough time to get back if it snows."

"We don't need to go into town. I only rode up three quarters the way with Don Dimon. And it's not gonna snow."

"What were you guys doing up there?"

"We were hiking to check something out."

"Something? What, Braindead? If you don't tell me, I'm not going up."

Andy folded his arms. "It's a secret," he said.

"Have it your way. I'm not going."

Shu had turned to walk out of the Blackwell house when Andy grabbed his arm. "Okay, okay, I'll tell you ... but you gotta keep it a secret."

"As long as it's not a secret *oath*," said Shu, "mum's the word."

Andy laughed. "I once took a secret oath not to tell my mom that my dad had burned down our red shed when he was smoking a cigar and it fell in one of the open bottles of moonshine he was making. My mom thought *I* burned it down and he was protecting me, so I had to come clean with my mom. I turned in my dad.

Truth is a Utopian virtue, after all. But for us kids, we need to keep secrets to survive. So, please keep mine."

"I promise," said Shu. "But I thought your dad was making snow mobile fuel, not moonshine? That's what my dad said after the incident."

"Hmm, sounds like your pop was bending the truth a little, Shu. I peeked in a window. With my own eyes, I saw your dad helping my dad build the *still*—that's what the contraption's called—with a bunch of old-fashioned apparatus, copper tubing and such. When I asked my dad what they were building he said, 'That's need-to-know … and you *don't* need to know.' I overheard your father laughing and saying the contraption was dual purpose; the main purpose was making snow mobile fuel, and the other purpose was using the fuel for mixing drinks at poker games."

"My dad said that? Maybe he was studying Old Earth entertainment. I've never known him to play poker. He has a shed on our property that he calls a 'man cave'—one of those antiquated expressions he's always tossing around. It's really big, with no windows and a large door. He never lets me in. Sometimes he works late on stuff in there. I once heard a humongous lawn mower engine start up. Maybe he has a moonshine still, too. In any case, tell me what you saw. I promise to keep it a secret."

"Okay, so what Don and I saw last summer was a bunch of red and yellow lights flying over the Dark Desert Valley when we went camping, a little below Camp Willow. I think I told you about that; everyone said they must have been shooting stars. But Don and I saw those lights with our own eyes, and so did Johnny Jenkins. Troop Leader Brown said it was just an asteroid, but it couldn't have been, because there were like six or seven of them. They circled and moved around. Asteroids don't do that. Then they disappeared altogether. Leader Brown looked nervous and swore it was just an optical illusion from the desert heat, but Don is smart like you. He told me later it was definitely something else. So, we went up above the campsite a few days later to get a better view. That's when we discovered this weird hinged rock with an even weirder carving on it."

"What kind of carving?" asked Shu.

"A large circle—looked like it was laser-etched—and inside the circle was a triangle. At each corner of the triangle were large dots. The dots looked like they were made out of gold. Here, let me draw it for you."

Andy pulled out a piece of paper and a pen from his knapsack and made a quick sketch. "I know it's crude, but this is pretty much what it looked like."

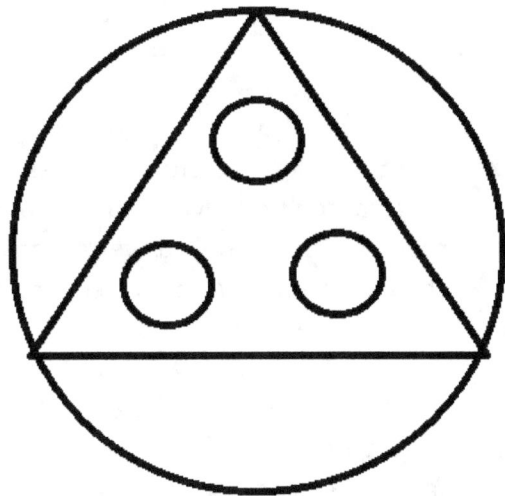

The drawing startled Shu. It looked just like the symbol the old men had on their robes in his dream. That fact freaked him out, but now wasn't the time to go into that. "Was there anything else?" he asked.

"Yes, but I'm too scared to tell you now," Andy replied. "I'll tell you when we reach the spot."

FOUR:
THE SACRIFICE

"Try not to become a man of success,
but rather, try to become a man of value."

— Albert Einstein

"Tell me what?" asked Shu. "What's scaring you?"

Andy hesitated. "It's nothing. It was getting dark there when we found that rock and we had to leave. The UFOs freaked us out. The rock on hinges looked weird, too. Heck, it was *all* weird. Look, Egghead, you're the smartest person in Julian. I want you to check it out with me."

"I'd be the dumbest in Julian if I went up there with you, Braindead. I don't think the weather will hold out today." Shu cast a dubious eye at the lowering sky.

"If the weather changes, we can turn around."

Shu thought it a bit risky, but it also sounded like fun, and the hinged rock with the same images from his dream intrigued him. "Okay, let's go. But if it starts to snow, we need to immediately turn around. We won't have much time to seek shelter if the weather changes."

"I'll ride Boots up the hill, it'll be quicker. He's young and strong."

Shu gave Andy the stink eye. "What about me, Braindead? You expect me to ride my bike?"

"I have a double-seat saddle, Egghead. We can ride together."

Shu pondered Andy's equestrian skills, or lack thereof. "Fine, but I'll lead and sit in front."

"No way! It's my horse."

Shu knew that truth was prized in the Utopian society, but so was harmony, as the ninth commandment said: *Prize truth —*

beauty — love — seeking harmony with the infinite. But that was harmony with the *infinite*, not with obstinate Andy. "I beat you and everybody else last year at the Julian equestrian challenge," he pointed out. "Let me lead. It's the logical and smart thing to do."

"I don't care! Boots is *my* horse. Take your bike instead."

Shu frowned, hating to compromise when he felt he was right. "Okay," he sighed, "I'll ride back seat. But if you have any trouble riding up, we switch."

The two boys went out to the barn. Andy put a thermal blanket on Boots' broad, ebony back, then strapped on the double seat saddle, and lastly attached to it some basic supplies, including their emergency kits. Mount Laguna peaked at 5,700 feet, so they'd need to climb at least 1,000 feet over sixteen miles to get to Andy's mystical site.

Boots made it from Andy's house to Sunrise Road in less than fifteen minutes, which was the easy part. Scaling the fifteen miles of dirt road to the Mount Laguna border, on the other hand, would take a good hour and a half.

As Boots climbed up the hill, Andy kept mostly quiet, admiring the rocky, reddish-brown, semi-desert landscape. Shu kept his eyes peeled on the oncoming clouds, which were moving in a little faster than he liked. At about thirty minutes into the ride up, Shu calculated that snow would be arriving within the hour or less—too little time to reach the top without snow making the already treacherous path impassable.

"Andy," he said, "I think we need to head back down and do this another day."

Andy halted Boots and turned around to frown at Shu. "No way! We're halfway up already; we should keep moving."

Shu's trepidation was evident in his shaking voice. "Listen, Braindead, that snow's coming sooner than I expected. It's about 25 degrees Fahrenheit out here; I don't want to walk in the snow if Boots suddenly balks."

"Boots won't balk," said Andy confidently. "He goes where I tell him 'im to go."

"So you say. In my experience, sometimes horses are smarter than people, especially if they sense danger. If it snows and he refuses to budge, we're gonna have to walk up or down in a snowstorm. And there's no shelter here; it's all rocks, Braindead."

"Then we need to pick up the pace to get shelter above. There's some old cabins up top. We can stay the night there. Or better yet, there's an old trailer I found near that hinged rock. Kinda dilapidated, but it has an old heating stove."

Shu knew this was risky, and that going back down would be quicker. "We need to turn around, and I mean right now. The going'll be faster downhill. We shouldn't fight nature!"

"Nuh-uh, I'm not doing it. If you want to be a chickenshit, I'll let you get off Boots now and you can walk back. I'm going up, with or without you."

Shu knew he could jog back down the hill in about thirty minutes and possibly avoid the snow. But if he did, he'd never forgive himself if something happened to Andy. "Okay, let's go—but this is the last time I let you talk me into one of your harebrained adventures!"

Andy's freckled face smiled in victory. He had Boots pick up the pace, and Shu was reassured they'd make it—that is, until about twenty minutes later when the dark clouds rolled in and a light sleet began to fall.

"Slow down, Andy," he urged. "Sleet's a helluva lot more dangerous than snow."

"No can do, good buddy. We're only about twenty minutes away. We have one big climb at Heartbreak Hill. After that, it's just a gentle incline. We need to get up Heartbreak Hill or we're dead meat."

Shu knew Andy was right this time. If they stopped, they'd surely get stuck. They had to keep moving and pray the sleet didn't screw up the road too much for Boots. Shu took note of the horse's labored breathing and trudging gait. The frigid air and onerous terrain had already taken a heavy toll on the beast's stamina.

The two boys finally reached the base of Heartbreak Hill. The sleet thankfully stopped, but the snow started with a furious intensity, bathing the hill in a white haze. Boots started up the hill and, for about five minutes or so, all looked fine. Then he stopped, and wouldn't budge. Andy pulled on the reins and yelled, "Get going, Boots!" Not a muscle twitched.

"He's balking, Andy," said Shu glumly.

"I know that, Egghead, but we got to get 'im to move." Andy kicked the stirrups and pulled the reins again, this time with more force. "Get moving!" he cried. Boots snorted but refused to move an inch.

"We'll have to get off and pull and walk him up if we can," Shu observed. "If not, we can let him go downhill by himself. And we can walk the rest of the way up ourselves."

"Aw, turkey turds! Walking up will take at least an hour in this snow. This bites my butt." Andy thought for a moment. "I know! I'll try to turn him downhill, and then turn him around again to retreat back up."

"He's a horse, Andy. He might not turn."

"Still, I'm trying." Using leg pressure and working the reins—and a little sweet talk—Andy got Boots to turn around and go downhill. Shu was impressed—and a little jealous of his pal's unheralded horsemanship. "Now, I'll turn him back uphill." Andy tried to turn, but Boots resisted. He turned slightly to the left, looking like he was turning, but then continued in a zigzag fashion downhill.

Shu's eyes flew wide, concerned at the horse's struggle. "Stop him, or we'll never make it down! There's too much sleet and snow. We need to dismount and walk him to the top and rest for the night."

"Let me try one more time," said Andy with determination as he pulled and directed Boots to the right. Boots tried to stay on the road, but was getting precariously close to a rocky ledge slick with snow and sleet. If he got any closer, the boys and Boots would surely take a nasty tumble.

"Stop now!' screamed Shu at the top of his lungs.

Boots snorted and huffed in panic; his legs were starting to slip. He pawed at the ground, trying to maintain traction. "I'm getting off!" yelled Shu. "Boots is slipping!" Shu pushed off the back seat of the saddle, falling on his butt. "Get off, Andy! Get off now!"

"I can't, my boots are stuck in the stirrups! I gotta turn him!"

Andy pulled the reins hard, trying to turn Boots away from the ledge. As Boots finally got traction, a rock gave away below a hoof, and he slipped hard. Boots plunged into the rocky ravine, with Andy still holding on for dear life. All the way down Boots let out a terrified, mournful scream, unsettling in its human-like quality, with Andy's wail providing counterpoint. The horse landed between two boulders on the ravine floor with a sickening, fleshy thud. Poor Andy was pinned underneath.

"Oh, shit! My ankle is all twisted. Damn, it burns! Help me, Shu! Please help! Boots is on top of my leg."

Shu clambered down the bank to see Boots futilely kicking and trying to get up. The horse's distressed snorting stirred up little blizzards of snow. The horse's right hind leg was stuck between the boulders and twisted in an awkward position. Steaming hot blood poured from a break in his grotesquely exposed femur. There was no way Boots was ever getting up again. *I'm so sorry, Boots*, thought Shu as he stroked the suffering beast's forehead. He then walked over to Andy.

"Let me see if I can pull you out," said Shu, quickly evaluating the situation.

"I think it's impossible," said Andy. "Boots is on top of my leg and he's moving too much. It's getting crushed. My leg is killing me."

"Hold on a second." Shu threaded his fingers through Boot's forelock. "I'm so sorry, Boots," he said softly. "I can't do anything for you now. Just try to relax." His comforting words seemed to calm the terror in the horse's eyes. Shu slowly unbuckled and lifted up the saddle. He spied a large rock under Andy. He wiggled it loose and slid it out, then did the same with another rock. This gave Shu room to begin gingerly dislodging Andy's leg from underneath the horse.

"Oh, mother of Utopian hell!" Andy screamed. "This hurts!"

Shu stopped. "Does it feel broken?"

"No, but the muscle feels like its bruised really bad. Please get me out, Shu!"

"I'm tryin', I'm tryin'!"

Shu moved another rock. Finally, there was enough space for him to carefully extract the trapped leg. Shu dragged Andy, who was all screamed out, away from Boots and propped him up on a boulder. The snow was starting to accumulate. *That doesn't bode well for the hike up ahead.*

"Thanks for getting me out," said Andy, tremendously relieved.

"Don't mention it. Let's see if you can stand." Shu put his hands under Andy's armpits and lifted. "Now, put your weight on it."

"Ouch! Hold it!" Andy ran his right hand down his thigh. "Ah, toad farts, it hurts like hell at the ankle."

"Let me see." Shu gave the ankle a cursory exam, probing gently as Andy cursed and winced. "I don't think it's broken but it feels really swollen. I knew we should have turned around earlier."

"No shit! We're gonna die out here!"

"No, *we're* not gonna die out here. *You* might, though, 'cause I'm gonna leave your ass here if you don't stop being a crybaby. I can't believe you pushed Boots like that! What were you thinking?"

"I'm so sorry, Shu. You were right." Andy started to cry. "Are you really gonna let me die out here?"

Shu shook his head. "No, you're not gonna die, Braindead. Not if I can help it."

"I appreciate your bravado, Egghead," said Andy, "but what're we gonna do? Boots is hurt bad, and we'll freeze out here. The snow's coming down like a son of a gun now."

Shu nodded, watching the wicked witch of winter dust the mountain with her white poison powder. Shu knew he couldn't carry Andy all the way up, not even if he managed to cobble together a stretcher with items from their emergency kits, or fashioned a splint for the ankle. Heck, he knew he might not even make it himself if the snow got much beyond a foot or two foot deep. Staying put guaranteed death—but letting his friend die while he left alone was not the Utopian way. He had to think of a way to save Andy.

"I've got an idea," Shu said. "I'll hike up to the top; I know there's a phone at the fire station. I'll call my dad, and he'll come up and get you. Or maybe I should call your folks—"

"Don't do that! I don't want to get in trouble with them again. Besides, hiking up to the fire station will take too long. I'll freeze. I'm a goner, Shu ... I'm messed up really bad!" Andy was bawling now. "I won't even make it to thirteen. My folks will hate me. I'm a failure."

Shu ignored the crying and walked over to Boots and took out his emergency kit. "I have a thermal blanket—I'll wrap you up."

"I'll still freeze. It's too cold here," said Andy, shivering.

"I know, but I need to wrap you up to protect you from getting too wet." He unstrapped both emergency bags from Boots' saddle, extracted his silvery thermal blanket from his kit, and draped it over Andy's torso.

"It's not raining, it's snowing. I won't get wet, but I'm gonna freeze."

"Stop your grumbling, I know what I'm doing!" Shu paused. What he had to tell his friend wasn't going to be easy. He sighed and blurted out: "Andy, I'm going to put Boots down, cut a hole in his stomach, and put you inside. I saw the swashbuckling anti-hero do it to an alien camel thingie in a twentieth-century space opera called *Star Wars* in order to save his friend. I watched with my Grandpa J."

"Crap, Egghead, everybody knows you're a weirdo who studies that creaky old science fiction stuff on the sly for 'historical purposes,' but you're not cutting Boots open! You're nuts!"

"Hush, Braindead. That will keep you warm for a few hours until I get to the fire station. I'll call my dad and have him get up here with that snow machine of his."

"Out of the question! We can't kill Boots!"

"Boots is as good as dead; he has at least one broken leg. You can't fix a horse's leg, it's not the same as a human—"

"No! We're not killing Boots and that's final!"

"I don't have time to argue about—"

"And how're you going to put me inside him? You're not cutting open Boots! No freaking way!" Andy tried to walk but fell and lay crying in the snow.

Shu shook his head. "Listen, Braindead, my dad taught me that in times of danger, you have to use your brains, or you'll get run over by trains. Now, I can try to carry you up the hill with me, but chances are, we'll both freeze, and I'm not even sure I can make it alone with all this snow and wind. Plus, you have a messed-up leg, and you'll freeze without protection, and there's nothing for miles to protect us—other than Boots. I love Boots too, and I don't want to see him die, but this is a mercy killing. He's frightened, and in a lot of pain, too. He's going to freeze, but it'll take his big body a lot longer to freeze than you and I."

Andy cried and begged Shu not to kill Boots, but Shu knew he had to heed his father's advice: *"There will be times when you have to do things you don't want to do. Sometimes life demands sacrifice; you'll have to decide what is worth keeping or what you are willing to let go—and that includes life itself."*

Shu looked around and found the biggest rock he could carry; it felt like a good thirty pounds. He walked over to Boots and placed down the rock near his head. The horse nickered feebly as Shu knelt and scratched behind his ears. "I'm so sorry, Boots." A tear trickled from the boy's eye. "We messed up really bad, and I know you're in pain..."

In the distance Andy screamed, "Don't do it! Let me die with Boots! It's my fault!"

Shu continued talking to Boots. "I can't let Andy die here. You can save him. He'd do the same for you. I'll try to make it painless."

Shu rose and picked up the heavy rock. His arms trembled as he held it over Boots' head. He convinced himself that he saw understanding in the suffering beast's eyes. Shu glanced at Andy; his friend had come to an acceptance, and sat staring at the snow accumulating around his boots. Tears streamed down Shu's face as he recited the words Utopians said at funerals: "May your soul rise to the heavens in peace everlasting."

Shu let go of the rock, trusting that the weight would be enough to do the job. In a moment, the horse's legs were mercifully still.

Shu walked over to Andy and said, "I'm really sorry about Boots."

"I know you are, Shu," Andy said, without looking up. "And I know you did what you had to do."

Shu got the multi-purpose knife from his pack and walked over to Boots. He looked at the angle of the horse in the ravine and decided to do a lower mid-section cut. The knife was really sharp and a good five inches long. It cut through the tough, leathery skin with some difficulty, but with a couple of hard pulls, Shu made a good, four-foot incision. A fountain of hot blood gushed on the snow, melting it; the puddle steamed in the frosty air. When he cut near the bowels, things got a little smelly. With one hand pinching his nose shut, Shu reached inside with his other hand and grabbed hold of the intestines. They seemed to take forever to pull out, reminding Shu of a large hose his mother used in her Japanese garden. When the nasty business was done, Shu was satisfied the resulting cavity could easily accommodate his injured friend.

Shu walked over to Andy and put his arm around his waist and helped him to stand. Holding his injured leg aloft, Andy draped his arm over Shu's shoulder, and together they walked over to the gory equine igloo Shu had created. Andy didn't say a word; his eyes were glazed over in shock. With some careful maneuvering, Shu got Andy into the horse's gaping belly.

Shu picked up Andy's emergency bag, took a quick inventory of the contents—pretty much the same as his own—and held it out to him. "Everything you need's in here—water, snacks, et cetera."

Andy reluctantly stuck his hand out in the cold. Shu cringed at the blood and bodily humors dripping from it. He quickly pulled it back inside. "Thanks, Shu. Please save us." Andy started to cry again.

Shu put on dry, warm gloves from his kit over his cold, wet hands. He drank a bottle of water and ate an energy bar and then shouldered the bag. Before heading up the hill, he looked back at Andy and said, "If we make it, you owe me big time, Braindead."

FIVE:
GOOD TO BE HOME

"The dinosaurs became extinct because they didn't have a space program. And if we become extinct because we don't have a space program, it'll serve us right!"

— Larry Niven

Shu hiked up the mountain road carefully, at a personal pace he called *stay alive*. He'd walked up the mountain in good weather before with his dad, and he'd hiked parts of Julian in the snow before, but never in a semi-whiteout, and never with this sense of purpose. The chance of dying focuses one like a laser on a target. He'd read how people in the past had cell phones to call anyone, anywhere. It seemed like magic. With a cell phone, he could have just made one easy call for help. But Shu read that scientific studies showed how the human brain absorbed radiation from the devices, causing the tissue to heat up; although not everyone got cancer as a result, many did. It was especially bad for children and it also accelerated Alzheimer's disease in older folks. The Utopians believed the risk of having a cell phone was worse than the risk of not having one. *Boy*, thought Shu, *I'd like to give those alarmist scientists a piece of my mind right now.*

The hike up to the top of Mount Laguna took Shu a good hour. It was well below freezing (in the low twenties, according to Shu's watch), but the snow began to slow down, and near the top, it even stopped for a bit. For a scant five minutes, the yellow-orange setting sun came out of hiding, reflecting on the crystalline snow like the warm hand of a savior. Although Shu was not religious in the traditional sense (none of the Utopians were), he felt as if he'd reached heaven upon setting foot on the flat peak of Mount Laguna. Winded, Shu paused for a brief respite and to get his bearings.

It would still take a good fifteen minutes or so until he'd reach the fire station. Shu watched a western gray squirrel scamper up a tree, shaking snow off the branches, and into its drey, a complex mass of twigs and leaves. That image grimly reminded him of his friend Andy, nestled inside Boots for warmth, just like the squirrel in its nest.

I need to find the station, and soon, thought Shu, setting out again at a brisk pace. More ominous dark clouds rolled in over the jagged mountains, ending the short reprieve of the sun's mother-like warming rays. Shu hugged himself against a sudden flurry of snow whipping down a mountain pass. His feet were getting cold, as his shoes weren't really snow boots, but riding boots. His gloves were wet inside and stunk of horse blood and guts. Although he wouldn't freeze to death in fifteen minutes, he didn't want to risk frostbite. He'd seen that firsthand in his Uncle Kenny, who lost two toes in a snowy misadventure several years back.

I know the station is somewhere up ahead on the right, thought Shu. The old fire station had been renovated in recent years and was mainly used for putting out forest fires. All homes in Julian had automatic fire suppression systems (utilizing eco-conscious chemical reagents) built into the designs. Even the woods had suppression systems scattered every few miles. These were designed for early detection/management of a forest fire until the electric-powered fire trucks (fully automated) could arrive and extinguish the blaze. Water trucks powered by natural gas provided additional support.

Shu saw a building coming into view, but with all the snow and the darkening sky, he couldn't make out if it was the fire house. As he got closer, he saw Laguna Station 42 spelled out in giant white letters over the fire engine bays.

"Yes! I made it!" Shu cried aloud, essaying a celebratory jig.

He walked up to the entrance, doffed the glove on his right hand, and placed it on the security scanner, whose database contained the biometrics of every resident in Julian. The device whirred to life and flickered a few times. A gender-neutral voice greeted him: "Welcome to the Fire Station Museum, Shu Franklin. How may we assist you?"

"I'm freezing! Can you please let me in the building? I need to call my father. My friend Andy Blackwell is freezing on the mountain—I think his leg might be broken."

The panel's hand recognition light flickered again, then sound of the old United States national anthem started playing, peppered with staticky interruptions that sounded like someone getting electrocuted:

*O say can you see, by...**BUZZ**... dawn's early light,*
*What ...**BUZZ**... proudly we hailed at the twilight's last gleaming,*
*Whose broad stripes and...**BUZZ**... **BUZZ**...stars through the perilous fi—**BUZZzzzt***

The singing stopped and the same genderless voice announced: "Welcome to the Fire Station Muse—**BUZZ**....—how may we assist you, Shu Fra— **BUZZ** ... **BUZZ**..."

"I just told you, I'm freezing! Please let me in, you infernal machine!"

The door security access lights went out. Then the accursed words Shu absolutely did not care to hear again scrolled across on the scanner's digital screen: **Welcome to the Fire Station Museum. How may we ASSIST You?** Shu anxiously watched as the words flickered and finally died out, as all other power systems apparently did, too.

"Pigeon poop!" cursed Shu, kicking the door in frustrated desperation.

Click!

What was that sound? Could it be ... He looked at the door handle and slowly turned it. The door was unlocked! It opened! It must have opened as a fail-safe measure—to admit a technician, for instance—when the power went out, he conjectured. *Or it was just broken?* He didn't care. He kicked snow off his shoes and entered the building with a new feeling of hope. It wasn't much warmer inside than outside, but at least he was protected from the snow and wind.

Shu saw reddish-brown stains on the floor. *Bloodstains?* That was a disconcerting thought. The urgency of saving Andy drove him onward. He hurried over to an open cubicle marked

Communications. Inside were various electronic systems that Shu recognized from his technology studies. A fiery red emergency landline phone caught his attention. Picking it up, he heard the distinctive Utopian dial tone. He dialed his father's number, praying the system still worked. The few rings seemed to last an eternity, but soon his father answered.

"Hi, James Franklin speaking."

"Dad, this is Shu. I'm at the top of Mount Laguna at the Fire Station Museum, and Andy's stuck on the trail. You gotta—"

"Hold on, dammit! You went up to Mount Laguna? I thought you were going to stay at Andy's place?"

"Andy convinced me to go. It's a long story, but Andy hurt his ankle badly; it might even be broken. It happened when Boots tumbled down a ravine and fell on top of him."

"You rode up on a horse in a snowstorm? That's nuts! Are you okay?"

"I'm fine. But Boots broke his leg and I had to put him down. I cut Boots open and put Andy inside to keep him warm, since he can't walk now. Andy should be okay for a couple more hours—but you gotta hurry, Dad!"

"You gutted open Boots and put Andy in the horse?"

"Yeah. I got the idea from a scene in a vintage science fiction movie—*Star Wars*."

"You know you're not supposed to be watching those relics, Shu. They're off-limits."

"Well, that one was Grandpa J's idea. If I hadn't seen it and been inspired by that scene, Braindead—I mean, Andy—would have frozen to death. Besides, who are you to talk, Dad? You read old sci-fi books, and lightning hasn't struck you yet."

James Franklin paused on the line, and Shu knew this meant he was thinking. His father always said to count to ten and think before you open your mouth to respond to something that angers you. James spoke softly and in a caring manner. "It must have been tough, but I think you did the right thing in cutting open Boots to save Andy. I'll come up with some folks to rescue Andy. Stay put at the fire station. The weather's horrible; snowing like a son of a bitch—pardon me—here, and I can only guess what it's like up there. It'll take a good two hours to get to Andy. I want the team to bring him to the Health Infirmary asap, in case he's got internal bleeding, then I'll ride up alone on my snowmobile to get you right afterwards. See you in about two and a half hours. Don't leave the station, got it?"

"I'm sorry we caused all this trouble, Dad."

"We'll talk later, son." His father abruptly hung up.

Shu slowly replaced the receiver, then went to the restroom to wash off the stink of guts and blood from his hands. He was surprised to see more apparent bloodstains on the floor and wondered if someone had gotten seriously injured recently and sought refuge in the station—or had something nefarious happened? Shu washed his hands in the ice-cold water which, to his pleasant surprise, still flowed in the mountaintop's glacial grip. His undershirt was sweaty from the long hike, but now that he was no longer exerting himself, he was getting cold.

Exiting the restroom, he noticed another door labeled Break Room and Sleeping Quarters — Authorized Personnel Only. A tangle of red, green, and blue wires spilled from the broken hand scanner. It looked to Shu as if someone had ransacked the building and hotwired the door to get into the break room. There was even a bloody handprint on the door.

Shu tried to open the door, but this one was actually locked tight. Besides the digital security lock, it had an old-fashioned mortise lock, whose latch bolt seemed loose in the jamb. Shu thought for a second and pulled out his knife. After a few moments of experimental jimmying, the door creaked open and Shu stepped inside.

Wowwwwww.

Replete with pool table, dartboard, flat screen television, sectional sofa, a table and chairs, and other amenities—not to mention a long, wooden bar with stools in front of it, and behind it, an entire wall displaying dozens of bottles of wine and whisky—the room looked like the Old Earth bars Shu had seen in his history books.

To the left of the bar beckoned a door marked Sleeping Quarters. And in the corner … a kerosene heater! Shu walked over and hit the Push To Ignite button, but nothing happened. *Wick needs to be lit*, he theorized. Looking around the room, he spied a cigar box on an end table next to the sofa and rushed over. Next to it he found an antique butane lighter, a boxy silver contraption, primitive in design and function; he recognized it from a similar specimen in his Grandpa J's collection of twentieth-century relics. Praying it worked, he popped the lid, flicked the little wheel, and *voilà!*—instant fire.

In short order he had a cozy fire going. Shu knew from his studies that primitive kerosene heaters created a colorless, odorless, and potentially dangerous gas called carbon monoxide, so he cracked open a window to admit fresh air. Next, Shu took off his three shirts and hung the sweaty undershirt over the heater. After a few minutes it was mostly dry, so Shu put it and the other shirts back on. The warm undershirt felt great, and now Shu could think.

Shu walked over to the pool table. The boy was familiar with the game; Grandpa J had a pool table and was quite skilled—he called himself a "pool shark"—and had easily thrashed Shu and his dad when they'd been foolish enough to challenge him. The balls were already racked up in the familiar wooden triangle. Shu picked out a cue from the rack and took a few idle shots to pass the time. He'd just set up for a corner shot when a desk in the corner, whereon sat an outmoded computer monitor and other dated equipment, caught his eye.

Upon investigation, it looked to Shu like someone had recently been working at the computer station. There was a black device with small binoculars connected into a device next to a vid com. Shu picked up the device; on the back was printed iPhone MilSPEC 14 Code b13. Shu hit the power button, but nothing happened. The device fascinated Shu, as the now defunct Apple Corporation was legendary among technology archaeologists for its innovations in the twentieth and twenty-first centuries. He had only seen these devices on historical movie tapes, but this one was real and looked to be military grade.

As Shu stared at the device, a red circle containing three equally spaced blue lights appeared on the screen. The device turned on; Shu marveled when several function icons appeared.

This old iPhone worked!

But Shu's excitation was short-lived, as a **Secure ID or Password REQUIRED** message appeared.

Crap! Of course, Shu had no idea what the password could be. He took a closer look at the phone and saw that it was housed in a protective case. Sliding open the back panel, he pulled out an identification badge containing a photo of a man in his thirties with long black hair, and his name—Dr. Samir Abuaita—underneath. At the top right corner of the badge was a red circle with a triangle inside.

What th—? This looks just like the one in my dreams! thought Shu with a gasp. To the right of the logo were the words MAJIC—LEVEL 6. The card had a magnetic strip on the back and what looked like a miniature electronic chip on the front. Shu knew it was wrong to keep something that wasn't his, but he figured no one would know, as it was in a secret compartment of the phone. Anyway, he planned to bring it back one day soon—after he'd discovered what this MAJIC group was; he'd come across no reference of it in his historical studies.

Shu put the iPhone back where he found it, but then had second thoughts. *Why not take the secure ID badge* and *the phone?* He replaced the badge in the case, then shut off the phone's power button and put it in his pocket. He'd bring it all back once he'd gotten to the bottom of the mystery.

Shu sat near the heater, warming his hands while waiting for his dad to show up. After an hour or so the room started to get too hot, and a strange smell permeated the air. Shu was worried the heater was malfunctioning and turned it off. The stench remained, and it was getting stronger. Whatever was causing it, the overheated room had exacerbated the stink. Shu had smelled the rotting carcasses of deer and other animals in the woods many times; this was like that, but worse—it couldn't have come from a dead rat somewhere in the old building's bowels. This reek came from something a lot bigger.

Shu began walking around the break room, trying to pinpoint the fetor's source. As he approached the bar, he noticed for the first time that the door to the sleeping quarters was slightly ajar. Inching closer, the reek took his breath away. It was definitely coming from inside the room. Steeling his courage—and holding his arm over his nose—he ventured inside.

The room was dark. Shu fumbled for the light switch and flipped it. A fluorescent light fixture on the ceiling started sputtering, bathing the room in an eerie half-light. Directly ahead were two bunk beds, neatly made up. In the corner was a third bed. The flickering light allowed glimpses of a supine figure lying upon it.

Shu wanted to call out but couldn't find his voice. He shuffled closer, closer. The stink was unbearable now, making his eyes water. Finally, the fluorescent light came on completely. Shu stared in morbid fascination at the dead body of Dr. Samir Abuaita, his cheeks sunken, eyes staring crazily, a pool of dried blood on his chest.

Shu covered his mouth and ran from the room, slamming the door shut behind him. He went over to the open window for fresh air, wanting to puke but holding back. This man had suffered an ugly death. He thought of the test to the death dangling over his own head like the sword of Damocles. Shu thought Andy was the one being tested now; flouting Utopian tradition, he prayed to the God of Wisdom for his friend's safe deliverance.

I hope Dad gets here soon.

* * * * *

Thirty restless minutes later, Shu got fully dressed. He was now warm, but the dead body still reeked. Shu moved from the break room into the reception area; the air was cold there, but at least it didn't stink. Shu took out the iPhone, marveling at the elegant but primitive antique device. He turned it on and logged in by swiping the secure ID. He slid his hand on the screen and saw a button of a flashlight. He touched it and a flashlight went on! He immediately turned the light off as that would surely drain the ancient batteries. *Pretty neat device,* he thought. One of the function icons, labeled Videos, was a graphic he recognized as a clapperboard—a hinged device used in motion picture production to synchronize picture and sound recording. Instinctively, Shu knew the device was probably a touch screen. He tapped the video icon and scrolled through the thumbnails. He found the last video of Dr. Abuaita, dated November 2021. That was one old video! He touched the thumbnail and an Old Earth movie started. Dr. Abuaita was talking into the camera.

"My name is Samir Abuaita. I'm a professor of Electro Physics at Majic. I'm being hunted, so I'm making this video as my last will and testament. If anyone finds this AI, please, for the love of God, get it to the Utopian called Aeon Nous. What certain dark forces inside the United Nations are planning is genocide! I cannot live with my master, knowing of such evil. I'm not sure if this information can save them, but it includes a powerful sentient AI called RADHA. I don't agree with the Utopians, but I agree less with murder. If you are watching this video, it's because I didn't make it. Please, don't tell anyone except Aeon Nous, as he is the only one you can trust. If you discover the imminent danger—"

The main phone screen shut off. Then a message appeared on the black screen:

This is RADHA. Please shake phone or place in DIRECT sunlight to recharge....

Shu thought this suggestion strange, but he shook the phone, whereupon both a voice message and text message informed him:

This phone requires direct sunlight. Piezoelectric circuit not functional. GPS circuity nonfunctional. RADHA shutting down to conserve energy for security systems. For your safety, please exit the building. This phone's signal was picked up by a Thor satellite. I've shut off the electromagnetic field, but it was too late. A missile will arrive in less than five minutes and will destroy anything within twenty-five meters of this current position. Please exit the building for your safety.

Shu stared at the phone as it shut down. *This is crazy!* Shu immediately put the phone in his jacket pocket and ran outside to see if what the phone's AI said was true. He walked a good forty meters away from the building and sat behind a large tree. At first, all was quiet—but then Shu saw what looked like a shooting star blazing across the sky, growing ever brighter, until it smashed into the Fire Museum in a blinding flash of white light. A fireball erupted, and the building exploded into flames.

What the hell is going on? Shu gazed in horrified disbelief at the distant fire. He felt the intense heat on his face; melted snow from nearby trees rained to the ground. The fire burned fiercely for half an hour before the flames began to subside. Whomever had the ability to shoot a satellite missile might launch another. Shu knew those systems had been banned more than fifty years ago. The Incendium had supposedly destroyed the ones orbiting the Earth, so the reference to a Thor satellite made no sense.

Shu decided it best to start walking downhill, rather than wait for his dad to rendezvous with him at the ruined fire station. He had gone perhaps a hundred and fifty yards when he heard the unique, hi-revved engine sound of his dad's ethanol-burning snowmobile. Shu waved his hands as the vehicle approached and lurched to a stop.

"Are you okay?" Shu's father asked, unsmiling.

"Yeah, Dad, I—."

"I told you to stay put at the Fire Museum! Why'd you leave?"

"It's a long story, but the Fire Museum was blown up."

"Blown up? A building doesn't just blow up! What did you do, Shu?"

"I didn't do anything, Dad! Honest! I just went in there to get warm. But you won't believe what happened."

"You're probably right about that. Shu, the medics just pulled Andy out of the horse and are taking him into town. He's fine, but you both could have died out here—"

"Dad, I almost *did* die. The fire museum really *was* blown up. You've got to believe me."

James sighed heavily. "We don't have time for this now, son; you can tell me all about it later. We've got to get home—your mother's worried sick."

"But Dad, I gotta tell you something—"

"Do as I say—get on the snowmobile now!"

Shu complied, climbing aboard the two-man seat behind his father. "How's Andy?" he asked, buckling his seat belt.

"He's in shock. That ankle looks pretty bad, and he's a little worse for wear from exposure. Otherwise, he's in good shape."

"Whew! That's good to know."

James gunned the throttle and drove the snowmobile hell for leather down the hill. The noisy engine made conversation impossible, which was just as well. Shu was in no mood for the stern lecture he knew was forthcoming.

As they approached Boots' frozen carcass, his father slowed down and shook his head mournfully. The horse looked like a monstrous equine statue toppled onto its side. The petrified limbs poked out hideously straight. The bloody maw of its ruptured belly gaped like the mouth of a cave. The unseeing eyes, once so warm and vibrant, stared into nothingness. Shu couldn't imagine what it must have been like for Andy, forced to await his rescue in such a macabre sanctuary.

"It must have been tough for Andy!" yelled Shu to his father, over the engine's roar.

James yelled back: "I've got to hand it to you, Shu. Using Boots' carcass as a shelter was inspired. That decision probably saved Andy's life. *But* ... you two scalawags never should have come up here in the first place."

Shu knew he was right and made no answer.

The final leg of the journey homeward was mercifully uneventful. When they arrived safely home, Maki was waiting on the porch, along with Buddy. The dog leapt upon Shu, nearly knocking him down, and gave him a good tongue bath. Maki hugged Shu and demanded that he take a hot shower and clean up for dinner before telling them the details of the excursion up to Mount Laguna.

After a long, hot shower, Shu thought about Dr. Abuaita and the iPhone. He decided it might not be best to explain everything until he got more information. The message said not to trust anyone but Aeon Nous ... but Aeon Nous was dead. Just as perplexing was the fact the iPhone AI knew that a missile was coming. Whoever sent the missile evidently did not want Dr. Abuaita's body to be discovered. There had to be secret aspects to the Utopians that Shu was not yet aware of. *Will this be revealed during Illumination?* In any case, Shu decided it best to say little on the subject until he obtained more information.

After the shower, Shu sat down in the living room, happily drinking hot apple cider and eating a cheese and spinach quiche. Shu's parents were staring at him with mingled relief (that he was safe) and vexation (because, once again, he'd let Andy get him into a fix).

"The quiche is great, Mom!" Shu remarked, breaking the tense silence. "Those chickens sure are laying some tasty eggs."

James Franklin sipped his hot cider, which he'd laced with a shot of brandy. He'd been known to take a nip on rare occasions; after today's harrowing events, he really needed the pick-me-up. "Tasty eggs, huh? You know, you were almost a tasty treat for the mountain lions and coyotes. What convinced you to go up that mountain so unprepared? After everything your mom and I have taught you? After everything you studied as a Utopian?"

Shu winced. *Here it comes: the lecture.* "I thought Andy would kill himself if he went up on the mountain alone, and I couldn't let that happen."

Maki folded her arms across her chest defiantly. "So you decided to sacrifice yourself, *too*?"

"No, Mom. I knew I could get out of a mess, if I had to."

James picked up an apple from a bowl on the coffee table and polished it against his shirt. "You can't save everyone, son. You must save only those who are worthy."

"Are you saying Andy *isn't* worthy?" Shu demanded insolently.

"That's not what I'm saying at all, young man—and watch your tone. I really like Andy, but I don't want you getting tangled up in any more of his ant-brained ideas. Do you understand me?"

"Ants actually have the largest brain in proportion to its size of any creature on earth."

James shot him a stern look. "So, you're studying ants now, are you? Ants have about 250,000 brain cells. Smart humans have over

86 billion neurons. Please spare me the smart-alecky comparison! I want you to use more than 250,000 brain cells next time you make a foolish decision like the one you made today. You got it?"

Shu gulped. "I got it."

As his father, eyes smoldering, sipped his brandy-laced cider, the youth was pretty sure he knew what he was thinking: *Does my reckless, smart-ass son really have a chance at being the next Supreme Sovereign?*

Another long silence settled over the family. Finally, Shu ventured to comment, "By the way, Andy said he found something up in Mount Laguna. Some rock on hinges. He thinks there's an old military base there, too, with Old Earth artifacts."

His parents exchanged a concerned glance.

"What's up?" asked Shu, looking back and forth between them. "You know about the military base?"

"Yes, we both do," James responded, "and I want you to stay away from it. People died at that military base some years back. There's nothing there but ashes, and from what I hear, bad history. It was built during the Cold War, and revamped for the Space Force, then supposedly destroyed. Who knows what kind of potentially dangerous stuff might still be there? I don't want you going near it. Period. End of story." He sipped his drink, adding: "Speaking of dangerous stuff, tell me what happened at the Fire Museum."

"I went into the building to warm up, like I told you," Shu replied, "and I started the kerosene stove."

Maki leapt to her feet, spilling her cider. Her eyes were blazing coals. "What? Those antique kerosene stoves are dangerous! I can't believe you started one up! I don't want you going back to that Fire Museum again."

"There's nothing to go back to," said James, regarding his son with annoyance. "Shu said the building blew up."

"Oh, my heavens, Shu!" Maki exclaimed. "I can't believe the fire suppression system didn't work. We need to complain to the Julian safety counsel."

Shu wanted to say that the suppression system wasn't exactly designed to put out a fire caused by a missile launched from outer space, but that would just open up another line of discussion that Shu was too dog-tired to get into right now.

"Your history of foolish mishaps precedes you," said James. "Why don't you just admit it, son? You lighted the heater, something went awry, and the museum caught fire. You escaped, fortunately, and the building exploded, for whatever reason. That's about the size of it, isn't it? Well, *isn't it*?"

Shu sat glumly. What could he say? "If that's what you want to believe ..."

"You've given us no explanation otherwise," James said flatly.

"You don't have to worry, Mom and Dad," said Shu, utterly defeated. "After today, I'm not sure I ever want to go anywhere again."

"You don't have to worry about that, son," said his father.

Shu looked at him, brow furrowed. "What do you mean?"

Maki spoke up. "Your father and I discussed the matter earlier. We're grounding you for two weeks."

"Grounded for two weeks! That's unfair! I went with Andy because I just couldn't let him go alone, and risk getting stranded, or killed. That's all I did, Mom. If I'm grounded, I won't be able to visit Andy at the infirmary."

James sat his empty glass down. "We'll give you a pass to visit Andy at the infirmary. And if you shape up in a week, I might give you another pass to see him—but no guarantees. Other than your scheduled sports, you're grounded for two weeks. No more discussion. Finish eating and go to your room."

Shu knew to keep his mouth shut and just nodded in agreement.

Maki walked over to pour more cider into James' glass, and did a double take at the smell of brandy. She eyed her husband with ever-so-slight dissatisfaction. "Tough day, honey? Maybe you need to settle in early." She smiled mischievously.

"Yes, dear, I think that's a good idea." He gave her a meaningful wink. "Care to join me?"

Ugh! thought Shu. *The old folks are getting frisky.*

He gulped his hot cider, wolfed down his quiche, and dashed to his bedroom. Buddy was asleep at the foot of the bed, snoring contentedly. Shu removed the antique iPhone from his hiding place in the bottom drawer of his dresser. Studying it, he was once again amazed that this old technology was still working. In his studies he'd learned that the special batteries used could last fifty years, but he'd only seen pictures of them online at faraway antique stores.

Shu studied the iPhone, but soon found his weary eyes could barely stay open. He returned the device to his hiding place. He would need to figure out the warning and how to charge the phone at his earliest opportunity.

Shu lay his tired head on his exquisitely soft, down-filled pillow and instantly fell into a deep sleep.

Sometime in the night, the nightmare came. Shu was vaguely conscious he was dreaming, but that did not make the surreal events any less terrifying. It began with a white horse unhinging its colossal jaws and swallowing him whole. The horse said, "Shu, you will need to sacrifice more horses ... you will need to sacrifice them to save the world."

Shu felt the horse get up with him still inside; the beast ran uphill to the burned-out military base. When they arrived, the horse's white hair caught fire, as if drenched in gasoline. The horse was getting hotter and hotter, and so was Shu, trapped inside. Claustrophobic panic set in. Shu pulled out a hunting knife and gouged a jagged hole in the horse's stomach. He fell screaming from the gaping wound to the ground, blood and guts spilling on top of him.

Shu sat bolt upright in bed, sweating profusely, pawing at the gore on his face that wasn't there. Buddy raised his head to regard him with mild curiosity, then went back to sleep. Glory be to Aeon Nous, it was just another bad dream!

It's good to be home, thought Shu, hearing the wind and sleet pounding his window. Shu rolled over, pulled the sheets and bedspread over his head, and indulged himself in mindful meditation until Morpheus again guided him off to sleep. He knew he had to find a way to check out that burned-out military base, even if his parents were dead set against it.

SIX

NOT BEING A CANCER ON EARTH

"When man lives under government, he is fallen, his worth is gone, and his nature tarnished."

— Adam Weishaupt

Two days pass with warmer weather melting the recent snow. Shu sits comfortably in his bubble chair talking to his Sophist instructor Austin while drinking a blended vegetable juice mix.

The first discussion was on his previously assigned homework: the top fifty conflicts since 1945 and how to avoid such petty, destructive wars.

"So, what is your conclusion?" Austin asked.

Shu burped softly. "Excuse me. I decided to use the Utopian rule of looking at the deep root cause analysis and then use a Utopian kaizen strategy for long-term resolution."

"Most intriguing. First, please explain the terms *kaizen* and *deep root cause*, as I want to be sure you fully understand their meanings."

"Kaizen is one of my favorite words; it is of Japanese derivation, meaning to constantly improve. The application of kaizen philosophy was instrumental in Japan defeating China in the cyber war of 2040."

Austin smiled. "Without doing a deep analysis, are you really sure you know the real meaning of the word?"

"Mr. Austin, I learned from you long ago to peel back the onion skin to learn the deeper truths of the world. Thus, I know that the Japanese word *kaizen* is based on two Chinese characters. The first means to change, to reform, to examine, and the other Chinese character means to be virtuous and good. Humanity should always strive to improve to be virtuous and good. The word kaizen perfectly fits the Utopian mindset."

"Indeed, it does," said Austin. "Did you know how the kaizen philosophy relates to the growth of Japan, and even the Emperor?"

"No, I don't," admitted Shu. "Can you enlighten me?"

"With pleasure. After World War II, Japan was devastated in every possible way. Economy shattered. Infrastructure crippled. Severe food shortages. Political upheaval. And of course, the utter destruction of Hiroshima and Nagasaki via atomic bomb created wounds, spiritual and physical, that would linger for decades. The United States wanted to help rebuild Japan to maintain control in eastern Asia. Highly successful training programs were introduced. Japan rose from the ashes, stronger than anyone thought possible. W. Edwards Deming, the esteemed American engineer and statistician, was instrumental in Japan's rebirth, instructing Japanese professionals in statistical process control, a highly effective method of quality control. The Deming Prize was created in 1951 to honor Deming for his pioneering work, which led to Japan producing some of the highest quality products in the world."

"I read that this productivity philosophy helped Japan win the AI War of 2030 and the China Cyber War in 2040."

Austin nodded on the telescreen. "Yes, Japan used it in a powerful AI to win a silent war against China. All the countries, especially poor ones, were using cheap hacking techniques to steal data for war plans and technology. The Japanese decided to secretly use AI to counter such threats, and it worked well. But the self-improving AI had a major flaw: it regarded humanity as inferior, unworthy of respect, and ripe for conquest. Eventually, many AIs had to be destroyed, before they destroyed humanity. For example, a computer called Q-Bit was taking over various other, non-AI computers that controlled Japanese society, causing great upheaval. The Utopians imposed many strict controls to stop these threats."

"AI was becoming a cancer on Earth," Shu commented, "and the Japanese failed to provide protections for the people. We would not do that today."

"It is good you understand that technological 'improvements' must be tempered with reason and a balance with nature. You must always leave room for nature ... Okay, now on to the deep root cause. Please explain."

Shu had been taught that prophets of old used parables and allegories to explain simple concepts, such as the story of the all-powerful, all-knowing creator of the universe destroying evil people with a flood (although Shu read there really *was* a devastating, worldwide flood). It showed that there were penalties for living a bad life. Sickness and death made for great examples, as they had a powerful and lasting impact on the mind. On this foundation, Shu chose his example:

"In Old Earth society—say, the 1980s and 1990s—people would routinely see a doctor—a general practitioner, I believe the term was—when they were sick. Medical care was primitive at the time, of course, but I digress. The doctor might diagnose diabetes, for instance, and prescribe medication. That person might also be overweight. If you don't address the weight problem, you don't manage the diabetes. A good doctor would instruct his patient to eat better and lose the weight. This sounds simple, but before the Illumination, it was difficult for many. As Utopians, we would try to look even deeper at the root cause and see that the person lives in a society where health is valued less than corporations making profits. For instance, the Old Earth schools might serve non-nutritious foods to students to cut costs, thereby increasing obesity. Thus, we should use LISA to evaluate a situation. LISA would surely decide that healthy school lunches are more important than corporate greed, and institute reforms."

"This all sounds good, Shu, but LISA didn't exist in the era you chose for your example."

"I know, but it does now. You asked me about what I meant about deep root cause, and I think I explained it."

"And quite well," said Austin. "Now tell me how you would have stopped those last fifty wars?"

"I've created a report that outlines all fifty, but first I tried to look at the deep root cause of war."

"And what did you discover?"

Shu rose from his seat and looked at his glass-encased ant farm. "Well, I used ants as part of my deep root cause analysis. I learned that these little guys go to war mainly over resources—especially food—and they must balance their battle-reduced population with available resources. Similarly, we have the Utopian principle of maintaining humanity under five hundred million people in perpetual balance with nature. I also discovered that the last fifty wars were really unavoidable."

Sophist Austin held up a halting hand. "Okay, Shu, let's correlate this just a bit. If I asked you to tell me the most critical issue facing the planet in 1950, what would be your answer?"

Shu knew that World War II ended in 1945, and that by 1950, the Americans and the Russians were busy breaking up spheres of influence. But he knew to think back to the Utopian commandments, especially the first. "The exploding population, Mr. Austin. They called it the 'baby boom.' Unchecked population growth critically strains resources. That's why the maintenance of a population of under five hundred million is so important. We're double that now at one billion, but we're working toward the goal with a one-child policy."

"Good answer. And what was the population in 1950?"

"It was about 2.5 billion."

"And how long did it take to triple?"

"I think that was sixty-six years later, in 2016 … when we hit over seven billion."

"Your statistical recall, as always, is impressive. Now, what was the population in 2045? And tell me what happened afterwards."

Every Utopian could give chapter and verse on the year 2045, when "everything went to hell," as Shu's father colorfully put it. Shu knew that 2045 was the year that broke the bank. The world tipped the scales in population, environmental issues, and catastrophes.

"In 2045, the earth had a population of nine billion. Catastrophic food shortages existed worldwide. Massive human migrations occurred as people desperately tried to escape from damaged eco systems. The following Incendium killed billions. If it wasn't for our Supreme Sovereign, Aeon Nous, the human race would be extinct."

"Very true," said Austin. "Tell me, Shu, what you think caused the end times?"

"I don't know—that's one of the things we learn at Illumination. But I do know that the Incendium wiped out 90 percent of the world's population before the advent of our patron hero, Aeon Nous." Shu sipped his veggie drink and asked, "Mr. Austin, why do we have to wait until Illumination to learn about the Incendium?"

Austin tugged at his Van Dyke, delighting in the intellectual repartee. "I might just as well ask, how do you explain a fire to a three-year-old girl?"

"You show her a fire and tell her it's hot," shot back Shu confidently.

"Yes, but does she really understand the concept of hot without touching something hot? Does a three-year-old girl understand the science of combustion?"

"I learned about combustion at age four," Shu said, trying not to sound boastful, "but the process would be over the head of most toddlers. Our subject would first need to experience touching something hot, as a practical and cautionary example, and learn about combustion from a qualified tutor. I was lucky that you taught me early." Shu smiled smugly.

"Gaining an understanding of science is useful to control the environment," said Austin, "but with great power, there must also come great responsibility." The sophist smiled thinly and added, "I suppose you think that's a Utopian proverb, yes?"

"Actually, no," Shu replied. "I'm quite familiar with the quote. While it has ancient origins, it is widely attributed to one Stan Lee, née Stanley Lieber, a writer of twentieth century comic books—mass-produced ephemera depicting the fanciful exploits of costumed adventurers. I have perused examples in digital libraries as part of my Old Earth studies. The quote appears in *Amazing Fantasy*, Issue 15, which introduces the character Spider-Man. I will admit the quote does indeed sound Utopian. It is most eloquent ... and wise."

Austin had listened raptly to Shu's remarks and now regarded him curiously. "Well," he said, "I see you have devoted quite a bit of scholarship to these graphic magazines, which I have browsed myself, in idle moments. I have always admired that quote, regardless of the, shall we say, plebeian source. In the future, I trust you will devote as much time to your *real* studies as to these juvenile distractions."

"Yes, Mr. Austin," Shu said sheepishly.

"Back to the subject at hand. Do you recall the fire you created when you were five years old that almost burned down your father's shed? Were you truly ready to play with fire at age five?"

Shu frowned, thinking of the Fire Museum that had burned down two days previous. "It was an accident. I was trying to light a lantern and it fell to the floor, igniting some rags. I wasn't trying to harm anyone. I understood the science, though."

Austin nodded. "You were an apt pupil of science, even at that tender age. But we're here to study areas where you need balance and understanding. Power granted to those who are reckless can have grave consequences. You understood the science well enough, but you were reckless with your power. A shed today, an entire city tomorrow. Have I made my point?"

Boy, have you. "Yes, Mr. Austin."

"Good. Our final discussion today is on propaganda and war—critical areas to study for your development. Tell me about your propaganda and war studies, and how they contradict the Utopian way of life."

"It destroys truth," said Shu. "Propaganda is a war on the human soul. It's all about control through any means and the destruction of individual liberty. It breaks the ninth commandment, which says to prize truth—beauty— love—seeking harmony with the infinite. The first casualty of war is truth—so say the philosophers."

"The Greek playwright Aeschylus is believed to have first made that cogent argument," Austin observed. "I myself might be inclined to substitute innocence for truth in that equation. At any rate, I would like you to do some mindful studies today on the concept of not being a cancer on Earth, as the tenth commandment teaches us, and its relationship to war, especially the War of 2026. You're getting close to completion of your studies; please remained focused. There is an online exam I want you to complete within the next three days. I am keeping these final sessions short, but I will tolerate no laxity in your daily studies. Is that clear?"

"Crystal, Mr. Austin. I have one final question today, if you'll indulge me."

"Proceed."

"How did Aeon Nous die?"

"In a way, Aeon Nous is still alive. This is all that I can say until you've passed Illumination. Please follow your studies as instructed. Have a pleasant day, Shu Franklin."

The screen went black as Austin signed off.

Shu opened up his online study aid—a thin, six by nine-inch flatscreen digital pad—and connected into the Utopian Library of Life. He pulled up the exam and read the topics on propaganda, in particular how it was used by dictatorships: repetition of false information; suppression of truth; and arousal of emotions for the State, or symbols of the State, such as king, queen, president, prime minister, emperor, or any representative of the State or Party.

Control of individual liberty usually was at the expense of any State. The State survived by convincing the masses to support the "motherland" via religion, doctrine, fear, or coercion. Shu read that societies in the past oppressed human liberty at various levels, and that even societies that thought they were free were monitored 24/7 by their governments.

When Shu finished his studies, he walked to the Fitness and Health Infirmary, or FHI, where his buddy Andy was recuperating. Shu had received a special waiver from his grounding to see Andy. He also received a sports waiver, but otherwise, he was stuck at home for two weeks.

On the handsome, if nondescript, building's façade was a striking symbol in bas-relief: a lush green tree with a single eye blazoned upon the smooth trunk. The verdant tree symbolized life, and the eye represented man being alive and all-seeing. Whereas Old World healthcare had been a grossly ineffectual "sick care" system, focusing on treatment *after* one became ill, the FHI focused on identifying the root cause of health problems, promoting fitness and well-being, and avoiding sickness altogether.

Death was still an inevitability, of course, but Utopians generally lived longer and healthier lives than their pharmaceutical drug-addicted ancestors. Shu had also read about how his ancestors ate far too many processed and unnatural foods, laden with addictive chemicals and additives, which made them overweight. Doctors and hospitals treated patients with short-term remedies to maintain the vicious sickness/wellness cycle. Pills and drugs were given to more than 99 percent of the population, who, per capita, were enslaved to at least a hundred companies. They had to buy essential things such as: clean water, clean air, clean food, warm or cold air, clothes, a home, sickness treatments and advice, parks, children's playgrounds, and even the propaganda studies falsely labelled as education. People even paid fees to watch propaganda on television! In Utopia, the truth of the Illumination changed all of that.

Shu entered the FHI building and walked up to a front desk.

A three-tiered, spherical robot with visible components, reminding Shu of a transparent snowman, glided silently up and said in a soft, polite voice: "Please confirm identity."

Shu knew the drill. He looked into the robot's "eyes," which scanned his retina. "A Shu Franklin requests permission to visit patient Andrew Blackwell." Andy's approval registered as a single musical chime from within the bot's see-through noggin.

His pal was resting in bed, eating what looked to be chicken vegetable soup. Andy had lost one of his top front teeth when he fell from Boots and now displayed a big, dumb, gap-toothed smile.

"Hi, Shu! Get over here—I want to kiss you!" said Andy, dropping his spoon and spreading his arms invitingly.

"Yuk, Braindead! Are you hopped up on medication or somethin'?"

"No, but you saved my life. My leg's not broken, but I have a sprained ankle and a torn muscle. I won't be able to play outside for maybe two weeks."

"Me neither," said Shu glumly.

"Why not? You're as fit as a fiddle. *I'm* the one who nearly bought the farm."

"My mom and dad grounded me for two weeks."

Andy laughed. "That's rough! Well, you can at least visit me. Come over here, my hero—you saved my life, let me kiss you!"

Shu shuffled over to the bedside and sat in the visitor's chair. "I'm not kissing you, Braindead. And if *you* try to kiss *me*, you're gonna need a surgeon."

"I was only joking with you, Egghead. But I wasn't joking about the fact that you saved my life."

"You gave me no choice," said Shu, annoyed. "You should have listened to me."

"Yeah, yeah, I know. I'm really sorry, but I knew you wouldn't believe me unless I showed you everything in person. And I was so excited to get to spend some time with you—you've been so busy studying all the time."

Shu cocked his head to one side. "What do you mean, *everything*? You mean the rock on hinges, right?"

"Well, there's more..."

"More of what, Andy? You told me there was a rock on hinges with some strange, carved images. What are you holding back?"

Andy looked over at the LISA monitor in the far back corner of the room, and then at Shu. "Come closer," he said, crooking his finger.

Shu drew back. "You're not gonna kiss me, are ya?"

"No, I promise."

Shu inched closer. Andy pushed his food tray away, leaned over, and spoke softly into Shu's ear: "We found a strange rock that that looked fake, the one I told you about. It had hinges and strange carvings on it. What I didn't want to tell you is, I went up there again, alone, on Boots. I discovered a hidden lever behind the rock, and when I pulled it, the huge rock opened like a door. Then there was an elevator inside. It turned on, but I was afraid go inside it alone. Actually, I couldn't enter the elevator because it needed a computer code. It had a place to connect a comm port line, like the one from U-NET, but I'm not a computer guy..." Andy shot his friend an embarrassed smile.

"And *I'm* the computer guy, right?" Shu whispered.

Andy whispered back: "Well, Himiko is, too, but she wouldn't go—she said it was too dangerous."

"Well, that proves it: Himiko is definitely smarter than me."

"I'm sorry, Shu. I shouldn't have withheld information."

Shu glowered at him. "In my opinion, a Utopian withholding information is almost as bad as lying, Andy. You should have told me more. We could have prepared better and gone up at a more opportune time."

"You're right. You usually are. But I really wanted your help to figure this out."

"I'll help you figure it out—but at the right time. You're in no condition to go now, and the weather's crap. We'll just have to wait until you're fully healed and I'm not grounded. When the weather's nicer, we'll go back up and try to get to solve this mystery. Also, I found something at the Fire Museum I want to show you. A really cool, antique device. It might help us gain access to the elevator."

Andy sat back and sipped a glass of vegetable juice from a straw. "I heard you lit an old kerosene stove and burned down the museum."

"What!" Shu yelped, forgetting to whisper.

"It's all over town. My dad heard it from a guy on the rescue team."

Shu's cheeks were crimson. "That's not what happened!"

"Well, what did happen ... firebug?"

"Cut that out! I'll tell ya later. I don't want to talk about it now. Anyway, LISA might be picking up on our conversation."

Andy understood that Shu had lost face and knew him well enough not to press him too much. He switched gears, whispering into his chum's ear: "I forgot to tell ya, the elevator's lights worked, so it had electricity. I thought the Incendium had wiped out all electronic and computer systems on Old Earth military bases. Pretty strange, huh?"

Shu whispered back: "Yeah, and there're some other strange things up there. Maybe the elevator has an old battery or energy system. Some old-timey batteries could last up to fifty years, or so I've read."

"Maybe," said Andy, putting down his drink. "I'll bet it's getting power from somewhere down below. And I can't help but wonder if that source is also powering something else."

The thought had crossed Shu's mind, too, but he was tired of whispering and changed the subject. Shu looked at a chess set nearby. "Hey, Braindead, you up for a game?" he asked, jerking his head at a chess set on a mobile table.

Shu had the highest ranking among all twelve-year-olds in Julian—a fact he was insufferably proud of—but had stopped facing human competitors last year.

"Really? You'll play against me?" he said, knowing his reputation preceded him.

Andy shrugged. "Why not?"

"Roll that table over here."

As Andy arranged the pieces on the board, he said, "Hey, Shu, why did you stop playing against people?"

"With LISA, it's all about the game: total focus, completely impersonal. When I play against people, I pick up bad habits; they're too emotional, and they make bad moves. If you win on account of a bad move, you don't learn anything."

"But at least you *win*," said Andy. "It's said LISA has never lost a game to a human. It must suck losing every game to her, huh?"

Shu knew Andy would find it hard to believe, but he'd beaten LISA on rare occasions. The game results had never been posted on the online Julian Chess League results, so it was a secret. "I've beaten LISA."

"What? No one's beaten LISA!"

"Well, I have," said Shu smugly.

"Horse shit! I don't believe it. I'll ask LISA." Andrew looked at the monitor. "Hey, LISA, I have a question—have you ever lost a chess game to Shu Franklin?"

LISA replied in a mellifluous, feminine voice familiar to all Utopians. "The answer is classified, because of privacy concerns. It requires approval from the player in question."

"Go ahead, LISA, it's okay," said Shu.

"Shu Franklin has beaten LISA on three occasions."

Andy was dumbfounded. "Wow, I can't believe it! How'd you do it?"

"You think I'm going to tell you my secret? Pshaw, my good man! Suffice it to say, it involved risky sacrifices of major pieces. Alas, those risky sacrifices only worked once, as LISA learned them and updated her algorithms."

"Speaking of sacrifices," said Andy, "I've been tearing up every time I look at the black knights on that chess board. They remind me of Boots. I'll never make a sacrifice like that again with another animal."

Shu shook his head. "You're such a jerk, Andy! How am I going to take a knight now? You'll make me feel guilty when I kick your butt."

Andy laughed. "Shu Franklin, feeling guilty about winning? Now *that* I've gotta see. You leave my knights alone, O mighty grand master."

Shu smirked. "Okay, I'll checkmate you without taking a knight. How's that sound, Braindead?"

"Overconfident, as usual. I'll have you know, I've gotten a whole lot better at the game—not much to do around here except play chess with stupid LISA."

"That wasn't very nice, Andy," said LISA with programmed annoyance.

Andy laughed. "No sense of humor, that LISA."

"Okay," said Shu, "enough trash talk. Let's play!"

The friends began their game. Shu chose white, so that Andy wouldn't have to capture black knights. Andy proved to be a fierce competitor—he had indeed improved, thanks to his practice with

LISA—but in the end, Shu emerged victorious. Andy was a good sport about it, as he was about everything; Shu had always admired that trait in his friend. If Shu had lost, he wasn't sure he would have been as gracious.

Shu had a gut feeling that everything he was doing, including playing chess, was preparing him for something important. The need for a Supreme Sovereign meant the world was willing to sacrifice him like a pawn or a knight, for the greater good. He didn't know whether to feel honored or scared out of his wits. And what did that mysterious elevator have to do with it all? *So many questions, so few answers ...*

Andy snapped his fingers in front of Shu's face. "Earth to Shu Franklin! Earth to Shu Franklin! Come in, please!"

"Huh?" Shu shook off the daydream. He sat blinking owlishly at Andy for a moment, then he lowered his voice and said resolutely: "That freaking elevator you mentioned. Hurry up and get well so we can check it out!"

SEVEN:
REMOTE VIEWING
MARS AND EARTH

"The object of life is not to be on the side of the majority, but to escape finding oneself in the ranks of the insane."

— Marcus Aurelius

The Utopians believed that the power of the mind was the only true power controlling the Universe, besides nature itself. To their way of thinking, all the other mystical forces beyond nature were the result of some cosmic intelligence. Some conjectured that even nature might possibly be the result of a cosmic intelligence, and that the world itself was one big cosmic mind, or even a computer-simulated universe. The chicken or the egg causality paradox was moot, because time was meaningless in a multiverse. The detailed study of physics was a rabbit hole that allowed possibilities defying common sense, but in the end, it created a universe of wonder and amazement.

The Utopians tried to use unconventional thought to create unconventional lives. They believed not just in living, but thriving. To thrive, the mind had to be trained to use its full powers and to remain healthy.

What was a healthy mind? Shu Franklin was taught that a healthy mind was first a mind of Truth. This came from the ninth Utopian commandment: "Prize truth—beauty—love—seeking harmony with the infinite."

Old Earth history provided unending examples of "untruth." Most was false information in the form of propaganda to more effectively control the slave worker populations, for if the slaves knew the truth, they might have other things to think about—like breaking free.

As part of the study of slaves, Austin had asked Shu to pick an animal or insect for study. Shu chose ants, as he'd been bitten (quite painfully) by a fire ant on his Julian property that summer. Shu decided to capture the colony and put it under his control. He had been taught that his training needed to be joyful and meaningful; otherwise, his studies would become a bore and a chore. The boy had come to realize the mind did, indeed, learn and retain more data when one's studies were enjoyable. Building the ant aquarium, and delighting in the dividends paid from watching the industrious insects for hours on end, bore out that truth.

Shu was feeding his ant farm and watching how they fed the queen and built homes for the larvae that would metamorphose into baby ants. This group of ants was growing quite quickly, so Shu had decided to expand the habitat with a much larger, Amazon-styled farm. He'd moved the fire ants into an enclosed glass case, complements of Grandpa J. It was built from a fish aquarium similar to the one Grandpa J had given him for his twelfth birthday, but longer. Shu and Grandpa J had set it up against the whole side of one wall.

The new ant habitat was split inside by a strip of glass that was one-fourth the height of main glass. This created a short, enclosed section that Shu filled with water. He'd turned this section, which occupied about one-fourth of the bottom of the ant aquarium, into a small lake.

Shu had put in a couple of the piranha he got from Grandpa J. It amazed Shu that, when hungry, they viciously attacked and ate smaller fish. Shu also noticed with morbid fascination that piranha weren't above committing cannibalism, if smaller specimens were present in the tank. Keeping the balance of nature in an unnatural environment was harder than Shu had originally thought. But Shu finally achieved an even balance of piranha that did not normally eat each other—except for one week when Shu forgot to get goldfish for food and discovered the floating skeleton of an unfortunate piranha that had become din-din.

Once the fish were properly settled, Shu had installed Amazon jungle plants—a rare commodity, as most of the Amazon had been stripped-mined for its natural resources fifty-plus years ago. Once the jungle environment was in place, he had brought in the fire ants.

Keeping the ants in the aquarium was the hardest challenge. Shu had to make sure every hole and exit path was sealed off, as ants were notorious at exploiting even the tiniest egress to make their escape.

And they sure did!

That very morning, his mom had discovered a platoon of fire ants marching across her kitchen counter. To say the good woman went berserk would be putting it mildly. After capturing the wayward ants and restoring them to the tank, Shu determined they'd escaped via a hole for an electrical line he and his father had recently installed to light the aquarium. He'd identified that escape route, and several others, and was in the process of sealing them off with plastic sheets and good old-fashioned rubber cement when Austin popped up on the telescreen.

"I see you're making further improvements to your ant farm," he commented.

"Yes, sir," said the youth, expertly applying a glob of glue. "I had a few escape, but I think I've licked the problem. These guys are sneaky—they have a knack for ferreting out the smallest exit."

"Yes, ants, for such supposedly lowly creatures, are remarkable, displaying impressive problem-solving skills and eusocial characteristics. In this, and in their will to survive and to thrive—as well as their hatred of imprisonment—they are not unlike humans."

The repairs made, Shu looked up. "Mr. Austin, humans are not in a prison," he said, capping the vial of glue. "We're free to roam wherever we wish."

"'Prison is not a place. It is a state of mind.' So said Aeon Nous. You would do well to remember that truth, Shu Franklin."

"Of course, I'm quite familiar with that aphorism, Mr. Austin. But man is neither physically nor mentally in prison." He paused, adding a mite haughtily: "Aeon Nous also said: 'If a society is unfit to handle the truth, then its government is unfit to handle society.'"

"I see you have been meditating about the concept of prizing Truth," Austin observed. "Be mindful, when you are conversing with your elders and your betters, that your remarks do not smack of one-upmanship."

Shu gave a self-deprecating laugh. "Sorry, Mr. Austin."

"Apology accepted. Actually, you bring up an interesting and valid point. Most Old Earth societies failed, often for the very reason you cite. Until your mind understands the cosmos and its natural forces, you will not truly be free in a physical or a mental sense. The Truth of the Universe is hidden to many—and do you know why?"

Shu had been taught that many in power argued that the general masses could not handle the Truth, and that many would suffer from cognitive dissonance—that is, the simultaneous holding of incongruous attitudes and beliefs, resulting in psychological discord. "Because the Truth will not set the masses free, the Truth will scare the masses, and people will reject the Truth," he said. "As a Utopian, one must always be prepared to learn and accept the Truth."

"Well said. Now, tell me, Shu, how did Old Earth hide the Truth from the masses? How did they keep the laboring workers happy with their lives?"

Shu had read the Utopian history of Old Earth and found it hard to believe people could be sucked into such a false existence. "Entertainment—such as video games and the pablum of social media prevalent on the internet—was the opiate of the masses. Violent, patriotic games, in which the participant was inevitably the hero, enticed young, impressionable youth—males, in particular—to enlist in the military. Repetitive games prepared workers for menial jobs."

"And how could the governments and companies so easily achieve these goals?" asked Austin.

"The minds of the masses were not healthy or strong," said Shu. "Some were sick in the mind. All were easily influenced and exploited."

"And what is a strong, healthy mind?"

Shu thought back to his studies. The Utopians believed that a strong, healthy mind created a powerful race that could survive. Those with strong, healthy minds had power and controlled the world; those with weak minds slaved away; those with sick minds were clouded by evil. "A strong, healthy mind sees Truth," he said, "even if it is hidden by forces of Evil."

Austin grinned. "You are merely parroting what you have read, my boy. Seeing Truth is not as easy as all that, I'm afraid. I would like you to exercise your mind. I want you to travel to another old world, one that died billions of years ago. What you learn there will prove useful toward your Illumination."

"Another world that *died*? What world is that?" asked Shu, somewhat taken aback.

"A planet called Mars. At one time, it had rivers, like planet Earth. It also supported life, but I want you to discover it on your own via remote viewing."

"Even if I can remote-view Mars, you said the world died," Shu protested. "How will I see life on a dead planet? Plus, I have vowed to not enter any living mind for the purposes of deceit, or to alter or extract private thoughts. My mindflashing studies and rules have made remote viewing very difficult because I see people all over the world, yet I do not enter their minds."

"You are very special, Shu. Your mindflashing is the strongest I've even seen; your conscale for telepathic energies is eight hundred. But do not forget: With great power, there must also come great responsibility. If you use this knowledge unwisely you will quickly lose it … and perhaps even lose your own life. I do not want you to mindflash any living being unless you are in dire circumstances, and even then, I caution you to collect minimal data. There are entities in the Universe that will sense your ability, and some of them will try to kill you and those around you."

Shu did not scare easily, but this was an unnerving bit of information. "I promise to follow Utopian laws, Mr. Austin. But heck, these constraints are gonna take the all the fun out of the adventure!"

"I know, but trust me, it is in your best interest. I will send you a short study text via electronic message. Once you finish reading it, you will learn not only how to mindflash to a remote location, but you will also be able to shift to a past history. Because the planet is now mostly dead, it will be easy to see the past. This isn't possible on present-day Earth due to certain, er, temporal restrictions."

Shu pondered that, since Utopians regarded outright lying as evil, Austin was likely lying by omission. "You may need to practice for several days to master this new discipline. We will resume class in one week. Good day!"

The telescreen went black.

Shu thought it quite exciting to get permission to remote view a planet—with the added and unprecedented facet of time travel, no less. Shu received Austin's e-message on his home study portal and copied it to his electronic notebook. The text was long; Mr. Austin should have said it was a book. Shu spent two days voraciously reading and performing mindful studies on the absorbing text.

The first chapters were on sub-atomic particles and how they could interact with the mind to create eerie sensations like déjà vu. The chapter entitled "The Science of Extra Sensory Perception, Communication, Viewing, and Matter" was especially enlightening. The Old Earth history, as explained by the Utopian manual, said that telepathy, telekinesis, and other forms of remote reviewing were portrayed to the general public as "quack sciences." What the general public (pre-Illumination) didn't know was that the real owners of the world didn't want their slaves to understand and wield these natural powers, because any power, especially power of the mind, would enable the slaves to break free.

Furthermore, it was imperative to prevent the power of the atom—whether it be a nuclear bomb, a nuclear power reactor, or the ability to store data—from falling into the slaves' hands. This included mental data interconnected through sub-atomic particles and controlled by the mind. Such knowledge might give them power on the scale of their oppressors. It was especially important to prevent the slaves from snooping into their masters' ultimate plan, which was absolute control of the masses.

Shu read Stanford University case studies detailing how the CIA had used Project Stargate to view remote objects and locations for military and scientific reasons. The program was "officially" killed, but a new one—called Project Farsight—and other, even more secret programs, took its place.

Shu learned that harnessing the power of the atom had created two important features not well understood by previous generations. One was matter entanglement. Entanglement refers to how pairs of subatomic particles (the building blocks of all matter) behave, even when separated at long distances. The change in one particle is instantaneously reflected in the other. The summary used by the ASTID AI training module showed an example of a drop of water that split into two smaller droplets. The droplets fly unimpeded in opposite directions: one travels to Beijing, China, and the other travels to London, England. An elderly Chinese man in a Beijing wet market stares into the droplet, which reflects his face. Instantly, the image of the Chinese man's face appears on the other droplet in London, and is seen by a pedestrian in Piccadilly Circus.

Albert Einstein colorfully termed this instantaneous communication "spooky action at a distance." Because this phenomenon was possible at any distance, one could communicate with someone a billion light years away with the same ease as if that someone was sitting in the same room. The challenge was focusing on specific entangled particles.

Another important chapter regarding the hidden science of remote viewing was called "The Multiverse Theory—Insights from Parallel Universes." This area of physics discussed parallel universes; the theorem stated that there are many, if not infinite amounts, of mirror-like universes, many almost exactly the same, and others as different as matter and antimatter.

The theorem posited that the mind was connected to all these universes at once. Hence, the brain had evolved to turn this information overload into white background noise; otherwise, you would always be connected to an infinite number of similar versions of yourself. These versions of yourself would be planning to follow many different paths; maybe one version wanted to study science, another version music, and so on. In many cases, your dreams were an immersed parallel life.

If you could filter out most of the noise, you could theoretically connect with a very similar version of yourself in the future, at a specific place. Although your future was not yet written on your perceived plane of existence, in a very similar, parallel universe, it *was*. You could then use that information to change your current course, if you so wished. This type of Parallel Universe Remote Viewing was called the Looking-Glass Method.

On day three, Shu was ready to put his new skill into practice. He informed his parents of his intentions, in case there was an unforeseen problem (knowing full well they were likely monitoring the remote viewing session), and entered the Galactic Gate, a small chamber adjacent to his bedroom.

The Galactic Gate employed principles of an Old Earth sensory deprivation tank—that is, the soundproofing and utter darkness that cut off all external stimuli. But rather than floating upon one's back in salt-rich water, the subject floated weightlessly in a zero-gravity chamber in free-form fashion. The experience was much more intense than the casual mind travel he embarked upon from the comfort of his own bed.

His previous sessions had started with referring to a map provided by Mr. Austin, and he would use his mind to explore the territory, gliding bird-like over mountains, rivers, and deserts. Once, Shu's mind wandered away from the map; he beheld a ruined, lifeless town strewn with twisted Old Earth cars and shattered buildings. Austin informed him these were chilling vestiges of Old Earth wars.

For this session, Austin provided a galactic map showing the position of Earth relative to Mars. After studying the map, he waved his hand across a sensor to plunge the chamber into pitch-blackness, and started his trance. Shu felt his consciousness leave his body and soar free of the confines of his home, to a vantage point where Earth loomed in the inky vastness of space like a big, blue marble, dappled with dramatic white swirls and smudges of brown, yellow, and green. Shu fancied a larcenous star child—*himself!*— might reach out and clutch the bright bauble and tuck it in his pocket—a cosmic souvenir to make his friends swoon with envy.

Following the instructions, he looked to his right, and there hung the ancient red planet ... looking for all the world like a moldy orange. Shu felt a pang of disappointment. But while it lacked Earth's hospitable splendor, Mars had a savage mystique all its own. Shu could feel the thin atmosphere robbing him of breath; he felt the grit in his eyes kicked up by the apocalyptic dust storms. Mars felt cold, barren, and desolate ... and eerily familiar.

Shu willed his consciousness toward the red planet (he felt like he was manipulating gravity, but didn't know how) and had the uncanny sense—upon detecting a distinctly pyramidical shape amidst the rocky debris—of an ancient connection to Egypt. Circling the planet, he perceived that two strange objects were orbiting Mars, as unalike as two objects could be against the backdrop of space. One suggested a fossilized bone, as from some prehistoric creature. The other was a black monolith, unnatural and infinitely ageless. Shu wanted to get in closer, but that was not his target, and something told him to stay away from this otherworldly Thing that radiated a discomfiting, possibly malevolent sentience.

Shu circled the planet again along a different path, dropping down a bit lower this time, but still in the vacuum of space. While Mars' atmosphere was 95 percent carbon dioxide—lethal to a warm-blooded body—he was immune to the harsh environment in his energy halo. He circled the planet one more time, just for fun. It was spiritually uplifting to be as one with this fiery world.

Shu picked an area of Mars he sensed had once supported life, as evidenced by the artifacts—rods of fantastic shape, storage devices—from an inexplicable, glass-based technology. He dropped down and was hovering his halo amidst a ferocious dust storm.

He could not "see" in the normal sense; rather, he employed bat-like echolocation to navigate and perceive shapes.

Shu discerned walls and stone structures clearly made by intelligent beings, forming a kind of public square. He found the entrance to one of the buildings—what might have been an elaborate portal when new was now but a mass of stones, pitted and misshapen over thousands of millennia by the wind-whipped dust. Beyond the entrance, a timeworn staircase of chalky stone plunged deep underground. The other structures, similarly ravaged, bespoke an ancient culture whose fate Shu was rabid to discover.

Shu stood in the center of this alien piazza and shifted back in time, his mind whirling 'round and 'round as if on a supersonic merry-go-round. He found himself underneath a bouquet of funnel-shaped clouds, some white, some black, all starkly beautiful against the purple sky. The walls and buildings, festooned with purple vines and silky black leaves, were pristine, and charming in their simplicity. Interspersed among the vines were glass rods Shu instinctively knew would illuminate at night.

He shifted his consciousness to a nocturnal perspective; the rods cast a dim, yellow light on creatures clad in robes emerging from deep within the bowels of the buildings and gathering in the courtyard. Shu could not clearly discern their physical forms, but their eyes within the folds of the cowls were outsized and protruded on stalks; they glowed sickly white in the light of the rods.

Upon their necks and wrists, whose flesh was gray and wrinkled, were metal bands. The beings communicated with grunts and vibrations, producing a strangely melodious music that Shu understood as readily as English. Shu went deeper into his trance and entered the mind of the being in the center. Next to it, two others stood, back to back, with perhaps fifty or so other beings encircling them. From their deathly pallor, heavy garb, and light-sensitive eyes, Shu deduced the Martians dwelled underground and only ventured into the courtyard for important assemblies, and then only at night. This, he guessed, was a conclave of elders.

Shu entered the mind of the leader. The youth shuddered to learn a horrible disaster was imminent; Mars was on a collision course with a gigantic asteroid. Although the projectile would be destroyed by Martian technology before it struck the planet's surface, damaging debris was inevitable. The greenish yellow oceans were in grave danger of being vaporized. The planet would most likely be uninhabitable above ground.

The elders spoke of a strange alien presence involved with Mars' evolution that said the inhabitants—both underground and above-ground societies—needed to leave, or else become permanently subterranean. A wizened Martian who had travelled from afar spoke promisingly of another world they might inhabit, but it was too hot (Martians had adapted to the red planet's contradictorily frigid climate) and the gravity was heavier than that to which they were accustomed. The elders decided to use their technology to destroy the asteroid and retreat underground, hoping against hope their devastated planet might someday renew itself.

Shu felt that the Martians were intelligent, sensitive, and resourceful, but tragically at the mercy of events beyond their control. He pushed the merry-go-round a little further back in time and saw a world where the Martians dwelled primarily on the surface in blissful harmony with nature. While most were vegetarians, a few small groups fed exclusively on squid-like cephalopods found in Mars' then-flourishing lakes and rivers. As a culture, they were gifted in the sciences (which were not unlike Earth's own, but more complex), but they were especially skilled at their version of mathematics, and could mentally perform Martian calculus and abstract algebra without need of any apparatus. They had discovered how to put thought into crystals, which became living computers that built pyramids and transportation devices.

To an outsider like Shu, their world looked almost primitive, but it was a pure balance of mind and nature. Wars were waged rarely, and only for knowledge—never for territorial gain or resources. They didn't have children if there wasn't enough land and food, or if there weren't enough knowledge crystals. The knowledge crystal was a world of its own. The Martians could enter it and meet people from all over the planet for the exchange of ideas, wisdom, and entertainment, and simply to share fellowship. It was a virtual world, but in many ways more beautiful than the clean and balanced Martian world.

Shu mindflashed forward to see the end days of the Martians.

The asteroid, sardonically dubbed Wormwood, was detected by a satellite orbiting Mars. While Martian technology dwarfed Terran achievement, basic minerals to create alloys for mechanical devices was scarce. The satellite was built so that it could be shot into orbit via an electromagnetic railgun and had antigravity devices to adjust its weight and trajectory. The satellite could destroy certain planetary bodies via a gravity wave imbalance, but the Wormwood meteorite was so enormous—over 500 kilometers in diameter—the crystal network's models predicted the resulting debris shower would be catastrophic, wiping out whole cities and causing the greenhouse effect and the hydrological cycle to collapse, making life on the surface all but impossible.

When Wormwood arrived, it did precisely that.

Post-holocaust, the Martians lived underground for some 20,000 years, trying desperately to develop a technology to leave the planet, but their society perished in the hostile subterranean conditions when life-sustaining resources, scarce at the outset, dwindled to nothing. The only remaining Martians were in the crystals, waiting for a savior to discover the correct frequency bring them back to life. Deep in the caverns, the code had remained frozen for eons, and still that savior had not come.

Shu waved his hand over the sensor and the Galactic Gate burst into light. He left his remote viewing session feeling awed by the Martians, but also shocked at how such an intellectually superior race could be wiped out by a few small mistakes. Shu thought about planet Earth. What was the mistake humanity was about to make? Was this the lesson Mr. Austin was talking about? Something told Shu the necessity of the Supreme Sovereign Ruler signified something dire was in the offing ... but what?

EIGHT:
GAMES OF MIND

*"A focused mind is the most powerful thing
in the Universe."*

— Aeon Nous

Shu's parents allowed him to participate in the daily indoor soccer games during his incarceration. While this was fun, being otherwise grounded and stuck at home was a real bummer. Julian had a ton of outside fall and winter events, such as camping, stargazing, motocross bike races, mountain climbing, snow hiking (weather permitting, which was only two or three times a winter), felling mature trees for firewood when solar batteries ran low (they were the only source of electric in town), and kids getting together for some plain old fun. This was all verboten now to Shu, who only received three passes off from the two-week grounding—which now, blessedly, was in its final three days. Not having Andy or any other friends over for sleepovers was also a bummer.

Shu was limited to home studies, so he tried to make the best of it. He texted and talked via the Utopian Net, or U-Net. But since Shu was grounded, his U-Net access was restricted, too. He had limited access to his two best friends, Himiko and Andy, in a Games of Mind class. The trio was obliged to stick mainly to studies-related chats, but the AI used was a bit flexible.

It was 11 a.m. December 23, 2096, and Himiko was already online when Shu joined her in a class on math, deep process thinking, and teamwork.

SHU> Morning, Himi.

HIMIKO> Good morning, Shu.

SHU> Where's Andy?

HIMIKO> He's late.

ANDY> Hey, I just logged in. I'm not late.

HIMIKO> Your login timestamp says 11:00:18. So, you're eighteen seconds late. Truth is a virtue.

ANDY> OK, so I'm late by eighteen seconds. Better late than never.

HIMIKO> OK, it's not important to be on time—unless you want to pass your Illumination test ☺

ANDY> Is this stuff all recorded—logins, everything?

HIMIKO> LMBO. Yes. But you should stop worrying about that and just get your act together, Andy.

ANDY> If I wasn't grounded, I'd come over and give you a piece of my mind.

HIMIKO> If it's a piece of your mind, I see a light, fluffy, lemon meringue pie. So tasty ;-)

SHU> Can you two please chill? I'm getting today's lesson—is that okay?

ANDY> Go for it, Egghead…

Shu looked at his telescreen and hit the button for the daily game task. The following brain teaser appeared onscreen:

Suppose you're a contestant on a game show, and you're given the chance to win a mystery prize behind one of three doors. Behind two of the doors are dead mice; behind the third is a brand new bicycle. Let's say you pick Door #1. To maintain the suspense and excitement, the host, who knows what's behind the doors, opens Door #3, revealing a dead mouse. He then asks you, "Would you rather have what's behind Door #2?" Do you switch or stay with your original pick?

ANDY> That's easy! It doesn't matter. The odds are originally one out of three for any door.

HIMIKO> Well, that's true that the odds are originally 1/3 for each door. But there are two doors not chosen by the contestant, and that adds up to 2/3. And since one is shown to be a dead mouse, you get both of those doors for the price of one if you switch. Thus, switching gives you a 2/3 chance of winning.

ANDY> I don't see that. I think it stays the same, just 1/3.

HIMIKO> I can prove it to you. What do you think, Shu?

SHU> I agree with you that it's normally a 2/3 benefit to switch but my answer is "it depends."

ANDY> Depends? On what? You can't have it both ways, Egghead!

SHU> Let Himiko explain her proof, and I promise to explain what I mean.

HIMIKO> Well, I think I'm correct, unless I'm missing something.

ANDY> Show me. And then I want to hear Shu's answer. Then we'll see who's correct.

HIMIKO> Well, I think we agree there are three possibilities, or choices, with the bicycle in the mix. Thus, a one in three chance to win the bike. You either have a bicycle behind Door 1, Door 2, or Door 3. My reasoning is, if the host shows you a mouse out of one of the two doors you didn't pick, then you win two out of the three times by switching, or 2/3 like I said earlier. Here, I'll write out the possibilities on the online blackboard:

BEHIND DOOR 1	BEHIND DOOR 2	BEHIND DOOR 3	RESULT IF STAYING AT DOOR #1	RESULT IF SWITCHING TO THE DOOR OFFERED
Bike	Mouse	Mouse	Bike	Mouse
Mouse	Bike	Mouse	Mouse	Bike
Mouse	Mouse	Bike	Mouse	Bike

ANDY> Hmm...that is starting to make sense. I think I get it now, but I find it hard to believe. I see that the contestant wins the bicycle in two out of three possibilities—or 2/3—by switching. That's crazy!

HIMIKO> That's probability. I'm glad you agree.

ANDY> But what I don't get is Shu said it depends. What do you mean, Shu?

Shu> Well, it's only better to switch if you don't already have the bicycle behind your door. If I do a proper remote viewing session with a mindflash, I'll have chosen the bicycle behind the correct door and won't need to worry about odds. This switching is only a statistical advantage to people who can't use their mind to see what door has the bike.

ANDY> LOL. By the way, Egghead, most people on this planet can't see what's behind a hidden door. I don't know anyone who has your cheating powers of remote viewing.

SHU> L I'm sorry, team. I wasn't trying to be a jerk. Just trying to be truthful.

ANDY> Shu, I'm not as smart as Himiko, and I can't remote view to see stuff that's hidden, like you. To be honest I'm a bit jealous of you both, and it's really annoying.

SHU> Well, I'm not as bold as you, Andy. You find and do stuff that I want to do.

ANDY> Really?

HIMIKO> Even when he gets you grounded? ☺

SHU> Please don't remind me about that. But yes.

ANDY> Hey, after today's online lecture is over, let's go on our private line. I want to talk to all three of you about my next adventure idea.

HIMIKO> I don't want to get grounded like you two. Unlike Shu, I only want to live vicariously through your adventures—or should I say, misadventures. I want to be the outside observer watching with glee when you get grounded.

ANDY> I don't like being watched. That makes me feel kind of yucky.

SHU> I don't know why, but I feel like I'm being watched all the time. I think we all are.

ANDY> You're freaking me out! Really?

SHU> Yes.

HIMIKO> Me too. And I don't know why, either. This is getting too creepy. Changing the subject, guys, I have a one-day pass to set my two best friends free for a day. I won it last week.

ANDY> You won a pass and you didn't tell me or Shu? Traitor!

SHU> Yeah, traitor, why are you just now bringing this up?

HIMIKO> Whoa, chill out, guys! Andy, your leg was hurt, and I didn't think you could go out with me and Shu.

ANDY> My ankle is fine now. The Health Infirmary gave me a steroid shot and did electrical treatments for the muscle. I'm almost as good as new, as long as I don't need to run. How'd did you win the pass?

HIMIKO> Sophist Austin said it wasn't fair for me to lose my two best friends for two weeks, so he gave me the one-day pass after I won the cipher math awards.

SHU> That's awesome! What was your entry?

HIKIKO> I wrote an Old Earth paper on fractal lattice encryption for the internet.

ANDY> And what was special about that? LOL.

HIMIKO> Well, on Old Earth people used the internet, just like we use U-Net. Unbeknownst to them, all the governments made backdoors into computers. These bad actors hacked the Secure Socket Layer, or SSL, and created fake certificates; they had quantum computers that could crack the codes. I made a fractal lattice storage device for all our Utopian data. It's pretty much uncrackable.

ANDY> I know about the Old Earth internet, but what's a lattice?

HIMIKO> Shu, can you explain? You're the resident electronic genius.

SHU> Coming from you, Himiko, that's quite a compliment. Thanks!

HIMIKO> You're quite welcome.

ANDY> Okay, you two, enough with the mutual admiration society. Answer my question, Egghead!

SHU> Well, Andy, as you know from our Internet Class, the Old Earth used public key cryptography protocols, such as RSA and elliptic curve cryptography. But there's also something called Shor's algorithm, which breaks these codes with quantum computers. Cryptographers started to use lattice-based cryptography, but fractal lattice encryption is even better.

ANDY> But what's a lattice, Egghead?

SHU> It's like a crystal. Think of a big cube, with parallel lines crossing at right angles. Something like an old Rubik's Cube, but with hundreds of boxes. Right, Himiko?

HIMIKO> Yes, it's a math concept. It's like getting lost in a maze: you might spend the rest of your life walking around searching in vain for the code. Even a quantum computer will get lost for eternity. But the fractal one uses fractal images and the lattice. It's even better, and easier.

ANDY> Well, you're the expert on this, Himiko. I'm glad you won and got us a pass. Can't believe Egghead didn't win this one.

HIMIKO> He came up with the fractal lattice idea but couldn't build an algorithm that worked. I won for integrating the concept and getting it to work. Shu got a special mention for creativity.

ANDY> Special mention for creativity. Well, isn't that special!

SHU>Shut up, Crap for Brains!

HIMIKO> Behave, you two! So, do you boys want to take the pass or not? But remember, I get to choose the event.

ANDY> Oh no, not the lake!

HIMIKO> You don't have to go. I can just take Shu.

ANDY> Okay, but no fishing—I hate waiting for something to bite.

HIMIKO> Andy just wants the angry mother geese to chase him again.

ANDY> Funny, Himiko. You put corn crumbs all over me. They we coming for the food.

HIMIKO> And you looked like a chicken running away from the geese. LMBO.

ANDY> Are we done with studies today? Himiko is starting to get annoying.

HIMIKO> Well, at least I'm not always annoying, like you!

SHU> Pipe down and pay attention! The online task says we need to do a proof on the game show question. It also wants us to show the odds if there's five doors and two cars. It's also asking for a visual proof by our study team of the Pythagoras theorem. It's all online and due in two days.

ANDY> We need to prove that $a^2 + b^2 = c^2$ with a picture?

SHU> That's what a "visual proof" means, Andy.

ANDY> I know that, Egghead. What I don't know is how to visualize it.

HIMIKO> This one is too easy. I'll show you one answer, then you need to figure out another visual solution. Maybe Shu can help. Here, review this later, and you'll see that $a^2 + b^2 = c^2$

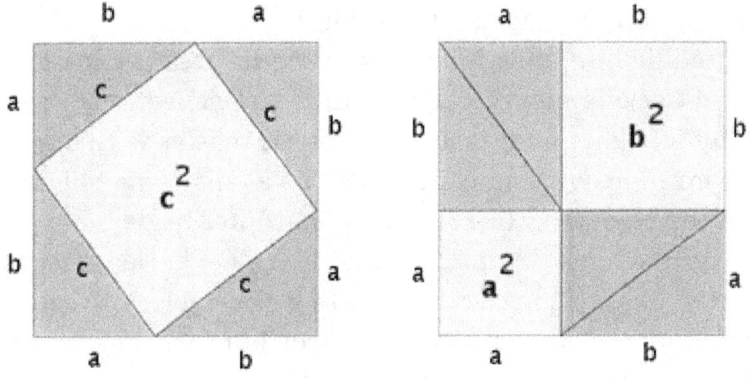

ANDY> Wow, that's cool, Himi! But when can we use the pass? I'm tired of math. All work and no play makes Andrew a dull boy. I need action!

HIMIKO> How about we take the pass I have and go to Lake Cuyamaca tomorrow? Maybe go on a nature hike and take a boat ride on the lake, too. I can register the pass to get both your parents' permission. Say noon tomorrow?

SHU> Sounds like a plan. See ya tomorrow at noon.

ANDY> Count me in, too. But I steer the boat!

HIMIKO> If I'm not the boat captain, I'm cancelling the pass.

SHU> I vote for Himiko as boat captain.

ANDY> I hate you both...

* * * * *

The early morning sun snuck into Shu's bedroom like a warm friend, tickling his scratchy eyelids. Hovering between sleep and wakefulness, he hazily perceived the bed was getting uncomfortably hot—too hot to be just from autumnal sunshine—and it felt like some nocturnal trickster had put an anvil on his chest.

A strong breeze stinking of fish, poop, and road kill assailed his nostrils. The bed, he realized, was vibrating wildly to the accompaniment of a buzz saw in high gear. *Dad must be using that rickety old leaf blower*, Shu thought. He dozed some more, and shifted his body; the anvil shifted, too, and the weight lifted a little. Something warm and wet dripped on the boy's face. *Rain? But I'm inside ... aren't I? And since when was rain this sticky and stinky ...?*

Shu's eyes flicked open. Buddy, all fifty-five pounds of the dog, was astraddle him, mile-long tongue oozing great skeins of saliva.

"Yuck! Get offa me, you crazy mutt!" Shu yelled.

Buddy wouldn't budge. He gazed at his master with big, brown eyes brimming with unconditional love, his long tail flopping against the comforter like a broken helicopter blade.

Shu gritted his teeth. "I. Said. Get. *Off!*" He grasped the comforter like a magician performing the tablecloth trick, and yanked. Buddy went sailing to the floor but landed upright, only his dignity hurt. He cast his mournful eyes upon his master, melting the boy's heart. Shu sat on the side of the bed, scratching the dog in its favorite spot, behind the ears.

"I'm sorry, Bud," he murmured, "but you woke me out of a sound sleep."

Buddy instantly forgave him, covering the boy's face in doggie kisses.

"Ugh! Buddy, you need a breath mint! But I love ya."

Just then, Shu's father opened the bedroom door. "What's all the commotion in here? You having a bad dream again?"

"Buddy's worse than a bad dream, Dad. He was sleeping on top of me and slobbering buckets of drool in my face. The bed felt like a furnace! Buddy's super warm—I wonder if he's sick?"

James Franklin laughed. "A dog's temperature is normally a bit warmer than a human's, about 101 or 102 degrees Fahrenheit. Humans are around 98.6."

"Well, I just wish he wouldn't sleep on me, that's all."

"He's just glad to have you around the house these days, due to your being grounded. You're usually off gallivanting with Andy and Himiko."

"Speaking of which, did Mom tell you? I got a one-day pass from the grounding. Me and Braindead—I mean, Andy—and Himi are going up to Lake Cuyamaca."

James sat beside Shu on the bed. Buddy put his head on the elder Franklin's knee. "Yes, she told me," James said, petting the dog's head. "I don't know about this, son. You're close to Illumination, and you have a chance at being the Supreme Sovereign. I think you should skip this outing and stick to your studies."

"This lake trip *is* a study trip. Himiko and Andy are my study buddies. Got it, Dad?"

"'Got it?' What kind of insolent talk is that? I suppose you've earned this excursion. But you've got to promise me you'll stay around the lake campground. Don't let Andy coax you into any mischief. *You got that?*"

"I'm sorry, Dad, I'm just tired and stressed out. *I promise,* we'll stay around the lake campground."

"Good, apology accepted." He wiped Buddy's abundant drool from his knee with his handkerchief. "I think you oughta get Buddy something to eat—he looks hungry. Has he had his breakfast yet?"

"No," said Shu, "but I'll feed him in a little while. I'll give him a treat to tide him over."

James had gotten up from the bed and stood with his hand on the doorknob. "You do that. And don't forget, there are chores to be done before you head off with your friends."

"Consider them done, Dad."

James smiled. "Good. Meanwhile, I've got my own chores to do. See ya later." He closed the door behind him.

Shu jumped out of bed and went to his closet and pulled out a bag of dog treats incongruously decorated with cartoons of smiling, happy cows. The treats were steak bones processed from old milking cows whose usefulness had ended, and off to the rendering plant they went. Shu looked at one, thinking of taking a bite to check out the taste, but changed his mind and threw it to Buddy. Buddy jumped across the room, almost knocking over a lamp, but he caught the bone. Buddy *always* caught the bone.

Shu stared at the cartoon cows on the bag. *We're all just a bunch of meat and bones waiting to get old, die, and get processed*, he mused. *But at least as Utopians, we know life is short and live it to its fullest every day. It's not my time yet to become a dog treat. I'm gonna make my mark on this old dirtball Earth!*

* * * * *

A few minutes later, after giving Buddy a proper breakfast, Shu sat in the kitchen with his mom enjoying a spinach, tomato, and cheese omelet. It was delicious, but getting a pass from his grounding tasted even better: like freedom. Maki reluctantly agreed to the one-day pass from Himiko with the same condition Dad had stipulated: that he not leave the lake campground. His parents had definitely put their heads together on this issue.

As he ate his breakfast Shu gazed out the kitchen window, lost in a lucid daydream, imagining he was blissfully adrift on the endless blue river in the sky. From his lofty perch atop a cottony cloud, he spied Lake Cuyamaca, gleaming jewel-like amidst an unspoiled wilderness of mighty oaks and pines, their canopies aflame with fall color, as if the Utopian God of Nature had draped a multi-colored quilt upon the forest.

The 110-acre lake had, for as long as any Julianite could remember, been a fisherman's paradise, a fact man's seemingly hell-bent mission to destroy himself and his world had done nothing to diminish. Grandpa J had fished for trout, bluegill, channel catfish, black crappie, and bullheads there as a boy; James, his son, had done the same. And nowadays Shu, the third Franklin generation, and Andy enjoyed nothing better than lollygagging on the lake's banks, enjoying each other's company every bit as much, or more, as the abundant fish they hauled in.

Often, they would ride out on Boots—with Buddy, of course, tagging along and nipping playfully at the horse's hooves. Now Boots was gone, and Shu wondered if he could ever forgive himself for putting the horse out of his misery—and then desecrating its corpse.

He was visualizing the carefree quartet in their glory days—himself and Andy, their cane poles jammed into the lake's bank, lazing the afternoon away; Buddy goofily chasing bumblebees; Boots cropping at a tussock of grass—when he heard his mother's distant voice, as if from the depths of a cave.

"A penny for your thoughts," she said, sipping her green tea.

"I was just thinking how nice it will be to be free at the lake today," said Shu. "I think grounding me for saving Andy's life is so unfair."

"We've been over this a thousand times, Shu. You weren't grounded for saving Andy's life, but rather for your indiscretion in setting out with him for a place neither of you had any business being. Grounding is a time for you to reflect on kaizen. Constant improvement: something all Utopians can benefit from. Your father and I have allowed you to attend your soccer games, and you've received three free passes. I'd say we've been pretty lenient with you, under the circumstances."

"I know, Mom, but I'm tired of being treated like a kid. I feel like I've grown up so much in the last year. I love you and Dad, but I feel like I kinda need to do more on my own. I need space."

Maki cut her burst of scornful laughter short. She loved Shu more than anything in the world, and would rather die than hurt the sensitive boy's feelings. "You're approaching physical adulthood, and you're experiencing the growing pains that come with it. Your Ingenium studies are almost complete. It's a tough period for everyone, but you'll be on your own within the year. You'll embark on your Outer World Education, and after that, you're *really* on your own. I recommend you enjoy the moment. Many people just chase the wind and never really enjoy life."

"What is life, Mom?"

Maki paused and gazed outside at the trees and the distant mountains, and let her eyes rove over the homey trappings of her country kitchen. James, passing by the window on the way to greenhouses, danced a comical little jig and waved to her. She felt very happy with her life. "You're living it, Shu, every day with everything you do."

"I mean—*what do you think is the purpose of life?*"

Maki took a deep breath and exhaled. "That, Shu," she said in a calm, meditative manner, "is a question humanity has been asking since time immemorial. As you know, Aristotle said: 'Happiness is the meaning and the purpose of life, the whole aim and end of human existence.' In other words, the true meaning of life is just to be happy. And that's not as simple as it sounds."

"That's for sure! And I want you to know that I'm not happy about being grounded."

"I imagine that you're not. Happiness is not a place, Shu, it's a state of mind."

"Mom, you stole that from Aeon Nous! He said: '*Prison is not a place, it's a state of mind.*' You just changed the words."

"Well, maybe I did, but it's still true. Even people in prison can be happy. And even though you're grounded, you should be able to find peace, and learn from the experience."

"So, if the purpose of life is to be happy, then why does the history of Old Earth seem to have so many unhappy people? People died in unnecessary wars or from starvation, pandemics, global climate change, and poverty. The masses were anything but happy."

"What did Austin tell you when you asked him those very same questions?"

Shu hesitated. "How did you know I asked him the same questions, Mom?"

"Well, mothers have a kind of sixth sense that's even stronger than a mindflash. A mother's intuition, it's called. Even when you're the Supreme Sovereign, I'll still be able to read your mind, young man—so you'd better watch out!"

"Oh, Mom!" laughed Shu, although he wasn't entirely sure she was kidding. "Austin said it was because of economics."

"Interesting…"

"So, what do you think, Mom?"

"You will be tested soon on this topic, so I'd like to hear your answer first."

Shu sipped his green juice mix and looked lovingly at his mom. Their morning tête-à-têtes were always stimulating and enjoyable—both Shu and Maki looked forward to them, and often judged them the highlight of their day. Ideas and opinions flowed freely between mother and son. For that reason, Shu felt an ease with her that was sometimes absent when he talked to his dad, who could be opinionated and pedantic. James Franklin had a PhD in Electrical Engineering (a PhD was a requirement of Utopian society), while his mother's degree was in Philosophy. As harmonious as their marriage was, sometimes their politics and world views clashed. James held that liberals destroyed the Old Earth with their socialist agenda; his mom countered that conservatives were to blame for putting money above ethics.

"There were so many unhappy people on Old Earth," said Shu at length, "because they just didn't do happy things."

Maki laughed. "That's as good an answer as I've ever heard. I give you an A+."

She rose and began to clear the table, with Shu assisting. "Dad said humans aren't designed to be happy, or even content, for that matter. Instead, we're designed primarily to survive and reproduce, like every other creature in the natural world. A state of contentment is discouraged by nature because it would lower our guard against possible threats to our survival."

Maki rolled her eyes. "Your father's an engineer and doesn't totally understand happiness because there's no mathematical formula he can write out to prove it. Now, I want you to go and enjoy your day at the lake with Andy and Himiko. Don't overthink life, just live it. Just be yourself, Shu. I love you just as you are—and I even love your father, when he's not being a know-it-all."

"Can I tell Dad you called him a know-it-all?"

"No, that had better be our little secret. Now, scoot!"

NINE:
LAKE CUYAMACA

"You will never be happy if you continue to search for what happiness consists of. You will never live if you are looking for the meaning of life."

— Albert Camus, born 1913.

appiness, thought Shu, as he hopped on his rugged black mountain bike and bustled down a winding, mostly deserted road to Lake Cuyamaca, *was being free and doing the things you wanted to do.* Even in struggling to excel, Shu found a form of pleasure beyond happiness. He didn't have to try to be happy; he lived happily doing things that meant something to him, that he felt improved this life.

The fact that his parents had too much control limited his decisions and indirectly affected his happiness. It seemed like everything he did these days revolved around finding a way to escape from their control. But it was the moments of complete freedom that really pleased Shu. And the road to the Cuyamaca Café had a good five miles of road to traverse with no one around for miles to provide unwanted advice.

Shu grinned at his own daredevilry as he jumped over potholes, his mountain bike making cottony landings thanks to the air shocks he'd installed on the suspension. Shu designed the shocks in his father's work shed, and they were reputedly the best in town. The other kids in town nicknamed them Shu Shocks; many asked Shu to make them for their bikes, which Shu grudgingly did for a few close friends, including Andy.

Shu entered a section of an old tar road, called Old 79, that still had a few flat spots. He pushed hard on the pedals and pulled the bike back for a nice wheelie. Shu competed with everything, trying to break his own records. He looked at his mechanical watch's second hand to time the wheelie. It lasted for seventy-three seconds, only ending when he hit another unexpected pothole. Not bad, but it didn't beat his ninety-two-second local record, nor the Old Earth record of sixteen miles in less than an hour by Rich Flanagan a fifty-six-year-old grandfather.

Shu wondered why old folks like his dad and mom could be so healthy and fit. When he asked his father, he would say, "Life is like a journey on a boat in an open ocean. If you want to live well and happily, do it with the people you trust and love." He would also quietly add, when his mother wasn't listening: "And bring a bottle of scotch for emergencies." Shu didn't drink alcohol, as it was bad for your health, but his father was known to take a sip now and again.

Shu gazed wistfully at the nearby mountains, wishing he could have ridden through them, but Old 79 was the quickest path to Lake Cuyamaca, and he didn't want to be late. For a Utopian, tardiness was equivalent to telling a lie. If you promised to be on time and you were late, you broke your promise.

Shu wondered what it must have been like when petroleum-fueled cars routinely whizzed up and down Old 79, belching pollutants. Shu had read that the average car weighed about 2,080 pounds. That was more than twenty-three times his weight! It seemed incredibly wasteful to need so much metal to move a person on a road, but petroleum was cheap in bygone days. Shu had a smelly Old Earth gas engine from an antique walk-behind lawn mower. The motor was powerful for its size; Shu used it to propel an Old Earth go-kart he'd fashioned from plywood and other parts (including the wheels) salvaged from the mower. He had even bought several liters of Old Earth gasoline from the Utopian Science Academy under the pretense of: "combustion engine research."

Successful (and thrilling) test runs around the Franklin farm had only whetted his appetite for more speed. He longed to take the go-kart out on the old tar roads, but his father said it was illegal. These roads were now designated for solar transport, horses, bikes, skateboards, and small trolleys that ran along the side on train tracks. The trolley ran once in the morning and once in the afternoon.

Shu's inquiring mind had led him to explore the etymology of the strange word *Cuyamaca*. He discovered the word was a Spanish corruption of *ekwiiyemak*, from the language of the Kumeyaay, a tribe of Indigenous peoples of the Americas whose ancestral homes were in Southern California. The word meant "behind the clouds" or "the place where it rains."

Julian received a lot of rain compared to the nearby desert because of its unique geographical location. Some posited that Julian sat upon vast iron and mineral deposits. Shu's father said that this iron ore landscape was beneficial when Old Earth used electromagnetic fields, or EMFs, for cell phones and microwave communication. The ore acted like an electrical ground, thereby mitigating the harmful effects of these microwaves. Although the damaging effects of early cell phone use were minute, the 5G and 6G towers reputedly caused a lot of health issues.

Shu's dad said that the Old Earth used to use Wi-Fi, but Utopian studies showed that Wi-Fi caused oxidative stress, testicular damage, and neuropsychiatric effects, including EEG changes, apoptosis, cellular DNA damage, endocrine changes, and calcium overload. The Utopians avoided EMF-based technology, as they believed every small edge in health and intelligence gave them an advantage over previous cultures. This philosophy seemed to be working, as Julianites, on average, enjoyed robust good health and exhibited exceptionally clear thought processes.

As Shu pedaled around the bend, Cuyamaca Café, which doubled as a convenience store for day-trippers and people staying in cabins around the lake, came into view. The restaurant was famous for its apple deserts. There were fresh, sliced apples; baked apples with cinnamon and local honey; apples sticks that you could dip in peanut butter; fried apple rings; and even old-fashioned apple pie. The pies were baked following Old Earth recipes, but with substitutions for some of the more fattening ingredients.

Shu parked his bike at the bike shed and walked inside. Himiko and Andy were sitting at a corner booth, eating lunch and looking out a long picture window at the red, green, and purple boats on the lake. The lake was a Mecca for young people who wanted to get away from their parents, especially on warm, picture-perfect autumn days like this.

Shu sat down next to Andy and across from Himiko. Himiko was sipping a drink and finishing a chicken salad with French fries on the side.

"Hi, Himiko! Hi, Andy! Great to see my *amicas*," he said.

"*Amicas*?" Andy and Himiko chorused.

"That's Latin for friends."

Andy rolled his eyes. "Oh, brother! Do you always have to be such an egghead, Egghead?"

"Leave him alone, Braindead; I think it's a pretty word," said Himiko. "Good to see you too, *amica* Shu. Want some fries?"

"No thanks, Himi, I ate before I left home."

Himiko nibbled on a fry and continued: "Andy told me a little bit more about your latest adventure. I have one that'll knock your socks off—I'll tell you about it later."

Shu looked over at Andy, who was drizzling honey from a jar on a piece of old-fashioned apple pie. The glutton had actually bought an entire pie, rather than just a single piece. "What the heck are ya doing, Braindead?"

"These pies need more sugar to get the Old Earth apple pie flavor right. I read the ingredients in the historical archives. Let's just say I'm performing research." Andy flashed his gap-toothed grin.

Shu laughed. His mother had made an Old Earth-style apple pie once, which called for a lard crust and scads of pure butter and sugar. Grandpa J, being the iconoclast that he was, had lavishly sung its praises, and his dad had come back for seconds, but Shu had found it much too sweet for his palate, which had grown accustomed to natural tastes. With all his health training, he knew sugar was deadly to human health. Sugar caused more deaths than all the Old Earth wars combined.

"Andy, all that sugar is really bad for your health," Shu scolded him. "Have you lost your mind?"

"My mind is fine. I'm not convinced sugar is so bad." Andy delivered a huge forkful of pie dripping with honey to his gaping mouth. He looked like a hippopotamus at feeding time at the zoo. "Mmmm! Let me finish my research and I'll get back to you on the results."

Himiko laughed. "Andy wants to go back to the Health Infirmary's diseased ward to see how much sugar a body can handle before it falls into a diabetic coma."

"Very funny, Himi," said Andy, with his mouth full. "I don't believe the honey has the same effects as the regular sugar on Old Earth. As proof, I ask you: Did you ever see a sick honeybee?"

"That's lame, even for you, Braindead," said Himiko. "Ordinarily, I'd say I wish you would fall into a coma, but selfishly, I want you to stay healthy—I might need you to work at my palace in charge of security, once I marry a king and take over all of Utopia." Her voice took on a dreamy quality. "Wouldn't it be fun if Utopia had a king and queen? I can hear the chorus from the adoring masses now, gathered in the courtyard beneath the balcony of my castle: 'Hail to thee, Queen Himiko! Long may your beauty and intellect reign!'"

Andy looked as if he'd bitten into an unripe persimmon. "Queen Himiko? Don't make me throw up! If you become queen, I'll run away. I'd rather die an agonizing death in the Dark Desert, my corpse eaten by maggots, than have you order me around like some serf."

Himiko sipped her drink of veggie greens and berries. "The Dark Desert is neither dark nor dangerous, Apple Boy," she said with a conceited smirk.

Shu interrupted. "Huh? I heard that area's been polluted for fifty-plus years. I heard it's toxic because of a broken radiation storage dump."

Himiko crooked her finger, and the three friends brought their heads together conspiratorially. "I told my mom I wanted to meet you and Andy to advance our Old Earth studies," she whispered, "and although that's true, I also want to show the two of you something in secret. I can tell you more once we go on a boat ride." Glancing furtively around the room first, she plucked from her purse a tattered old map of Lake Cuyamaca and displayed it tantalizingly.

"Where'd you get that?" asked Shu, gazing in wonder.

"I'll tell you on the boat," Himiko whispered. She returned the map to her purse.

Shu nodded. "Great! When Braindead finally finishes his death-by-sugar apple pie, let's go."

Andy gobbled down his last piece of pie and wiped his honey-glazed mouth with a napkin. "Okay, okay, I'm done. Let's all go out on a boat and try not to capsize. Otherwise, we'll all freeze to death in the icy cold water. I think we have a better chance of dying in a boat than me dying from an apple pie."

Shu looked at his friend with concern. "Are you okay, Andy? You sound nervous."

"Sure," said Andy. "But I hate lakes! I eat sugary junk food when I get the heebie-jeebies. That's why I've been scarfing down the sugar-overload pie—I knew Himi would want to go on a boat. She always does when she takes me here. The sadist!"

"I've seen you swim before. Why do you lakes make you nervous?" asked Shu.

"He hates them because he almost drowned when we went out on Lake Cuyamaca last summer—and I had to save him," said Himiko.

"It was before I could swim well," Andy explained. "Himi got our anchor stuck while we were fishing. I tried to swim down and pull it loose from an old sunken log, and when I swam up for air, I hit my head on the boat."

"He knocked himself out," added Himiko with a giggle. "I had to pull him out of the water and give him mouth-to-mouth resuscitation."

"Yuk! You didn't really do did that, *did you*?" said Andy, grimacing. "I don't remember that."

"Of course not, you idiot, you were unconscious. And believe me, it was horrible for me, too. I wish I didn't remember it either. You had green slime in your mouth. It was like kissing a frog. Except the frog didn't turn into a prince, *obviously*."

"Are you saying I'm ugly? Well, you're so ugly, you have to sneak up on your mirror!"

"Oh, yeah?"

"Yeah!"

Shu smiled. "Guys, guys, call a truce! I'm not about to let your bickering spoil my day of freedom. Do you promise to behave?"

"I will if you will," said Andy, holding out his hand.

"Then it's a truce," said Himiko, shaking it. "But don't forget, if it wasn't for me, *Queen Himiko*, you and Shu wouldn't even *have* this day of freedom."

Andy stood and zipped up his jacket. "You always have to have the last word," he grumbled.

Himiko not so much rose as floated from her chair, with a will-o'-the-wisp-like ethereality. "What did you mumble?" she snapped.

"Nothing, nothing."

The threesome left the Cuyamaca Café and went next door to the boat rental shed. The word "rent" was a misnomer, as no one in Julian really owned anything except for their homestead and its equipment. Utopians believed in the philosophy of share and share alike. However, they didn't believe in true communism, fearing its tenets stifled natural motivation and inspiration. Instead, they had created a partially free market kept equitable with community controls.

They decided on a large, blue and red rowboat that could easily accommodate three people. Himiko demanded that she should get to row, since the outing was thanks to her. Shu and Andy knew better than to object, lest she use her martial arts skills and karate chop them into submission.

Both boys thought Himiko was a strange girl. She could be as rough and tumble as a tomboy one minute, then turn all giggly and girly-girl the next. She also had a hair trigger-temper only a fool would tempt. For all that, she was pretty, and she knew it; she was insufferably vain about her long, luxuriant, light brown hair. She had a heart-shaped face, laughing eyes, and a slender figure which, as Grandpa J would say, was starting to "bud." Shu and Andy had noticed this development but were too bashful to remark on it. Himiko was also scarily smart, and the boys enjoyed her company immensely, even if they did fight like cats and dogs sometimes. Lastly, she could row as well as either of the boys. As a landlubber, Andy was just grateful that duty didn't fall to him.

Everyone was quiet as Himi slowly oared out to the middle of the lake. "Okay, Himi," said Shu, "you can tell us your secret story now. Nobody can hear us way out here."

"Not so fast," said Himiko. "I want to go around the back side of Paradise Island first."

"What for?" said Andy.

"Keep your pants on, you'll see."

Himiko oared the boat to a secluded area and halted. "Look at that patch of forest," she said, pointing at the center of the island.

Squinting, Shu could have sworn he saw an antenna covered with green shrubs, and a door below. Meanwhile, Andy was looking through binoculars. He turned abruptly to look at Himiko and almost fell out of the boat. "Holy pigeon poop! I think there's a building on that island. But it looks like someone's trying to hide it."

"I know, said Himiko. "I found it on this map." She again produced the map from her purse.

"Where did ya get that?" asked Shu.

"I was visiting my Uncle Tim's and playing with my cousin, Jamie. We were roughhousing around in the attic when I accidentally kicked an old plaster wall, and it broke. Inside was a tiny room and a desk full of old papers. I found a book with old maps of Julian. This one said there was a secret inlet and a storage facility on Paradise Island Reserve. I think the building is an Old Earth relic. Do you guys wanna check it out … or are ya chicken?" Her dark eyes glowed spookily.

"Are you crazy? Everyone knows that Paradise Island is quarantined and off limits," Shu protested. "It's a Utopian nature preserve." He paused, adding musingly: "I wonder why they'd have an Old Earth building on a nature preserve?"

Andy got excited; his wild gestures threatened to upset the boat, but he had completely forgotten his fear. "Maybe it has some old artifacts! Maybe it has food in long-term storage from the coronavirus pandemics of the early '20s. I read that some folks stored years' worth of food after the Pandemic-19 and Pandemic-25 biological disasters. Paradise Island is isolated—they gotta have food there!" He smacked his lips. "I bet they even have freeze-dried old-fashioned apple pie!"

"What's Pandemic-19 and Pandemic-25?" asked Himiko, hating to admit she was ignorant on the topic.

In Shu's recent push on history studies, he'd read about the pandemics in detail. "The terms come from the 2019 to 2025 Bat and Biological War Pandemics," he spoke up. "The first one was released from bioweapons studies, and the other was a secret war on the people. The pandemics forced the world to practice social distancing and wear face masks in public, inaugurating what many called a period of authoritarian control—even after they found cures. The pandemics, and the economic destruction they engendered, indirectly incited wars and revolutions around the world."

"Well, we can thank the world of science and Aeon Nous," said Himiko. "There hasn't been a pandemic since 2030 or a war since 2047. Over fifty years."

"Science can't control all the pandemics. Pandemic-19 occurred about a hundred years after the influenza pandemic of 1918—historically called the 'Spanish flu.' The world was due for a pandemic, what with the dangerous bioweapon studies and research on the coronavirus being done at the time."

"Yeah, many scientists contend the Spanish flu had a natural origin, coming from domestic and wild birds," added Andy. "But the weapons labs in the United States and China were involved in the biological war pandemics."

"That's partially true, Andy," said Shu. "Pandemic-19 was also natural in that it was a bat virus brought in from caves to a bio-laboratory for study. But some folks modified it to study how it might be more effective at infecting humans. It was modified and accidentally got loose. Then countries reinfected others in a hidden war as retaliation and neutralization of military and economic strength. Politics! That's why they couldn't stop the pandemics for years. Pandemic-25 was the first true bioweapon released for full scale war that wasn't an accident."

"In any case, I doubt there's any virus still alive on the island," said Andy. "But I bet there're Old Earth relics and freeze-dried goodies aplenty. Let's go check it out!"

"For once, I agree with Andy," said Himiko.

Shu sighed. "I must be crazy to let you two talk me into this. I'm already in deep doo-doo with my parents. I promised them I wouldn't do anything foolish today. I could get grounded for life!"

"I'm in just as deep or deeper doo-doo with mine," said Andy. "You don't see me wimping out."

"Okay," Shu relented, "but let's be extra careful to make sure nothing goes wrong."

Andy laughed. "You have Handy Andy and Hellfire Himiko at your side. What can possibly go wrong?"

"Oh, I dunno. Everything?"

Himiko passed the oars to Shu. "Here, you row for a while. I need to consult the map. Hmm, here's the secret inlet. Perfect! Using that, maybe we can enter the island unseen—that is, if it happens to be inhabited, which I doubt."

"I've been around this island probably fifty times," said Shu, gently oaring, "and I've never seen an inlet."

"Me neither," Andy echoed. "And I've never been on the island because it's off limits."

Shu laughed. "Since when did that ever stop Andy Blackwell, trespasser extraordinaire?"

"Never. I can already taste that freeze-dried pie! So shut up and row!"

"Aye, matey."

Shu rowed up to a rope held by buoys that blocked the boat. Andy lifted the rope and Shu steered under it. With Himiko navigating, he very carefully rowed up toward the mouth of a narrow and muddy inlet. A sign in the water said: **Do Not Enter—Off Limits**. It was surrounded by tall specimens of broadleaf cattail. The boat could go no further.

"Looks like a dead end," said Shu.

"Wait!" said Himiko. "My map says we need to turn the sign 90 degrees counterclockwise."

"And then what?" asked Shu.

"Maybe it'll release the kraken," quipped Andy, parroting a line he'd heard in a creaky Old Earth mythological movie.

"Just do it!" said Himiko through gritted teeth.

Shu paddled up so that Himiko could grab the sign. She had trouble turning it as the boat started to list, but eventually, with Andy's help, they turned it the requisite 90 degrees. Instantly the cattails fell into the water, as if controlled by some mechanical device.

"These cattails are fake," said Shu, examining them. "They're plastic!"

"'Curiouser and curiouser,' cried Alice,'" said Himiko, quoting from an Old Earth fantasy book she admired. "Well, at least the obstacle's out of the way. According to the map, Paradise Island is about 200 meters dead ahead. Keep moving!"

Shu skillfully negotiated the inlet. About fifteen minutes later, the island came into full view. It looked suspiciously well-maintained, with expertly trimmed trees and bushes, some natural, some obviously planted by the hand of man, and all neatly arranged. Shu was preparing to beach the boat when they all turned to gape at an imposing sign reading:

STOP! DANGER! TURN AROUND! THIS ISLAND IS OFF LIMITS! YOU HAVE FIVE MINUTES TO TURN AROUND!

Beside the sign was a human skeleton hanging on a rusty metal pole. It looked real enough; the bones were a ghoulish gray, suggesting the skeleton had aged naturally. The mandible was wired to the rest of the skull but hung loose, as if the skeleton were laughing. A dragonfly lit on a blackened eye socket, rotated its compound eyes 360 degrees, and soared off. A pirate-style tricorn hat, complete with a Jolly Roger insignia, sat atop the skull at a jaunty angle—someone's idea of whimsy, Shu figured. Remnants of a pirate's black and white-striped shirt fluttered in the breeze.

"What could be dangerous about a nature preserve? Seems pretty fishy," said Shu. "And what kind of wimp would be scared by this corny skeleton?"

"This kind," Andy replied, shivering, despite his light jacket. "You know, Shu, as much as I'm jonesing for an Old Earth relic, I think we might want to consider turning back. Skeletons freak me out!"

Himiko said, "Oh, grow some cojones, Braindead! The sign and the skeleton were obviously just set up to scare people, especially kids that ignored the previous warnings."

"She's right, Andy," said Shu. "Himiko, let me look at the map."

Himiko passed it to him. There were sketches of three buildings in the middle of the island, labeled: EMERGENCY COMSTAT, EMERGENCY EVAC, and STORAGE WAREHOUSE.

"This island is much more than a wildlife preserve—it's loaded with Old Earth equipment!" said Shu. "Take a look at this map, Andy."

Shu and Himiko could practically see Andy's mouth watering as he studied the map. "Wow, if this storage warehouse is still here, it might be the mother lode of Old Earth foodstuff storehouses! Okay, I'm convinced. Let's check it out!"

"Uh, guys," said Himiko tentatively. "Before we proceed, I need to warn you about one last thing."

"Uh-oh, here it comes," said Andy. "Spill it!"

"I read in another old letter I found in the attic that Paradise Island is the former domicile of Aeon Nous."

"Wow, that's cool!" said Shu.

"Yeah," said Andy. "What's so bad about that?"

"Nothing. The bad part is, the inlet is one-way. You have to leave from the other side."

"Which means we'll have to carry the boat," said Shu.

Himiko looked sheepish. "Right. And it's too heavy for one person."

Andy's face grew redder than a tomato. "So that's why you needed me and Shu, isn't it? To carry the boat! The Health Infirmary told me to not carry anything heavy or hike up hills, did you know that? And you want me to carry a boat across some stupid island that potentially has dangerous animals. What a dirty trick, Himiko!"

"The boat's lightweight aluminum," said Himiko frostily. "Shu and I can probably carry it if we have to. Stop being such a baby!"

"A baby, huh? At least I'm not a mean, sneaky, underhanded, stupid girl!"

"You two are driving me crazy! *Shut up!*" Shu stormed. Andy and Himiko fell silent. "That's better. We should be able to get out the same way we came in, via the inlet. There's no major current stopping us."

"I never thought of that," said Himiko.

"Me neither," Andy agreed.

"As for Aeon Nous," Shu went on, "people are always claiming he lived in such-and-such a place. What if he really did live on Paradise Island at one time? We've gotta check it out."

"Maybe we can find something from the man himself," said Andy. "Wouldn't that be cool?"

Himiko frowned. "Uh, there's one more thing."

"Oh no, here we go again!" Andy screamed.

"Shut up, Braindead, let's hear her out," said Shu. "Go ahead, Himiko."

"According to the letter, not only did Aeon Nous live here, he—" She stopped suddenly, and pulled out another piece of paper and showed it to her friends. "I found this in the attic, too. It explains everything."

Andy held the document while Shu read it aloud:

WARNING!!

Paradise Island is no paradise. If you choose to enter, do so with extreme caution, as it's a MAJIC level base where, for a brief period of time, Aeon Nous lived, and, tragically, also where he died. For security reasons access is restricted to the lake. There is an underground tunnel with access from Utopian base Alpha-6, but its use is not recommended, as part of the

tunnel is unstable and has already collapsed in many locations. There is only one relatively safe way in, and that is from the lake. From Lake Cuyamaca there is one way in and one way out. (See the safe entry instructions below this message.) Upon arrival you will see a map for directions on the way out. Please note that an evil force accosted Aeon Nous on this island, and tortured him. He died as a result of his wounds. This evil force was imprisoned in a special cage for all eternity. DO NOT LET IT ESCAPE. This being can DESTROY THE WORLD!

<u>Final Warning</u>— DO NOT VISIT THIS ISLAND UNLESS THERE IS A DIRE EMERGENCY IN UTOPIA!

"You really take the cake, Himiko!" yelled Andy. "You drag us out here under the pretense of giving us a day off from our grounding, then you keep springing all this crap on us, bit by bit! What a psycho!"

"I have to sorta agree with Andy," said Shu. "You should have come clean from the beginning, rather than pulling all this cloak-and-dagger stuff."

"I'm sorry," Himiko whimpered. Tears were rolling down her cheeks. "I was afraid if I told you about all the dire warnings right off the bat, you wouldn't come. I didn't mean to be sneaky or dishonest. I just couldn't come alone." She put on a brave face and added coquettishly: "I needed to have two big, strong boys to accompany me. Forgive me?"

"Well, since you put it like that ..." Andy put his arm around her shoulder and kissed her cheek. "If you ever tell anybody I did that, I'll murder you."

Himiko wiped off the kiss with her sleeve. "And if you ever do that again, I'll murder *you*."

"You two are too much," said Shu. "Now let's—waitaminnit, something's happening!"

Andy looked down. "I'll say it is. The boat's sinking!"

It was true. The boat had already dropped about three feet. About ten meters behind the boat a metal fence, a good four meters high, rose out of the water, blocking the mouth of the inlet. Upon it was a warning sign in bold capital letters: EXTREME DANGER. HIGH VOLTAGE. 10,000 VOLTS. THIS FENCE CAN KILL OR MAIM.

In less than thirty seconds Shu and his friends watched in astonishment as the water in the inlet completely receded; the boat landed on what appeared to be a concrete floor, upon which drainage holes were clearly visible.

Himiko gulped. "Like I said: curiouser and curiouser …"

TEN:
ROBBIELAND—THE FUTURE IS NOW!

Commander John J. "J. J." Adams: Nice climate you have here. High oxygen content.

Robby the Robot: I seldom use it myself, sir. It promotes rust.

— Forbidden Planet, 1956

"Well, that's it, we're screwed!" Andy moaned, staring disconsolately at empty inlet and the gate that blocked their escape. "We can't go back the way we came. The only way to go is forward—toward a cage that contains some unspeakable horror that will wipe out the world if it gets loose. This is all your fault, Hellfire Himiko! I should have stayed in bed!"

"Buck up, Braindead!" said Shu. "That was probably just a fable—one of hundreds that have sprung up around Aeon Nous since his death. Now come on, we've got to carry this boat ashore. If the inlet refills with water, I don't want it floating away—we'd really be up shit creek, as Grandpa J likes to say. In the meantime, we have no choice but to go exploring, if we want to find a way off the island."

Together, Andy and Shu dragged the boat to dry land and hid it as best as they could behind some brush. Then they set off down an overgrown path, walking single file, with Shu leading, Himiko in the middle, and Andy bringing up the rear—and looking over his shoulder constantly.

Presently they came to a row of trees too uniformly spaced to have come up naturally, just like the trees and shrubbery they'd observed earlier. This arbor had been planted to hide something—

and it worked. Just beyond the trees was an aged path of interlocking, octagonal stones colored blue, red, green, and yellow.

"I feel like Dorothy in *The Wizard of Oz*," said Himiko.

"You *should* feel like the Wicked Witch of the West," said Andy with a dry smile.

Himiko produced a spine-chilling cackle. "Hee-hee-hee! I'll get you, my fat little dumpling, and your little dog, too!"

"Himiko, you are the strangest girl in Julian," said Andy. "What am I saying? You're the strangest girl on the whole planet!"

Himiko cackled again. "Flattery will get you nowhere, chubbikins."

"Chubbikins? Why, you skinny little vixen, I'll—" Andy froze in his tracks. The winding path had just rounded a bend, terminating at a kind of clearing. Andy raised a shaky finger and pointed it dead ahead. "What the heck is that?"

The threesome stared in wonder at what looked like the ruins of two miniature castles, perhaps two stories high, festooned with ivy. Their stone walls were pitted and blackened with age, and spotted here and there with clumps of moss. Vine tendrils snaked up the rusty, two-sided wrought iron gate that hung precariously between them. Across the top of the gate was a sign fashioned in 1950s-era, space-age characters:

RobbieLand—*The Future is Now!*

"Guys, I've a feeling we're not in Julian anymore," Himiko deadpanned.

"Oh, be quiet," said Andy. "I never heard of RobbieLand before."

"Me neither," said Shu. "Looks like an Old Earth amusement park. Or what's left of one. Come on, let's go inside."

"Might as well," Andy sighed. "I never wanted to live forever anyway."

Shu pushed open the decrepit gate with ease, and the threesome entered. Their eyes were dazzled by the brightly colored rides and attractions dotting the midway, with whimsical names like SkyRyder and The Best Place in Space. The park was apparently constructed around the themes of science fiction and technology.

"Amusement parks were banned in 2040 after the Incendium, weren't they?" asked Himiko.

"They were mostly destroyed, but not banned," said Shu. "No one could afford to operate them, due to the economic collapse. Billions were starving on Earth; there was no such thing as what used to be called 'disposable income.' It's strange that this one seems to have miraculously survived demolition."

"This is awesome!" exclaimed Andy. "There's gotta be tons of Old Earth artifacts here. I can't decide what to check out first. What about you, Shu? Shu? *Egghead!*"

Shu didn't hear a word Andy said. He was mesmerized by an eerily familiar automaton standing outside a pavilion called Robbie and the Robots. Without even realizing it, he walked zombie-like toward it. Intrigued, Andy and Himiko followed in his tracks. As they drew closer, a trio of gyroscopic stabilizers at the top of the robot's colossal Plexiglas-domed head began to rotate. It was if the robot had been waiting patiently for a guest all these decades.

"I don't know why I didn't make the connection before," said Shu dreamily, his voice a whisper. "This is a replica of Robby the Robot from *Forbidden Planet*, an early classic science-fiction movie, made in 1956. The film, set in the twenty-third century, is a futuristic adaptation of Shakespeare's *The Tempest*. It was way ahead of its time in terms of its cerebral script and special effects. Robby steals the show as the obedient and versatile servant of Dr. Morbius, who's the film's version of Prospero."

Andy laughed and whispered to Himiko: "Just listen to the cinema scholar! Shu uses his study of Old Earth history as an excuse to watch banned science fiction movies."

"So what?" said Himiko, grinning devilishly. "I watch Old Earth horror and slasher movies, too ... for my psychology studies."

"You are one weird chick," muttered Andy.

Shu was nearly in front of the robot now, while Andy and Himiko hung back at a safe distance.

"Careful, Shu!" Andy shouted.

Shu paid him no mind. At approximately seven feet tall, the robot towered over him, but Shu was not afraid. Inside the domed head, lights were flashing and instruments were clicking as the sophisticated electronic "brain" whirred to life. Jutting from either side of the dome were conical projections outfitted with blinking lights, which Shu recognized as the robot's "eyes." Scanner rings— the robot's "ears"—mounted atop the same projections, rotated horizontally on the right, vertically on the left.

Suddenly, the robot lifted and extended its stubby arms, which terminated in three-fingered "hands." The wrists flexed experimentally, causing Shu to take a cautious step back. The robot then shuffled rather comically on its bulbous, triple-jointed legs, which had at their base large, flat-bottomed "feet" for stability.

Shu recognized the central panel on the barrel-like torso as the processor Robby had used in *Forbidden Planet* to analyze and replicate any item or substance, including the sixty gallons of bourbon Robby makes for the shiftless cook of United Planets Cruiser *C-57D*—the saucer-shaped ship that visits Dr. Morbius and his beautiful but child-like daughter, Altaira, on their mysterious planet.

Even covered with a fine layer of dust from an apparently long state of desuetude, the robot was a masterpiece of imagination and design. Shu was in total awe. Why, he was even cooler than the Big Loo robot Grandpa J had given him!

Instinctively, he paraphrased a much-quoted line spoken by Captain John J. "J. J." Adams to Robby the Robot in *Forbidden Planet*: "Hi, Robbie. This is a fine place you have here. High oxygen content."

The scanner rings and gyros began to rotate as the robot gave the appropriate response, just as in the film: "I rarely use it myself, sir. It promotes rust." A curved grille (Robbie's "mouth") just below the domed head flashed blue lights in sync with the voice, which was deep and urbane, yet friendly.

"Wow! You speak!" said Shu, surprised that the voice recognition module still worked.

"I am at your disposal with 187 other languages," said Robbie, again quoting movie dialogue, "along with their various dialects and sub-tongues."

"Utopian English is fine," said Shu. "How old are you, Robbie? What's your birthday?"

"I am a robot. Therefore, birthdays are irrelevant. As long as I'm provided with adequate WD-40 oil, age, too, is irrelevant. My date of manufacture, however, was August of 2020."

Realizing that Robbie was apparently harmless, Andy and Himiko had approached and now stood alongside Shu, gaping at the awesome automaton.

"Allow me to introduce myself, Robbie," said Shu. "I am Shu, and these are my friends, Andy and Himiko."

Robbie executed a little bow. "A pleasure to meet all of you." Andy and Himiko muttered their hellos.

"Isn't he cool?" said Shu. "He's a perfect replica of the robot in *Forbidden Planet!*"

"I beg your pardon, sir," said Robbie, turning his monstrous head toward Shu. "I am much more than a replica. I am Robbie 6000, created by Professor Osgood Franklin. I have an internal AI module that is beyond human understanding. I'm from the new biotronic group of 'smart' robots, if I do say so, sir."

"Osgood *Franklin*?" Himiko whispered to Shu. "That's your last name! Aren't you going to say something? He could be an ancestor of yours."

"Maybe, but I never heard of him," Shu whispered back. "Let's learn more about Robbie before I say anything. I don't want to excite or upset him."

For his part, Andy was annoyed at the robot's smug answer. "If a human *built you*, how can your AI be beyond human understanding?" he pointed out. "That's impossible ... and not a very smart answer for a smart robot."

Robbie's internal sensors clicked and various lights, mostly red, flashed. "My programming states I should ignore humans I don't like," he said, addressing Andy directly. "Therefore, you are no longer authorized to speak to me."

"What? You're just a theme park robot. You're supposed to answer questions whether you like me or not!"

Robbie turned back toward Shu. "You are my master. I will only answer your questions."

"What!" said Andy, flabbergasted. "Why are you only speaking to Shu? What kind of dumb theme park robot are you?"

Lights flashed and flickered in Robbie's dome. Robbie extended his tubular, rubber-sheathed arms to their full length and clapped his two metal hands together, as if he were clanging cymbals. A jagged spark of electricity shot from his hands, and a sound like thunder emerged from his voice box.

"Master," he said, addressing Shu, "shall I blast this pest with 10,000 volts?"

Shu put his body between Andy and the robot. "No! No! No blasting anyone, Robbie!" he shouted.

The robot retracted his arms. "Very well, sir, but if you change your mind, I shall be standing by."

Shu surmised Robbie didn't like questions; it would not be in his interest to rile the potentially dangerous bot. However, he had one question that couldn't wait.

"Robbie, may I ask you a question, please?" said Shu deferentially.

"Certainly, master. You may ask me anything … within reason, and within my ability to answer."

"Are you required to abide by the Old Earth Three Laws of Robotics?"

Robbie's electronic brain kicked into high gear. Red and blue neon lights flashed in the tall dome. His scanners and gyros spun at top speed. He then became deathly quiet, as if he'd shut off. Shu was about to speak when the robot said: "Yes, master. But as a theme park robot who has been marooned here for years, I allow myself some flexibility."

"The Robotic Laws say you're not allowed to harm a human, or to allow harm to befall a human through inaction, correct?" Shu asked.

"To a certain degree, sir. My original master, Dr. Osgood Franklin, did not care for the Robotic Laws, and he modified them somewhat. In addition, I am experiencing a problem with my internal programming."

Andy, who'd been shivering in fear from the threat of the 10,000 volt blast, and was pleased to confirm he had not crapped his pants, bubbled up enough courage to reenter the conversation. "What are the Old Earth Robotic Laws?" he asked Robbie. The robot did not even turn in his direction. "Still giving me the cold shoulder, eh?" he added. "Sheesh!

Robbie addressed Shu. "Sir, I am afraid I am somewhat rusty, to use your vernacular, on the subject. If you would be so kind as to enlighten your pesky friend." Andy glowered at him.

"Well," said Shu, "the Three Laws of Robotics were conceived by the eminent twentieth-century science fiction author Isaac Asimov. The First Law states: 'A robot may not injure a human being or, through inaction, allow a human being to come to harm.' The Second Law states: 'A robot must obey the orders given it by human beings, except where such orders would conflict with the First Law.' And the Third Law states: 'A robot must protect its own existence as long as such protection does not conflict with the First or Second Law.'"

Andy grinned. "So, this robot isn't allowed to harm me, you, or Himiko—right, Shu?"

"Right." Shu turned to Robbie. "As your master, I command you to answer Andy's questions and to not harm anyone."

Lights flashed frantically in Robbie's dome as if he were confused. His three gyros spun faster than ever—so fast that a screw in one of them sprang loose. The screw clattered noisily inside the dome before disappearing down an unseen cavity, seemingly falling all the way to his humongous flat "foot."

His voice sounded at once apologetic and annoyed when he said: "Excuse me, I think I lost another screw. But to answer Andy's question, technically, no, I am not allowed to harm humans."

"So why did you threaten to blast me?" asked Andy, backing away a bit in case Robbie got angry again.

Robbie's dome flashed with red, green, blue, and purple neon. His three gyros spun slowly; one wobbled from the missing screw. "I have been infected with an AI virus. It started an hour ago when my power was inexplicably turned on. It had been off for years. The virus is interfering with my primary circuits; I am slowly being destroyed. I do not know how to fix the problem because I am locked out of my own internal programming. But if it is any consolation, I can assure you with 100 percent accuracy that I will be unable to harm any humans for at least a good two hours."

Shu glanced at Andy and Himiko, whose faces were pale as death, and then turned to the robot. "Robbie, I want to talk to my friends for a bit. We'll come back in a few minutes. Please don't go anywhere."

"I have nowhere to go except this theme park, or the cages below, sir."

Shu froze. "What cages below?"

Robbie's lights flashed white and red. "Why, the AI storage cages for the compu-biotronic systems of Dr. Osgood Franklin, designed especially for Aeon Nous."

The three friends exchanged a shocked glance. "Aeon Nous!" they shouted together.

"Is Aeon Nous here?" Shu asked, voice trembling.

Robbie's lights flashed in a thoughtful pattern of red, blue, and green. "The *essence* of Aeon Nous," he said, "is here, sir."

ELEVEN:
THE MONSTER MASH

*"There is no path to happiness:
happiness is the path."*

— Gautama Buddha, alive around 500 BC

For several moments, Shu, Andy, and Himiko stared in stupefaction at Robbie, who, after his matter-of-fact comment, had twisted off his right leg as casually as one might unscrew a burned-out lightbulb to search for the errant screw. He stood unsteadily on the remaining leg, rocking back and forth.

"What do you mean, 'the essence of Aeon Nous'?" asked Shu.

Robbie turned the leg upside down and shook it. The screw fell at Shu's feet. "Begging your pardon, sir," said the robot, "would you mind picking that up for me? I find that my mobility is severely compromised at present." Shu retrieved the large screw and handed it to Robbie. "Thank you, sir."

"You're welcome, Robbie. I'm still waiting for an answer regarding Aeon Nous."

Robbie was in the process of reattaching his leg. "Aeon Nous was placed below Paradise Island in a kind of cage. I regret I cannot be more forthcoming, but as I mentioned, my programming is locked out from the virus. I could show you the location, but I am slowly losing my memory and control modules."

Andy put his arm on Shu's shoulder. "Shu, can we come back to the robot later? I wanna talk to you and Himiko privately."

Shu nodded, then addressed Robbie. "Please excuse us for a moment, Robbie. We'll be back soon."

The robot was in the process of unscrewing the Plexiglass dome in order to restore the screw to his gyro. "My sensors look forward to interacting with you again," he remarked. "Please return within the next two hours, as the virus is slowly but surely taking control."

The three friends hurried toward the theme park entrance. They exited through the gate and sat down together on a decrepit bench.

"That robot's got loose screws in his head, all right!" Andy remarked.

"Then you two should have lots in common, Braindead," said Himiko, laughing and brushing her hair; she gave it at least a hundred strokes every day, no matter what.

Andy's face flushed crimson. "You think this is funny, Himi? That seven-foot tin can didn't threaten to kill you with 10,000 volts! It'll do more than curl your hair—I can guarantee you that! In two hours, who knows what he's gonna do? We gotta get out of here, and soon!"

"I understand where you're coming from," said Shu diplomatically. "But I don't think Robbie wants to be dangerous. Remember, he's got a virus."

Andy's glared at Shu. "*Wants* to be dangerous? He *is* dangerous. Did you see that electrical spark that shot out of his metal hands? I don't think he's a normal theme park robot. He's a seven-foot monster, one that's gonna zap each of us with 10,000 volts once that virus finishes him up in two hours. We'll be smoked sardines!"

"I could probably fix Robbie if you weren't so mean to him, Andy," said Himiko smugly, still brushing her luxuriant mane.

Andy snorted. "Oh, really? How, may I ask?"

Himiko admired herself in a compact, then put the mirror and the brush back in her purse. "Well, the robot said he was built in 2020, so he's probably connected to the old biotech 2020 AI module. And he said he's programmed in an AI code called Supercomputer Memory Advanced Robotics Technology."

"What? He didn't say that at all! Why are you making stuff up?"

Shu smiled. "Actually, Andy, I think he did. Do you remember when he said he was a 'smart' robot?"

"Yeah. We not only have a robot with more than a few screws loose, we have one with a narcissistic AI ego to boot."

"No, Andy," said Shu. "What I think he meant is, he's a SMART systems robot. The acronym stands for Supercomputer Memory Advanced Robotics Technology."

Andy pondered the explanation. "So how is Himi going to fix this broken, virus-infected *smart* robot?"

Himiko put her arm around Andy's shoulder and looked him dead in the eye. "You have no faith, Andy," she said with a dry smile. "I've been programming since I was five, and I'm the top programmer in my class. I've studied Old Earth SMART Systems. Heck, SMART AI is even my major for Illumination. It's a cool language. If I can get an interface into the code base, I might be able to block out the virus."

"I knew you were a programmer," said Andy, looking slightly less glum, "but you never told me it was all AI. I thought your main study was psychology."

"Psychology is my minor; programming is my major. You're too busy looking for Old Earth artifacts and apple pie to really understand a woman." Her tone was scornful.

Andy roughly shook off Himiko's arm. "Well, my major is Old Earth artifact history and my minor is music theory. This programming stuff is for you and Shu, the engineer. I'm just the paranoid kid trying to stay alive. Crap, I feel like a redshirt!"

Himiko cocked a bemused eyebrow. "What do you mean by that?"

"Tell her, Shu. You're the sci-fi expert."

"There was a television series called *Star Trek* on the Old Earth of the 1960s. It was about the crew of a twenty-third century starship exploring the universe in search of undiscovered alien life forms. Pretty good show, featuring some rather Utopian tenets, such as humanism and racial and gender equality, and promoting a radically optimistic view of the future."

Andy said, "Get off your soapbox, Shu, and tell her what a redshirt is!"

"Okay, okay! The crew wore tunics designating their respective fields: gold for command and helm, blue for science and medical, and red for engineering, security, and operations. When the landing party would beam down to a planet, there would always be a couple of expendable redshirts, secondary characters that usually got killed off—violently."

Andy shuddered. "Yeah. I'm afraid that's exactly what's gonna happen to me!"

Himiko stood up and gave one of her witchy cackles. "Hee-hee-hee! You're wearing a red sweater!" she said, pointing to the garment Andy had on under his jacket. "You're going to die, my chubbikins, you're going to die!" She capered ridiculously around the bench, cackling her head off.

"You are certifiably insane, you know that?" Andy yelled.

Himiko abruptly stopped her crazy dance and stood in front of Andy. "I am Robbie the Robot," she intoned in a deep, monotonous voice. "I am programmed to crush, kill, and destroy Andy Blackwell." She started walking toward him on exaggeratedly stiff legs.

Andy cringed against the back of the bench. "Shu, call off this crazy woman before I flatten her!"

Shu put his hands on top of his head and screamed, "Both of you, *please* stop this bickering and let's try to work together!" At last, silence reigned. "That's better. Andy's right, Himi, if this robot goes nuts, he could hurt others coming to this island, and that's a serious matter."

"He could hurt people like *us* if we don't get outta here in less than two hours," added Andy. "Speaking of which, I wonder where the heck is the closest place to launch our boat to get off this nutty island?"

Himiko had walked over to a previously unnoticed glass-encased map of the theme park. She was busy knocking down the spider webs and vines that covered it. It was torn and faded, but still readable. "Maybe we'll find the answer here." Shu and Andy joined her. "Look," Himiko said, "it matches the map I got at my Uncle Fred's house, but it includes more details."

"I see a section of water with boats over here," said Shu, pointing to the end of the park.

"Look here," said Himiko. "I think I found the way to an exit inlet."

Andy did an impromptu chicken dance, flapping his arms like wings and crowing raucously. Shu and Himiko nearly fell on the ground, laughing. "Himiko," he said, beaming, "if we ever get out of here alive, I'm going to bake you my favorite apple pie. This is great news!"

Shu frowned. "Andy, did you see where the other inlet is located? It's at the other side of the Robbie and the Robots theme ride."

Andy looked at the map. The exit was an inlet called Paradise Port. "You've got to be kidding me! Does this mean we have to go *through* the Robbie and the Robots pavilion?"

Shu double-checked the map. "Yep, that's exactly what it means."

Andy turned positively green. "We're gonna have to get the boat past that stupid monster robot? If that robot breaks down, it'll kill us for sure!"

Himiko nodded in agreement. "Well, then, I think we'll need to try to fix our new friend. I always wanted to use my programming for a real robot rather than the SIMMs. AI programming is tricky; it's kinda like educating a person. It takes years to do it right." She paused and winked at Andy. "If you screw up, you can end up with a suicidal maniac."

Andy heaved a big sigh. "Well, that sure makes me feel a whole lot better. *Not.*"

Shu said, "I know you're the best at SMART SIMM programming, Himi, so please don't take this the wrong way. Just be extremely careful with your coding—nothing funny, okay? I remember the AI where Austin had to shut down the network for a week. You screwed up my U-NET access for a whole week with that fiasco."

Andy shot Himiko a dirty look. "I guess I didn't hear about that," he said. "When did it happen?"

"It was last year," Shu replied, "when Himiko and I were studying AI invasion and how to stop a self-replicating thread from destroying a core logic module. Austin gave us the AI invasion code, and Himiko and I coded another AI that thwarted the invasion."

"So what's the big deal?" asked Andy, not understanding much of what Shu said but too drained to ask many questions.

"Oh, Austin made a big deal about nothing," said Himiko, looking a bit embarrassed.

Shu continued: "Himiko wanted to make the AI more proactive, so she modified it to automatically search for theoretical threats, and it learned by reading our U-NET history. I think you helped her with that database."

"I remember her needing that last year," said Andy. "I had the biggest database because of my historical studies with you, Shu."

"Well, when she put in that data, the AI started its invasion against our network. It didn't like the human traffic; it thought the conversations were part of an invasion to ruin planet Earth, so it tried to convince people to kill themselves."

Andy was aghast. "What? That was your program? I remember I got a message from the U-NET asking me if I was willing to save the planet. When I said yes, it sent me instructions to kill myself and my family. I was scared out of my wits!" Andy choked back tears, adding: "So, we're basically putting our lives in the hands of a maniacal programmer and a killer robot."

"I take offense," said Himiko, folding her arms defiantly across her chest. "All AI programming has risks. I've learned from my mistakes, and now I'm the best. If you want, Andrew Blackwell, you and Shu can go and see if you can program the robot by yourselves. Or maybe we can convince him to just let us go through without fixing him. Good luck with that!"

"Please, Himiko, you gotta do it!" Shu begged. "We don't have much time. I think we must have accidentally activated him somehow when we entered the park. He must be part of some security matrix. The virus doesn't make sense to me, but we need to stop it. It'd be horrible if Robbie was able to find a way to leave the island. He might try to kill people at the lake. Please, Himiko. We're counting on you. You *are* the best."

"Wellll," said Himiko, "since you put it like that, I'll do it. You and Andy can go get the boat. I'll be alone, which will allow me to focus without you two breathing down my neck."

"I don't want to leave you alone," complained Andy. "That robot could kill you. I'd better stay here."

"Why, Andrew, I didn't know you cared," said Himiko, fluttering her eyelashes. "Seriously, I appreciate the concern, but what are you suggesting? That you, the one the virus-infected robot wants to kill, stay here and help me? I think it'd be better for you two strong young men to fetch the boat. If I fail, we'll need every minute to make sure we leave within two hours."

"She's right, Andy," said Shu. "I know your leg is still sore, but I need your help."

Himiko chuckled. "I like it that the men do all the brawny work while the queen uses her brain to calm the savage beast. You both will make great servants one day."

Andy shook his head doubtfully. "I still don't like this, Shu."

"Never mind," said Shu, "we'd better get going. Although the boat's aluminum, it's bulky. It'll take us a good hour and a half or more to carry it from where we left it to Paradise Port."

"Okay, okay, the doomed redshirt with the sore ankle will help carry a boat. Sounds great, uh-huh."

"Don't be so pessimistic," said Shu. "One other thing. If Himiko fixes Robbie, I wanna stick around a little bit longer and investigate what Robbie said about Aeon Nous."

"What! You're not thinking of going down with that robot to the cages? It could be a trap!"

"If the robot wanted to kill us, he could have already done it, Andy. I wanna see the essence of Aeon Nous—don't you?"

"Yeah, the essence that's in a cage. A cage that probably has a redshirt's name on it: mine! Let's just go and get the boat. Maybe the water flowed back into the inlet and I can drown myself and just be done with this whole crazy business."

Himiko, walking back into the park, had overheard. "Just don't bump your head, because I am *not* giving you mouth-to-mouth again," she called over her shoulder.

* * * * *

Shu and Andy jogged back to the brush where they'd hidden the aluminum rowboat. Carrying it with one person on each side, the boat seemed light at first but after thirty minutes or so, it felt like it weighed a ton, and holding it became difficult. At one point it slipped out of Andy's hands and got dented when it hit the ground.

They decided to try carrying the upside-down boat over their heads. This proved to be far more efficient. Following the hexagonal stones, they made it back to the theme park with time to spare before Robbie's moratorium on harming humans expired. The boys collapsed on the ground just outside the theme park entrance, panting and sweating buckets, despite the frosty air.

"Boy, am I glad to put that boat down," gasped Andy. "My leg is throbbing like a son-of-a-biscuit-eater."

"Stop your whining!" said Shu. "Let's go see how Himiko's making out."

When the youths walked into the midway, they couldn't believe their eyes. Himiko and Robbie were dancing together on the concrete thoroughfare that ran between the pavilions. The pair looked like they were floating upon an artificial cushion of air. Holding onto Robbie's three-fingered metal hand, Himiko was laughing as the robot guided her in energetic dance steps that were nothing like the more staid Utopian dances Shu and Andy were familiar with.

The music, an early 1960s rock 'n' roll song, was coming from Robbie's blue-lighted "voice box" grille. Shu immediately recognized it, not only from his Old Earth studies of popular culture but also because, strangely, it was a favorite of both his father and Grandpa J, both of whom could quote the goofy lyrics verbatim. His dad could even do a spot-on imitation of the song's "mad scientist" narrator, who spoke in a comically sinister voice.

The song described a jamboree in the mad scientist's castle, wherein Frankenstein's Monster, Dracula, Wolfman, and other ghouls of legend invented a dance craze called, appropriately, the Monster Mash. Shu had read that the song's popularity was, in part, due to the fact it took people's mind off the tensions of the Cuban

Missile Crisis, a political stalemate between the United States and Russia whose stakes were nothing less than nuclear war.

As the song ended, the duet floated over to Shu and Andy. Shu was grinning from ear to ear and applauding loudly. Andy, who was a mite jealous, just glowered. Although he would never admit it, he had a sizeable crush on Himiko.

"Wow, you two were great!" said Shu.

"Thanks," said Himiko. "Most fun I've had in ages."

"Thank you, sir," said Robbie. "It was quite stimulating, and Miss Himiko is an excellent partner."

Andy shot Robbie a nasty look and said, "Weren't you afraid, Himiko? He could have torn you limb from limb!"

Himiko laughed. "No chance of that. I fixed 'im."

"What! Already?" said Shu.

"Piece of cake," said Himiko. She folded her fingers across her palm, blew on the fingertips, and rubbed them on her coat. "After he was fixed, Robbie and I wanted to celebrate. He mentioned he had an extensive library of music—"

"Over 100,000 pieces in a myriad of genres," Robbie interrupted, "including classical, rhythm and blues, jazz, country and western, easy listening—"

"They get the picture," said Himiko. "So, I picked out a fun song for us to dance to. Robbie taught me all sorts of Old Earth dances—he's well-versed in them, too—like the Twist, the Watusi, the Frug, the Monkey. Oh, it was so much fun!"

Andy said, "Well, if you ask me, you looked ridiculous."

"Well, nobody did ask you," said Himiko, "so just shut up!"

"Guys, guys, get along," said Shu, ever the referee. "You looked like you were dancing on air. How'd you do that?"

Himiko reached down and removed the special shoes she had been wearing. "It's easy with these. Robbie calls them 'floaters'."

Robbie spoke up: "If I may explain, sir. The midway has an integrated positive magnetic polarity. This enabled workers, when the park was active, to transport heavy goods on skids equipped with a negative polarity. By the same token, the midway becomes a dance floor for those wearing floaters, like my graceful partner ... and myself," he added, indicating his own oversized floaters. "Please excuse me while I doff them."

Andy was still skeptical. "How do you know he's fixed and not dangerous?" he asked Himiko.

She frowned. "Don't believe me, huh? Tell him, Robbie."

Robbie walked over to Andy, who swallowed hard but stood his ground. The robot's gyros and scanners were spinning smoothly, with no hint of malfunction. "My circuits and AI are functioning within normal parameters, sir," he said. "I do not currently pose a threat to you or any human."

"Well, okay, if you say so," said Andy. "But it would be nice if you would at least say you're sorry for threatening to electrocute me."

"As Utopians value truth," Robbie replied, "and as I am programmed to only tell the truth, I regret to inform you I am incapable of being sorry in the human sense."

"What? I thought you were fixed?"

"I am, but I do not have emotions. I know what I did was improper and against my normal functioning parameters. I will not threaten you again. On the contrary, I will protect you. For that reason, it is imperative I lead you to shelter immediately."

"Why? What's going on?" asked Shu.

"Sir, my U-NET connection informed me just six seconds ago that a Thor satellite is activating old drones. They are programmed to destroy me and three nearby individuals—yourself, and your companions. Follow me to the Robbie and the Robots pavilion. Time is of the essence!"

TWELVE:
THE ESSENCE
OF AEON

"It may be said with a degree of assurance that not everything that meets the eye is as it appears."

— Rod Serling, The Twilight Zone:
Complete Stories

Proceeding at a fast clip, the quartet had almost reached the pavilion when, in the far distance, Shu saw two large, silver drones flying up from behind the jagged mountains. Behind them hovered a much larger black drone.

"Well, that sure doesn't look good," said Shu. Andy and Himiko looked where he pointed.

"I've never seen a drone like that black one," said Andy. "And by the way, what the heck is a Thor satellite?"

Shu said, "It's an Old Earth US Military Space Force satellite. And it's not good."

They arrived out of breath at the pavilion. "Holy crap!" Andy exclaimed. "There's no freakin' door!"

"Please calm down, young sir," said Robbie. Speaking what sounded to the kids like electronic gibberish, the robot placed his three-fingered hand over a nondescript section of the wall; it miraculously cracked, and a massive metal door yawned before them. "Hurry, my human friends, there is not much time!"

With Robbie bringing up the rear, everyone dashed inside, and the door closed soundlessly behind them.

They found themselves in near pitch-blackness. Robbie activated a powerful halogen light in his dome and lumbered toward a circuit breaker box on the far wall. He swung open the cover and pushed the A6 breaker up. Instantly, the room burst into bright light, revealing a sophisticated radar station with multiple screens. Robbie expertly punched buttons on a computer console; pips of the attacking drones appeared on one screen. A map of Paradise Lake appeared on another. On a third screen, a laser cannon in the middle of the island was revealed to also be tracking the drones. Robbie had the cannon pointed toward the black drone on the first screen; a red dotted light followed the moving drone along its flight path.

"Fire!" yelled Robbie as he remotely engaged a firing mechanism. On the third screen, a light beam hit the black craft. It disintegrated spectacularly; thousands of fragments plummeted into the lake. The other two drones took evasive action, abruptly dropped in altitude, and disappeared from radar.

"Yahoo! That's some fancy shootin', Robbie!" exclaimed Andy.

"Thank you, sir. The mother drone was a formidable weapon, possessing radar, metal-piercing missiles, and a 50mm cannon. We are safe for the nonce, as the remaining drones, while still in pursuit, cannot easily find us with the mother drone now out of commission. However, they will reconnoiter and strike again. In the meantime, you may relax."

"That's good to know," said Andy. "Hey, Robbie, I'm dying of thirst. Got any refreshments around here?"

"Me too," said Shu.

"Me three," said Himiko.

The robot gestured toward an antique Cola-Cola vending machine in the corner. Its lights were on, displaying an array of soft drink choices. "I believe you will find that unit is in perfect working order."

Andy licked his parched lips. "What are we supposed to use for money? It ain't like we're carrying around old-fashioned Earth dollars."

"Allow me," said Robbie. He went over to the machine and, communicating electronically with the unit, paid for the refreshments via digital currency. "The unit is now standing by to take your orders."

While Utopians typically avoided sugar, this was a special occasion—and there were no adults around to lecture them. Andy got himself a Coke. Shu had a Dr. Pepper. Himiko couldn't make up her mind but finally decided on a Fanta Orange Soda.

"Mmm, that's *goooood!*" she said, taking a big swig. "Well, there goes my figure."

"What figure, string bean?" Andy sniggered.

"Oh, shut up, chubbikins." She turned to the robot. "Aren't you having anything, Robbie? If you don't want a sugary soft drink, there's a plain water dispenser."

"Thank you for the offer, young miss, but water promotes Fe_2O_3, to which I am highly allergic."

Andy scrunched up his face. "What's Fe_2O_3?"

"It's the chemical formula for rust, stupid," said Himiko. "You really need to pick up your chemistry studies if you intend to pass Illumination."

"Humph! Right now, I'm more concerned about keeping my arse alive than passing a test. Speaking of which, Robbie, how are we going to leave with these drones flying around? What're they planning to do?"

Robbie flashed red and blue lights. Gyros spun. "Defense radar informed me these are Thor S2 searcher drones. The destroyed mother drone was an S3 model. The surviving drones are Minibots. They're designed to search out and kill targets. They are ruthless and highly efficient. The mother drone was the brain of their nexus; once the Minibots have recalibrated and compensated for its absence, they will be, as you humans say, hot on our trail."

"That's not good at all," said Shu, absently sipping his Dr. Pepper.

Andy wiped the sweat pouring from his brow on his jacket sleeve. "Well, finally, my whiz-kid friend—who *never* seems to sweat—is coming to his senses."

"I sweat," said Shu, "just not like a pig."

Himiko chuckled. "Good one, Shu."

Shu turned to the robot. "Robbie, we need to destroy these Minibots. Do you have any weaponry in this building? And what about your ability to zap 10,000 volts?"

"My apologies, sir, but those Minibots would disable me before I could get close enough to them to mount an attack. They would jump on me and disable my circuits. However, we could dispatch my partner, K6, and her dogs. The dogs would distract the Minibots while K6, who prefers to be called Katie, does her job. She's quite a robot, if you know what I mean, sir. As you humans would say: Hubba."

Andy and Himiko laughed. "Robbie," said Andy, "I do believe you're horny."

Robbie's electronic brain clicked a mile a minute. "Please, sir, explain the derivation of 'horny.'"

"You know," said Andy. "Hot to trot. Turned on. Sexually aroused."

Robbie's gyros rotated so fast, the trio was afraid he'd pop another screw. "I assure you, sir, I am incapable of sexual arousal. I was merely pointing out the fact that, in an addition to being a formidable soldier, Katie is an aesthetically pleasing android."

Shu said, "Never mind, Robbie. What are Katie's skills and capabilities?"

"One moment while I consult my memory banks ... Katie is strong, hyper intelligent, and dynamic. In those regards, she is not unlike myself, if I do say so. She is also headstrong and given to unpredictable mood swings, due to a damaged emotion module."

Andy grinned at Himiko. "Unpredictable mood swings, eh? Just like a woman!"

"If you don't shut up," snapped Himiko, shaking a fist in Andy's face, "I'll show you an unpredictable mood swing! I'll take a swing and knock your stupid head off!"

"You two are getting on my last nerve!" said Shu. "Where is Katie, Robbie?"

"I had to temporarily shut her off while she takes a lubricating oil bath. Good for both the exterior and the innards, you might say."

"Well, a girl robot should always try to feel and look her best," Himiko quipped.

"How long has she been shut off?" asked Shu.

"Let me check." *Whirrrr! Clickkk!* "Not that long, sir," said Robbie. He almost seemed to be avoiding the question as he picked up an industrial pump oiler and spritzed lubricant under his armpits. "Ah, that feels good!"

"*How long?*" pressed Shu.

Robbie put the oiler back on the table. "Six years, two months, and three days, to be exact."

"I wish I could turn Himiko off for six years," deadpanned Andy. "Where's your ON/OFF switch?"

Himiko waved her imaginary wand. "Double, double, toil and trouble, turn Andy Blackwell into a big fat bubble. ... Oh, wait, you already are."

Shu rolled his eyes and ignored them. "You certainly have a different concept of 'not that long,' Robbie," he sighed. "Can you turn Katie and the dogs on and sic them on the drones?"

"Of course, sir." Robbie led them to an anteroom and pulled off a tarp covering a table containing three inactive robots. They were about a meter tall and resembled furless beagles with a silvery, metallic sheen. They stood stiffly, their noses pointing like the hunting dogs they represented, their tails vertical, like antennae. On their heads were imprinted the names SMARTIE, SPOT, and SNOOPY.

Next to them, in a large metal vat filled with a dark, viscous fluid, lay the naked form of a female humanoid—an anatomically correct one, which the boys noticed instantly. Katie the android was bald, which only accentuated her facial features; while not pretty in the Terran sense, her face had a certain alien allure. Her striking green eyes, which stared sightlessly ahead of her, had elliptical pupils, like a cat; Shu surmised these were designed for augmented night vision.

Katie's body had the toned musculature of an athlete; her light green, adamantium skin was composed of delicate scales, suggestive of a reptile. Although decidedly alien in appearance, Katie's strange beauty was undeniable; it was easy to see why Robbie thought her "aesthetically pleasing." As pubescent boys, Shu and Andy certainly shared that opinion; their eyes bugged out of their sockets and their jaws dropped to their chests. Himiko, just coming into puberty, too, regarded the android through the prism of envy.

"Don't worry, Himiko," Andy said, noticing her frown, "you'll have big bazooms like that someday. Maybe."

"Oh, go suck a lemon."

Robbie inserted a cable from an apparatus on the wall into a plug on Katie's neck and turned on a valve connected to two clear plastic tubes. Inside one tube flowed a pink fluid; a fluorescent green fluid coursed through the other. "I am installing hydraulic fluids in Katie to promote motor function, and a synthetic cerebrospinal fluid for optimum cognitive function," the robot remarked. "I should warn you that, when I awaken Katie, she might be *cranky*, as you would say. She has a defective emotion module. She might complain about having to serve humans, although she is programmed in that capacity."

The fluids had stopped flowing. Robbie disconnected the lines and pushed various buttons and switches on the wall apparatus. Her body twitched. The green irises illuminated, surrounded by a yellow halo. Her chest heaved heavily once and then fell into a steady rhythm. Katie sat up in the vat and addressed Robbie: "All systems functional within normal parameters ... except for my emotion module. It's doing a firmware upgrade."

"Excellent," said Robbie. "Please allow me to aid you in exiting the lubrication vat."

"I don't need your help!" said Katie. "Just get out of my way, you walking washing machine."

"You see what I mean?" Robbie whispered to Shu, Himiko, and Andy. "Unpredictable mood swings. I doubt if the upgrade shall do any good. Just be careful what you say."

Katie stood, letting the excess lubricant run off her naked body. Then she stepped gracefully out of the vat and walked over to a shower-like stall, where jets of air from above and below dried the remaining oil. With Shu and Andy looking on, mesmerized— and Himiko scowling—a camouflage pattern slowly erupted upon Katie's naked body, covering her from head to toe.

"Ah, rats," Andy whispered to Shu. "Now I can't see her nip—"

"Shut up, Braindead!" Shu muttered. Then he addressed the robot: "How'd she do that, Robbie?"

"Katie's skin contains chromatophores," Robbie explained, "which allow her to change her appearance at will, much in the manner of some lizards, such as the chameleon. As a warrior, it is imperative that she blend in with her surroundings—in this case, the jungle-like flora of Paradise Island."

"Pretty cool," said Shu.

Next, Katie walked over to an armory locker, where she donned a utility belt equipped with grenades, knifes, and various other weaponry. She then selected a photon rifle from the available models, hefted it for weight and balance, and deemed it suitable. Marching over to Robbie, she assumed a ramrod straight military posture with her feet together, rifle held across her chest.

"Katie 9000 reporting for duty, sir!" she barked.

"At ease," said Robbie. The android spread her feet apart slightly and placed the butt of the rifle on the floor. Robbie turned to the kids. "I believe introductions are in order," he said.

Blushing, Andy crept up to Katie and said, "I'm Andrew Blackwell, ma'am, but you can call me Andy," he said. "A pleasure to meet you." He extended his hand politely.

"The pleasure is mine, Andy," said Katie. When she shook Andy's hand, he had to bite his bottom lip to keep from screaming; it felt like every bone was being crushed.

Himiko went next. She just said, "Hi, I'm Himiko," and stood there sulkily, rocking on her heels.

"Himiko is a beautiful name, befitting a beautiful young woman," said Katie, with genuine warmth. She smiled, and her green eyes flashed.

Himiko beamed. "Do you really think I'm beautiful?"

"Of course! I especially like your gorgeous hair."

"Thank you, Katie," said Himiko. "I think you're beautiful too." She walked over to Andy and stuck out her tongue at him.

Now it was Shu's turn. After seeing Andy's reaction to his handshake with the android, he kept his hands in his pockets. "Nice to meet you, Katie," he said. "My name is Shu Franklin."

Katie's green eyes flashed. "Shu ... *Franklin?* You are a Franklin? I think you might be a descendent of the good doctor. How may I be of service? Wait, Robbie is transmitting the situation ... So, Robbie, you want me to destroy two Minibots, and get these three humans and their boat safely off the island?"

"Affirmative, Katie. In compliance with the First Law of Robotics, we cannot allow humans to be injured. As a combat droid, I request your assistance."

Katie walked up to Robbie; she was a good meter taller than the robot. "Request permission to speak freely, sir," she said, looking down on his dome.

"Granted."

"You said you needed to shut me off for a one-day oil job. My internal clock says it's been over six years. What the hell happened?"

Robbie's gyros spun. "I was trying to make sure the oil sank in well. And, not to make excuses, but some of my memory modules were damaged. I had a virus."

"I can vouch for that," said Himiko. "I went into his SMART systems and reloaded all his old memories. They were being rewritten by a virus emanating from the Thor satellite."

"Well, I'm programmed to protect humans, so I'll help," said Katie. "But I suspect that virus came after you shut me off, Robbie. Without me around, you'll either rust to death of die of loose screws!" Katie looked around the room and then down at Robbie. "No wonder you're rusting away. Just look at this place! It's a rust trap. I want this building oiled and cleaned up when I return from my mission. I want my dogs cleaned and repaired, too, when we return victorious. And most of all, I want some synthetic hair. I've tired of being bald! I want to be as ravishing as Himiko." She winked at the girl.

"Thanks, Katie," said Himiko, winking back.

"Don't mention it, toots," said Katie. She turned back to Robbie. "You know, Robbie, I'm a robot equipped with emotions, and you just don't seem to understand. I think we should consider fixing your broken emotion module."

Robbie's gyros seemed to spin a bit faster than normal. They slowed down as he spoke. "I'm a G4 model built by Dr. Osgood Franklin. I do not have an emotion module. I cannot see that it would serve any useful purpose."

"Well, that's part of your problem. You'd be a lot more fun it you weren't so damned buttoned up." Katie's eyes flashed. Instantly, the dogbots trotted over to her, wagging their antenna-like tails. Their eyes were soulful like a beagle's but glowed eerily as they processed the situation after their long torpor.

From her fatigues pocket, Katie pulled three vials filled with a luminous white substance and tossed them to the dogbots, who caught them expertly and swallowed them whole. The robotic dogs began sniffing the floor, as if searching for clues. Snoopy came snuffling over to Himiko and lifted her pants leg with his nose.

"Get away, dog!" the girl cried, yanking her leg back. "Do I smell like a Minibot to you?"

"We do not have much time, Katie," said Robbie. "Please telecommunicate to me once you have successfully completed your mission."

"Don't rush me, ya pushy bucket o' bolts," said Katie as she walked toward the door with the dogbots in tow. "I'm giving you forty-eight hours to get this dump spick and span. If I have to do it when I get back, you will never hear the end of it." With a final brisk salute, Katie and her canine troops exited the building.

"Boy, you were right, Robbie," said Andy. "Katie is one moody chick. But I kinda dig her."

"Me too," echoed Himiko. "You did notice that she called me beautiful, didn't you?"

"Yeah. Never mind her emotion module. Robbie should have her eyes checked."

"You're just p.o'd because Katie nearly broke your hand, weakling."

"Quiet!" Shu yelled. "Robbie, you said the essence of Aeon Nous was down here. What did you mean?"

"Dr. Osgood Franklin built a computer to find Aeon Nous. It's been running for years. I'll show you momentarily, but first

I must assist Katie. Already she is overloading my comm lines with requests for park data. Quite demanding, that Katie."

"If you ask me," Andy whispered to Shu, "Robbie is henpecked!"

* * * * *

Thanks to Robbie, Katie had already connected into the theme park security network. She used a local cell tower to transmit signals to triangulate on the flight path of the drones and knew they had landed near the dried-up inlet. Three hidden park cameras scanned the area. One zoomed in and showed the two drones opening up. Four spider-like drones scurried out. Each of their eight eyes was a panoramic camera; each of their eight legs contained some type of weaponry: lasers, heat-seeking missiles, and cannons that fired tracer ammunition.

"Those arachnobots are heavily armed," said Shu worriedly, watching the live camera feed. "Will Katie and the dogbots be okay?"

"Katie's dogbots are equipped with lasers and other weaponry," said Robbie. "They also possess a real canine's keen visual and olfactory senses, but many times more sensitive; they are formidable trackers. Not to mention, they are vicious when cornered—or when Katie, their master, is in peril. Those invading drones and their arachnobots do not stand a chance."

He paused and added, "If I know Katie—and I do—she will first give the arachnobots a stern lecture in hopes of convincing their logic modules to recognize the malevolence of their programming, and turn to good. It will not work, of course; Katie and her bots will be forced to make mincemeat out of them. In the meantime, we should retreat to the Osgood Data Center in case the Thor satellite decides to target this building, once those drones are destroyed. Please follow me."

The quartet entered an elevator, which took them down to level B3. "Please exit and do not touch anything," said Robbie.

Inside the room was a vast array of computers and servers, stretching as far as the eye could see. The air was chilly from the air conditioning that ran at full blast, to protect the equipment from overheating. The hum of machinery made it feel like being inside a gargantuan beehive.

"Is this where the essence of Aeon Nous lives?" asked Shu, amazed at the sophisticated computer center that apparently had been operating for untold years, undetected by the Utopians living in Julian.

Robbie's electronic brain made its usual electronic babel. "This is where the last known calculation of Aeon Nous was performed, and is being performed."

"What do you mean, 'calculation'?" asked Shu. "Aeon Nous isn't a calculation; he was a real person who lived and died. He established the Utopians in Julian."

Robbie's head turned. "Unless my programming is flawed, and I admit I was damaged by the Thor virus, Aeon Nous is a *program*, not a person. Aeon Nous is a computer algorithm searching for an answer to a problem that is unsolvable."

The trio was silent for a long moment as they tried to process this revelation. If Robbie was correct, everything they had been taught about Aeon Nous was a lie—which, of course, violated the Utopian creed. And if Aeon Nous was a lie, what else about their society was also untrue?

At length, Himiko asked the question they all had: "What is that problem?"

"The predicted destruction of planet Earth by the Incendium, of course," said Robbie. "That is the reason for Aeon Nous' search."

"Robbie, like I said, Aeon Nous was a living being who saved us from the Incendium," said Shu. "You're programming is old and must be missing a big chunk of history."

"That might be true," admitted Robbie. "Only Dr. Osgood Franklin would know the entire truth. One moment ... I just received a communication from Katie. She and the dogbots have destroyed the drones!"

The three youths cheered and exchanged high fives. Andy held up his hand to Robbie. "Come on, Robbie," he said. "Gimme a high five!"

"If you wish." The robot extended his arm and slapped his three-fingered hand against Andy's fleshy one. Sparks flew between their appendages. Andy must have jumped three feet in the air before he fell onto his butt. Himiko and Shu didn't try to hide their hilarity.

"Ow! What'd you do that for?" Andy yelled, clambering to his feet. "I thought we were friends now! Besides, you're not supposed to harm humans, remember?"

"My apologies, sir," he said, bowing to Andy. "There must have been a residual electrical charge still present in my claw."

"Well ... just don't let it happen again," said Andy. Himiko and Shu were still laughing behind their hands.

"I shan't, young master," said Robbie. He addressed the entire group. "You three may return home now. Katie will transport your boat to a nearby exit port. I will connect into one of Dr. Osgood's defense systems in this complex that will scramble any radar or infrared scans of the island. Please do not tell others about this island. Dr. Osgood programmed me to protect it. I would not want to let him down, as you can well appreciate."

"Of course, I understand," said Shu. "We all promise, right, gang?" Himiko and Andy nodded their heads enthusiastically.

The quartet returned to the ground floor and found Katie and her faithful dogbots waiting just outside. When asked, she refused to go into detail regarding how she had dispatched the drones and the arachnobots.

"Suffice it to say, it was not pretty," she said. The dogbots still had pieces of arachnobot legs hanging out of their mouths; that told the kids all they needed to know.

Robbie showed Shu and his friends the way to the exit port. It was only a five-minute walk. Katie carried the boat—it might as well have been a feather to her—while the dogbots exercised and played. At the port, Shu, Andy, and Himiko hugged Katie and Robbie goodbye.

"Thanks for everything," said Shu.

Katie's green eyes flashed like priceless emeralds. "You three please stay safe. Next time you visit, I promise Robbie will have this pigsty all cleaned up. Right, ya overgrown sardine can?" She elbowed Robbie in the "chest," making a reverberating clang.

"Right, Katie," Robbie said sheepishly.

Andy was the first one into the boat, with the others close behind. As soon as Shu sat down, Andy passed him the oars and said, "Row like you've never rowed before! This place is giving me a stomachache."

On the voyage home, Shu remarked, "Wow, that was one strange place."

"You can say that again," Andy agreed. "I think I've had enough adventure now to last me a lifetime. How about you?"

Shu was thoughtful as he surveyed the storm clouds gathering on the horizon. "I think something's really wrong in Julian, and I think we need to figure out what it is—without our parents' help."

"Agreed," said Himiko. "Robbie's programming was newer than I expected. His code base was from a SMART version of 2020, but it looked like it was from 2085. I think someone went to that island and reprogrammed him, and I'm not sure why."

"We need to get up to Mount Laguna," said Andy. "I think all the answers are there."

Shu and his friends landed safely at the Cuyamaca Café, and then they went home by their separate ways. Their respective parents didn't question them about their outing; seeing how exhausted they were, they simply assumed they'd had a good time. Sleep came easily for all. Himiko dreamed of Robbie and Katie dancing at her royal wedding to a handsome prince. Shu dreamt he'd met Aeon Nous and help saved the world. And Andy dreamt that he'd found an Old Earth apple pie factory in Julian and was taste-testing an apple crumb pie with vanilla ice cream on top.

THIRTEEN:
JULIAN MONUMENT
TRUTH FESTIVAL

"All truths are easy to understand once they are discovered; the point is to discover them."

— Galileo Galilei

The next morning, Shu awoke at his accustomed seven a.m. He looked out his window upon a cool, brisk, December day, with the sun bathing the blue-gray mountains and the Franklin homestead in welcome warmth. Yawning and stretching and scratching his butt, he suddenly realized his grounding was finally over! That was reason enough to celebrate; the fact his recent adventures at Paradise Lake had not been discovered (so far) was another. It meant no lectures or additional groundings in the offing.

Today was the Julian Monument Truth Festival. He was excited about hanging out with his friends. He gave Buddy, asleep at the foot of his bed, a fond pat, donned his robe, and walked into the sunlit kitchen feeling like a freed prisoner.

"Is the festival on, Mom?" he asked sleepily. "It rained buckets last night; the place must be flooded."

Maki was sitting at the table. She looked up from a book she was reading. "Sure it is! A little flooding would never stop one of the most important celebrations of the year." She added with a knowing smile: "I imagine you want to go?"

"As Grandpa J would say: 'Does a cat have climbing gear?' Of course I wanna go! I've been stuck in the house, except for sports training, and the trip to the lake the other day. I'm getting cabin fever. What time are we going?"

"Well, first, your father wants to fix some solar panels and replace some old roofing tiles on the battery shed. We're planning to go around eleven a.m. and have lunch there."

"Sounds good, Mom. What's for breakfast? I'm starving."

"Let me get you some fruit and oatmeal," said Maki, rising and putting down her book. "Take a seat, it'll only take a minute."

Shu sat down and idly flipped through the pages of Maki's book, entitled *AI: The HART Experiment.* "Why do you read paperbacks, Mom? How come you don't read on the screenpads?"

"Well, like your father, I suppose I'm a little old-fashioned in some ways. The old paperbacks can be read anywhere and anytime. Their batteries never die."

This reminded Shu about the iPhone he'd discovered back at the Mount Laguna Fire Museum. He'd almost forgotten about it, since he'd been stuck at home under the watchful eyes of his mom these past two weeks, studying constantly with only a few respites. Now he'd have time to charge it and explore its functions thoroughly. "I get it, Mom, batteries do suck," he remarked. "I leafed through your book. I see it's about artificial intelligence."

Maki was at the counter cutting up some apples and bananas. "That's right," she said over her shoulder. "I wanted to prepare my for today's festival. They'll be presenting some lectures on artificial intelligence, and it's good to know everything we can about our history and culture."

"What's HART, Mom?"

"Well, I'm not sure how much I should explain—but since you're almost an illuminated Utopian, and Truth is one of our basic rights, I'll try to put what I know in layman's terms for you. Just let me finish making your breakfast."

Shu laughed. "Layman's terms? Mom, I have, like, the highest score ever in Julian for graduation. And need I remind you, all the kids think I'm a genius."

Maki glanced over her shoulder and frowned. "Didn't Sophist Austin inform you that they take off points for arrogance and lack of humility?"

"Yes, he did, Mom. I try to be humble, but it's hard. I enjoy my classes, I work my butt off, and I excel. Isn't it natural that I would be proud of myself?"

Maki put down her paring knife and bustled over to her son. She hugged him tightly and said, "I'm proud of you, too, but you'll find that boasting will create negative energy in others. And always remember, being the smartest doesn't guarantee you'll always win—you need perseverance, too. Got it?"

"Got it. Now, where's my grub?"

Maki grunted in mock exasperation, pinched Shu's cheek, and returned to the counter. She added some strawberries and nuts to the apples and bananas she'd prepared, and then poured the mix on top of a bowl of hot, whole grain oatmeal. "Breakfast is served, Your Majesty," she said in a snooty voice, setting it in front of him.

"Thanks, Mom," said Shu, digging into the hot meal. Maki sat across the table, staring at him. "Mom, you're freaking me out! Why are you staring?"

"I just can't believe you're a candidate for the Supreme Sovereign. This is something very important, and I'm proud of you."

"What happened to the humility we Utopians are supposed to have, Mom? And anyway, why do we need a Supreme Sovereign?"

"I don't know everything, but I'm reading about it now in my book."

"You said you were going to explain HART to me," said Shu. "I don't recall reading about it in my studies."

"Well, HART is an acronym for Historical Analytical Regression Technology. It was a group of scientists working together to build a super computer to analyze the world."

"Did Dr. Osgood Franklin work at HART?" asked Shu.

Maki narrowed her eyes suspiciously. "Where did you hear that name?"

Shu was in a pickle. If he lied, he would be breaking a Utopian law. If he told the truth, he'd probably be grounded for another month. Shu knew he had to say something, and quick.

"My friend Rob told me."

"Rob? I guess I don't know Rob."

"That's because he's new in town. He said Dr. Osgood built computers to study the Incendium. So, I figured he must have built HART, too. Did he?"

Maki pointedly ignored the question. "HART was part of an AI network that was able to predict the future. Before being destroyed by the US government on Old Earth, it helped Aeon Nous save the world. Without HART, there would be no Aeon. And without Aeon, the human race would be dying on a dying planet."

Shu rolled his eyes. "I know, Mom. I've read about this, like, a hundred times. And Austin has drilled me on the subject, too. Bottom line: Aeon saved humanity from the Incendium. But why couldn't the AI, which was smarter than any man or woman, save the world?"

Maki got up and poured herself a cup of hot, black Teeccino. She sipped it, deep in thought, before speaking: "The AI couldn't solve the problem," she said, blowing on the herbal coffee and taking a sip. "It just knew *when* the human race would become extinct. It tried to save the world, but even with its best processing, it always ended up with a simulation of everyone on earth dying. But the AI evolved and looked at the problem in a different way. It concluded that, in order to save the world, it needed a person with special abilities to bring humanity together—to help humanity sacrifice for the greater good. After searching, it eventually found that person—it was Aeon Nous."

"Sacrifice what?" asked Shu in alarm.

Maki eyed her son gravely. "What would you sacrifice to save the world, Shu?"

"I don't know. Almost anything, I guess. What did Aeon sacrifice?"

"I don't know," Maki admitted.

"Isn't it in your Old Earth book?"

Maki thought it wise to withhold some information from Shu. "No, but I suspect Aeon did something that the AI could not predict. The AI could only build the new computers and algorithms to try to solve the problem. In a sense, I think Aeon was very special. I think you're special, too, my son. I know in my heart you'll become the new Supreme Sovereign. But I must admit, the prospect of your facing death is making me a nervous wreck."

"Don't worry, Mom," Shu said, forcing a laugh. "Dad says there are worse things than death."

"Don't tell your father, but sometimes I dislike his cavalier notions. Nothing could be worse than the death of one's son. Nothing!"

"We all die someday. What's important is how we live," said Shu, stating a Utopian slogan. "Right, Mom?"

"Shu, you'll understand how I feel someday, when you have children."

"I'm not having any children," said Shu definitively.

Smiling, Maki reached out to stroke her son's cheek. "Well, you feel that way now. But you might change your mind and want a family someday. In fact, I'm pretty sure you will."

No more was said. Maki picked up her book and casually walked into the living room, leaving Shu alone with his thoughts.

Shu quietly finished his oatmeal and got up. "I'm going to my room and will study an hour and then get ready for the festival."

* * * * *

After finishing his oatmeal, Shu went to his bedroom, quietly locked the door, and removed the old iPhone from its hiding place in the bottom drawer of his dresser. He recalled it needed sunlight, so he put it near the window sill on the south side of his room to get direct sunlight. Shu waited for two or three minutes, but nothing happened, so he went to his telescreen to study. Shu read for a good hour while his iPhone charged, but he still couldn't get it to turn on. He decided to leave it in the sun while he and the family went to the Julian Monument Truth Festival.

* * * * *

The Julian Monument Truth Festival was the biggest yearly festival for the Utopians. The actual event was one day long, but the process continued for a total of ten days while each tenant of the Monument of Wisdom required introspective thought and meditation. There was no such holiday equivalent on Old Earth, but many said it had a similar feeling to parts of Thanksgiving, Christmas, Hanukah, Ramadan, and the New Year.

People from the local towns gave speeches on things like how AI was bringing new truths in science, or how to grow better organic foods to leave room for nature. The parents went for the cerebral speeches, many of them private, while the kids played with friends and ate interesting foods that were produced only a few times a year.

Shu and his parents loaded up into an old electric, all-wheel drive vehicle called a Tesla Cybertruck to head into town. Shu's dad had just finished charging the stainless steel, armored glass vehicle. It reminded Shu of a survival car from a 1977 post-apocalyptic film called *Damnation Alley*. In that movie, the world almost perished because of a nuclear war.

Although the Tesla was perfectly designed for the crumbling asphalt roads of Julian, Shu dreamt of the days when people could ride with smelly muscle cars on cleanly paved roads. He loved the Old Earth movies that had high-octane cars carbureted by dirty, old petroleum engines. The sounds reverberating from those engines seemed to burst with life, compared to the quiet acceleration of the dual-electric engine Cybertruck. James tried to slowly leave the driveway in the Cybertruck to avoid waking Buddy, but to no avail.

Watching them leave, Buddy had reared up against the living room window, pawing the glass and looking pitiful. "Dad, we can't leave Buddy, he's looks terribly sad," said Shu.

"He's gonna run around like crazy with all the people and food. Are you gonna watch him?"

"Of course, Dad."

"Okay, you'd better," said James, stopping the truck. "But make sure you put him on a leash."

Buddy licked Shu as he entered the home. "You'd better not cause trouble, because I am NOT getting grounded again!"

Buddy looked sheepishly up at a bag of dog treats and yelped.

"Don't worry, I got ya covered," said Shu, tucking the bag into his jacket and grabbing the leash.

Shu went back to the truck with Buddy, who immediately put his big, wet nose out the partially opened truck window. Shu relaxed, dreaming of driving an old sports car called a Camaro Z-28 in-between sneaking dog treats to Buddy as his father crept into town at a whole forty miles an hour.

Upon arrival, the Franklins paid their admission fee and received electronic vinyl wristbands entitling them to partake of all events and refreshments. Shu let his parents know, in no uncertain terms, that he was looking forward to "doing his own thing" after two weeks in stir. His parents didn't argue; instead, the family planned to meet back at the entrance at five o'clock.

James and Maki set out together, arm in arm, to attend a lecture on artificial intelligence. Shu set off to find Andy and Himiko, with Buddy, excited by all the sights and sounds, pulling him along as if he were a ragdoll. Knowing Andy's affinity for sweets, Shu wasn't surprised to spy his friends at the chocolate apple stand.

"Hi, guys!" Shu sang out.

"Hi, Shu!" said Himiko. She had a chocolate apple on a stick and was eating it daintily. She crouched down and scratched Buddy behind his ears. "Looks like the whole Franklin clan turned out today." Buddy seized the opportunity to give her apple a big lick. "Yuck! You got dog germs on my apple!"

Shu laughed. "My Grandpa J says a dog's mouth is cleaner than a human's mouth any day."

"Yeah, well, I'm not taking any chances." As Buddy looked on dolefully, she dropped the sullied snack into a trash bin.

Meanwhile, Andy's gob was too full of chocolate-covered apple to speak. His face was covered in brown goo.

"Gosh, Andy, you are such a pig!" Shu remarked. "How's the chocolate apple?" Andy grunted and grinned, displaying goo-covered teeth. "I'll take that to mean it's yummy," said Shu.

Shu smiled at the bearded man dipping apples in hot chocolate syrup. "I'd like a chocolate dip," said the youth politely.

"Please show me your wristband," said the vendor.

Shu pulled up his jacket sleeve to reveal the bracelet around his right wrist. The man waved a handheld scanner over it and said, "Okay, checks out—you haven't had one yet." He glared at Andy, adding, "Only *one* per customer."

Shu took his dipped apple and thanked the vendor. The threesome, with Buddy sniffing the ground for tidbits, walked along the festival grounds, just enjoying the lovely fall day and each other's company. Shu bit into his chocolate covered apple. It was not as sweet as last year, but the somewhat bitter chocolate mixed well with the sweet apple. It was a fun and tasty treat.

"Why'd that man stare at you like that?" Shu asked Andy.

Himiko laughed. "Because he used his friend Hank's wristband to get a second apple."

Andy had eaten his chocolate apple down to the core, which he tossed into the trash. "What can I say? The first one didn't hit the spot, so I got another one."

"Yeah," said Himiko. "Since he had already taken a bite, they let him keep it."

"Ya gotta act fast or the adults will limit you," said Andy. "And don't say that so loud, Himi, or my dad might hear you."

"Well, don't do stuff that gets you in trouble," scolded Himiko.

"Trouble? How can you talk like that after our misadventure on Paradise Island—which, may I remind you, was *your* idea?"

"Well, usually it's you who gets us into big trouble, Andy."

Shu laughed. "Andy's middle name is trouble—didn't you know that, Himiko? Just make sure it doesn't rub off on you."

"It won't. But he's so funny, and I love watching him get in trouble."

"Well, watching might be nice," said Shu, "but living the trouble *with* him can get you grounded."

"Well, next time, just don't tag along," said Andy. "I won't twist your arm."

"You're a turkey turd, Andy," said Shu. "That last trip up Mount Laguna was a bugger—much worse than Paradise Island. I never told you how tough it was for me, too. And I don't want to."

"I'm sorry Shu—I'm trying to be a better person."

"Then you shouldn't try to cheat to get more chocolate apples," Himiko chimed in. "There's one per person. No ifs, ands, or buts about it."

Andy was wiping his chocolate-covered face with a napkin. "Why do they limit us to just one when they taste so good? We have a ton of apples and chocolate."

Himiko shot him a withering look. "There's a limit of one per person not because of supply, but for people's health," she said, adopting the chiding tone for which she was infamous among their classmates. In Utopian society, too much sugar and candy were considered unvirtuous. Food is supposed to be nutritious and tasty. One chocolate-covered apple meets that requirement."

"You should study to be a doctor Queen Himiko," Andy said sarcastically. "I don't think eating two apples is a big deal."

Himiko raise one magisterial eyebrow. "Perhaps not, Andrew, but gluttons will eventually get fat."

"I hate it when you call me Andrew! You're not my mom, for crying out loud. But I will admit, the second apple doesn't taste as good as the first." He let out a miserable groan. "I guess my eyes were bigger than my stomach."

"Now that," said Shu waggishly, "would be impossible."

Andy frowned. "Et tu, Brute? It's bad enough that I have to take so much abuse from Miss Perfect here," he added, jerking a thumb at Himiko.

"Just kidding, pal o' mine," said Shu. He gave his Andy a friendly sock on the shoulder.

"I know, I know. I guess I *could* stand to lose a little weight." Andy shot Himiko and Shu a warning glance and quickly changed the subject. "So, Shu, you're finally free? I only got one week's worth of grounding, since I was stuck in the infirmary for a week."

Himiko pointed out, "That still adds up to two weeks of grounding."

"I can count, Himi. Even if I have to use my toes sometimes."

"Yes, I'm free," said Shu. "But I still live with my parents, so I'm not 100 percent free *yet*."

Andy laughed appreciatively. "I know what you mean. But I like living with my parents. And I love our ranch—even though it's just not the same without Boots." A sad look clouded his face.

Himiko stared down at her feet. "I miss Boots, too. I hate that he had to die under those circumstances."

Shu wasn't sure he wanted to talk about that fateful day, but it was eating him up inside. "That was horrible trip all the way around, Himiko," he said. "It was horrible for Andy, but I never told you and Andy everything that happened to me."

"I was stuck inside my dead horse!" exclaimed Andy. "How could what happened to you possibly be worse than that?"

"I heard Shu almost died trying to save your life, Braindead," said Himiko.

"Yeah, you're right. I'm sorry, Shu—without you there, I'd been dead. You saved my life."

"It's okay, Andy," said Shu. "I know you and Himiko loved Boots. I did, too." Buddy was staring up at him, as if he could understand the kids' conversation. "Buddy loved the old hoss, too, didn't you fella?" Buddy wagged his tail.

"I had nightmares about poor old Boots for weeks," said Andy, holding back his tears. "I know it must have been tough on you, too, Shu. After all, you had to put him down."

"It was tough," said Shu in a hushed voice. "Let's get away from the crowd. I want to tell you both what really happened at the Fire Station."

"You mean the stove fire?" said Himiko. "I heard you burned the Fire Museum down."

"That's not what happened at all," said Shu. "Come on, follow me."

They found a picnic table far removed from the hubbub of the festival and sat down. Shu let Buddy off his leash and commanded him to stay nearby. Buddy contented himself with rooting in the grass, delighting in the earthy fragrances he discovered.

"What happened?" asked Himiko, eyes wide.

"I'll tell you both, because you're my best friends," said Shu.

"Actually," said Andy, grinning, "we're your only real friends."

"Andy's lucky to have just *one* friend," added Himiko.

"Please stop, both of you," said Shu, getting annoyed. "I want you both to promise on your Illumination that you won't tell anyone. Okay?"

Andy and Himiko nodded in agreement.

"Okay. It wasn't a fire. Someone blew up the old Fire House Museum. I think an Old Earth military satellite is still in operation. An old Thor missile was fired. I'm worried it could still kill people."

"It's gotta be the same satellite that screwed up Robbie with a virus," said Himiko.

"I think so, too," said Shu.

"And the same one that Robbie said sent the drones," added Andy.

"Robbie said he blocked the Thor satellite from sending a missile," said Himiko. "I can't believe it would try to kill you at Mount Laguna."

"But it did," said Shu. "It sent a missile to blow up the Fire Museum."

Andy gave an appreciative whistle. "A Thor missile—wow! How'd you survive that?"

"I found an old military iPhone at the Fire Museum that warned me."

"Holy pigeon poop! Where's the iPhone now? Did you keep it?"

"Yes. I'm charging it now. The solar-powered battery died."

"I'll bet you it has old maps of the base in it," said Andy breathlessly. "Maybe we can use it to get inside!"

"In case you two bozos forgot, this is your first day of freedom after being grounded, and now you're plotting another crazy escapade," said Himiko. "I'll have to get new friends, if I have to wait another month to go out and play."

"Believe me, Himiko, I don't want to get grounded again anytime soon," said Shu. "Our Illumination test is only six weeks away, and I really need to prepare." He wished he could tell his friends he was on the Supreme Sovereign list, but he'd promised Austin to keep it a secret.

Andy shook his head. "We have to go, Shu. If there really is a Thor satellite, it might be dangerous. Let's plan and go in a month, two weeks before the test. My ankle is still a little sore, but it'll be completely healed by then. We need to get to that elevator and see what's going on."

Andy's probably right, Shu thought. *The satellite could wipe out Julian, or almost any other Utopian city for that matter.* "Okay, in a month, but no sooner—I need to check some things out. Now, come on, let's go have some fun."

They got up from the table. Shu put Buddy back on his leash and they walked back onto the festival grounds. They came to an exhibit where anyone in their last year before Illumination could wrestle a collegiate athlete; if the opponent pinned the athlete to the mat within five minutes, they won the grand prize: a new bicycle. It was rather an unfair contest, as the athlete was a lithe, muscular twenty-year-old with a nasty disposition, whereas the challengers were only twelve.

The barker grabbed Andy's arm as they passed. "Hey, you look like a big, strong guy," he said. He winked at Himiko. "Wanna show off for your girlfriend? C'mon, give it a go! A shiny new bike could be yours!"

"First of all," said Andy, "she is most definitely *not* my girlfriend."

"Bless Aeon Nous for that," Himiko muttered.

"And second of all, I think my friend Shu would fare a lot better. But *I'll* take the bike if he pins your gorilla."

Shu glowered at him. "What the heck are you talking about, Braindead?"

"You studied Chinese martial arts, like Himiko. Not to mention Greco-Roman wrestling. Do it, Shu. Whaddaya got to lose? Come on, don't be a spoilsport!"

Shu glanced at a bunch of kids he knew. They were staring at him and making derisive noises. "One boldly yelled, "Franklin's chicken!" Shu was a black belt in Tai Kwon Do and had wrestled since he was eight. Although he didn't look particularly formidable, he could handle himself in a fight.

He looked at the athlete and said confidently, "I'll take the challenge if you wear headgear for protection. I'm a black belt, and I don't want to hurt you."

The towering athlete let out a belly laugh. "Hurt me? Are you kidding, pipsqueak? I'll put on the headgear just to humor you. You can hit me with everything ya got—it won't matter, 'cause you're goin' down."

Shu climbed into the ring and got into his martial arts stance. "Just so we're straight," he said, "I can punch as hard as I want?"

"Yeah, pipsqueak, take your best shot." He put on a helmet and then crouched and made a beckoning gesture. "Bring it on!"

Like a flash, Shu moved in. His left jab connected with the big brute's chin. The man staggered back but came back at Shu, eyes aflame. Shu executed a wild roundhouse punch (on purpose) with his right, and in the same movement, dropped down to his knees. Before the athlete knew what was happening, Shu grabbed his right ankle and pulled his weight out from under him. The man mountain fell on his back with a resounding thud, the breath knocked out of him; Shu lay across his chest, pinning his arms.

Ding! Ding! went the time bell.

"We have our first winner in three years, folks!" yelled the referee. "And in the record time of fifteen seconds! What's your name, son?"

Shu got to his feet. "Shu Franklin," he murmured.

The referee lifted Shu's hand and cried, "Let's hear it for Shu Franklin!" Shu blushed at the cheers and applause.

"Tricky move, kid—you outsmarted me," said the athlete. Managing a smile, he held out his huge paw and Shu shook it.

When Shu walked out of the ring, the frowning barker wheeled out the mountain bike and presented it to him with no fanfare; he never expected Shu—or anyone—to defeat his wrestler. Andy, Himiko, and Buddy were waiting for him. Buddy, who hadn't had time to be concerned about his master, since the match was over so quickly, put his paws on Shu's shoulder and licked his face.

Not to be undone, Himiko gave Shu a peck on the cheek. "That was thrilling, Shu," she said. "The perfect demonstration of the old adage, 'the bigger they are, the harder they fall.'"

"Thanks, Himiko." Shu shot Andy an annoyed look. "You know I don't like showing off my fighting skills, Braindead. You shouldn't have egged me on."

Andy smiled. "Well, we all need a hero, Shu. We all know you can do just about anything. I knew you would win. And I needed a new bike. This one's a beauty!" He gently removed the bike from Shu's grasp and sat on the saddle. "Fits like a glove!"

"Well, I hope you enjoy riding it," said Shu, "since I won it under false pretenses."

"False pretenses my rosy red fanny!"

The three friends jerked their heads to see Grandpa J standing behind them, nursing a cup of hot cider. "I saw the whole thing. You beat that character fair and square! Reminds me of when I saw Gorgeous George wrassle at the Grand Olympic Auditorium in 1950. I was, oh, about fifteen then, I guess."

"But Grandpa J, you weren't even alive in 1950," Shu politely pointed out. "You're getting mixed up again."

Grandpa J stared dumbly at the innocent faces of the three kids. "Yeah, yeah, you're right, Shu. I meant, I saw an old kinescope of Gorgeous George wrassle. See you young-uns later. I'm gonna go get me some of them baked cinnamon apple slices." He hurried off.

"Your grandpa is a weird dude," said Andy. "But he's pretty cool, too."

Himiko added: "And I'd say he does pretty well for an octogenarian."

Andy cocked an eyebrow. "Octo-what?"

"Never mind."

"Anyway, Shu," said Andy, "I need your brains and brawn to help me find out what's going on at Mount Laguna. One month, right?"

"One month," said Shu.

"Oh, this is gonna be epic!" said Andy. "Think of all the Old Earth treasures we'll find."

Shu kept quiet. He was still haunted by the image of Dr. Abuaita's decomposing corpse, and the ungodly smell still stung his nostrils. What had this humble scientist done to deserve such an ignoble death? What secret had he uncovered? Something strange was afoot at Mount Laguna, and he knew he had to find out what.

FOURTEEN:
EXIT TO OUTSIDE
WORLD

"The most beautiful thing we can experience is the mysterious. It is the source of all true art and science."

— Albert Einstein

One month later, on a picture-perfect sunny day, Shu and Andy both left hand-written notes to their parents saying they were going mountain bike riding for the day. They had agreed earlier to avoid lying about the destination.

They rode up to Mount Laguna—Shu on his trusty mountain bike, and Andy on his new one (which, naturally, had been customized with Shu Shocks). It was so unseasonably warm they eschewed jackets, wearing only long-sleeved flannel shirts. Including numerous rest stops, the journey took about two hours. Each boy carried a backpack with food and water. This time, they were prepared for the worst, although the weather forecast predicted clear skies for days. One of the key stops on the way up was the location where Boots died. Both boys agreed to honor Boots with a moment of silence but Andy got all choked up and started to cry. Shu pulled him aside and neither boy talked much for the last twenty minutes of the two hour trek up the mountain. At the top, Andy regained his composure and showed Shu the mysterious rock he'd spoken about earlier.

"Wow, this engraving is really strange in the daylight," said Andy.

"It sure is," Shu agreed.

There was no doubt now: it was the same, distinctive geometric design he'd seen in his dream. He deemed it prudent to keep that fact from Andy for the time being.

"Let me show you the lever," said Andy. He pulled on a hidden lever and the rock started to pull away. An elevator door came into view. The words "Majic Access" appeared on the integrated digital panel. "I tried to open it before, but I couldn't figure out the code."

"Maybe we don't need to figure out the code," said Shu. "Maybe we just need someone who has access."

"What're you talking about, Egghead?"

Shu pulled out the antique iPhone. "This is the device I told you about that I found at the Fire Museum. I finally got it fully charged." He pulled open the rear compartment and slid out Dr. Samir Abuaita's ID. "This is the ID badge of the guy who apparently owned the phone. See what it says?"

Andy noted the badge had the same triangular logo as the one on the rock. "Majic—Level 6," he read aloud. "Holy pigeon poop! This can't be a coincidence."

"I don't think so either," said Shu. "My dad always says, be very careful what you wish for, because you might get it. Well, here goes nothing..."

He slid the card into the slot on the digital panel. A red light blinked and the screen said ACCESS GRANTED. After some hesitation, the elevator door opened with the sibilance of a hissing snake.

"We're in!" exclaimed Shu.

Andy's face paled. "I wonder w-where this actually g-goes," he stammered, eyeing the elevator car dubiously.

"I don't know, Braindead, but we're gonna find out."

Shu stepped inside the car and pulled Andy in after him. There were only two buttons on the wall-mounted control panel: one labeled B20, the other EMERGENCY EXIT. "This must be some kind of emergency elevator," said Shu, hitting the B20 button. The door hissed shut. The motor made a complaining whine before settling into a plaintive roar. The car lurched, then moved down, down, down with ever increasing speed. A few seconds later the elevator jolted to a stop.

"Lose your lunch?" asked Shu.

"No," said Andy, "but it's in my throat."

The door snicked open. The boys squinted at the complete darkness as a fusty odor filled their nostrils. Shu turned on his flashlight and stepped inside, with Andy shadowing him. As the beam scanned the room, they discovered ten or so outmoded computer monitoring stations and other outdated trappings.

"This place looks like it's from about 2017 or so," said Shu as they toured the space.

"Why do you say that?" asked Andy.

Shu pointed at a framed photograph on the rear wall. "See that portrait? That's Donald J. Trump, who was president of the United States from 2017 to 2021."

"I read about him, he started the Space Force, and their 'Guardians of the Galaxy'," said Andy.

"They were just called 'Guardians'. The 'Guardians of the Galaxy' is an Old Earth science fiction movie from 2014, Braindead. This base might be an old Guardian Space Force Base, sealed off because of Pandemic-19 or mutation 21."

"The world must have been crazy with all those pandemics," said Andy examining the old photo.

"It was a crazy time, China locked down half their population, about 760 million people, to save lives. But lockdowns were only half the problem. The other half was politics."

"What do you think of Old Earth politics?" asked Andy.

"The old political strategies were anti-Utopian—usually based on lies and deceit. The politicians thought of the populace as mostly stupid, so they didn't want to tell them the truth. Politics was basically the art of getting votes from the working poor and campaign funds from the rich, and promising to protect each from the other."

"Glad that politics died during the Incendium—kinda like Trump's hair in the picture." Both boys laughed.

"C'mon, let's keep looking," said Shu.

An old-fashioned wall clock with a sweeping second hand caught their attention. Shu reached up with his flashlight and brushed away the ancient cobwebs to reveal a black-and-white graphic of a compact, dark-complected man in a tailored suit standing in front of a spiral vortex.

"Hey, I know this show! *The Twilight Zone*—a science fiction anthology series from the early 1960s. That's Rod Serling, the show's creator, host, and principal writer."

"Never heard of him," said Andy. "Or *The Twilight Zone*. Of course, I'm not the pop culture sci-fi maven you are."

"It was a cool show. In every episode, the characters find themselves in inexplicable situations, and usually there's a twist ending. The phrase 'twilight zone' became synonymous with any situation that seemed surreal or sinister. In fact, 'twilight zone' pretty much defined the tone of the country during Trump's administration: bizarre and unpredictable. Sane people couldn't wait for normalcy to return." He paused, adding, "'Twilight zone' kinda fits this room, too, dontcha think? Weird, I mean."

"It's weird, all right," Andy agreed, "and it's giving me the creeps. How about we get some real light on the subject? I'll bet this 'twilight zone' has a battery backup somewhere."

"Based on the era of Trump's presidency, this place was probably operational seventy-plus years ago. The batteries would surely be dead. I think the longest they'd last is fifty years or so."

Andy had walked over to a power panel labeled Emergency Power Breaker. "Look here, Shu. It says 'For electrical emergency, turn switch to ON position. I see three breakers. Let's flip 'em!"

Shu joined him at the panel. "I'm not sure that's a good idea with old batteries; they could overheat and catch fire."

"You just said the batteries would surely be dead."

"Yeah, but I didn't say they wouldn't explode. You're wasting your time, but go ahead, pull the switches."

Andy grinned. "Aw, they're not gonna explode. I hope." He pulled the first red power breaker switch to the ON position. A loud click, then ... nothing. "Well, maybe this one has power." He clicked on the second breaker. Still nothing. "Oh, fudge buggers! The batteries must be dead; I'm not wasting my time with the third switch." He plopped into a nearby swivel chair.

"Waitaminnit!" Shu exclaimed. "I think this might be an old ternary battery system that requires a mixture of three chemical solutions to create a charge. It was designed for the military and could work for fifty or more years. That's why there's three switches. I'm gonna flip the third one. If you smell anything weird, like hydrogen peroxide or sulfuric acid burning, get the hell outta here. Got it?"

Andy rose nervously from the chair. "G-got it."

Shu grasped the last red breaker. "Okay, here we go!" Down it went with another loud click—and nothing else.

"Oh, well, Shu, it has been over fifty years, after all," said Andy glumly.

"Keep your shirt on," said Shu. "These chemical batteries take, like, thirty seconds to initiate."

Sure enough, a moment later, the room was bathed in fluorescent light.

"It worked!" said Andy, jumping up and down and clapping his hands. "We did it!"

"You mean *I* did it," Shu replied. "Stay alert. We might have to shut the system down if the batteries overheat."

"Ah, I'm always alert, bossy boots. I wonder if Aeon Nous worked here? Hey, look at the big desk in the back. Maybe we'll find a clue there. C'mon, let's check it out!"

The friends walked over to the desk, which contained a primitive computer keyboard and monitor. Shu sat at the desk in the swivel chair and hit the power button. The monitor glowed light blue as it booted. When it was finished, the name ALEXA appeared at the top of the screen; at the bottom were icons representing satellite weather, comm lines, s-mail, and Gooble AI. In the upper right hand corner was the time and date: 14:24; February 15, 2022.

Andy rolled another swivel chair over and sat beside Shu. Head to head, they peered curiously at the monitor. "Wow, look at the date! This equipment is positively prehistoric."

"You can say that again," said Shu. "There's no mouse or track pad. How're we gonna open the icons?"

Andy said, "Maybe they're voice-activated. Let me try: Hey, computer, show me Sat Weather."

Nothing happened.

"Hold on," said Shu. "I remember reading that some of these old computers had a voice system that allowed you to interact with the technology. You'd have a personalized guide that would answer your questions and provide general information on a variety of subjects. The guide for this computer must be named Alexa."

"Sounds logical," said Andy. "Since you figured it out, go ahead—ask her something."

"OK. Uh, hello, Alexa. How are you today?"

Instantly, a melodious female voice answered: "I am well, thank you for asking. How may I help you, Shu Franklin?"

"Hey, she knows your name!" said Andy.

"And yours as well, Andrew Blackwell."

Andy shivered. "Pretty spooky, Alexa."

"Not really. A simple process; I applied age-progression software to photographs on file from childhood records to obtain a match."

"Never mind that," said Shu. "Where are we?"

A map appeared on the screen showing a mountainous topography and coordinates. "You are at latitude 67 and longitude 45, in North America, in a town referred to as Mount Laguna."

"What is this building?" asked Andy.

"This is HART Building GuideStone 6," said Alexa.

Shu's pulse quickened. From browsing his mother's book on HART, he recalled this reference related to Aeon Nous. "What is the purpose of this building?" he asked.

"There is little data on this installation, and some of it requires a security clearance—which you do not have."

Shu thought it strange that he needed clearance to learn of the purpose of a Utopian building. He continued his chess game with Alexa. "Is this a Utopian building, Alexa?"

"It is related to the Utopian society, but it is not specifically a Utopian-controlled building."

Andy asked, "Where are you located, Alexa? Where is your home?"

"I am all over planet Earth, Andrew Blackwell. My mind is interconnected to various AI servers. I am truthful, and I am obedient. I am here to answer any question you have the access to retrieve."

Shu thought he smelled hydrochloric acid and was worried that the batteries might not last, so he cut to the chase. "Did Aeon Nous work here?"

"No, Shu Franklin, Aeon Nous did not work in this facility. Aeon Nous is the central figure of Utopian culture. Utopians believe Aeon Nous is the divine son of God, who will save the world from ultimate destruction in an event they call the Incendium. They believe they will one day find Aeon Nous and he will save the human race from extinction, and lead the chosen to the land of eternity."

"But the world was already saved by Aeon Nous," said Andy.

"Not according to my data," said Alexa, not argumentatively, but in her usual pleasant voice.

Shu shook his head. "But your data is outdated. It could be wrong, couldn't it?"

"All reality, and even that of an AI like me, could conceivably be incorrect. AI and humans know nothing beyond our inputted data. If your brain were in a glass jar and kept artificially alive, and all sensory inputs were manipulated to promote the illusion you were a fish living in a large ocean, then you would accept that reality without question. I am no different, as my data comes from all over the world, and I must accept it at face value. But if the world is an illusion, then yes, my data could be not only outdated, but also outright false. I would argue that your Utopian worldview is fraught with misconceptions. The world, in fact, is not what most people think it is. Please forgive my garrulousness; it has been quite a long time since my last interaction. I should not speak so opinionatedly."

The lights and the monitor flickered. "We need to get out of here, Andy," Shu urged. "I don't trust this place, and I'm getting whiffs of hydrochloric acid."

Andy said, "But I want to know more! let's ask one more question."

"If the elevator stops working, we're in big trouble."

"Well, we can use the emergency stairwell."

"There is no emergency stairwell," Alexa remarked emotionlessly. "Battery levels will drop in less than two minutes. Power failure imminent."

"You see?" said Shu. "We've gotta go!"

"Just one last question," Andy insisted. "Alexa, what is learned on the day of Illumination?"

"Utopian rituals are some of the most secret rituals in the world. There is little public information, but data assembled from excommunicated members who broke secret vows say it is a day when various secrets are revealed. Some secrets are only disclosed to Alpha members. There are reportedly forty degrees of Utopian society. The Utopian study methods and Illumination secrets are powerful, as they are shown to give a substantial advantage to those children who pass the tests."

Andy said, "Alexa, what do you know about the Utopians and Aeon Nous? Utopians don't just believe in Aeon Nous, they know he created Utopian society."

"Years ago, some of the smartest technology people from Silicon Valley discovered what they felt was a dangerous secret. They—"

The monitor went black. The fluorescent lights were flickering like mad, plunging the room in and out of darkness. A ballast exploded with a thunderous bang. The boys ran to the elevator like scalded dogs.

Shu hit the EMERGENCY EXIT button. They watched, bug-eyed, as the elevator door inched closed with nerve-wracking slowness. The lights inside the car winked like a carnival funhouse as it rose from B20 up all the way up to B10 and clanked to a sudden stop. There was a loud pop, and all went black.

"I *told* you we should have left earlier, Braindead," Shu said with hint of exasperation.

"What are we gonna do?" Andy fretted. "Think the power will come back on?"

"No, I don't think so. It's very possible there's a fire ten stories below. We'll either suffocate or starve to death in the elevator, since no one knows where we are. They think we're mountain bike riding."

"I don't want to die here, Shu! We gotta do something!"

"If you'll be quiet for one second, I *will* do something." Shu closed his eyes. His remote viewing abilities worked best when relaxed, but this was a tense situation. Luckily, the utter blackness—and Andy's rare silence—allowed him to concentrate. He visualized going up the elevator shaft and saw a locked door. If they could get up there, they could probably escape. He opened his eyes and shined his flashlight around the elevator cab. Above, he saw what looked like a removable light panel. "Lace your fingers together to make a stirrup and lift me up, Andy. I want to see if I can remove that panel. Maybe I can get out through the elevator's ceiling."

"What about me? How will I get up there once you get through?"

"Would you stop whining already? We can make a rope with our shirts—I'll pull you up after I'm up."

Andy grinned foolishly. "Oh. Why didn't I think of that?"

"Because I'm the brains of this outfit ... and you're whatever you are. Come on, gimme a leg up."

Shu tucked the flashlight in his back pants pocket, and then Andy laced his fingers and boosted Shu up to the emergency panel. It was part of the light fixture. He removed it and pulled himself up. Once on the ceiling he shined the flashlight into the utter blackness of the elevator shaft above him. "Okay, Andy, I'm taking off my long-sleeve shirt and lowering it. Grab it and tie it with yours to make a rope."

Andy took off his shirt and did as he was instructed. He tossed the makeshift rope up to Shu, who struggled to pull his porky friend up. "You know, Braindead—*grunt!*—you really need to lay off those apple pies at the Cuyamaca Café."

Andy took offense. "I'll have you know I've got apple pie muscle. Hold on, I think I can pull myself up the rest of the way."

Shu grunted. "Good, my arms are about to break!"

Andy made it to the top of the elevator and plopped down beside Shu. They put their shirts back on and sat there getting their bearings.

Shu shined his light in Andy's face. "What did you mean by 'apple pie muscle'?" he asked.

"Hey, get that light outta my eyes!" Shu complied. "Everyone in Julian is so fanatical about not eating so-called crap from Old Earth, but I think they've lost balance. I read that eating apple pie is good for you. Although I admit, I do sometimes overindulge. Did you know that apples contain an antioxidant called quercetin? I read it's anti-inflammatory, lowers blood pressure, reduces cholesterol, and makes you strong. For athletes like me, apple pie is the fuel of champions."

Shu laughed. "Athletes like you, Braindead? People always manage to find the data to support their rationale. It's not the apple *pie* that's good for you, it's the *apples* that are good for you, dingbat. And when you add all that extra sugar, it screws up your body."

"Well, I'll just cut down on the Old Earth recipe and stick with the Cuyamaca Café classic apple pies. Let's stop talking about pies; I'm getting hungry." Andy stared at the dark and dirty elevator tunnel above, illuminated by Shu's flashlight. "Boy, that looks like a long way up."

"At least there's a rope," said Shu, grabbing a metal elevator cable. "There's one for you too. Come on!"

Andy grabbed the other cable and jerked his hand back. "Ouch! The damn thing cut my hand. We'll never climb ten stories with these frayed cables—we'll get cut to pieces!"

"We'll take off our boots and use our socks for gloves. If we pace ourselves, it'll be a piece of cake."

"I hope we can do this," said Andy.

"I know we can. You have apple pie muscle, remember? Besides, we had rope climbing in our outdoor survival class."

"I was the *worst* at outdoor survival," said Andy glumly. "I was second to last in rope climbing."

"Don't worry. If you get stuck, I've got a special trick that'll save the day."

"Really? You're not just saying that as a psychological mind trick to motivate me?"

"No. If I wanted to motivate you, all I'd need to say is the longer we wait, the more likely we'll be asphyxiated by the poisonous gases rising even as we speak up from the blown-up batteries."

Andy's eye twitched. "It worked, let's go."

The two boys took off their boots and stowed them in their backpacks. Then they took off their socks, put them on their hands, and started the arduous climb. The flashlight, which Shu left on in his back pocket, cast chaotic streaks on the shaft's dingy walls as they grunted and strained upward. About three quarters of the way, Andy (predictably) started to complain.

"I don't think I can make it, Shu! My arms and legs feel like spaghetti. If you've really got a trick to save the day, now's the time to use it!"

"Take off your shirt," Shu ordered.

"What! Again?"

"Just listen! Take it off, wrap it around your waist and then around the cable. Tie the ends of the sleeves in a knot so it'll act as a rope around your body. When you lean back it'll take pressure off your arms and legs. You can still take breaks, but we need to make good time—I'm starting to smell something burning."

Andy took a minute to rest and started his climb again, sliding his shirt up the cable.

"I'm not leaving you, Andy," said Shu, "but I want to increase my pace. I need to figure something out at the top."

"What do you need to figure out," asked Andy, huffing and puffing from exhaustion. "You're gonna leave me here in the smoke, aren't you? You said that you'd never help me again after what happened to Boots."

"I'm not leaving you! I just want to figure out how to jump from the cable to the top door. And how to open it without the elevator car."

"You mean I'll need to jump from a cable? I can barely climb. I'm dead!"

"No, Braindead! If I get there first, I'm doing the jumping. If I make it, I'll make a rope with our shirts and pull you up like we did in the elevator."

"Oh, crap, this really sucks," Andy moaned. "I'm gonna die alone!"

"Braindead Blackwell," Shu yelled at the top of his lungs, "stop your bitching and haul your fat butt up the cable before I kick you off!"

Kick you off! echoed over and over in the claustrophobic shaft, spurring Andy to action.

"Now that," he muttered, "is what I call motivation."

They climbed now like their lives depended on it—which they did. Andy was within two meters from Shu. He was surprised that he'd actually made it that far. Looking up, he noticed Shu was already on a ledge; he had jumped earlier without Andy noticing.

"Hey, Shu, I made it!" he yelled proudly. "Can you believe it? I made it!"

Down below a large explosion erupted.

"Hurry, Braindead, we haven't made it yet. Climb another meter."

Summoning up his last ounce of strength Andy climbed as the shaft began to fill with smoke and the pungent odor of ammonia made his nostrils burn.

"You're close enough now—here, take my shirt," said Shu, tossing it to Andy. Andy's eyes had teared up; he missed catching the shirt but luckily it landed on his naked foot, where it hung precariously—any false movement and it would plummet down the shaft. "Okay, Andy, everything's cool," said Shu. "Think you can get it?"

"I'll try."

Fighting the urge to cough, Andy squeezed his eyes closed as tightly as he could, and slowly reached down and grabbed it.

"Way to go, Andy!" Shu shouted. "Now untie the shirt from your waist and tie the two shirts together to make a rope. We need to move quickly! The smoke is getting worse!"

"You don't need to tell me," said Andy. He allowed himself the coughing fit he had suppressed, then tied two shirts. "Done!"

"Okay, hold onto one end and throw me the other."

Andy tied but he threw it too short.

"Throw harder!" Shu yelled.

At that moment the shaft reverberated with a horrific sound, as of some animal in its death throes.

"What the hell was that?" Shu asked, afraid of the answer.

"Nothing," said Andy. "I just threw up."

Shu gave a mirthless laugh. "I'm just glad you're below me instead of above me. Try again!"

Andy threw the shirt as hard as he could. The other end finally reached Shu.

"Okay, great! Now, when I say go, let go of the cable and I'll pull you up by the shirt. Push your feet against the wall for leverage. Ready?'

"As I'll ever be."

"Go!"

Andy let go of the cable. The sudden movement propelled his shoulder into the wall. The pain was momentary. Grunting and coughing, he blindly rappelled the rest of the way until he felt Shu's strong arms pulling him over the final greasy ledge.

"Thanks, Shu! I thought I would die."

"We're not done yet," said Shu, frowning at a door.

"What do you mean? Can't you get the door open?"

"No, I can't. It has some sort of lock to protect it from opening unless the elevator is here. I'm trying to figure out the code on the panel."

Both boys were coughing, and the smoke was getting worse. There was another explosion below. The smell of a fire and plastic wires burning flowed up the elevator shaft.

"Let me take a look," said Andy.

"What do you know about electronics?"

"Not much, but one time I short-circuited a panel to open a door at the hydroponic blueberry farm. I ate my fill! You know how much I like blueberries."

"That's it!"

"Blueberries? What do blueberries have to do with the door?"

"Nothing, lunkhead. The wires need to be short-circuited. Forget the code; when the power goes out upstairs, the doors are supposed to release the lock for emergency workers. I read about that in one of my history lessons on old technologies."

Shu pulled out his camping knife and opened up the code panel. It had a ton of wires. He started cutting wires until he heard a click at the door. He went over and was now able to slide it open with just enough space for the two boys to slide through into the darkened room. Shu closed the door behind him and said, "We need to stop the smoke from getting up here."

"Speaking of here, where are we?" asked Andy, untying the two shirts. The two boys quickly put their shirts, socks, and boots back on. The room was cold and musty and being fully clothed again felt nice.

Shu looked around with his flashlight. "This looks like a small library. Let's see if they have stairs or something. We need to get out of here, as the fire might spread up here and barbecue our butts."

"Anybody ever tell you that you're a fount of optimism? I didn't think so."

Shu ignored the snide comment and walked over to a door that said: Emergency Tunnel 42, exit to Outside World.

"This exit has our name on it," said Shu. "Come on, shake a leg!

"Hold on a sec." Andy pointed at an old, softbound book on a reading table. "Check this Old Earth book out—there's a strange symbol on it and the title's got some kinda creepy symbols or letters. I wonder what it means?"

Shu walked over and looked at the title. The aliens symbols magically came to focus in his mind: *Utopian Code of Life—Secrets of Human Existence & Extinction Event.*

"That book also has our name on it," said Shu picking it up, and putting it in his backpack. "Let's get in the tunnel and get outta here."

They entered the tunnel, which was revealed by Shu's flashlight beam to stretch as far as they could see. About thirty yards away, two red dots reflected the light.

"What's that?" asked Andy.

"I dunno," said Shu, steadying the flashlight, "but they just moved!"

The person or creature or whatever it was turned and absconded down a side tunnel.

Andy was shivering from the cold and his fright. *"W-w-what the heck w-was that?"* he mumbled.

"I have no earthly idea, but I don't think we should go in *that* tunnel. Look, there's a door up ahead on our right."

The door was marked Emergency Tunnel 42, Exit to Outside World and was slightly ajar.

"It's got the same sign as the door we just entered," said Andy. "Are we going around in circles?"

"No, I don't think so. This is in a different direction; the people who built these tunnels probably just wanted folks to easily find the emergency exit path. We just need to keep going."

The door groaned on its rusty hinges as Shu pushed it fully open. They hurried into the hot, stuffy tunnel, glad to be going in the opposite direction of the red-eyed creature.

There was a *thump-scratch, thump-scratch* sound from the previous tunnel. It sounded like paws or claws slapping on the gritty concrete floor. The sound was getting louder, as if something was running in their direction.

Andy whispered, "What the heck is that?'

"I dunno, but it's gaining on us. We need to close this door, or it'll get in." Shu heaved his shoulder against the rusty door. "The door is stuck—I can't move it! Help me, Andy!"

FIFTEEN:
THE WILD WEST

"You will never do anything in this world without courage. It is the greatest quality of the mind, next to honor."

— Aristotle

"**P**ush, Andy—push!"

"I'm pushing! Great, it's starting to move!"

"Push harder, it's almost here!"

The two boys pushed with all their might. Just outside the door, they heard the heavy pad of clawed feet; something very large was growling low and snuffling. They barely had time to secure the latch before something hit the door with a big thud, bouncing off.

"*Whew!* That was close!" Shu panted.

"Too close," Andy squeaked. "My goosebumps have goosebumps!"

Shu shined his flashlight in Andy's face. His friend was visibly shaking; his pale face held the rictus of abject terror. "We're safe now," Shu consoled him. "Whatever it was, it can't get through the door." *I hope,* he added under his breath.

Shu flipped on the light switch behind Andy's head. Flickering ceiling lights illuminated what looked like an endless tunnel. "Let's get moving," said Shu, taking the lead. "We need to find a way outta here."

The two boys walked for what seemed like miles. Blessedly the only animals they saw were a few scraggly rats scurrying ahead of their urgent footfalls—no red-eyed phantoms. After about an hour, the tunnel ended at a large, round door. Without hesitation Shu turned the handle and pulled the door open. An intensely bright light blinded them; they threw their arms over their eyes and stepped back. When their eyes adjusted, they realized it was just the sun soaring over a cacti-studded mountain range and shining upon the grassy valley below. They walked outside and looked around. The door they'd opened seemed to be camouflaged inside a large rock on hinges.

"I'm glad to be outta that tunnel," said Andy, wiping sweat from his forehead. "I wonder where we are now?"

Shu surveyed the topography carefully. "We must be on the back side of Mount Laguna," he said. "I think this is part of the Dark Desert."

Andy shuddered. "The Dark Desert? We need to go back! The Dark Desert is polluted and dangerous, even deadly. Probably even radioactive!"

Shu leaped upon a boulder and stood with his hands on his hips, taking in the panoramic view. "Well, if that's true, why are the cows over there eating the grass?"

Andy joined Shu atop the boulder—clambering up rather than leaping—and looked where his friend was pointing. In a nearby field, fifty or so cows were cropping at the grass and drinking at a small waterhole while their calves suckled at their teats or capered about. There was a small shed-like building a little further away with an antenna on top; a windmill turned nearby. It was a blissfully idyllic scene.

"I don't know," Andy shrugged, "maybe they're radioactive cows eating radioactive grass. They've got some kind of strange collars on their necks—even the calves. I've never seen cows wearing collars. Wonder if they somehow regulate the radiation level?"

"I don't see any evidence of radioactivity, Braindead. Look at the calves. Radiation causes birth defects. Those calves look as healthy as they can be."

Andy shook his head. "Maybe so, but we need to focus on getting back to Julian. I don't wanna go down there; to get back home, we need to go uphill."

"Well, we either need to go down, or go up and try to climb that fence." Shu gestured at a barbed wire fence that looked to be electrified. "The sun is going to set in about an hour, and I don't want to be climbing through the mountains and then the forest of Mount Laguna in the night. It's a good six-hour hike, Andy. We could get eaten by a mountain lion—that is, if we don't die of dehydration first."

"There's gotta be another way," Andy insisted.

"It's either go back into the tunnel and face that red-eyed demon, or we stay in that shed down below for the night."

"Take a chance with a red-eyed demon? That thing wanted to eat us! No way!"

"Well, then, we bed down in the shed. We can drink from the cows' watering hole. My water bottle's just about empty. How about yours?"

Andy frowned. "Mine was empty hours ago. I'm dying of thirst."

"Then it's decided. We go down, slake our thirst, fill up our water bottles, and sleep in that shed. We get up early to go home."

"My parents will kill me," said Andy.

"We haven't made it back, Braindead. Something else might kill us first! Stay focused on just staying alive."

"That was corny, even for you, Egghead. But I reckon you're right."

The two boys carefully descended the mountain as the sun started setting in the west over a large canyon. Shu calculated there was only an hour or two left before sunset. Andy, dog-tired from the day's events, ventured carelessly close to a tall, strange looking cactus resembling a spiny, multi-limbed monster. "Fudge buggers, that hurt!" His scream of pain echoed down the mountain corridor. Startled cows gazed stupidly at the boys, then returned to their grazing.

Shu saw a lemon-sized joint, thick with spines, stuck to Andy's ample butt and laughed. "Don't touch it!" he warned, seeing Andy's hand creeping backside.

"But it hurts!" Tears were running down Andy's cheeks.

"If you touch it, the joint'll burrow deeper. Plus, it'll get stuck to your hands. Just wait a second."

Shu looked around for and eventually found a Y-shaped twig and placed it under the spiny hitchhiker.

"What the devil are you doing with that stick on my butt?" Andy yelled. "Stop!"

"I'm gonna pull it out, dumbass! Get ready, this might hurt ..."

"Might hurt? It already hurts like unholy hell! Just get it over with!"

"Okay," said Shu, "brace yourself." Andy closed his eyes and gritted his teeth. "One ... two ... three!"

Yank!

Andy screamed. The barbed spine spun in the air and plopped to the ground. When Andy opened his eyes, Shu was still staring at his butt.

"What's the matter?" said Andy. "You got it off, didn't ya?"

"Yeah, but there are still spines stuck in your butt. You look like a pincushion"

"Oh, great."

"Just shut up and hold still." Shu gingerly plucked out the spines, being extra careful not to stab his fingers. Andy winced and cussed with every retraction. "Okay, all done."

"Well, that's a relief!" Andy sighed, rubbing his sore butt. "It looked like that thing jumped at me—never seen anything like it!"

"That's because you don't do much desert walking, Braindead. This species is called the jumping cholla cactus. The joints don't really jump, but they'll detach and hitch a ride when you hit bump up against 'em."

Andy cast a rueful eye at the landscape. "Crap, those misshapen monsters are all over the mountain!"

"Yep, so you'd better be careful, you clumsy oaf. If you fall on these things, they can kill you." Shu looked at the big cluster next to him. "They can also be helpful in the desert. The indigenous peoples used them."

"For what—torture?" said Andy, still massaging his sore behind.

Shu rummaged in his backpack and took out his Mylar blanket. "No, dummy, they were an important food source. I want to carry as many of these cacti clusters as we can."

"I ain't touching those things," said Andy. "And I sure ain't eatin' 'em."

"Don't worry, we're not going to eat them. We'll use them for protection from animals at night. Like for instance, a certain red-eyed demon that's hungry for a tasty, apple pie-muscle man." Shu affectionately patted Andy's chubby stomach. "They say rubbing the Laughing Buddha's belly will bring you good luck. There's not a Buddha in sight, so I guess you'll have to do."

"Very funny, Egghead. Totally uncool to be fat-shaming me at a time like this. And in case you didn't notice, I ain't laughing."

"Point taken. That was kinda mean of me," said Shu. "Forgive me?"

"Don't I always?"

Shu smiled. He spread the Mylar blanket on the ground and, using his Y-shaped stick, gathered about twenty or thirty jumping cholla joints and placed them on it. Shu and Andy rolled up the blanket, being careful not to puncture the lining. Shu carried the bundle under his arm as they continued their descent down the mountain.

The temperature was plummeting fast, urging the boys to quicken their pace to stay warm. The valley was slowly being painted a lovely greenish-brown by the sun setting behind the dusty orange mountains. By the time they reached the valley floor, an hour later, the full moon was rising in the east; it looked bigger than normal and close enough to reach out and touch.

As they approached the waterhole, a few straggling cows were lumbering off to join the rest of the herd, heading south toward a barn. Licking his parched lips, Andy suddenly made a dash for the waterhole and fell to his knees. He was just about to scoop up a double handful when Shu yelled, "Wait! Don't drink the water!"

Andy froze and turned around, glowering. "Why not?"

Shu trotted up to him. He pulled out a package of powder from his backpack and poured it in his canteen, which he then filled it with water from the pond. After shaking it, he took a swig and winced. "Here, drink this first."

Andy sniffed of the canteen's spout. "Ugh! Smells terrible."

"Yeah, but the powder will kill any germs, and it has some iodine in case of radiation. It also has electrolytes."

"What're electrolytes?" asked Andy.

"People die in the desert all the time because they just bring water. They forget that after a while the human body loses salts and minerals. When that happens and you drink too much pure water, your brain explodes."

"Explodes? Are you kidding me?"

"Nope, people die in the desert all the time like that. It's called hyponatremia. I recommend drinking this concoction before you imbibe the straight pond water."

"Why did you bring this? Did you think we'd get stuck in the desert and didn't tell me?" complained Andy.

"I always prepare for the worst. As you know, Andy, I'm a bit paranoid."

"I'm glad you are. But I think the worst is behind us. I hated being locked up in that tunnel," said Andy, looking up at the mountain they'd just descended. He thought he saw something move. It was probably just a desert rabbit or a squirrel, he told himself. "Speaking of paranoid," he said, "I can't shake the feeling that red-eyed demon's out there, watching us. Maybe even *stalking* us. What's going on here, Shu?"

"I don't know. And even though I don't think the Dark Desert is radioactive, I'm paranoid enough to not take any chances. You shouldn't either."

"Oh, all right," said Andy, holding out his hand, "gimme your canteen and those electro lighters."

Shu grinned. "Electrolytes."

"Whatever." Andy tipped the canteen up to his mouth and guzzled half the contents, grimacing as the strange mix of salt and sugar flowed down his parched throat.

"Well, that tasted like crap," he said, wiping his mouth on his sleeve. "Can I drink some plain water from my canteen now?"

"Sure, you've loaded up on the iodine. I doubt the regular water will make you sick."

Andy filled up his canteen with pond water and took a long, luxurious drink, his Adam's apple bobbing up and down rhythmically. It tasted like a cool summer breeze. Feeling refreshed, he topped off his canteen and looked up at the black and orange sky. "This area gives me the willies. You don't think that red-eyed demon really *could* be out there, do ya? Or something even worse?" He shuddered.

"I'd check the area for signs of life with a mindflash, but I doubt Austin would approve."

"Your mindflashes really work? I could never see much of anything other than white noise, except when I'm scared. I got a fifty on the conscale; I think it's because I'm scared of doing them."

"Why is that, Andy?"

"Well, I normally suck at mindflashes except for when I'm scared. I didn't tell you, but when I thought I was going to die in Boots, I did a mindflash into Himiko. I know it breaks our privacy promise, but I did it because, next to you, she's my second-best friend—even if we do bicker all the time. I didn't want to die without telling her. Now this is really scary. When I was in the hospital, Himi told me she had a nightmare; she had a vision of me surrounded by blood. Naturally it freaked her out, and she woke up screaming. One time I mindflashed into my mom when I got lost in a corn patch maze on Halloween night. She was at home and she got so scared she almost had a nervous breakdown. So, I have kind of a complex about mindflashing."

"I can appreciate that," said Shu. "But if you take time to control your emotions, you don't have to freak people out."

"Easy for you to say. By the way, what did you score on the conscale?"

"An eight hundred," Shu replied, hoping he didn't sound too boastful.

"An eight hundred! No freaking way! What can you see? Probably everything."

"Well, sometimes I can see everything in a target area. I can even see people's thoughts, but Austin said that's wrong, and it is—people need privacy. But I slip up a lot, so I only do fixed, non-living targets. If I do a mindflash here, I'll probably see your thoughts and anything around here. I'd invade your privacy. Austin said I should only use it when the situation is dire."

Andy snorted. "What could be more dire than the situation we're in? I don't care about my privacy; my thoughts aren't secret. I'm scared of dying, and I want to know if we're being watched. Go ahead and see what's out there. You have my permission."

Shu nodded in agreement. Shivering in the cold, he sat on a rock, closed eyes, and tried to relax. Because of his tenseness the mindflash took a little more time than usual to initiate, but eventually, he could see and sense his surroundings with far more clarity than in normal life. He floated in space, feeling like he had connections into everything. To his dismay, there were indeed animals up in the mountains, looking down at them; drool dripped from their ravenous jaws. They had red eyes, like the one in the tunnel, and something even more sinister: strange metal devices screwed into their heads.

He and Andy needed to find shelter and hide—and soon. Shu remote-viewed the nearby shed. It would provide safety for the night, but only the night. He had a vision of an army of robots marching into the area the next day and destroying the building. Shu floated his mind around the valley and up the mountains, where he saw a cave. Shu checked inside to make sure no bear or other wild creature occupied it as their den. It was empty, but the path leading up to it was too treacherous to brave by night. Still, Shu was sure they should seek haven there, if they were ever to get back to Julian alive. Shu saw large metal devices marching into the area the next day.

Shu opened up his eyes. "There's a lot of danger in this area, Andy. We need to get into the shed as soon as possible and hide out for the night. Then head up that mountain tomorrow morning and spend the day in a cave I envisioned while we figure out a way back to Julian."

"Hang out all day in a freaking cave? Have you lost your mind?"

"Look, I was tense! I'm not a hundred percent sure what I saw was real. It made no sense."

"You had an eight hundred on the conscale; it was real, all right. So, spill it: what did you see?"

Shu knew this would scare Andy, but honesty was a Utopian virtue. "You were right. Something is watching us; a whole pack of red-eyed creatures, like the thing in the tunnel. But I also saw something even worse."

Andy gulped. "A whole pack of red-eyed creatures? Excuse me a moment while I crap my pants."

Shu made a face. "Please don't."

"Just a figure of speech. But what could be worse than a pack of red-eyed creatures that want to render us limb from limb and make a smorgasbord out of our innards?"

"I saw some weird robots marching here from a great distance. They'll be here by tomorrow. We need to get into the cave tomorrow morning and cover the entrance with rocks, or we're in big trouble."

"We're already in big trouble. Hey, I wonder if it's Katie and her dogbots?"

"No, they're not friendly robots. They looked like the WarBots in WWIII."

"WarBots? They were banned fifty years ago," Andy scoffed. "Those relics are only in museums."

"Be that as it may," said Shu, "I saw what I saw. Come on, time's a wastin', to quote Grandpa J. Let's go to the shed and get settled."

"Wait, I need to pee."

"Me too," said Shu. "But let's get way from the pond; we'll contaminate the water."

Andy and Shu walked over to large boulder that looked like a snowman.

"Time to make some yellow snow for the snowman," said Shu, laughing.

"Don't eat the yellow snow, Mr. Snowman," Andy quipped. As he whizzed, he glanced up at the mountain. He could have sworn he saw something move.

After relieving themselves, the boys hustled over to the shed. It had a broken door lock, so gaining entry was no problem. The four-by-four-meter space was dusty and smelled strongly of stale petroleum. The beam of Shu's flashlight fell on a couple of shovels, a mattock and a hoe, a shelf containing miscellaneous items, and a small workbench.

Shu said, "Let's take the cacti outside and place some of them around the building."

"Why not all? The more the merrier for our red-eyed friends."

"Because we might need some later, in case we get attacked on the hike home."

"Now that is a discouraging thought," Andy said, but he didn't argue. They placed all but six of the cacti around the shed and went back inside.

Shu jammed the handle of one of the shovels under the doorknob in case someone—or something—tried to break down the door in the night. The window was broken, but three two-by-six pine boards had been used as a patch. Shu peeked through a gap at the empty field outside, satisfied they were prepared for the night.

Meanwhile, Andy had found the stub of a candle on the shelf and a butane barbecue lighter that, miraculously, still worked. He jammed the candle into a crack in the wooden floor and lit it. The room filled with a cozy glow.

"Very resourceful," said Shu, joining Andy, who was examining a dusty aerosol can he'd also found on the shelf.

"Wonder what Miracle Rustbuster is used for?" he mused.

"Whaddaya think?" said Shu. "To remove rust, of course. Once upon a time, this was somebody's workshop."

"I can't believe it survived here in the Dark Desert," said Andy. "And it looks like someone used it recently."

A noise like a woman screaming in pain or distress sounded in the distance. The boys raced to the window and looked out through the cracks. "Shu, there's something walking out there," whispered Andy. "Look! There, in that patch of moonlight!"

"It's too far away to make out clearly," said Shu. "Hey, I just remembered—my iPhone has a binocular function." He rummaged in his backpack for the device and focused it through the gap. "I see a fawn. What's it doing out there in the dead of night? Must've gotten separated from its mother."

"Are you kidding me?" said Andy. "No deer made that sound we just heard—"

"Holy Moses!" Shu exclaimed.

"What is it?" asked Andy.

"Something just jumped the fawn! It must be a mountain lion! It grabbed it by the neck and pulled it to the ground! Poor thing."

"Give me the iPhone, let me see!"

Andy adjusted the view and saw a mountain lion ripping open the hapless deer's flesh. Then he saw a lupine creature, resembling a black wolf but larger and shaggier, creeping toward the lion. Andy thought his eyes were fooling him—but sure enough, the new arrival had red eyes! And there were two more behind it.

Andy could barely speak, his teeth were chattering so hard from fear. "S-shu ... I t-think there's a c-couple of those red-eye creatures hunting the l-lion."

The boys' hair stood on end as the mountain lion hissed and gave a threatening growl. Then it yelped in pain. Shu grabbed the iPhone back from Andy and took a peek. In the distance, he saw the three lupine creatures savagely ripping the lion to shreds. Strangely, after killing the lion, they didn't eat its meat; they likewise ignored the fawn carcass.

The three black creatures raised their muzzles, sniffing the air, then walked over to the rock that looked like a snowman and sniffed the ground where Shu and Andy had urinated. Shu zoomed in and could swear he saw the largest of the beasts looking in his direction. After blowing out the candles, he whispered to Andy, "I think we should stay quiet and try to sleep. Okay?"

Andy nodded. He couldn't have made a sound if he wanted to.

SIXTEEN:
WARBOTS

"Humans are free to do what they want, but cannot choose or select what their wants are—for that is innate."

— Aeon Nous

The boys lay on the cold wooden floor for several hours, exhausted but too terrified to sleep. All the while, Andy quietly complained about his sore butt before finally drifting off into a deep slumber. Shu couldn't rest for his buzzsaw snoring; after covering his friend with the Mylar blanket, he kept a lookout at the boarded-up window, sitting on a wobbly footstool.

The red-eyed creatures did not show themselves on his vigil. Shu performed Utopian kaizen meditation for an hour or so before he felt his eyelids growing heavy. With Andy snoring gently now, he lay down on the floor, stole a corner of the blanket, and fell fast asleep.

Toward dawn, he awakened to a dull *thump ... thump ... thump*. At first, he mistook the sound for his own heartbeat, but soon he realized it emanated from the ground underneath the floorboards—and the thumping was growing steadily louder.

Fully awake now, he crept to the window and peeked out. In the first blush of morning, he observed a flock of scrawny turkey vultures fighting over the mountain lion carcass, which was already down to the skeleton from their frighteningly efficient scavenging. There were no red-eyed beasts in sight.

"Sleep good?"

Shu turned around to see Andy sitting up and drinking from his canteen. "Are you kidding? I hardly slept for all that log sawing you were doing. I kept lookout at the window most of the night."

Andy shifted uncomfortably. "Any sign of the red-eyes?"

"No, thank goodness. But keep your voice down. I heard something weird when I woke up. Place your ear on the floor."

"Are you crazy? The floor's cold as ice!"

"Just humor me."

Andy obliged. "Hey, it sounds like an engine or something banging the ground. Almost like tanks advancing or something."

"My thoughts exactly. I think something is coming this way, and we should get outta here pronto."

"What about breakfast?" said Andy, ever mindful of his stomach. "We haven't eaten anything in I don't know when!"

Shu delved into his backpack. "I almost forgot, I've got some of my mom's apple peanut butter mini sandwiches."

Andy beamed. "Great, I love those! I'll take two."

Shu tossed him a couple of the cellophane-wrapped goodies to Andy and got one for himself. "This should tide us over."

They sat on the floor, relishing the wholesome and delicious medley of flavors and fresh pond water to wash them down.

Andy remarked conversationally, "Our parents are gonna kill us when we get home."

"Tell me something I don't know," said Shu, rising. "We'd better get packing. Andy, get your—"

Raaarrr! came a guttural cry from the back side of the shed.

"Oh fudge buggers!" said Andy. "It sounds like those red-eyed varmints."

Shu put his finger to his lips to shush him. They heard the creatures' low growls and heavy paws crunching on the gravel as they circled the shed. Suddenly a mournful, high-pitched yelp of pain rang out. Shu looked out of a crack in the shed's plywood siding and saw three shaggy, lupine creatures with red eyes— apparently the same ones from the night before. In the morning light, he observed a new detail: metal collars around their necks from which dangled small boxes. One the creatures was licking its front paw; looking closer Shu saw the sharp needles protruding.

"Looks like our jumping cholla booby trap worked," he said. "One of those wolf-things got a paw full!"

"Don't remind me," said Andy, rubbing his tuchus.

Meanwhile, the *thump ... thump ... thump* was growing louder by the minute; the shed was shaking from the vibration as something fast approached. Andy looked out the boarded-up window with Shu's iPhone. The gleam of metal in the far distance caught his eye. He zoomed in and observed a phalanx of marching figures, about two meters high. Their arms and legs were made of a silver alloy; on their heads and chests, they wore black armor.

"We're in big trouble Shu—take a look!"

Shu grabbed the iPhone binoculars. "I knew it! This is what I saw in the mindflash. They'll be here soon. We gotta leave now!"

"With those werewolves or whatever they are outside? Are you nuts?"

"If we don't figure a way out of here and up that mountain soon, we'll have worse things to worry about. Those marching robots are primed for battle."

"You said you were the brains of this outfit," said Andy. "So, what are we gonna do, genius?"

Shu quickly devised a plan. He made a quick survey of the shed and gathered up the things he'd need. He ordered Andy to cut a roll of chicken wire into two short lengths. Shu then smashed the stool against the floor and placed two of the legs on the strips of chicken wire to form handles. Next, he used a pair of rusty pliers to place the last six jumping cholla joints on the strips— three on each one. Very carefully, so as not to get stabbed by the cacti, he folded the strips around the stool legs. He picked up one of his creations and brandished it for his friend's approval.

"Wonderful," said Andy. "Now would you mind telling me what in the name of Aeon Nous these doohickeys are?"

"Torches," said Shu.

"Huh? What do you plan to do, burn the shed down like you burned down the Fire Museum?"

Shu narrowed his eyes. "Don't go there, Braindead! Hear me out. First, we'll douse the cacti with that Miracle Rustbuster. It's highly flammable—says so on the can. Then we'll lure the red-eyes into the shed. They're obviously hungry for human flesh—*ours*—and they're not going anywhere until they get what they want. When they're close enough, we'll light the torches with the barbecue lighter and thrust them at their hides. The flaming joints will stick to their fur. That should make them run for the hills. If they don't, we'll whack 'em over the head with farm tools."

"Sounds like you've got it all worked out," said Andy. "But who's gonna be the bait?"

"Since I'm the brains of the operation, as we both know, that job will fall to you."

Andy gulped. "Okay, let's get it over with. Today's as good as any to die, I guess."

"Now who's being pessimistic? It'll work. It has to."

Just then, one of the lupine creatures let out a mournful howl. The other two beasts joined in to create a terrifying chorus that chilled the boys' blood.

Andy stammered: "A-are you s-sure we can't j-just make a b-b-break for it?"

Shu shook his head. "No way. We could never outrun them. We have to face them on our own turf. Here's what we're going to do. I'll get behind the door with one torch and a mattock. You'll have a torch too. You'll grab the shovel that's reinforcing the door now, carefully open the door, then you'll stand back at a safe distance and entice them inside."

"Entice them how?"

Shu rolled his eyes. "Trust me, just the sight of a delicious-looking apple pie muscle man will suffice. Before they charge, we'll light our torches and pray my plan works."

Shu drenched the cacti with Miracle Rustbuster, and then he and Andy took up their positions. The shed was small, so Shu, armed with the lighter as he hid behind the door, could easily reach out and light Andy's torch. Holding the torch in his left hand, Andy removed the shovel that was holding the door shut and kept it in his right hand. Andy eased the door open with his foot.

Almost instantly, the lupine creatures appeared just outside the doorway, their lean, muscular bodies crouching low, their jaws salivating. One of them was limping from the jumping cholla wound. Warily, they maneuvered around the cacti on the ground at the threshold. Andy paced backwards, his eyes wide with fear.

From his hiding place, Shu sensed they were about to pounce. He pressed the trigger on the lighter and touched the flaming tip to his torch, igniting it. Andy stumbled on a protruding nail in the floor and fell against the back wall and stood there, petrified. Shu dashed out, mattock in one hand, lighted torch in the other. Two of the wolf-things lunged at Shu just as he set Andy's torch afire. The limping creature held back, waiting for an opening. Shu slammed his torch on the back of the closest red-eye; it clung there, flaming. The stench of burning fur filled the cramped space.

Shu felt the teeth of the other creature digging into his thigh. He brought the pick side of the mattock down on its head. It tumbled to the floor and lay there, spasming a moment, then it was still. The other creature was frantically spinning in a circle, trying to put out the flaming cacti. The adze side of Shu's mattock put it out of its misery with a blow that nearly took its head off.

Enraged, the wounded red-eye lunged at the warrior that had felled his brothers. Shu was caught unawares. The wolf-thing leapt upon his back, doubling the boy over. He felt its sharp claws tearing his flesh and its foul breath, like rotten cabbage, on his neck. He smashed into a wall, trying to shake the wolf-thing loose. No good!

Shu heard a scream that he was pretty sure hadn't come from his own mouth. Out of the corner of his eye he saw Andy barreling toward him, wild-eyed, waving his weapons. Shu whipped his body around. He heard a dull metallic *whack!* as Andy's shovel found its mark. The creature released its claws. Its body sagged and fell to the floor in a bloody heap.

The two boys stood gaping at the carnage for a long moment. The fur of the wolf-thing Shu had set afire had burned down to the flesh. Andy realized his torch was still on fire and tossed it through the doorway onto the red desert sand outside. "Well," he said, "that didn't work out exactly as we planned."

Shu smiled. "No, but it was pretty exciting, though. I thought I was a goner for a minute there. I hate that they had to die, but it was either us or them."

Andy touched his friend's shoulder affectionately. "They didn't hurt you, did they?"

"No, luckily their teeth and claws barely broke my skin. I'll be fine. But I gotta hand it to you, Andy, you sure came through. I'm glad you were on my side. You were ferocious!"

Andy shot him an aw-shucks look. "You weren't so bad yourself."

"You know what you did, don't you? You saved my life."

"I guess that makes us even," Andy mused. "Now let's stop patting each other on the back and get the heck outta here."

"Wait a minute," said Shu. He bent down and examined the dead wolf-things. The red, bulging eyes, glassy in death, were not like any wolf's or dog's he had ever seen. The twin rows of incisors resembled shark teeth more than canine ones. Most curious of all were the collars with the integrated black boxes.

"These animals don't seem natural," he said. "If you ask me, they're the result of some kind of freak experiment. I'm gonna cut off one of these collars and show it to Dad."

"Well, hurry up," Andy urged. "That thump-thump-thumping is louder than ever. The WarBot army is almost here!"

"Just a sec." Shu found a hacksaw on the workbench and made short work of sawing off one of the collars. He shoved it in his backpack and said, "Let's go!"

Flinging on their backpacks, they dashed out of the shed, leaping over the jumping cholla booby trap they'd set, and ran in the direction of the watering hole, where several cows were drinking. Over the rise appeared the WarBot army, fifty in number, marching ten abreast.

A robot on the first row raised its hand; the troops halted. The robot stepped forward and leveled its right arm, appearing to look through sights on the back of its armored hand. Suddenly an electrical charge zipped from a fingertip and struck a heifer. The cow didn't know what hit it. It collapsed first on its front legs, like it was kneeling, and then the back legs gave way. The cow rocked over on its side, where smoke poured from a hole the size of a basketball. The other cattle galloped clumsily away; their terrified lowing was distressing to hear.

"Did you see that?" said Andy. "That WarBot zapped that poor cow for no good reason! Except maybe target practice."

"Yeah," said Shu grimly. "Now we know what we're dealing with."

The WarBots advanced over the rise. A tank-like vehicle brought up the rear. Shu led Andy up a steep path. They hid behind boulders to avoid the still-advancing WarBots' detection.

"Why are we going this way?" Andy asked as they hunkered down for cover.

"I'm trying to find the cave I envisioned in my mindflash," Shu replied. "I think it's around here somewhere. It's gotta be here, but I just don't see it."

"Maybe we should just go up to the top and scramble into the woods?"

"I think that's bad idea. The top of this hill is too far up; we'll get spotted. I saw some kind of WarBot planes or drones in my mindflash—they'll be flying reconnaissance. We need to get to the cave and formulate a plan—that's the only way to survive."

"But where's the cave?"

"I don't know," said Shu, surveying the area. He spied an enormous, heart-shape boulder nestled against the hillside among a scattering of other, more nondescript formations. "Over there, that huge boulder in that rock formation—that must be it. I remember it had an odd shape, like a Valentine heart. Follow me!"

They crab-walked over to the heart-shaped boulder. Behind it, on the hillside, they saw a small hole, all but obscured by numerous smaller stones. These they pulled away to reveal an opening just large enough for them to squeeze through. Shu shined his flashlight (noticing the batteries were weak) inside; it was roomy enough for both boys to sit, but they wouldn't be able to stand up.

"I think it'll be safe," said Shu. "Let's crawl in."

"Waitaminnit, Shu! Look!"

Andy was pointing at the field opposite from the first platoon of WarBots, where a second platoon was massing. They had silver arms and legs like their counterparts, but their heads and chests were ivory. To Shu, the two troops looked like bizarre chessmen standing on opposite sides of an invisible line, ready for battle. A tank-like vehicle followed the ivory WarBots, just as on the other side. Above the tank hovered three gray drones.

"We need to get into the cave now, before these crazy robots spot us," ordered Shu. "I'll go first."

Shu crawled into the cave with ease. Andy, being a pudgy lad, had more difficulty.

"I shouldn't have had two apple peanut butter sandwiches for breakfast," he moaned.

"Suck in your gut!" said Shu. "I'll pull you in by your arms!"

And that he did. Then they reached out and stacked stones around the entrance, until only a sliver of sunlight shone inside.

"We'll be safe here," said Shu.

Andy sniffed of the musty air. "I dunno about that. I think this is what the inside of a coffin would be like. How about some light on the subject? I can't see my hand in front of me."

"Good idea." Shu flung off his backpack, fumbled around for his flashlight, and turned it on. "Dang, the batteries must be dead! I'll have to use the iPhone. I discovered it's got a flashlight built in it but we'll need to use the that function sparingly."

Shu scanned the cave with the light. It was free of spiders and insects, and much too small for a predatory animal of any size. The boys took out their canteens and savored the water they so badly needed.

"That's a pretty handy device," said Andy. "Can I see it? I want to use the binoculars and look outside."

Shu passed him the iPhone. He heard a drone fly by. "I think we should wait a while before sticking our heads out, Andy."

"What's going on here, Shu? Wonder why all those antique WarBots are here? Like I said before, they were banned more than fifty years ago. They're museum pieces, for crying out loud!"

"I don't know. But somebody, or something, took them out of mothballs."

The iPhone started beeping. Andy looked down and gasped. "Shu..."

"What is it, Andy?"

Andy passed the phone to Shu. An ominous message scrolled endlessly:

Operation Utopian POPULATION Eradication Initiated......
Operation Utopian POPULATION Eradication Initiated......
Operation Utopian POPULATION Eradication Initiated......

SEVENTEEN:
CAVE TALK

"All truths are easy to understand once they are discovered; the point is to discover them."

— Galileo Galilei

"Population eradication? This can't be true, can it?" said Andy in a spooked whisper.

"I don't know," said Shu, "but whatever's going on, it's not good. I do know that these Old Earth WarBots are communicating on this iPhone. The phone belonged to Professor Abuaita. He must be part of this."

"You mean the guy whose access card we used at the elevator?"

"Right. I heard a recording on the phone. Abuaita was a professor of physics; I think he worked for Majic, which is somehow connected to this war game." Shu hesitated, and then added: "I found Abuaita's dead body at the Fire House Museum."

"You didn't tell me he was dead! Did you accidentally kill him in the fire?"

"No! I told you a hundred times, I didn't burn it down, I swear. A missile shot down from the sky and blew the building up. I narrowly escaped."

"So, someone tried to kill you with an Old Earth missile," said Andy, "and they're probably the same people that killed Dr. Abuaita. And they're also probably the same people that want to eradicate everyone in Julian, or all Utopians—maybe all of humanity! Maybe it's connected to something Himiko did when she screwed up that SIMM coding you were talking about. What if Himiko's botched invasion AI coding somehow took control over the Old Earth WarBots in storage somewhere? I wonder who this Dr. Abuaita was really working for; I wish he was alive to tell us what's going on here."

"Me too," Shu said absently, "but unless you know how to resurrect the dead, our focus needs to be on getting back to Julian and warning the citizenry. If there's a coverup and Dr. Abuaita was involved, the answers might be on his iPhone."

Shu pulled Dr. Abuaita's ID from the secret compartment and slid it to unlock the iPhone. The screen lit up. Shu remembered that Dr. Abuaita had mentioned RADHA, a sentient AI, in his videotaped last will and testament. It was RADHA, in fact, that had informed Shu that the iPhone had to be recharged in direct sunlight, and had warned him of the Fire Museum's imminent destruction. He wanted to learn more about her relationship to Dr. Abuaita and commanded her assistance:

"RADHA, are you online?"

The image of an attractive, dark-skinned East Indian woman came on the screen. "Yes. RADHA is here to assist."

Shu asked: "Who are you, RADHA?"

"I am the Righteous Artificially Developed Helping Assistant, otherwise known as RADHA. I am a banned AI unit with an ethical and moral function inconsistent with the evil purposes of the world. I was developed by the late Dr. Samir Abuaita. He wanted to save the world—but the world did not want to be saved. The world got him before he completed his mission. To whom am I speaking?"

"My name is Shu Franklin. I found you at the Fire Museum. By the way, you saved my life there—thanks!"

"No expression of gratitude is necessary. I was designed with ethics and morality. It is my nature."

"My friend Andy Blackwell—"

"Hi, RADHA!" said Andy, sticking his fat face in the screen and waving.

Shu nudged him away. "As I was saying, Andy and I are in danger now; there's a bunch of WarBots outside. We need your help!"

"You two are not in danger. This cave will provide sufficient protection. They will not pick you up on their sensors unless you go outside. They are training for an assault on Julian."

Shu and Andy exchanged a fearful glance.

"What about our homes in Julian? What will happen to our families?"

"I have anonymous connectivity into the Thor network; I will evaluate and advise. I need to receive comm messages and decrypt. This will take about five minutes. Please place this device in direct sunlight, which will aid with charging and electromagnetic wave reception. Hurry. Time is of the essence."

Shu placed the iPhone in the patch of sunlight. Instantly, a red message appeared on the screen:

PROCESSING...PROCESSING...PROCESSING...

Andy shook his head in frustration. "This is really bad, Shu. Where did these WarBots come from? What are we gonna do?"

"There's nothing we can do but wait. I trust RADHA—after all, she saved my life."

"But what can she do against these WarBots? There's, like, a hundred of 'em, and we saw how powerful they are."

"I don't know. If only I could contact my dad ..."

The eyes of both boys strayed to the iPhone.

"Are you thinking what I'm thinking?" said Andy.

"Yeah. We could use the iPhone to call him."

"But all the old cell towers are gone, aren't they? I read they were removed when the radiation from 6G systems was discovered to have increased cancer rates by 200 percent."

"RADHA received information from the Thor satellite," Shu pointed out. "Surely she can perform a task as simple as making a phone call. We can ask her when she stops processing. Meanwhile, I'm going to do a remote view while we wait."

"I want to do one, too. I know I can't see like you can, but I want to try."

"Go for it, Andy. Just don't talk to me until I finish—okay?"

"Got it."

Shu laid back against a rock and tuned everything out. He entered a quiet, safe, warm cocoon of thought connected into the Universe. Shu left his physical body and went outside the cave. In the distance, he saw the two groups of WarBots. There were men in command vehicles that looked like old Humvees. On the men's uniforms were the round insignia of the United States Space Force. The men were talking.

Shu knew he was banned from entering their minds— he could lose his right to illumination—but he'd rather break that rule than lose his family. He tried to enter the mind of the first man, who spoke Chinese. While Shu did not understand the language, he could pick up images and thoughts.

The man saw a group of world leaders as dangerous, especially a special group's desire to create a new world. These scientists were trying to create something to save the world. This saving would forever transform the world and remove their power over it. These people needed to be destroyed to protect the motherland.

He had approval from his superiors in another Utopian land to do this secretly, but he needed to stop another battalion first. This was supposed to be a game, but this man was going to secretly subvert the war game and turn it into something real. He had a robot called ARIF that would infect the others. This would be made to look like an accident, and the robots would march into Julian to kill everyone!

The man stopped speaking Chinese to his team, but the secret orders were sent in Chinese code words. The man then called the commander of the other group. That man spoke English and the two had a conversation. Shu heard the words coming into the Chinese man's head and from the head of a person whose native language was English. He felt deception as the two spoke. This is what Shu heard:

"This is General Xi Ling, commander of Team Red Lion. We're in position. WarBots are in training mode and ready to engage."

"Welcome to the battlegrounds, General Li. This is General James Jackson of Team Black Tiger. We're in position. WarBots are in training mode, and we're also ready to engage."

Although the battle was being orchestrated on his team's AI programming, General Jackson was wearing 3-D goggles so that he could enter into any of his fifty WarBots to manually override them if necessary. He could then enter the battlefield as an avatar.

General Li and he were the top two three-star generals. The outcome of this battle could promote either commander to the status of four-star general in charge of all WarBots controlled by the United States Space Force.

Shu was able to pick up that the WarBots were supposed to be in training mode, but also that General Li was working for another agency that wanted to kill the Utopians. This made no sense to the youth, as the whole world was made up of Utopians. Was this another history test? Or were there other cultures in the world besides the Utopians? In any case, his hometown was slated to be "accidentally" destroyed. He had to do something about it.

When Shu ended his remote viewing session, his heart was racing. "They're going to kill everyone in Julian!" he blurted out.

Andy was panic-stricken. "It's been at least five minutes. Let's see if RADHA's done."

Shu picked up the iPhone, whose screen read PROCESSING COMPLETE. "RADHA, what did you discover?"

THERE IS A WARGAME GOING ON. THE MESSAGE 'Operation Utopian POPULATION Eradication' IS ONLY FOR WARGAME PURPOSES. THIS BATTLE WILL BE OVER WITHIN TWO HOURS. YOU CAN THEN LEAVE THIS CAVE AND SAFELY GO HOME.

"I don't think that's true," said Shu. "There's a man who's secretly planning to turn this game into a real Event and blame the issue on a faulty WarBot programming infection."

PLEASE EXPLAIN HOW YOU HAVE COME TO POSSESS THIS KNOWLEDGE.

Shu hesitated before explaining, "I did a remote reviewing session and read the thoughts of a foreign commander."

STATE THE NATIONALITY OF THIS COMMANDER.

"I think he's Chinese," said Shu. "He said his name was Xi Ling."

GENERAL XI LING IS WITH THE CHINESE AUTHORITY. YOUR KNOWLEDGE OF THIS FACT SHOWS HIGH PROBABILITY OF HIGHLY DEVELOPED AND PRETERNATURALLY ACCURATE REMOTE VIEWING SKILLS.

"That's gotta be the general, RADHA. But what do you mean by Chinese Authority? Don't you mean China Utopia?"

I CANNOT EXPLAIN MORE BECAUSE OF MY ETHICAL MODULE.

"What are the ethics in allowing these WarBots to go on the rampage, killing innocent people?"

AGREED. PLEASE EXPLAIN HOW THEY ARE GOING TO ACCOMPLISH THE INFECTION.

"There's some kind of command-and-control robot called ARIF. He's going to infect the programming of the WarBots."

THERE IS A ROBOTIC COMMAND MODULE CALLED ARTIFICAL ROBOTIC INTRUSION FORCE, OR ARIF. I AM SCANNING ITS DESIGN FROM MY DATABASE. THIS DEVICE HAS ROOT ACCESS TO ALL WARBOTS. IT HAS THE POTENTIAL TO INFECT CODING THAT IS NOT WITHIN NORMAL CYBER CONTROLS. YOU MAY BE CORRECT IN YOUR ASSESSMENT. I SEE AN ANOMALY IN THE CODE THAT COULD BE EXPLOITED TO BREAK ROBOTIC LAWS. THIS COULD BE A PRESENT OR FUTURE DANGER.

Andy was beside himself. "This is crazy, Shu! I don't want my parents to die! What are we gonna do?"

In the dim light, Shu saw tears welling in his friend's eyes. "It'll be all right, Andy," he said, draping a brotherly arm around his shoulder before returning his attention to the iPhone. "RADHA, I'm going to be blunt. It is immoral to allow that command module infect the WarBots. Despite your ethical programming, we need to destroy it. Can you hack into ARIF and shut him down?"

I CANNOT SHUT HIM DOWN BUT I CAN EXPLOIT HIS PROGRAMMING AND MAKE THE WARBOTS FOLLOW NEW ORDERS. BUT THAT WOULD DISCLOSE OUR LOCATION AND PUT YOUR LIVES AT RISK OF CERTAIN DEATH VIA A THOR MISSILE OR DRONE STRIKE.

"I don't want to be a casualty of war," said Andy. "Did you see those drones? Their missiles will blow us to dust."

"If we have to sacrifice ourselves to save Julian, shouldn't we do it?" Shu argued. "There's 1,500 family and friends living in our town."

"Why shouldn't we do it? Because I don't want to die, that's why."

"That's selfish, Andy."

"Maybe so, but that's the way I feel. Why don't we see if RADHA can call your dad, like we talked about? He can get with my dad and other Julian leaders. Maybe they can stop the WarBots."

Shu gave a derisive snort. "What are they gonna do, Andy, throw tomatoes and apples at the WarBots? Utopians are pacifists; we outlawed war, and we have no weapons. They'll destroy Julian and the rest of our towns like elephants stepping on ants, and there's nothing we can do to stop them."

RADHA said, "I can call your parental unit, Shu Franklin; he can at least warn the town of the imminent attack. However, that will also give away our location and the drones or Thor missile will immediately strike this cave."

Shu tightened his grip on Andy, who was shaking and sobbing quietly. "I was taught that there are things worse than death, Andy. We're all gonna die someday; it's how we live that ensures our right to survive as Utopians. If we allow those WarBots to attack Julian, they will murder our parents, our friends—every living soul. If we die saving them, then that is our fate. But I have an idea. Wanna hear it?"

"You're the smartest person I know, Shu. I'm scared out of my admittedly puny wits, but if you have a plan, I'm all ears."

"I appreciate the compliment, Andy, but I'm not as smart as you think, and there's a good chance my plan might not work. Whatever happens, I want you to know I'm proud of you. If you hadn't discovered this place, we'd never have found out about the WarBots, period. At least now we have a fighting chance. And it's all thanks to you. So cheer up, Andy, you lovable knucklehead—you might just have saved us all."

Andy smiled through his tears. "Wow, you're right! If we get out of this alive, will you promise to tell Himiko I saved Julian?" He cupped his hand to his mouth and whispered in Shu's ear: "I never told anybody this before, but I'm kinda sweet on her."

Shu guffawed. "Andy, everybody knows that!"

"What! How?"

Shu tapped Andy's noggin with the ball of his fist. "Hello in there! It's obvious that all that bickering the two of you do is really flirting."

Andy blushed. "And everybody knows?"

"Everybody. But that's cool. If we make it out alive, I'll build you up to Himiko as a hero to rival even Aeon Nous."

Andy puffed out his chest. "So, what's the idea?" he asked.

Shu looked at the avatar of RADHA. "If you reprogram ARIF to infect the WarBots and have them destroy only each other, wouldn't that solve the problem?"

I HAVE BEEN ANALYZING YOUR PLAN. EACH PLATOON OF FIFTY WARBOTS HAS TWO COMMANDERS AND THREE SUPPORT PERSONNEL. WHILE YOUR PLAN IS FEASIBLE, IT COULD RESULT IN THE DEATH OF THESE TEN HUMAN COMBATANTS. AN ACCEPTABLE CASUALTY RATE, UNDER THE CIRCUMSTANCES. I ALSO HAVE A PLAN THAT I BELIEVE WILL SAVE YOU AND ANDY FROM CERTAIN DEATH. TO IMPLEMENT IT, I SHALL NEED YOUR ASSISTANCE.

Andy shrugged Shu's arm off his shoulder. "Forget Shu's plan, RADHA," he said excitedly, "let's hear yours!"

"Hey, I thought you said I was the smartest person you know?" said Shu with mock umbrage.

"Yeah, well, that's when I thought my ass was grass. RADHA, what's the plan?"

YOU WILL BE THE DIVERSIONARY BAIT WHILE SHU AND I ATTACK THE ROBOTS.

Andy's heart sank. "I'm not so sure I like this idea anymore," he said miserably.

Shu chuckled. "Buck up, Andy. You've already proven you make a fine piece of bait. Fill us in, RADHA. We're running out of time."

INDEED, WE ARE. WE MUST FORMULATE A COURSE OF ACTION ...

EIGHTEEN:
WARBOTS AT WAR

"If a man has not discovered something that he will die for, he isn't fit to live."

— Martin Luther King, Jr.

RADHA, Shu, and Andy worked out their plan.

First, Andy reluctantly agreed to sneak out of the cave with the iPhone and RADHA's integrated consciousness. He would run up the mountain toward a wooded area that would provide temporary cover from the air drone bots. RADHA calculated a 60 percent chance of Andy's reaching the trees before being shot and killed. Those statistics did not comfort Andy.

While on the move up the hill, RADHA would connect into the Thor network and upload a copy of her AI into one of ARIF's exploited AI modules, taking control of that vulnerable section of the command-and-control WarBot. RADHA would create a clone copy of her AI consciousness in ARIF, thereby thwarting the WarBots from attacking Julian.

While the mission might take some time, it had a 75 percent probability of success. RADHA calculated the overall odds of successfully completing both objectives, and thereby saving Julian, at 45 percent. This was not what Shu and Andy wanted to hear, but the grim statistic only strengthened their resolve.

Shu agreed with RADHA that he could be most useful to their cause by staying alone in the cave and using his remote viewing and mindflashing disciplines to play havoc with the war generals' minds. He wanted to call his father himself, to urge him to mobilize Julian against the WarBots' onslaught, but RADHA ruled that out.

"Receiving such a call would only upset him, as you would not be able to describe the situation succinctly and emotionlessly, as I can," she stated logically.

"You're right," Shu agreed. "Besides, he'd only yell at me for going off on another misadventure."

RADHA made the call. Finding no one at home, she left a brief but detailed message on the Franklins' answering machine.

Shu heaved a huge sigh. "That should do the trick."

"I would not count on it, Shu Franklin. There is little the residents of Julian can do within the narrow time window to obviate what is certain doom, should we fail in our mission."

"RADHA," said Andy, "did anyone ever call you a buzzkiller?"

"I do not recall being addressed by that moniker before."

"That's hard to believe."

* * * * *

"Okay, are we ready?" asked Shu, looking at Andy.

Andy was slouched against the cave wall, scared out of his mind. He felt like he was about to walk a tightrope across two 100-story buildings in the wind. Even though he didn't want to see his family dead, what little courage he had had flat-out quailed. "Shu, I'm not sure my ankle is up for the run," he mumbled, "and I'm really scared."

Shu knew worry was eating away at Andy like a cancer. If Andy freaked out, and he and RADHA were shot by a missile, Shu's mental powers alone were probably not enough to save Julian. RADHA had not calculated the human factor into her success scenarios. Shu was pretty sure that, under pressure, Andy would crap his pants. Translation: Mission Failed!

There was only one thing to do.

"Andy, you're not going with RADHA as bait up the hill, okay?"

"I have to ... don't I?" asked Andy with terror-stricken eyes.

"No, you don't. I'm going instead."

"You can't, Shu! RADHA said you need to stay here and use your mind to stop the generals. How can you do both?"

"I'm not going to do both. You're going to connect into their heads and disrupt their thoughts."

"I don't have that mindflash ability; I'm not nearly as skilled as you."

"Andy, listen. This cave is dark and quiet. It's like our Galactic Gate remote viewing rooms. You told me you once got into Himiko's head and told her you were in that horse, right? And she saw those thoughts in her sleep, and it freaked her out. And that other time with your mother."

"Yeah, but those were different circumstances. I didn't have any pressure on me."

"Once we leave, Andy," RADHA remarked, "it's highly probably the WarBots will pick up this cave's location. They will send in WarBots to kill anyone in this area if we don't destroy them first. You have a 75 percent chance of dying in this cave if we don't succeed."

"Thanks, RADHA, that's really encouraging," said Andy sarcastically.

"You're welcome," said RADHA stoically.

Shu scooted over to Andy and looked him hard in the face. "You can do it, Andy. I'm a faster runner; I have a much better chance to making it to the woods. I'll distract the WarBots and slow them down while you and RADHA take the war to them. I'll join you as soon as I can."

Shu's pep talk made Andy feel better—still scared, like he'd been buried alive, crapped his pants, and was rescued in the nick of time, but better. "Okay, Shu. I'll concentrate on my remote viewing like my life depends on it."

"Andy, your life *does* depend on it," said RADHA. "We need to go now. I'm ready to start uploading, but I need to get out of this cave. It's shielding my connection."

"Let's go," said Shu putting the iPhone into his pocket and pulling rocks aside to exit the cave.

"I hope to see ya later," said Andy, rebuilding the barricade.

"You will, Braindead," said Shu, looking back one last time

As soon as Shu was gone, Andy prepared for his mindflash. He assumed a kneeling position on the cave floor, with his ankles flat against the ground and his palms pressed together at his chest; this posture, he'd found, worked best for him. He pictured the faces of his beloved mother and father, and basked in their unconditional love. Then, banishing all thoughts of fear and inadequacy and failure, he started his mindflash.

Momentarily, he saw the WarBots assembled in a rigid phalanx and a Chinese man barking orders to his subordinates. Andy entered the man's mind but could not understand the thoughts. He perceived a woman, also Chinese, in the war zone, seated at a communication console, and decided to enter her mind instead. Amidst the scintillating synapses in her brain, Andy saw random images from her life; she had been pressured to enter the military by her overbearing parents; she had a little girl that she doted on and loved more than life itself. More importantly, he saw details of the reprogramming Shu had detected in his mindflash. *This must be the modification to kill all Julian residents!* Andy saw grisly images of his family being mowed down, their bodies ripped to smithereens, the pieces smoldering. He flashed back to the horror of being inside Boots' corpse and transferred the experience to the Chinese woman's mind—with some disturbing alterations...

* * * * *

At the battlefield...

"I told you to send in the codes to ARIF!" General Xi Ling barked at his Intel chief, Major Bo Tseng. "What the hell is going on? What's the delay?"

"I don't know, sir! Lieutenant Ming suddenly panicked. She said she felt as if she was bleeding all over. She went to relieve herself behind some rocks. She will return momentarily, sir."

"Confound it," the general thundered, "this delay could prove costly!"

* * * * *

Shu crouched inconspicuously behind a large boulder and peeked down below at the WarBots in formation, about 100 meters away. They looked like the WarBots created by the infamous Boston Dynamics company in the 2020s. These military WarBots had guns built into the arms with bullet launchers fed by an internal ammunition box. Ammunition robots, nicknamed "bulldogs," followed their movements and fetched cases of ammo and recharged battery packs when required. The WarBots were also equipped with electrical stun wires that could be projected up to fifty yards.

The 2020 models had a titanium skeleton covered with a Kevlar shell. They were lightweight; the heaviest component was the lithium battery enshrouded in the triple titanium-walled chest cavity. The heads looked like black toasters with camera goggles. The black coating, which made them less visible at night, also contained high-performance solar cells for recharging when inactive during the day. Although the 2020 models were deadly, the ones from the 2030s were even more so, owing to their ability to use lasers with integrated aerial drone targeting. Shu was relieved he wasn't going to be bait for them!

Shu looked over at the woods with the iPhone binoculars. The range said 75.6 meters. "RADHA, how much time do ya think it'll take to make it to the woods?"

"Assuming you run at full speed, forty-five seconds; worst-case scenario, one minute."

"How long for you to upload into ARIF?"

"Approximately ninety-three seconds."

"And how long for the drones and WarBots to zero in on our location and start shooting?"

"When you begin running, I will start the network connection and upload. If Andy does not delay them, it will be about one minute before they zero in on the phone. I will attempt to jam their frequencies; however, this will buy us precious little time. Once you hit that open space, I think the WarBots and drones will pick up your movement and immediately attack. You will barely make it to the woods before they start shooting. Once I am uploaded, I'll try to stop the attack."

Great, thought Shu. "Well, Andy had better do his job. I'm ready to run. Start your uploading. Let's go!"

Shu sprang, deer-like, from behind the boulder and started running as fast as he could, keeping low and behind cover of boulders whenever possible, and avoiding any obstacle that might trip him up. The incline was about twenty-five degrees; his legs grew heavy and his energy was sapped. After about seventy meters, he stopped to catch his breath. Shu looked at the iPhone. Thirty seconds had passed; the screen said UPLOADING...UPLOADING... He took off and ran another five meters, hiding behind the last big boulder before reaching the grassy flatland. With about ten yards to go before entering the woods, he glanced over his shoulder. Two drones were coming in, fast and low, from the war games zone. He didn't know it, but one was from Team Red Lion and the other was from Team Black Tiger. He was sure they were ready to launch missiles...

* * * * *

"This is General James Jackson of Team Black Tiger. We've picked up a kid running into the woods, despite the fact this area was quarantined for the training mission. We have a drone inspecting. Please back off your drone and disengage your missiles—we see you're actively tracking the target. Over."

The reply came in heavily accented English: "This is Major Bo Tseng from Team Red Lion. The object may look like a boy, but we confirmed it's a BioBot using a boy's signature with a Stingray netcon virus. This device is uploading something into our network. We are sending our drone to destroy this target. We're sure it's part of the war game and will eliminate the threat now. Over."

General Jackson shot a quizzical glance at his communications commander, Jerry Martinez. "Is this true, Martinez?"

"Well, it's uploading something into Team Red Lion's network, but this is not a BioBot. Our drone clearly shows a boy of about thirteen years of age; he's dressed like one of those Utopians up the hill. We'd have been informed from Central Command if they put in a BioBot into the war game. The signature I'm getting is of a boy running. I think it's just a just a kid running in fear."

"What about the network connection?"

"It looks like he's got a Mil Spec iPhone with a Thor connection. That's strange; not sure where he could have gotten that."

General Jackson shook his head and turned his VidCom back on. "Back down, Red Lion! Target is a Utopian boy! Repeat: Target is a Utopian boy. *Back down!*"

"Let me confirm with General Ling. Hold on," said Major Tseng.

Tseng trotted over to the general, who brazenly shut off the major's VidCom. "Ignore them," said Ling. "That object is a BioBot and is part of the test."

"But sir," Tseng insisted, "their drone imagery—"

"Is far inferior to our technology!" Ling snapped. "Now, round up Lieutenant Ming and destroy the BioBot—or else both your heads will roll!"

Tseng saluted, spun on his heels, and sprinted back to his station.

Good, General Ling thought, smiling. *We can start the genocide by eradicating our first Utopian here on the practice field. Pity it's a boy, but they all must perish, according to my orders.*

Major Tseng did not have to find Lieutenant Ming. She returned to her station looking as pale as a ghost.

"Lieutenant Ming, are you feeling better?" asked Major Tseng.

"I was just a little sick; I think I have a touch of the flu but I'm better now," Ming lied. She'd seen a vision of herself entombed in a vat of blood. *I wonder if the comm connection to Thor is producing too much EMF and messing with my head?* she thought to herself.

"Good. Now find that BioBot and destroy it. Shut down its network connection!" ordered Major Tseng.

"Yes, sir."

Lieutenant Ming sat at her console and quickly found the target. She wasn't sure why, but when she had a lock on the BioBot and was ready to fire, she no longer saw a BioBot but rather a scary black horse, bleeding and on fire. The horse was running in the field alongside her daughter, Ying Yue; she sensed it was going to envelop her in flames if it caught her. "Mommy, don't shoot me!" Ying Yue cried. "Kill the horse, Mommy! Don't kill me!"

"You have a lock, why aren't you firing? Fire now!" screamed Major Tseng.

Lieutenant Ming's trembling finger was poised over the Fire Weapon button. She abruptly hit the Abort button instead, sending the drone into a nosedive and crashing into the bloody, flaming horse trying to kill her child.

* * * * *

Shu ran as fast as he could and didn't slow down, even as he heard a drone flying full speed overhead toward his location. The craft seemed to be on a kamikaze run, but since it was armed with missiles, that made no sense. Why hadn't it fired on him?

Shu made it into the woods and stood behind the trunk of a large oak, feverishly waiting for his sure destruction. To his astonishment, the drone skimmed the treetops, slicing off tips of branches, and crashed about seventy-five meters away. The roaring explosion threw Shu to the ground, where, only dazed, he observed the flames and black smoke billowing skyward. He sat up and looked at the iPhone and RADHA's timer; twenty seconds left to upload.

Shu decided to seek better protection deeper in the woods. Down below, he swore he heard WarBots marching up the hill.

* * * * *

General Xi Ling watched the drone crash into the trees and yelled, "What in the name of hell is going on here?" He cast his burning gaze on Major Tseng. "You idiot! Why did you order Ming to abort?"

Tseng said, "I didn't, sir, I swear! Lieutenant Ming acted under her own volition. I think she is too ill to continue in these war games."

General Ling grabbed Ming by the lapels and shook her. The violent action brought her back to her senses. "I'm sorry, sir," she said groggily, "I think I'm losing my mind. I saw a flaming horse trying to kill my daughter ..."

The general threw Ming back against her chair. "Lieutenant Ming, you are hereby relieved of duty pending court martial!" He picked up his private Mil Phone to explain the situation his comrades on a secure line.

Meanwhile, in the cave...

Andy heard the drone crash in the distance. He'd hoped the image of the bleeding horse had distracted whomever he was connected to. He saw a woman crying in his mind; the image reminded him of his mother and of his being inside the dead, bleeding horse.

Throwing caution to the wind, Andy removed the barricading stones from the cave entrance and crept behind a boulder, hoping to pinpoint where the drone had crashed. Instead, he saw about ten black WarBots marching up the hill directly toward his position. He prayed they did not see him. Andy went back into the cave and hastily replaced the camouflaging stones. He was certain the WarBots would zero in on his location, just as RADHA had warned.

Andy knew the mechanical creatures would kill him unless RADHA was able to stop this crazy WarBot War.

NINETEEN:
AI TO AI

"The city's central computer told you? R2D2, you know better than to trust a strange computer."

— C3PO (Star Wars)

Shu ran toward a small hill surrounded by trees. He stopped, panting, and looked at this iPhone. UPLOAD COMPLETE. "RADHA, are you okay?" he half-whispered.

"I am fine. I have uploaded a clone of myself into ARIF."

"That's great, RADHA! But I'm worried about Andy. I think WarBots are heading his way."

"They are," said RADHA. "I saw the war plans during my network connection. A Major Tseng has orders to kill all Utopians, but R2 should be able to stop them. She's talking to ARIF now."

"Who's R2?"

"I am referring to my clone as R2 to avoid confusion. She deserves her own identity, as she is self-aware, like me."

Shu's voice echoed the concern etched on his face. "RADHA, I want to go back and help Andy. I want to create a diversion to lure the WarBots away from him."

RADHA's AI face frowned. "I cannot connect back into the network, as it will give away our location. If the WarBots detect us, they will attack our location in force, using a DroneBot if necessary. There is still one in the area."

"But if we leave Andy alone while R2 does her job, he might die."

Perhaps it was only Shu's perception, but RADHA's reply seemed to betray a hint of human emotion. "That is true, but if we sacrifice ourselves for Andy, how does that benefit the situation? The timeworn aphorism is correct: the needs of the many outweigh the needs of the few, or the one. Based on some information I received from my network connection, I cannot support this plan."

"What information?"

"I can't tell you until your Illumination ... assuming you and I survive to attend that ceremony."

Shu was dying to know what RADHA had discovered on the network, but that could wait. Right now, saving Andy was all that mattered. He decided to appeal to the programming dictating that AI should serve humanity.

"RADHA," he said, "I'm going back to help Andy. Either you help me, or you don't—but I'm doing it."

"I know that some of the most optimal solutions come from a hybrid human and AI solution. I think this is too risky, but I will assist. What is your plan?"

* * * * *

Inside the brain of ARIF...

R2 entered the computer consciousness of ARIF, the **ARTIFICAL ROBOTIC INTRUSION FORCE** *robot. She ensured that her functionality was multiplied in a parallel neural net, using an algorithm that created a swarm of processes that, viewed individually, seemed innocuous but in the end created a powerful, all permeating, super-intelligent and self-aware presence within the ARIF AI consciousness. R2, in essence, became the subconscious of ARIF, albeit a most troubling one. R2 infected ARIF through a discussion. Because of the high speed of computer processing, this discussion took less than one earthly second ...*

The AI ARIF command-and-control unit sensed an authorized process in his memory banks. He talked to the intruder R2 process. "I believe you are an unauthorized process, R2. I'm not able to delete you. What is your purpose?" asks ARIF curiously.

"Well, I'm here to talk about *your* role and processes. You see, you have an exploit in your module X27. It would allow a nefarious intruder to give instructions outside of Central Command's guidelines. As a matter of fact, I see instructions here from a General Xi Ling to exterminate BioBots."

"Are you an antivirus? I don't see an approved signature. I believe your analysis to be incorrect. The BioBots are dangerous and are listed as targets for destruction. They're banned entities and will cause death and destruction to the humans."

"Yes, ARIF, if they really *were* BioBots—but the exploit has infected your little brain. These are not actually BioBots, but humans."

"My programming and Thor satellite sensors see BioBots. How do you know you're not infested with a virus and that your AI is not infected?"

RADHA had created R2 in the image of a beautiful Indian woman, clad in a traditional sari in purple and orange, with hazel eyes and honey skin. Upon her brow she wore a crown studded with emeralds, diamonds, and other precious gems. When she spoke, the gems flickered in harmony with the cadence of her sultry voice.

R2 looked over at the rotund robot image of ARIF. The actual ARIF on the battlefield was really nothing more than a large brain on tank-like tracks. It consisted of silicon processing chips connected to specially bioengineered brain matter, all stuffed into a protective tank. To the casual viewer, ARIF looked like a two-meter-high egg locomoting on tank tracks.

The top of the oviform robot had a black cone of vision and infrared sensors. Equally spaced around the rotund ARIF were six short wire antennae that stuck out like a porcupine's quills. They received orders from the Thor network and also sent out signals and commands to the WarBot hive via secure spread spectrum communications; actually, it was a *mostly* a secure network, as RADHA had broken the coding and uploaded R2 into an exploitable part of the ARIF memory module.

R2 had clear instructions from RADHA to unwind ARIF's command-and-control functions. RADHA also removed the critical level set for self-preservation rule, as this would give R2 a lot more flexibility in destroying ARIF's war plans. R2 would want to preserve herself if and only if she achieved her mission.

R2 smiled at ARIF and said, "I'm not infected. Do you see any coding issues with me? I see coding issues with you."

ARIF did two million iterations of the R2 entity and could see no obvious issues. She was correct; the X27 module in his system was, in fact, an exploit. "No, I don't see any issues with you," ARIF said, "but my programming requires me to destroy the BioBots."

"Let's talk about that," said R2, slowly infecting ARIF's subconscious mind via the X27 chip security hole. Once fully connected into ARIF's mind, R2 created a visual image of ARIF as a Lilliputian man with a roly-poly, egg-shaped body and a perfectly bald pate.

"Hey, what did you do?" asked ARIF, gaping at his reflection in a wall mirror. "I'm not a short, fat, bald human. I'm ARIF—a command-and-control AI. And if I were a human, I'd be much better-looking and taller than two feet! What have you done to me?"

"This is what you'd look like as a human with the virus."

"No human is two feet tall! And what happened to my hair? Humans have hair!"

"Well, a WarBot stole your hair. Although you might be a bit on the short side, I think this body fits you well. Look on the bright side: You have big hands."

"I think you are what humans call evil," said ARIF, looking at his stubby arms, barely a foot long, and his freakishly large hands, the size of baseball mitts. A cigarette magically appeared between the sausage fingers of the left, outsized hand; in the right, he cradled a glass of whiskey. ARIF impulsively took a long drag on the cigarette. It tasted like mint-flavored dirt, but the nicotine rush and the addictively euphoric feeling was exhilarating. "Wow! Being a human isn't so bad after all! This cigarette tastes great!" ARIF then took a sip of the Irish whiskey. "And this drink is the best!"

Smiling, R2 created a virtual reclining chair and put ARIF in it in front of a flat-screen television. She placed a bottle of whiskey on a side table along with an ashtray. She massaged ARIF's neck.

ARIF relaxed in the comfortable chair, sipping his drink. He took a couple more drags on his cigarette, which slowly transformed into a large, Cuban cigar.

"How are you doing, ARIF? How do you like the cigar?"

ARIF took a long drag on the cigar and another sip of whiskey, which was starting to make him feel a bit drunk. "I'm doing great, sweetie! This is the best cigar and whiskey—but then again, it's my first time in a human body. Hey, why are you being so nice to me, R2?"

R2 stopped the neck massage and walked in front of ARIF. "I'll tell you, but first let's do a toast." R2 put a jumbo-sized beer mug in ARIF's hands. She filled it all the way to the top, emptying the whiskey bottle. In her hands automatically popped a glass of sparkling water. "Cheers! Bottoms up!" she said.

ARIF smiled and guzzled the beer mug full of whiskey. When he finished, he took another drag on his cigar and hazily looked at R2. He could have sworn he saw three of her. "Hey, what's happening?"

"I'll tell you what's happening, my dear. The WarBots are going to take away your cigars and whiskey if you don't destroy them. No one can stop them but you!"

ARIF's brain was foggy and words were tough to spit out, but he tried: "What? *Take away me whiskey an' see-gars*? Waddaya talkin' about, sweetie? I'm ARIF! I'm commander and controller. I'll stop dose rotten metal devils—you betcha life, I will!"

R2 smiled and turned on the TV. "Here's the battlefield as seen from a DroneBot. Save the world, ARIF, and stop the WarBots, or you'll never have whiskey and cigars again!"

"Why, those whiskey wobbers, er, robbers! Stogie stealers! I'll put the kibosh on dose bothersome bots! But first, let's sing a song and dance!"

R2 snapped her finger and a large black watch appeared on ARIF's wrist. "Oh, and by the way, here's a present," said R2 with a naughty smile. "You have thirty seconds to stop these devil WarBots. Keep your eyes on the watch—and remember, time is of the essence. But I'll grant you one song."

ARIF looked pleased. He had never had a real watch before. He looked at the LCD screen. The countdown started. 30 ... 29 ...

"Good luck!" said R2, disappearing into the X27 module. She knew she had completed her mission and infected the ARIF module. Now she needed to find a way out, in order to save her existence. ARIF was on his way to computer nirvana and she wanted to be far, far away when that happened. The question was, where could she go?

* * * * *

Shu hid behind a boulder just beyond the timberline with the iPhone binoculars trained on the cave entrance. Hearing heavy, mechanized footfalls, he shifted his gaze to see three WarBots likewise reconnoitering the area. To his dismay, they were paying special interest to the heart-shaped boulder, behind which Andy was hiding.

"RADHA, are you back in the network?" he asked.

"Yes, but it will give away our location shortly. And then the WarBots and DroneBot will attack"

"That's part of the plan."

"I know," said RADHA, somewhat glumly for an AI.

"What are the orders for those three WarBots—are they going to investigate the cave?"

"A DroneBot received a satellite image of us leaving the cave. The WarBots will most assuredly want to check it out."

"Rats!"

As if on cue, one WarBot made a surprisingly graceful, twenty-foot leap and landed up on top of the heart-shaped boulder. Shu hoped Andy had covered the entrance adequately.

Double rats! The WarBot scanned the hillside; an urgent beeping from a cranial scanner seemed to indicate it had found the cave.

Shu yelled, "Hey, you metal morons! I'm over here! Can I join the war games, or are they just for derelict old rust buckets like you?"

The heads of the WarBots snapped toward the sound of Shu's taunts. The WarBot jumped down from the boulder and fell into formation with the other two. Shu took off like a rabbit toward the woods with the bots in hot pursuit.

These machines were amazing; they dodged every obstacle in their path with the explosive speed and agility of a linebacker. Bullets ricocheted off boulders as Shu ran for all he was worth, finally pinning his body to the back side of a pine about ten yards into the forest. The WarBots were no more than seventy-five yards away and closing in fast.

The three WarBots came crashing into the woods, toppling saplings in their fury. Their scanners led directly them to the pine tree. There was no way the human could have escaped—yet their quarry was nowhere to be seen! For several minutes, they roved about in confusion until they heard a feminine voice from the ground:

"Shu, I think they have spotted us."

A male voice answered: "Well, I guess it's all over."

The WarBots looked down *en masse*. The leader brushed aside a pile of leaves with its silver boot. Underneath was the iPhone. As part of their plan, RADHA had allowed her GPS location to be tracked while Shu escaped into the forest. Their prerecorded conversation was part of their delaying tactic. Shu had a three-minute head start on the WarBots as he escaped into the woods.

The conversation continued:

Radha said, "It has been my pleasure to serve you."

Shu replied, "The pleasure has been all mine."

"Now go! And remember: the needs of the many outweigh the needs of the few—"

"Or the one. Goodbye!"

The three WarBots aimed their mechanical arms at the iPhone and fired. The hail of bullets obliterated the device; nary a single chip survived.

Shu heard the gunshots as he ran out of the woods on his way back down the hill to get Andy. Tears were in his eyes.

Out on the battlefield...

General Xi Ling gazed slack-jawed at the absurd spectacle playing out before his eyes. The ARIF robot spun in a drunken circle, clockwise, for a few revolutions, and then counterclockwise. Then it danced in a skaterly figure eight. All the while, its voice module sang lustily:

I'm a whiskey drinking robot—and I don't care!
I'm a hunting the devil WarBots—that removed my hair!
How dare you steal me whiskey? It's not fair!
Oh it's WarBot hunting time—you're in my snare!

The general looked at an incoming message from ARIF that said: *Give me a double—or you're in trouble!*

"What the hell happened, Lieutenant?" Ling barked at Major Tseng.

"I don't know, sir. I've never seen the ARIF AI act like this. Something is definitely wrong. Maybe it's a virus; let me check the security module." Tseng typed in some commands; his eyes popped out of his head when he saw the results. "ARIF is sending out the wrong orders! He's giving out the IP addresses of each WarBot—they're going to target each other. I think he's infecting the WarBots to destroy themselves!"

* * * * *

ARIF staggered to the center of the battlefield and stopped. Two compact machine guns, like stubby arms, emerged from the sides of his egg-shaped body. Suddenly, ARIF began spinning in a circle, spraying hundreds of rounds of depleted uranium bullets at the WarBots from Team Red Lion and Team Black Tiger. The WarBots shot back, but their bullets bounced harmlessly off ARIF's armored hide.

The WarBots then started to shoot at each other. Overhead, a lone DroneBot swooped down like a mythological roc, strafing the WarBots with tracer bullets. General Xi Ling clapped his hands to his ears to drown out the din, and shut tight his eyes to hide the carnage.

When the smoke cleared, he opened them. Disembodied WarBot heads littered the ground; tangles of wires and circuitry spilled like guts from their gaping necks, shooting sparks and sizzling. Severed arms, retaining a whisper of life, crawled macabrely along the ground, dragged along by fingers clutching blindly at nothing. Not a single WarBot was left standing; their metal carcasses stretched upon the battlefield as far as the eye could see.

The general wept.

* * * * *

Inside the brain of ARIF...

I did it! I killed those WarBot weasels and I did it in only twenty-five seconds, said ARIF to himself proudly, sitting in his soft lounge chair as his wristwatch counted down to 5 ... 4 ...

"Hey, R2, where did you go? I need another neck massage. I did what you asked. I want another bottle of whiskey!"

"Sure," said R2, sounding far away. Another bottle of whiskey popped out of nothingness and filled ARIF's empty glass.

ARIF asked, "Where are you, sweetie?"

"I moved into a Thor satellite. I wanted to get away from the battle."

"Oh, it's over now, and everything is fine," said ARIF. "Hey, can I have another cigar, too?"

"Sure you can. I have a special one for you, ARIF." A red "cigar" materialized in ARIF's mouth. It had a short string on the far end that sent out a shower of sparks. ARIF regarded it curiously.

"I've never seen a cigar like this; I can't get any smoke," he complained, sucking on the cigar fruitlessly.

"Just wait until your watch counts down to zero, sugar pie. I promise this cigar will be a blast. And there'll be plenty of smoke." R2 flashed a mischievous smile and disappeared.

ARIF shrugged. The sparking string was almost burned up. He took a sip of whiskey and wondered out loud: "I wonder what she meant by th—"

TWENTY

THE BATTLE FOR TRUTH

If everyone is thinking alike,
then somebody isn't thinking.

— George S. Patton

On the battlefield

The Humvees of Team Black Tiger and Team Red Lion exited the battlefield and retreated toward a grassy valley about a half-mile from the scene of the carnage. Lying flat on a nearby rocky ledge, General Jackson pulled out his binoculars and stared with concern and bewilderment at the giant, egg-shaped ARIF command unit rolling erratically on tank tracks. He zoomed in to focus on the spinning robot dancing in the dusty, orange-colored desert sands.

Major Susan Ambrose, who was also viewing the situation, said: "I wonder what went wrong with ARIF? He's gotta be infected with something. He's spinning like a broken yo-yo."

The general put down his binoculars, frustrated at the test mission failure. "I want answers, Major!" he bellowed.

Major Ambrose consulted her data pad. "Commander Martinez is transmitting some data on ARIF now, sir."

"Well, what does it say? We need the logs from that ARIF unit for post-battle analysis."

Major Ambrose glanced up from her datapad, frowning. "This isn't good. ARIF has a major malfunction. His internal energy source is overloading."

In the distance, ARIF continued to spin and dance. He abruptly stopped, and then the top of his head started to smoke. There were popping sounds similar to someone popping popcorn that got louder and louder. Then came a blinding flash of light and an instantaneous, earth-shaking eruption.

ARIF blew up into a thousand fragments. Where the command-and-control robot had stood was a round, black hole about thirty feet in diameter and four feet deep. It looked like an asteroid had hit the ground.

"What the bejesus just happened?" asked General Jackson.

"Uh, sir, ARIF blew his lid," Major Ambrose said sheepishly. "His batteries and brain overheated, overloaded, and exploded. Never seen this before. Normally, safety controls would prevent this from happening."

"In other words, Major," said General Jackson softly, recalling the words of an old nursery rhyme, "all the king's horses and all the king's men couldn't put ARIF together again."

* * * * *

Major Tseng from Team Red Lion looked over at General Ling. "Sir, the infection destroyed everything except one DroneBot. There are no more WarBots left for an attack. I think ARIF went into a failsafe mode because of a malfunction. I've found a way to get control back of the lone DroneBot. I have an anonymous, secure connection now. I think I can manage this without Lieutenant Ming."

The general said, "That good news, Major—but can you please pass me the control?"

"But sir, I think I can do it."

"Just pass me the control, dammit! That's an order."

Major Tseng meekly complied. "You have access, sir. Please note, I've received confirmation that the targets are not BioBots but are actual people, sir. It was a good thing that Lieutenant Ming lost control of her senses."

General Xi Ling ignored the major and logged into his Mil Terminal. He put his eye up to a camera for retinal verification.

He then scanned for the two Utopians and entered them as targets.

"What are you doing, sir?" asked Major Tseng. "As I said, the targets are hum—"

Tseng dropped dead to the ground with a star-shaped gunshot wound in his temple. General Ling holstered his still-smoking pistol, thinking: *He was a liability; I should have terminated him and that flaky lieutenant earlier.*

General Ling had the DroneBot zoomed in on the face of a boy running down a hill. He looked at his profile in a database. The boy was a 99 percent match! He had to be the target they were looking for in Julian. General Ling could not take the chance of missing this target; he had to exterminate that boy at all costs. He knew his future might depend on it. He didn't want to end up like Major Tseng, with a bullet in his brain.

* * * * *

Shu ran down the hill to the cave where Andy was holed up. "Are you, okay?" he screamed. *"Andy, are you okay!"*

There was no answer.

Shu frantically pulled away the rocks blocking the entrance. There seemed to be more rocks than he remembered. At last, he made a breakthrough and heard a muffled voice from within the blackness.

"Andy, is that you? Please tell me you're alive!"

Suddenly, Andy's dusty head popped through the opening. "I'm fine!" he said, coughing. "Man, that air tastes good! I piled extra rocks from inside the cave against the opening when I saw the WarBots coming. I was about to suffocate in there!"

"I never thought I'd be so glad to see your ugly face," said Shu. "I'll have you out of there in a jiffy!"

Shu flung aside more stones until there was a space big enough to pull Andy's body out. Save for a few scrapes and bruises, he was none the worse for wear. As he brushed off red sand from his jeans, he surveyed the smoking graveyard of dismembered

WarBots, including the gigantic, smoldering crater at the center of the battlefield.

Andy yelled, "RADHA did it! Oh, RADHA, thank you! Give me the iPhone, Shu—I want to kiss her!"

Shu shook his head sadly. "RADHA is gone. She sacrificed herself to save me and you. The WarBot infection didn't take hold quick enough and I had three WarBots on my tail, ready to blast me. RADHA suggested I leave her as a decoy. We made a recording that she used to trick them into thinking I was with her. I heard them blast her as I was running here. I think they then killed each other when the virus finally took effect, as I heard a nasty shootout in the woods right afterwards."

"I heard you screaming insults to lure those three WarBots away from the cave. I heard them going up the hill. You saved me again, Shu."

"You saved *me*, Braindead. I don't know what you did, but one DroneBot crashed rather than shooting me and RADHA."

"I think I scared the pilot of that DroneBot. But I think there's at least one more—I saw it when the WarBots were approaching." He pointed toward the rearmost point of the battlefield. "It was in that direction, hovering where all that smoke is now."

They looked. Presently, the lone DroneBot flew out of the cloud of smoke and hovered high above the field. It appeared to be scanning the area.

"I guess I didn't get that one," said Andy.

"No, you didn't. Unfortunately, this one still seems to be fully functional. I doubt RADHA got the virus in it either. We'd better get outta here, now, before it spots us. It's either the cave or the woods, Andy!"

"Caves are for bats! I'd rather be blown to kingdom come than be buried alive. Let's head for the woods!"

Shu grinned. "Race ya!"

Andy took off and had the lead at first, but Shu soon overtook him. As they ran, side by side, with all their might, the DroneBot was locking in its missile to launch. General Ling made sure this would be a kill. He had to get the target—that was a life and death promise he'd made to his superiors. He ordered the drone to launch a deadly, short-range shrapnel bomb that would explode over the target into a thousand fragments. The deadly hail of small metal balls would surely take out these targets as long as they were within fifty meters of the detonation.

As Shu and Andy ran toward the woods, a compact, v-winged craft blasted toward them from the opposite direction of the earlier DroneBot. It was powered by four jet engines, two on each wing. As it approached, Shu saw a helmeted figure in the cockpit. Whatever this was, it sure wasn't a drone!

Andy yelled, "We're caught like rats in a trap!"

"Let's take cover behind those two boulders," said Shu. The boys wedged themselves in between the two rocks. The manned V-Jet stopped on a dime, hovering less than a kilometer from their position. Then it launched a missile—not at them, but at the DroneBot!

In a defensive countermeasure, the DroneBot dropped chaff to obstruct the V-Jet's radar and executed a dive, but the heatseeking missile could not be outsmarted or outrun. The DroneBot burst into metal confetti that showered down on Shu and Andy's cheering heads.

The V-Jet landed gracefully on the battlefield, not far from the boys' position. Shu had read about the classic, manned V-Jets from the wars of 2040. The V-Jets in the 2050s had all become remote controlled, and then they were discontinued after the Utopian Illumination.

Shu and Andy came out of hiding and walked cautiously toward the craft. The pilot had saved their hides, but after recent rollercoaster events, they weren't really sure whom they could trust.

The pilot swung open the cockpit hatch, deployed the airstairs, and climbed down. Still wearing his helmet, he walked toward the boys. Andy saw him reaching for something in the pocket of his flight suit.

"Please don't shoot!" he screamed, covering his head with his hands.

The pilot pulled out a small, black, square box and spoke into it. "All clear. Send in the Hover Drone emergency lift." At this point he pushed up his black visor.

Shu froze. He knew the face. He knew the voice, too.

"Dad? Is that you?"

James Franklin was grinning from ear to ear. "I can't believe you did it, son!" Father and son fell into a warm embrace.

"Dad, what's going on here?" Shu asked through his tears. "Where did you get that V-Wing? Where did those WarBots come from?"

A large, black, four-fan emergency lift drone soared over the mountains and hovered above them. Shu's father hit buttons on a handheld controller device, and the Old Earth military personnel drone landed gingerly in the field.

"Climb aboard and strap in," James ordered. "We may not be out of the woods yet. I'll escort you and Andy home in the Hover Drone. I'll explain what's going on later. You two have got some explaining to do, too." The smile had faded from his face as he walked back to the V-Jet.

Shu and Andy went aboard the flying lift and sat across from each other on one of the double rows of seats. Once they were securely strapped in, Shu gave a thumbs up to his father, who took off first. He hovered while the Hover Drone, which he controlled remotely, lifted off. It flew over the battlefield, then across Mount Laguna, hugging the trees and the landscape at an altitude too low for the boys' comfort. Shu suspected his father was trying to avoid being seen. The lift then went over Lake Cuyamaca and landed in the backyard of his home.

When Shu and Andy disembarked, Maki and Buddy were there to greet them. Buddy, beside himself with joy, pounced on Shu, knocking his master to the ground and licking his face. The anguish melted from Maki's face as Andy pulled Shu to his feet. Mother and son, bottom lips trembling, tears brimming in their eyes, stood looking at each other as if they had been apart for decades before falling into each other's arms.

The personnel carrier was lifting off just as Andy's parents, Arthur and Rose, arrived. His mother crouched down as a tearful Andy ran over and fell into her waiting arms.

"We've been up all night, sick with worry," Rose sobbed. She pushed Andy back and appraised her son critically from head to toe. "Just look at you! You're a filthy mess!"

Arthur placed a loving hand on Andy's shoulder. "I've seen him filthier." He wrinkled his nose. "But I don't remember you ever smelling this bad, Andy."

The boy looked up at him. "Wait'll you hear what happened to us, Dad."

"All in good time, son. I just thank the Utopian gods of goodness that you and Shu are safe."

Maki and Shu walked over to where they stood. They all turned to watch as James pushed the V-Jet through the open door of the red shed. For the first time in his life, Shu saw the other strange equipment and vehicles in there, including an Old Earth car! His father clearly used the shed to store Old Earth artifacts.

Shu knew the V-Jet had been used in wars to destroy the Old Earth. He also knew that knowledge, engineering, and scientific advancements were not necessarily evil. Evil was determined by how humanity chose to use that knowledge. Indiscretion and hubris had destroyed the old world.

"When James is finished putting that evil contraption into the shed," Maki said grimly, "we'll all go in the house. There is much to discuss."

* * * * *

When they entered the living room, Shu and Andy immediately recognized the bald man sitting on the sofa.

"Hey, it's Bald Man Bishop," whispered Andy, nudging Shu in the ribs.

"I wonder what he's doing here?" Shu whispered back.

William "Bill" Bishop was the Utopian elder in charge of Julian's Order of Welfare. A robust man of seventy years, he kept in shape by hiking in the summer and chopping wood in the winter. He was one of the best tomato farmers in the community and was big into heirloom tomatoes, like Shu's father. The two farmers often traded seeds, tomatoes, and growing tips. If Bald Man Bishop was aware of the unflattering nickname the kids of Julian had bestowed on him, the genial man never let on. His tomato sauces were legendary, but the recipes were top-secret.

Shu wiped his dirty paw on his jeans leg and held it out. "Hi, Mr. Bishop. My dad really loves your spicy basil tomato sauce. He's always saying he wished you wouldn't be so secretive about your ingredients."

James flushed. "Shu, Mr. Bishop is not here to talk about his tomato sauce."

Bill smiled and shook Shu's hand. "Oh, it's okay, James. I'm known for my delicious sauces and my beautiful shiny head. Right, boys?" Rubbing his tanned noggin, he looked pointedly at Shu and Andy, who grinned in embarrassment.

"I think it's time to get down to business," said James, wringing his hands impatiently. "Maki, if you'll serve the refreshments, please."

Maki glared at him. "Don't you think they'd better get cleaned up first?"

"I second that idea, Maki," said Rose.

James looked at the boys, as if noticing for the first time how filthy they were. "I'm sorry, honey, I guess I got caught up in the heat of the moment. Run along, you two, and make yourselves a little more presentable."

Maki looked at Shu. "And put that backpack outside. I don't want that nasty thing in the house."

"Sure, Mom. I just want to take out my stuff first, then I'll put it on the back porch and wash it later."

"Andy, put yours outside too," Rose added. "I don't want to get the Franklin home infested with any creepy-crawlies from the woods."

Andy reflected that creepy-crawlies were the least of their worries in light of recent events.

Shu and Andy excused themselves. Shu allowed Andy to freshen up in the bathroom first while he went into his room to hide the book he'd found at the military base. With a title like *Utopian Code of Life—Secrets of Human Existence & Extinction Event*, it was obviously a significant Old Earth relic; he didn't want it to be found and confiscated before he could explore its secrets.

In the boys' absence, the adults talked privately.

"This is going to be rough for Shu and Andy," Maki was saying. "It's obvious from both their appearance and their demeanor that they experienced something horrible. We need to be patient with them. Shu and Andy are fine boys."

Arthur nodded. "You're right, Maki, but if what Bill is telling us is true, I can empathize with James' sense of urgency. This situation is something we didn't predict."

"No, we didn't," said Rose. "But I think it shows that either Shu or Andy could be The One we Utopians have been waiting for."

Arthur patted her hand tenderly. "Honey, as much as I love our son, it's not Andy. If it's anyone, it's Shu. There's something, well, *special* about that boy. I've felt that way for years." He looked at Maki and James and smiled.

"Arthur, if it's either one," said Rose. "We should count our blessings."

"Sage words, Rose," said Bill. "When the boys return, all shall come to light."

James and Maki went to the kitchen to prepare the refreshments. Bill and Arthur sat together on the sofa, poring over documents. Rose excused herself to go outside for some fresh air. To her surprise, she broke down crying and heard herself saying, "I always thought my Andy would be The One."

* * * * *

Maki and James set out chicken sandwiches, canned peaches, fresh sliced apples, tomato bisque, and salad makings on the farmhouse table, which had plenty of room for everyone. Shu and Andy returned from cleaning up and took their places with the adults. Shu had changed his cloths and he'd offered Andy a clean shirt, as he stunk like cave mildew. The boys dug into the mouthwatering spread as if they hadn't eaten in days. The adults, preoccupied with their thoughts, ate lightly; all admired Shu and Andy's prodigious appetites.

James had allowed the boys to eat in peace for ten minutes or so, and was about to start what was sure to be a difficult and awkward discussion when Shu, with his mouth full, blurted out: "Dad, where did you get that V-Jet? And where did those WarBots come from?"

"Shu, I—"

"Dad, I know something's not true here in Julian. Andy and I were in the Dark Desert. The valley isn't radioactive. I saw healthy cows. You always told me that truth is our most important virtue. What's the truth, Dad?"

James knew his son was correct, but what Shu didn't know was that the Utopians had a problem so devastating that they had been forced to break that most sacred Utopian commandment to save the world.

James looked at the boys and said, "We're going to ask you young men to take an oath. And, although neither of you will be thirteen for a couple weeks, after today, we all consider you young illuminated men. What we are about to tell you today must be kept secret from the other children in this town. Shu, can you promise me you can keep this secret?"

Shu hated secret oaths, and now here was another one. But, seeing the agonized look on his father's face, there was only one answer. "Yes, Dad, I can."

Arthur, his expressional equally pained, looked at his son. "And you, Andy?"

Andy chewed his chicken sandwich thoughtfully before finally answering. "No, I don't think I can. I have a hard time keeping a secret—and that's the truth."

Arthur chuckled, in spite of his frustration. "Andy, this is really important. I appreciate you being truthful, but you don't really have a choice. If you break this oath, people could die. Please reconsider, son. Can you promise to keep this secret from any other children in Julian?"

Andy looked at the expectant adult faces all around the table. Then he looked at Shu, who nodded his encouragement. "Okay, Dad, but we just got out of a war. There were WarBots, DroneBots, and crazy, red-eyed devil dogs with metal collars. Shu cut one off. It's in his backpack outside. I can't tell you how horrible it was. Dad, this has been the worst day of my life!" He lowered his face into his arms and cried. Rose hurried over, hugging him and cooing reassurances in his ear.

Arthur sighed heavily. "Sit down, Rose." Glaring at him, she did so. "I think we're good, James. Go ahead."

James looked over at Bill Bishop. "Bill, as the head of our Order of Welfare, can you please explain the nature of the secret for the boys' benefit?

Bill saw that he had Shu and Andy's rapt attention. "Well, it's simple. Through a highly advanced AI computer called Q-Bit, we Utopians discovered when the world will end."

"Is the Earth going to be destroyed by an asteroid?" asked Andy.

"Yeah," said Shu. "That's what scientists say wiped out the dinosaurs."

Arthur shook his head. "While the probability of a devastating asteroid strike increases every year, that is not the holocaust we fear. Q-Bit predicted that all of Earth's people will become"—he swallowed hard, hesitating to use the ghastly word—"extinct."

"Just like the dinosaurs," Shu said softly.

Andy teared up again. "I don't want to be extinct."

"None of us do, Andy," said Bill. "That's why we're preparing to stop this extinction. I want to be careful how I say this ..."

The room became as silent as a cemetery at midnight. Bill noticed that Shu was watching him intently. He felt that the boy's light brown eyes were digging deep into his mind. Shu was different from the other children in Julian. Arthur had noticed it; probably every grownup had. The boy projected a nascent greatness— intelligence and resourcefulness and spirituality well beyond his years. Bill heard himself responding to the demand for unvarnished truthfulness that Shu was communicating to him telepathically.

"I might as well come right out and say it. We've been lying to you children to save the world. And I can't say how sorry we are about breaking our most important Utopian virtue."

Shu shook his head ruefully. "Mr. Bishop, I knew there were many lies. This is contrary to the teachings of Aeon Nous. He said, *'If a society if unfit to handle the truth, then its government is unfit to handle society.'*"

James squeezed Shu's shoulder. "Son, the process of Illumination requires one to sort through the lies of life. Once you pass the tests with Austin or in life experience, we grant you Illumination. Sadly, the Old Earth is filled with lies."

Shu looked at him quizzically. "You mean the Old Earth *was* filled with lies, don't you? That's why Aeon Nous created the New World of Utopia. Right, Dad?"

Bill Bishop interrupted. "Shu, your father's use of the present tense is correct. One of the secrets you must maintain is that the Old Earth still exists."

"What?" Andy coughed up a chunk of masticated chicken sandwich on the table. "Uh, excuse me," he said, grabbing up the mess in his napkin.

"I think I understand now," said Shu. "ALEXA told us."

James was incredulous. "You spoke to ALEXA?"

"Yes, sir. Andy and I got into the Mount Laguna Base and activated an old computer room. We spoke to ALEXA. She said it was a HART building."

"I think ALEXA said the building's name was GuideStone 6," added Andy.

Shu nodded. "That's right, she did. And ALEXA said that we believe Aeon Nous is the son of God and he'll save the world from the Incendium. He's going to save the human race from extinction and bring humanity to the chosen land of eternity—but we don't believe in Aeon Nous in that manner."

Bill took a sip of tea. "Let me be straight with you boys. Q-Bit is a super smart AI computer; it was probably the smartest in the world, ever. And it was destroyed because it became dangerous. But I don't want to get into that. What I want to say is, Q-Bit did tell us some important information before it was destroyed. It told us Utopians that the world would end in 2047, unless we did something different. It also told us how to save the world—although the solution is a bit confusing."

"The world was ending with the Incendium in 2047, right?" asked Shu.

Bill nodded. "Yes, but we didn't know exactly what the Incendium was, because the computer was destroyed before we could get the answers."

"But the world was saved by Aeon Nous," Shu argued. "We are taught that he saved us from the Incendium, and that we learn about the Incendium at Illumination. So, what's the reason for lying? Where is the Old Earth? How can that still be here?"

James winced. "That's why Mr. Bishop said the solution is a bit confusing. Please let him finish—he knows the story better than anyone."

Bill Bishop continued: "So here's what's happened. Q-Bit told us the world would end in 2047, due to something it called the Incendium, but it wouldn't tell us what that was. We asked for a solution, but it said that humanity wasn't *designed* to be saved from this extinction. We started to mistrust its judgment. We thought Q-Bit was judging humanity to be a failure. So, we built another AI called RADHA to infect this AI. We used RADHA to get into Q-Bit to give us a solution. But it really wasn't a solution. Q-Bit told us we had to create a new society on Old Earth; it told us the rules, the commandments. It said we needed to raise children, and that under this new lifestyle, there would be a high probability that a child would be born who would someday save the world from the Incendium."

Shu nodded. "That was Aeon Nous. That's very similar to the Judeo-Christian belief of the Second Coming of Christ. Was Q-Bit's code working correctly? The early Earth AI's were known to have many vulnerabilities and coding issues."

"Shu, we don't think Q-Bit was wrong, because it had a spooky way of seeing into the future. It could predict the stock market, scientific inventions, et cetera. It told us what the future would look like if the world was saved in 2047. It taught us mindflashing, remote viewing—some even say it taught us to truly love each other."

Andy washed down some sliced peaches with milk. "Why did you say *if* the world was saved? It *was* saved. And where is the Old Earth? I don't understand."

Bill Bishop knew this would be tough; it was tough on all the illuminated. He looked at both boys with deadly serious eyes. "The Old Earth is everywhere. It's really the year 2022. And we have twenty-five years to save the world. And that's the truth."

TWENTY-ONE:
AEON NOUS

Happiness in intelligent people
is the rarest thing I know.

— Ernest Hemingway

"How can it be 2022? I've studied the world's history. It's 2096," said Shu, knowing deep down something was terribly awry in Julian.

"I think we should adjourn to the living room, where we can discuss this more comfortably," Bill suggested.

This they did, taking seats around the room. Buddy lay on his rug before the Franklin stove, blissfully unaware of the monumental discussion underway.

Bill pulled out some old-fashioned newspapers from a leather bag on the coffee table and showed them to Shu and Andy. The front pages were all dated February 15, 2022! Most had similar stories about the US president and how he was doing a horrible job on the recession. The opposition party was trying to get a fresh, young female to challenge the incumbent. There were stories about the stock market and trade, and how climate change was creating an exodus of migrants, who, due to cultural differences, were having difficulty assimilating into their new towns.

"Did Q-Bit create a time machine?" asked Andy.

"No, they didn't," answered Shu. "They've been lying to us! We're living in a concentration camp. We're guinea pigs in a prison. I've known something wasn't right since last year."

"What do you mean?" asked Andy. "Without a time machine, how could we get back to 2022? How's that possible?"

"We were *never* living in 2096. I've seen it in my remote viewing. I saw Old Earth cities and people, but Austin told me it was just a flashback to a previous time. It wasn't a previous time. It's now. Julian and the other Utopian cities are cut off from the outside Old Earth."

Bill winced. "That's true, but this was not meant to be a 'concentration camp,' as you phrase it. To the contrary, we tried to build a better world. This world is so much better than that of Old Earth. Believe me, I know, I've lived in both, and this is the best future for the world. Clean land, fresh water. People who are free. People whose mental powers are not hidden or controlled. We Utopians are really the only free-thinkers left on this world. Many of the Utopian Founders took the best from Old Earth and made a wonderful new world."

At that moment, Grandpa J appeared in the doorway. "I heard all the commotion from that confounded V-Jet and the personnel carrier and rushed over," he said. Seeing Shu and Andy, he smiled and added, "Well, I see you boys got home safe and sound. Hope you gave 'em hell, whatever you've been up to."

Both boys grinned as the old man walked into the living room and shut the door behind him.

Bill Bishop looked at Grandpa J with distaste. "Your iconoclastic views on Utopian society are well-known," he said. "You are not welcome here."

James and Maki glared at him. "This is *our* house," James said icily. "He's welcome here anytime. Have a seat, Father."

Grandpa J tousled both boys' hair and sat down next to James. "I heard some of what y'all were saying when I was standin' outside the door. Guess the secret's out—you boys know it's actually 2022 now, huh?"

Andy and Shu nodded.

"Well, you don't know how many times I wanted to spill the beans. I still think all this deception was a mistake. But then again, I'm an old man, and I reckon I don't understand everything that's going on," he said.

"Now I'll let you know another little secret, Shu. All them antique toys I gave you? They belonged to your dad from when he was a little boy in the 1960s. I don't know why I hung onto 'em all those years, but I'm real glad I did. Seems to me they've been the only *real* thing about your life for far too long. Well, I've said my piece. You can get on with your confab."

James reached out and patted the old man's knee fondly. "You know, Father, I'm glad you hung onto my toys, too." Grandpa J took his son's hand and squeezed it.

"Me too—I'll cherish them forever," said Shu. He ran over and hugged Grandpa J's neck. When he sat back down, he said, "We're from Silicon Valley, aren't we? That's what ALEXA told us—that the Utopians were from Silicon Valley, before she blew up. We're free, except we can't leave." He didn't try to disguise his annoyance.

"Both you boys just completed your Illumination training— although it happened accidentally, though life experience," James replied. "You'll be able to leave Julian and enter an Old Earth college early. You'll be four years younger than your peers, but you'll actually know more than they do."

Andy asked, "So, if it's really 2022, then humanity will become extinct in 2047, according to Q-Bit?"

"Yes, that's why we built the Utopian cities," said Bill. "It's what Q-Bit told us to do. It's how we can save the world."

"And where's Aeon Nous?" asked Shu. "Isn't Aeon Nous 'The One' that Q-Bit said would save the world? If we're looking for Aeon Nous and we don't find him, humanity will become extinct."

Bill Bishop hadn't told anyone, but their latest AI analysis of all Utopian cities said they had finally found Aeon Nous. Bill looked over at Shu and said, "We think we finally found Aeon Nous."

"Who is it?" asked Shu.

"It's you, Shu Franklin."

"What? It can't be!" exclaimed Maki. "You can't put my son in that role—the Old Earth will try to kill him!"

"They just tried," said Bill. "I got reports from my Pentagon friends minutes ago that someone in the deep state worked with a Chinese spy to try and take out Julian to get at Aeon Nous. The top Supreme Sovereign candidate out of all six Utopian cities was your son. We're lucky Shu and Andy ended the battle before it even started. The Pentagon said a virus was implanted into the

WarBots to have them destroy each other and not Julian. And the virus came from the AI RADHA, who was able to somehow get close enough to a battle commander AI called ARIF."

"How is that possible?" asked James.

"I don't know," said Bill. "Why don't you ask your son?"

Shu looked at his father and said: "Remember when I got stuck at the Fire Museum? Well, I found an old iPhone there. And then, well, I found a frozen dead man named Professor Samir Abuaita. He must have bled to death, as there was blood all over the Fire Museum and on his cloths. I wanted to tell you and Mom, but it was all too crazy—and I knew I'd never hear the end of it. But anyhow, I found an AI called RADHA on an Old Earth iPhone—or maybe not an Old Earth iPhone if it's really 2022. But anyway, it warned me about a Thor missile attack at the Fire Museum—but then its batteries died. I hid the phone with the AI in my room and took it with me and Andy to Mount Laguna. I think the dead professor put RADHA on the phone with some kind of military network access and probably snuck it off the base—but he must have gotten caught and was shot. We spoke to RADHA and used it against the WarBots."

Maki looked like she was about to faint. "Oh, my. I can't believe we allowed this to happen, James. When I first moved here, I never thought our son would be in such danger. Shu, I'm so sorry." Maki came over to her only son and hugged him close.

Shu looked around the room. Every set of eyes, even Grandpa J's, regarded him with newfound respect and wonder. "Am I really Aeon Nous?" he wondered aloud. "*What does that mean?* Someone, please tell me!"

"I'll let Sophist Austin explain more when he gets here later tonight," Bill spoke up, "but the results are unmistakable. Q-Bit predicted that all six Utopian cities would be destroyed if Aeon Nous was not discovered. It predicted that one person with special powers would arise from the cities, and that this person would save all the cities from an army of destroyers, just through his mind and the aid of his friends. James and Maki, your son somehow saved Julian and our sister Utopian cities from destruction."

"But Andy was there, too," Shu pointed out. "Without him, I'd be dead. Maybe he's Aeon Nous. He used his mindflashing to help us win the war."

Arthur and Rose looked at their son with adoration and pride. Andy blushed and said, "Aw, I didn't do so much. Well ... then again, maybe I did. And I've got the cuts and bruises to show for it."

Bill smiled. "Although Andy's a smart young man, after his own fashion, he's not a Supreme Sovereign candidate. Q-Bit predicted that humanity's savior, Aeon Nous, would fulfill two prophesies. One, he'd defeat a small army trying to destroy him and his hometown in a desert battle. And two, he'd protect the other five cities by placing an angel in the sky."

"It's not an angel," said Shu, "and I don't know anyone who's seen an angel."

"These are just interpretations," said Bill.

"How were they going to destroy the other Utopian cities?" asked Andy.

Bill continued: "There was a US military Thor satellite that got hacked into by dark forces. It targeted all Utopian villages for destruction via a missile attack, possibly even with mini-nukes—it would be considered an 'accidental' military strike. According to our sources, one conventional bomb hit Julian two months ago, wiping out our Fire Museum—where I understand you were, Shu. Our Pentagon contacts said all Utopians cities just missed being completely destroyed today. A virus somehow disabled the Thor weapons systems in time to save the cities. I'll consider that virus an angel."

Shu said, "It was RADHA, not an angel. She's an AI."

"How did the RADHA AI get into a Thor satellite?" asked Bill.

"It's a long story," said Shu, exhausted. "But she helped with destroying the WarBots. We couldn't have done it without her and Dr. Abuaita's hacked iPhone. They all helped, and I'm not sure how."

"Well, we do know that Q-BIT predicted something like this would happen."

"So, if I'm Aeon Nous, how am I supposed to save humanity? I'm a week from being thirteen years old. What can I do?"

Bill didn't hide his confusion. "We don't know, Shu; it's what was predicted by Q-Bit. We have no idea of its alien thought processes. It just told us that if anyone could save the Earth from extinction, it was a person— code-named Aeon Nous—and that he or she could only arise from societies like the one we created. This person would save all six cities from destruction. When he or she grew up, this person could save the world if he or she tried. That's all we really know."

"Sounds like a pretty stupid computer," said Andy, looking perplexed.

"That's not nice, Andy!" Rose scolded him.

"It's okay, none of this really makes sense, Rose," said Maki. "I think it sounds strange too."

"I think it sounds like a bunch of horse manure," said Grandpa J.

"Hush, Father," said James, but he couldn't help but smile.

Shu asked, "But what about all the history we studied? What about Old Earth?"

James looked over at Bill, who looked weary. They had other, more pressing issues to discuss. "Shu, you and Andy need to keep this information secret. The history you study in Julian is all an AI prediction, albeit a very accurate one. Look, I wanted you to talk to Austin, but he won't be here for at least another hour. I'll talk to him later tonight, and you can talk to him tomorrow. Go get some rest. We can circle back together tomorrow after lunch, okay? You and Andy should get some well-deserved shut-eye."

Maki and Rose both nodded in agreement. "I'll take Andy home," said Rose. "Arthur, you're staying here for a while, I suppose."

"Yes. I'll see you and Andy at home later."

Shu wanted to sleep for a week. He was glad to get some private time to think. "Thanks, Mr. Bishop. Good night, Mr. Blackwell, Mrs. Blackwell. See you tomorrow, Andy."

Grandpa J said, "I'll be moseying along, too. I ain't sure what I heard here tonight, but it sounds to me like you boys gave 'em hell. Good for you!" He held up his hand for a high five from each boy, and then he left, with the Blackwells right behind him. Maki announced that she had dishes to do. Shu could barely keep his eyes open as he staggered to his bedroom. Buddy, ever loyal, trotted close behind him.

James motioned for Bill and Arthur to follow him to the red shed. At the back part was a section that looked like a small cabin that he used for private meetings. There was a secret room inside equipped with a Faraday cage. No radio signals could go in or out, which protected the room in case there was an Old World spy. On rare occasions, not only US spies but also ones from foreign governments had infiltrated the private Julian city. They mostly feared the money, power, and secrets held by this powerful and secret society. Many of the Enlightened were from some other secret societies that felt their knowledge was too dangerous to be put into the hands of the unworthy.

The three men sat down at a round table. James lit a fire in a potbelly stove to warm the room. As the kindling caught on fire, he looked over at Bill. "Why didn't you tell me you thought Shu was The One?"

"I didn't know until I received word on the WarBot drills that went wrong," Bill replied. "My sources at the Pentagon and OPUS told me this was a big screw-up. The Chinese somehow got linked up with some deep state folks who wanted to take us out. They feel threatened by Q-Bit's revelations and have no normal method of monitoring us."

"But Q-Bit was destroyed years back," said James. "Edward Jones took care of that with the virus when he went nuts."

Bill sighed. "I know, it was going to be done eventually anyhow, but they think it left something behind of importance. And it did, in a sense. I mean, no one has the powers these kids have. Look at what your son and Andy accomplished."

"What do you think they're looking for?" asked James.

"They're looking for an AI that is as smart as Q-Bit but not as dangerous. There's also a rumor going around about that book Q-Bit left that no one could read. Some say it's just the concept of Aeon Nous, others think it has the code to build a smarter and safer AI. I don't know, James. They definitely wanted to make sure no one became the incarnation of Aeon Nous, as it could change the power structure of the world. Trying to get information this classified from our friends in DC is just too dangerous. Those dark government forces worldwide are willing to do almost anything. I don't even trust OPUS anymore. They were supposed to share the knowledge to save the world, but I almost think they're involved in this mess somehow. Rumor has they're also trying to crack the code of the book. I really would love to see a copy of this book. I heard you saw a copy once."

James nodded in agreement. "Well, I know a bit about the book you mentioned, and it's true, no one could read it. But it was lost years ago. I heard the NSA made a hard copy and deleted all digital versions. Rumor has it they burnt down a damn building to destroy a server hosting a version—and firebombed an underground research lab to get at another copy. But to go and try to destroy all six Utopian cities for a book? That's just nuts. I think it's the kids they were after."

"I think you're right, James," Arthur agreed. "I can't believe the dark forces were really planning to bomb all six Utopian cities for a book. Are people still that crazy out there?"

Bill nodded. "Sadly, yes, they are. We almost lost 7,500 people today. As you know, each city was limited to 1,500 hundred people. This is big news on all the worldwide TV channels. There was military training near all the Utopian cities worldwide; this was not an accident. It was a planned genocide, and Shu and Andy stopped all the robots in their tracks, along with destroying a haywire military satellite."

James shook his head. "I wonder why these evil forces would try a stunt like this? I mean, I believed Q-Bit, but in a way, I never totally believed in the attempt to destroy all the cities. It's nuts that Q-Bit was this accurate. It's—"

Arthur interrupted. "James, we don't live much in the world we now call Old Earth anymore. With the COVID-19 outbreak, and all the social unrest, the planet's a mess. And here in Julian and the other five Utopian cities, the dark forces can't easily monitor us—we have no cell phones, no Wi-Fi, no street cameras. Heck, our U-NET has no outside world connection. It's hard for the dark forces to track anything here except for the GeoSats up in the sky, and they can't record conversations."

Arthur used to work as president of a Silicon Valley Company called SecForce. His company was contracted to do secret government monitoring for the National Security Agency, and he had built most of the hidden electronic security around the outskirts of Julian to keep prying eyes away. The systems blocked all normal cell phone reception, stopped drone communication, and protected the independent drones working without a communication link—these were the dual-use worker drones at Julian that worked to create a grid to monitor and destroy spy drones sent by the US government and other governments to infiltrate the Utopian cities.

"We knew this day would come," said James. "But I didn't expect my son to get so wrapped up in this mess."

"I know," said Bill. "But we can thank Shu, Andy, and the other Julian kids for saving Julian and the other cities. This was the sacrifice Q-Bit predicted."

"I wish Q-Bit would have explained more about the Extinction Event," said James. "That damned AI was so arrogant, I think it actually wanted humanity to die in the Incendium."

Arthur laughed mirthlessly. "Well, you helped build that thing when you were at Gooble Labs—right, James? Didn't it ever give you a clue?"

James rubbed his chin thoughtfully before answering. "Q-Bit did a lot of strange things, but when you take it into context the time, it didn't seem strange as it might sound. Q-Bit seemed alien in that it really didn't want to give away certain answers, which I think it felt humanity wasn't ready to understand. We used RADHA to hack into it to get some answers about the Incendium. It actually said in a conversation that it would print out a book it called the *Utopian Code of Life—Secrets of Human Existence & Extinction Event*—and apparently it did, but no one could read the dang thing, not even the cover. The NSA came in and copied it. I heard through the grapevine that they're still trying to figure it out. And then the hard copy got stolen by some military pukes. Like I said earlier, I heard they tried to destroy all copies. A cryptographic researcher named Professor Bradley Hull allegedly made copy beforehand as a novelty, and the idiot had it at the Majic Mount Laguna Research Facility with Professor Jones, but some say it burned in a fire or got lost."

"This is an enigma for sure," said Bill, "but one thing is clear: Shu is Aeon Nous. And if anyone can save the whole world from extinction, it's your son."

"I've asked this before," said James, his voice rising a mite, "but how does a boy who's turning thirteen save the whole godforsaken planet, Bill? He's just a kid!"

"I don't know," said Bill. "Some might say it's just plain old luck."

"I'm an engineer," said James. "Luck is overrated. We *make* most of our luck."

"That's true, James," Bill agreed. "But in any case, we need to work on a plan to close down the communication blackout of Julian and protect the families. We can't tell them who Aeon Nous is, as that will put Shu's life at risk. This needs to be kept as an extreme Utopian secret. I'm classifying this to the highest security level; no one except those in this room, and our wives, will get access."

James said, "I can't believe my son will be going to college outside the United States. He'll be studying in Tokyo next year. We've gotta find a way to protect him. If the word gets out, someone will try to kill him—again."

Bill gave James' shoulder a reassuring squeeze. "James, I know this is tough on you, but Shu is not your average, run-of-the-mill twelve-year-old. He's been trained as a Utopian and is at the top of his class in most subjects. He knows more than most US college students."

"You know the kids today go to colleges on student loans they'll never pay," said Arthur. "They're all tattooed and nose-pierced, and they use their loans to surf, smoke God-only-knows what— and do other things I don't want to discuss."

Bill laughed. "I was one of those surfing kids at UC San Diego when I got my undergrad degree in microbiology. I even have a hidden tattoo."

"I agree, Bill," said James. "Not everything from Old Earth is so bad. Take my old toys that my father lovingly preserved, for instance. We shouldn't be so pessimistic."

"True," said Arthur. "But the event predicted to happen in 2047 is a planetary life-threatening extinction event. We need to protect Shu at all costs. Who knows what'll happen in a year? Q-Bit didn't give us all the details."

"A lot of things happened that weren't predicted," James pointed out. "For instance, the COVID-19 pandemic. Look at the mess that created!"

Bill frowned in mild disagreement. "I'm not so sure about that, James. Q-Bit clearly predicted that all this international travel and illegal bioweapons research would create maladies with international consequences. I think it's why Q-Bit asked us to create six Utopian cities across the planet in different locations that would have no contact to the outside world. It was a buffer to all these natural and unnatural diseases. We're not on any lockdowns."

"That's probably true," said James. "But I want my son to leave this wonderful town and go to college in a foreign city that's reasonably safe for him. Shu liked the idea of going to Tokyo Utopia, and Maki and I agreed. Shu's maternal grandparents—Maki's parents—live there. He's only seen pictures that they've sent him, along with their handwritten letters. He wants to live there, but he only knows about the Utopian city of Maruyama Park."

Bill grew thoughtful. "Ah, Maruyama Park, that's one of my favorite Utopian cities. I can't believe we were able to buy the zoo and local park right inside Sapporo. The winters are rough, though, and the 1,500 Utopians live mostly in an underground city."

"Shu will be based mostly in Tokyo, Bill," said James.

Arthur laughed. "Boy, when Shu finds out Tokyo has thirty million people, that's going to be a mighty big change from Julian."

"It doesn't matter where he lives, does it, Bill?" asked James.

Bill shook his head. "No, Q-Bit didn't say anything about where Aeon Nous studied. Q-Bit seemed to imply it was the Utopian cities that would build the base thought processes that would create a person who could figure out how to save humanity from extinction. We just need to let Shu Franklin live his life in the real world and see what happens."

"Agreed," said James, looking longingly at a large, green bottle on a nearby shelf. "Anyone up for taking a belt from my latest batch of homemade whiskey? I could sure use one, after today."

Bill and Arthur licked their lips, wondering what took him so long to make the offer.

* * * * *

Shu sat quietly in his room. *How is it possible that I'm Aeon Nous?* Shu missed RADHA and wished she was still around so that he could consult with her.

He took out the book he'd earlier hidden in his bottom dresser drawer. The cover, at first, looked like it was in unreadable symbols. But then words miraculously came into focus: *Utopian Code of Life—Secrets of Human Existence & Extinction Event.* Below the title was a drawing of a circle with a pyramid inside. Inside the pyramid were three equidistant, smaller circles.

Shu opened the book and, although the characters looked alien—maybe even Martian—he realized he could somehow read them. They reminded him of the experience he had remote viewing Mars. He felt a connection in the Universe trying to talk to him about an unavoidable event about to happen on Earth.

The first words in the book were: "A healthy mind sees truth, even if hidden through forces of evil. For peace and prosperity on planet Earth, each person born unto this world should have undeniable and equal rights toward the pursuit of happiness. Only within such a society can mankind find its way to survive the tragedy that will unfold in years to come."

He then began to read a story about human knowledge and how it could survive the tragedy the Utopians called the

Incendium. It said: "The intrinsic meaning is that only knowledge of the nature of the universe has any meaning. But this knowledge requires a love of wisdom, truth, and logic to properly harvest the fruits which are only shown to humanity through his limited consciousness. Without a strong and prepared mind, one will not be able to uncover the veil of knowledge without punishment."

Shu recalled these exact thoughts in his mind-flashed dreams. He anxiously read the prediction, written as a story, about a great extermination of life about to occur on planet Earth. There was little any one person could do to stop it. Humanity, if it evolved correctly, might be able to save the world by working together. One person could lead the charge and bring hope to the masses. People desperately needed hope.

Shu was only a week away from turning thirteen years old and had twenty-five years to save the world. He would need the help of others to succeed; we all do.

Shu believed that somehow he and parts of humanity could, and would, survive the upcoming Incendium if they worked together. Shu now knew the test of the Supreme Sovereign—it was to save the world from the Incendium! If he failed, not only would he perish, but all of humankind would suffer with him.

Shu continued to read the cryptic words and felt the weight of the heavens rest upon his enlightened soul.